MW01674251

RUBRIC

A Novel by

GLENN A. BRUCE

RUBRIC

Second Edition Copyright © 2022 by Glenn A. Bruce
(Original First Edition Copyright © 2019 by Glenn A. Bruce)

All rights reserved. No part of this book may be used or reproduced in any manner whatsoever, without written permission, except in the case of brief quotations embedded in articles and reviews. For more information, please contact publisher at Publisher@EvolvedPub.com.

SECOND EDITION SOFTCOVER
ISBN: 1622538323
ISBN-13: 978-1-62253-832-4

Editor: Jenni Sinclaire
Cover Artist: Kris Norris
Interior Designer: Lane Diamond

EVOLVED PUBLISHING™

www.EvolvedPub.com
Evolved Publishing LLC
Butler, Wisconsin, USA

Rubric is a work of fiction. All names, characters, places, and incidents are the product of the author's imagination, or are used fictitiously. Any resemblance to actual events or persons, living or dead, is entirely coincidental.

Printed in Book Antiqua font.

BOOKS BY GLENN A. BRUCE

Banana Republic: Richie's Run
Race!: A Hei$t Story
Rubric
The Man
Versions of the Truth

DEDICATION

For all the victims who do not yet know they are.

Chapter 1

He sits nude and alone at his computer upstairs, the bedroom feeling more like a mausoleum than a home—unless he's dead and doesn't know it. Which he thinks might be better than the actual thing. But he isn't sure.

He scrolls through Facebook, Twitter, Instagram, and TikTok—pages and pages of young girls, barely women, telling the world where they've been, what they've been doing every moment of every day.

Where they'll be tonight.

He groans low. It's so easy—all so easy—and every bit of it hurts so hard.

They post pictures, happy, sultry, inviting—posed in what they'll be wearing when they walk out their front doors into the night. How they've fixed their hair, what perfume they chose. Who'll be there with them and when they plan to meet. How long they'll stay and where they might go afterwards.

"Here we are at Hannigan's Shenanigans last week. Going back tonight. Can't wait!"

"Anyone want to meet up at Cartel tonight? 10:30. See you guys there!"

"Checking out Posterz around midnight. Hear it's awesome! Be there or be somewhere boring!"

They post "Follow me!" links like breadcrumbs along the way, with real-time updates. Some have apps that do it for them. Wherever they go, there they are—online, on-air. Live!

Until they're not.

All too easy.

He takes a shower, but even scalding hot water and Lava bar soap doesn't wash away the filth. It never does.

The next thing he knows for sure, after some fleeting images in between, he's at the club and there she is, just like the pictures. Same clothes, same hair, same smile, same friends, same happy laughter posts. Every one of them a target and they don't know it, never even think about it. They live as if there's no tomorrow, just later tonight for more fun and some little sleep.

It's all he can think about. It's all he sees every moment of every day.

***

She senses something and looks toward the service bar in back, but there's no one there. Just some other young people her age, exactly like her. She doesn't even see them. Part of the landscape of her nights.

Her night is about to change.

She's out in the parking lot, going to her car, a little too drunk to get stopped but not too drunk to stay between the lines. Her judgment isn't impaired, she assesses quickly, so it'll all be all right. She won't get stopped; it's just a feeling she has.

She's usually right.

She's smiling, remembering the good times, all those good times in the last half hour of her life. It's really great, these great friends, these homies, her peeps—

And there he is.

What the fuck! Where the fuck did he come from!

He's just two feet away from her. Walked right up without her noticing, she was so caught up and lost in her happy thoughts. He could kill her right here and now if he wanted.

No waiting! First come, first gone.

No one else is in the parking lot. Not a soul. Just the two of them. *Fuck!*

She hazards a quick glance past him at her car. Close, but not close enough; and he's standing between her and it. Between her and escape. Her and freedom. Her and the rest of her life.

Life.

Tomorrow's night flashes across her eyes—her same friends, her same favorite drinks. Nachos with everything, piled high. The music, the wonderful music. The good life!

Life.

It's all going to be gone in seconds. Or will he knock her out and take her somewhere else? Rape her and beat her and rape her some more. Beat her senseless and kill her and rape her some more and...

He isn't making his move. He isn't moving. *He isn't moving!* And she realizes:

He isn't dead in the way; her car is off to one side; if she makes a break for it, he might not be able to catch her; she might make it to her car and –

Now!

She runs, fumbling, dropping her key at her door, looks back –

Where is he! Where the fuck is –

The key's in the door. Turning. It's open! She's in!

Slamming the door, hitting the locks, the power locks. *Thank god!* her father insisted on power –

She drops her keys again. *Shit!* She's bent over, digging. Digging! *Where are they? Where the fuck are they!*

Tap.

Tap.

Tap.

She sits bolt upright, eyes wide – no keys in her hand. He's at her door, right at her fucking door! She leans down, bending over, feeling around again, digging again. *Where the* fuck *are they!*

Tap.

Tap.

Tap.

She's not finding them. She's not fucking finding them. God damn them! God damn it! Goddam this whole night, this whole fucking goddam thing! This goddam life! This lie!

Tap.

Tap.

Tap.

She looks. She has no other choice. Not really. What she sees is as frightening as the blade she expected – the gun, the piano wire, the gag, the ether.

The badge.

That's what the tapping was. He was tapping his goddam badge on my window! What? Is he fucking going to arrest me?!

Now he's talking. What the fuck is he saying? What is he fucking saying at my window with his tapping fucking badge!

"Just a crack," he says.

What? What? What the fuck are you saying?!

"Open it. Just a crack."

He shows her how much he means with that badge, *that fucking badge in his hand,* motioning downwards at the top of her window, just an inch. *Just an inch.* Only an inch. With the fucking badge. *Just a fucking inch.*

Tap.

Tap—

Okay!

She'll give him a half-inch. That's enough to hear *whatever the* fuck *he has to say, this cop* asshole.

He won't be able to smell my breath, is what she's thinking. He won't know. She is *not* getting out of her fucking car, no matter what. She'll call her father first. She'll—

Fuck! Cellphone! Why didn't she think of it! Now she's digging for that.

Tap.

Tap—

Goddammit! Stop with the tapping!

Her eyes won't go any wider. He isn't going away. That badge, that *look.* That crazed "he doesn't give a shit" look. So, if he doesn't give a shit, *why is he here?!*

Just lower the window a half-inch, that's fine. Put the cell away. You won't need it. That's what he's telling her without words.

She's thinking if she calls her father, she'll have to explain why she's half-drunk in a parking lot outside a bar at 3:00 in the morning with a man outside her car window that she let follow her. Her father's always saying *Look around you; keep an eye for anything suspicious.* Anything like some guy, some man, *some asshole with a badge!*

Some cop. Probably a killer cop, a murderer. One of those cops that goes crazy, that you see on the news, who goes crazy and kills his wife or his family or both. Someone he didn't even know.

In a parking lot.

If she dials 9-1-1 and he *is* an insane psycho-cop, he'll just kill her anyway! *Shit!*

Tap.

Tap.

"Okay! But move back."

He stares.

"*Move back*!" she shouts.

She knows he can hear her just fine, but he doesn't move.

"Fuck."

Just a little mutter, a private one for herself, her sanity, her hope. She wishes she could open the window that half-inch—that she had the guts, the stupid confidence—enough to feel a thin slit of night air, to smell the freshness in her musty car, which reeks of her stale cigarettes she sneaks, the spilled beer from last month, some old fries under the seat.

Whatthefuckever.

"What do you *want*?" That's it. Sound tough, sound put-out; guys don't like that shit; he'll probably go away, back to his old hag at home *in the trailer park and fuck her pretending she's me, the perv.*

Why me?!

He isn't moving, he isn't emoting, he's just looking, staring at her as if she's already dead, a corpse in a car staring at him with panic and disgust at his old *disgustedness.*

"I *said,* what do you *want*?!"

He continues to stare at her like the *stupid dead bitch* she feels she already is.

She yells, confessing—what other choice does she have?—"I can't open the fucking window! I dropped. My. Keys!"

Oh sure, now he's gonna nod like he knew that all along and I'm a stupid fucking little cunt!

He leans closer, so she can hear. She still can't see him clearly with the mall light behind him. He's holding his badge name and number in his hand so she can't read that either. Is he even really a cop? Did he get his badge in some costume shop? Is he a Halloween *freak*?

He's going to talk. Finally! She can see his mouth opening to speak. *Okay! Say something! I can't fucking* stand *this anymore!*

What does he want? Money, purse, pussy? At this point she's ready to give any of it, all of it, just to be allowed to open that window and smell that fresh air and leave to live another night of anything other than this.

"What do you *want*!?"

He says, "Nothing. You're lucky."

"What the fuck is that supposed to mean?!"

"Don't advertise everything you're gonna do on your little blog site. The next time it may not be me," he says.

She shouts with hateful abandon, "And your fucking *point* is?!"

He's done.

He turns around, puts his badge away, and walks off.

She cannot believe this happened. She looks at her shaking hands on her shaking legs. There is one thing she hates worse than anything, and that's being scared, someone scaring her, *goddamyoufucker.*

This is not the time to mention it, so she says, real quiet, careful not to disturb this delicate balance of him leaving her in the relative safety of her Camaro, "Fuck you, motherfucker."

She has her keys. They were on the seat under her cute little loose summer dress with the blue flowers and key lime vines. She only now feels them and sticks them in the ignition and starts the car.

She squeals out of the parking lot as fast as she can go—which is almost too fast. She barely misses a light pole, then scratches out onto the street into honking traffic and is gone for home, for the safety of her home.

Wait till she writes *this* shit on her blog.

***

He has never looked back. He has walked to his car. He has gotten in. He is driving away. The things that can happen in this city, in this world, make him sad and sick at the same time.

So easy.

Chapter 2

Mark Young could still remember the day it all started. He'd worked a night shift and was coming home in early daylight. The usual. A paperboy was throwing *The Times Courier* on a few front lawns for those people who still read the paper, like Belton, the older man next door—always traveling somewhere with his wife, off to see the kids, the grandkids, old friends.

What a life, he always thought whenever he saw them wave and take off for the weekend, for the week, ten days. Retirement. The word started to sound as delicious and far away as a plate of *palusami* in Bora Bora, and no more likely.

Mark Young could still see the paperboy throwing the papers and remember thinking how strange yet comforting it was that people still read newspapers in this day of links and sites, blogs and social media—*fucking podcasts*—technologies that just pushed us further and further away from each other while pretending to bring us closer.

Bullshit. All bullshit. Too easy. So easy it becomes impossible.

Mark Young liked working nights alone. The department had adopted the format some years ago when so many murders happened at night and no detectives were on shift to respond. Dispatch was always calling the Homicides Investigations captain at home to ask who to call next. Captain Carter Corlius—"Si-Si-Si" some of the cops called him, because he never said no to a superior—got tired of being bothered in the middle of the night and began a rotation. His detectives complained more than they usually did—all but Mark. So, Mark Young became the Night Man.

Some nights were better than others.

There'd been no bodies called in, no murders, no rapes, no serious assaults, nothing to report, so Mark worked on reports all night. Cold cases had seemed appealing when he got to the office; but by 4:00 AM, making no headway got old. So, he switched to "Current Homicides." He had six on his desk. He'd be in court for months when they all hit.

Just before his shift change, someone reported a child's body out by the mall. A girl of twelve had been raped, murdered, and left nude—probably not in that order, Mark thought. Last seen by her parents, next seen by a garbage truck driver when he lifted a dumpster over his cab. He almost set it back down on the body, catching a glimpse at the last second and stopping. Though this wasn't the first body he'd found, it was the first child. He was shocked at the amount of blood around the small victim. He called it in then took the day off. Nobody knew where he was, but everyone was looking.

It will all be someone else's problem, the Day Shift, Mark thought, and turned onto his street feeling relief over that lucky break. Time on his side for once.

Dead kids were always tougher.

Coming home, Mark was glad he had a home to come home to—a wife, *his* kids. Most of the guys in Homicide were divorced or in the process. Murder is death on marriage.

He would remember feeling tired that morning, as tired as he ever had. Maybe his iron was low. Maybe his will to go on. Whatever, something was down on the stick.

He pulled into his driveway, thinking about nothing more than his waiting bed after a long shower and—

Bang!

Something hit his car, landed right on the hood and skipped up over his windshield, off to the right. A small bicycle—as if falling from the clear sky above. He wasn't aware that he'd reflexively slammed on his brakes, but he had. Now he was looking for the source.

Up, then left, to the angry neighbor.

What was the guy's name? They'd never met, but he hadn't lived next door that long—maybe a year, maybe less. Young guy, thirty, thirty-two—or older and holding up well—had a hard look, at least at the moment. He did his anger duty, glowered, then turned and headed for his front door. Went inside without a look back.

Mark got out of his plain-wrap detective beater and walked around to see. The hood was scratched, not bad for 188,000 miles. No one might notice, and if they did, say a city mechanic or another cop, a great story would evolve.

No one cared anymore about anything as meaningless as a dent or a scratch. Mark thought of the Miami cop who ran his black-and-white into a cement wall at fifty miles an hour while some lucky civilian recorded it all on his cellphone. Got a million hits on YouTube. Totaled the fucker; lucky to be alive. He was stunned all right. This? Some minor cosmetic scratch? Who looked at a hood anyway?

Besides, shit happens. People attack police cars all the time with keys and bottles, eggs and bricks. Guns.

Mark found his son's small bicycle and knew what had happened. It wasn't the first time. He headed down the driveway and toward the kitchen door at the rear of the house. Going up the steps, he could hear the family breakfast rush in full swing.

"Everyone's late, eat fast," his wife Anne was saying. "MJ, do you have your suit for practice?"

"Yes, mom," MJ said, with little tolerance for being checked on, and held up her swimsuit. It had the school colors, scarlet and gold. She said, "Hi daddy," without looking.

MJ was still eleven, but just barely, and already almost as tall as her mom; thin as a rail, like her dad had been at her age, gangly but strong.

"Mornin' sweetheart," Mark said as he came inside and kissed his daughter on the top of her head. She smiled, but still didn't look up from her YA romance novel. "Boys and girls with class in love in class and out," the cover promised.

Mark asked, "How's this one?" MJ was always reading.

She said, "They're about to go on a geology field trip and picnic. A lot can happen *there*."

Mark chuckled—partly because he enjoyed her enthusiasm and relative innocence, and partly because he or Anne always scanned the books before letting MJ read them. So, he knew that Barry tries to kiss Missy under the oak tree, and she kicks him.

"Mornin', sport," Mark said to his son.

Andy had just turned seven. He was a gentle kid—a towhead who still valued his mother's protection but wanted to be braver someday. Just not too soon. *When I'm a big boy*, he liked to say.

"Hi daddy," he said, looking up and smiling. "Are you gonna kiss Mommy now?"

"You betcha," Mark said, and followed through. He knew that Andy liked to see his father come home and hug his mother, give her peck on the cheek.

Anne said, "Thanks, you. I missed you last night."

"I miss you every night," he said. He knew not to take it further.

Anne, Mark's wife of seventeen years, was tall, thin, blonde, and intense. No one ever called her beautiful, except Mark in the early years.

But she was attractive in the strong way Mark needed at the time, and he fell head over heels.

Nothing much had ever gotten under Anne's skin until the last year or so when Mark went to nights full time. Most nights, he didn't get home till dawn. Some nights he didn't get home until after she had left for the day.

Sometimes, he didn't get home.

Anne said, "Andy," as a reminder to speed it up, even though she knew her son never changed his eating pace for anything or anyone. He had one speed. He took one bite, one spoon or forkful at a time, chewed until it was done, then swallowed. He did it with apples, with lasagna, with ice cream. It didn't matter to Andy; food was food, and he took his time.

MJ, on the other hand, shoveled whatever she ate, barely bothering to taste it. She was always reading—eBooks, paperbacks, comics, cereal boxes. She loved Nancy Drew for a while because Dad was a cop and MJ wanted to be one, too. Then she moved to youth adventure and some sci-fi for kids. Then she discovered the possibility of boys and went on a romance rip. Today's young adult novel was set in the dark ages of the 1950s. She didn't understand the lingo, but she understood the good looks and young lust. It was all she and her girlfriends talked about at school: boys. Anne had to dig that out of her, but she remembered her own girlhood passions and treated MJ's with due respect.

By the time Mom said to hurry up, MJ was already done and turning the page. She would probably rather have been texting a friend, but phones weren't allowed at the table, in the den, or in bed. That left the bathroom, but her mother was onto her.

So, she read a lot.

Andy had eaten one piece of toast and was starting on his egg. He could only eat one food type at a time and didn't like items on his plate touching one another. One time, Anne had made him "toad in the hole"—an egg cooked into a piece of bread with the middle torn out. Andy just stared. He wasn't comfortable with the concept or the name. Anne had to give him replacement Wheaties.

"Andy," his father said with a familiar tone.

"What'd I do now?" Andy said, and stopped eating to stare at his plate, certain he was in for it.

"Eat, Andy," Anne said.

Andy took a small bite of egg.

Mark said, "Left your bike on the neighbor's lawn again."

Without looking up from her book, MJ said, "Mr. Poopyhead?"

Anne said, "MJ."

"Well, he is!" MJ said, and Andy nodded. MJ said, low, "I could've said something worse."

"If you like the taste of soap," Anne said—though she had never done that to her kids and never would.

MJ said, "I hate his kids. They're mean." She had tried playing with them, even though they were *little*—the oldest was nine—but all they wanted to do was burn ants with a magnifying glass or throw rocks at birds or squirrels.

Anne said, "That's probably because *he's* mean, dear."

Andy said with no drama, "He ties them in the basement and beats them with chains."

Mark and Anne shared a smile. Mark said, "They don't have a basement, son."

Andy said, "Ethan said they did, and I heard them screaming all night one night, the whole night."

Anne raised her eyebrows. Her son slept harder than granite. Since the day he was born, he never missed so much as an hour of sleep time, unlike his sister who was a night owl. Many a night she had to be told to turn off the radio or put down the book, stop drawing. Those were the only times MJ whined, but she had a good whine when she needed one. Other than that, like her mother, MJ was unfazed by most anything except:

"Spider!"

Everyone in the room jumped, including Mark. MJ had pulled her feet up onto her chair seat and was pointing at the small moving dot on the floor.

Andy giggled and Anne looked at her husband with that, *Well?* look. The *It's your job* look.

Mark raised his eyebrows, took one step, and squashed the bug with his leather shoe. He removed his shoe and the bug went with it.

"Kind of anti-dramatic, isn't it?" he said. "After all that drama."

MJ stuck her tongue out at her dad.

He smiled and looked at the bottom of his shoe. "Hmm," he said. "A fly." He smiled at his daughter. "Not a spider after all."

"Thank *god*," she said even more dramatically, put her feet back on the floor and picked up her book again, immediately back into the story right where she'd left off.

Andy said, on seeing the dead bug, "I miss the dog." He always called Fluffy "the dog" because MJ had named him, and Andy thought it was a stupid girly name for a boy dog. Plus, his dad always said "The dog."

Mark told his son, "He'll wander back. They always do. It's only been a week."

"It's been two. He's dead," Andy said darkly.

Mark had explained *habeas corpus*—no body, plus no neighbor or passing driver had come to the door—"Did you have a Golden Retriever named Fluffy?" from the name on the collar—so, The Dog was likely still alive, just lost.

Anne said, "He'll find his way home, honey."

Anne checked on the breakfast plates. MJ's was clean—had been after the first thirty seconds—but Andy had only finished one-quarter of his egg. Anne said, "Go brush your teeth. You can have a pocket pita in the car."

"Okay," he said and hopped off his chair. He loved pocket pitas, as long as they were only one flavor—cheese or bacon, not both. Tofu or tomato. He left his egg.

Anne told MJ, "You too. And don't forget your homework this time."

MJ tore out of the kitchen as she always did, passing Andy in the hallway.

Mark said, "No running in the house." Not that he cared. He enjoyed MJ's high energy approach to everything—the opposite of her languorous little brother who took his sweet time with everything, which Mark also appreciated as it mirrored his own life tempo. MJ mirrored her mother's intensity, Andy, his father's unflappability. At first, they thought Andy might be autistic, but he just preferred an easygoing stroll through childhood, rather than a race. MJ ran everywhere; Andy sauntered. *He always stops to smell the roses,* as Anne said, enviously. She was more likely to think they needed pruning and fertilizer.

She said to Mark, "You want his egg?"

Mark said, "Sure," and sat down to eat it. "May I have some orange juice?"

"Sure," Anne said. As she walked past the refrigerator, she opened the door.

Mark nodded, grinning. She was a funny lady and a good mom. A solid partner.

On her way back in, with a purse on her shoulder, Anne grabbed the OJ out of the fridge, kicked the door closed with her foot, and set the gallon jug on the table by her husband.

"Thanks," he said. "Poopypants threw Andy's bike over the fence onto my cruiser."

Anne stopped. "You're kidding."

"Didn't say a word. Just scowled and went inside his house. About scared the shit outa me. Came outa nowhere. Wham!" Mark shook his head and poured some OJ into Andy's empty milk glass. He laughed about the incident in retrospect.

Anne wrinkled her nose. "How can you do that?"

"Laugh about an asshole?"

"Drink orange juice in a glass with milk residue."

"It's like a Creamsicle," Mark said. "You take after your son."

"Ha," Anne said. "He really did that? Threw Andy's bike over the fence onto your car?"

"Right on the hood."

"He didn't break Andy's bike, did he?"

Mark shook his head. "Cruiser took a ding."

Anne opened her purse and dug around in it. She said, "His wife spoke to me one time when I was taking the garbage out to the curb."

"I need to start doing that again, I'm sorry," Mark said.

"You weren't here," Anne said flatly, stating the obvious.

Mark asked, "So, what'd she say?"

"Not much. Hello, maybe. She seemed distant."

"Imagine that." Her husband throws bikes at cars.

"I tried to make small talk," Anne said. "Told her you were a cop, I used to teach, doing the paralegal now. We had two kids about their kids' ages. Well, Andy."

"She say what he does?"

"Sales, I think. Maybe. I don't know. She wasn't real specific about anything as I recall."

"Probably med'd up, living with that."

Anne nodded as Mark stood. She patted his hand and he kissed her on the head. Then he headed for the stairs, pulling out his badge and gun.

"Any excitement last night?" she asked.

"You don't want to know," he said, because he knew she didn't.

Chapter 3

Mark slept until 3:00 PM, then watched some television in the bedroom with the sound off. Someone was playing someone else somewhere he didn't recognize. He barely remembered when he used to enjoy sports.

Anne had dropped the kids off at a friend's house on the way home and was studying for her real estate license exam in the den when Mark came down.

"I didn't hear you come in," he said.

She nodded. Her six-hour day working as a paralegal—or, as she called it, "glorified *secretarianism*"—while the kids were at school, had taught her to be quiet and invisible. Her employers' clients didn't like to know anyone else was in the office. "Someone might hear their sordid tales, weaknesses, and spiteful greed."

The firm specialized in divorces—boring, tawdry stuff, as Anne saw it. But they also handled real estate issues for a few large investors, which she found far more interesting because it was straight ahead. Much less melodramatic. As a result, she'd developed an interest in commercial real estate, seen the potential, and was working that way.

Mark got a cup of cold coffee from the coffeemaker—at least it was today's—and a bagel that definitely was not. When he tried to bite into it and the crust gave as much as a good piece of oak, he threw it in the trash and opened the fridge.

"There's some leftover spaghetti and salad," Anne said from the den, sensing his need. Then she said, "Did you notice the front hedge is dying?"

"Dying?" He hadn't noticed.

She said, "I don't know 'dying' exactly, but it doesn't look healthy. Kind of brownish on the edges of the leaves. Maybe you should water it if you get a chance."

Mark said, "Sounds like it's dying," and made no further commitment.

Nor did Anne.

Mark dug the spaghetti out of the refrigerator and ate from the Tupperware container at the kitchen table. He didn't get two bites down before his cell rang. It was Jerome, his old partner before the department could no longer afford to send detectives out in pairs and switched them all to individual caseloads. "Yeah."

Jerome said there was a double homicide and the captain wanted him in early. Jim Jakes was out sick and everyone else was busy.

"*I'm* busy," Mark said. "I'm eating cold spaghetti."

"Mmmm," Jerome said, and hung up.

As Mark passed the opening to the den, he told Anne what he had to do. She nodded without looking. Once her husband took a call, he was committed. A kiss on her head and he was out the door.

The double homicide turned out to be more of a mutual deal. Two homeless guys had killed each other over a sandwich one of them had cadged from a college kid outside a Blimpie. The two older men had stabbed each other to death under an overpass, their shared home. Alcohol wasn't a factor, for a change.

When Mark arrived in the late afternoon, the murder site was relatively calm. Forensics had already come and gone. A uniform cop Mark had known for years said, "Must be nice, bein' able to take your time whenever you want."

Mark laughed and told him to fuck off. The cop returned the laugh and finally went for coffee. His job was over now that Homicide was here.

Officers had carefully preserved the scene for the investigating detective. Mark looked over the bodies, made a few notes about the weapons—one rusty Boy Scout pocketknife and one Sizzler steak knife—the fairly large amount of blood, the old clothes, the worn shoes, and the lack of wine bottles, then turned his attention to the object of desire. He flipped open the sandwich to find it empty. He looked up at the young female cop guarding the scene.

"It's just bread. Nothing in it," he said.

She nodded and looked away. She was new.

"I think you can go now," Mark said. "Tell the bag boys to take 'em away."

"I think they're women," she said.

"Okay."

"County?"

He said, "Unless they're taking hobos at Lucerne," the high-end hospital in Latchwood—a ritzy development with nothing under five million, several over twenty. They had their own healthcare. "Built it on sugar daddy bake sales," Anne used to say. "Ten-dollar croissants sold by two-dollar cupcakes with ten-thousand-dollar tits."

The young female officer headed for the coroner's van. Mark made a last note—"one solved, a thousand to go"—and put away his book. He started back for his car when he saw Jerome pull up and get out of his unmarked detective car, a relatively new silver Impala, smoking a Winston regular. Mark could see him putting the red pack away from all the way across the crime scene. He'd quit smoking himself twelve years prior, just before MJ was born, and never missed it. Anne was grateful.

Jerome, a thin, light-skinned black man around Mark's age, said, "They got your witnesses down at the station. Carina took their statements." He waited.

Mark didn't disappoint. "That should be colorful."

Jerome laughed, ground his Winston out on in the dirt, and lit another.

"What're you doing down here?" Mark asked.

"Slumming. I had a vehicular earlier"—vehicular homicide—"had to drive all the way out to Carrington with backup. Dude called it in said it was some homie, bald head and tats—"

"In Carrington?" Upscale for gang members.

"Ran the tag," Jerome said.

Mark said, "Carina lives in Carrington. Should've had her go. Might've made the national news." He grinned. Carina Beaulieu had a reputation for *embellishment.*

"She was busy with your eyewitnesses." Jerome shrugged. From his tone, Mark guessed Jerome hadn't wanted to go. Jerome always had other things to do—*more important* things. Then again, anything was more important than *this endless shit.*

Mark did a quick impression of Carina's interrogation technique. "'Would you say the color of the deceased's blood was more crimson or burgundy?'"

"Cerise," Jerome said.

"Nice," Mark said. Jerome could be quick. "So, the homie give you much trouble?"

"Wasn't home. Had to wait two hours."

"Did he come in guns blazin' with his banger buddies?"

"Ran over his own garbage can. Drunk as a monkey in a vat. Saw the black-and-whites and panicked."

Mark said, "So *then* he came out firing."

"Motherfucker was ninety-*two*. Didn't even know he'd run over the girl."

"But he was bald."

"Oh yeah."

"Tats?"

"Liver spots."

Mark chuckled. "You're lucky to be alive."

"Wouldn't'a been if I'd been sittin' on his garbage can."

"He's in county?"

"Carrington," Jerome said. "I gave it to local."

"Generous. Where'd the hit happen?"

"Bolton Heights."

"Same difference."

No one wanted those incidents. Every call to planned communities ended in harsh accusations. "Mr. Challers there on the right leaves his garbage cans out past three PM." "Mrs. Talley runs her sprinklers in the middle of the day." "Those new people over there are constantly leaving their garage door open! It's appalling!"

And the granddaddy crime of them all: "My neighbor's dog does its business in my yard and she never picks up after it, officer."

"It's in the bylaws!" Mark and Jerome said together.

Mark added, "Can you please arrest them, officer."

And Jerome said, "At least rough 'em up a little."

In Carrington, some old white geezer running over a teenaged girl downtown, then driving home with no clue, was the equivalent of a mass murder in the capitol. But he probably wouldn't do time—some compassionate judge would just take away his driving privileges.

Jerome watched the coroners' ladies carting off the body-bagged hobos and offered Mark a cigarette, a Camel. Mark declined, and started telling a joke.

"Hey, two homeless guys walk into a shelter and ask where the bar is. So, the nun says..."

***

The nightstand clock read 3:23 AM. Anne was snoring hard on her back when an unfamiliar loud noise cut through enough to wake her up with a jolt. She reached over to see if her husband was in the bed with her, unsurprised to find he wasn't.

She listened for a few minutes, heard nothing else, and went back to sleep.

***

Mark was at a bar in Conover. Two drunks got into it over a hockey score. The younger one hit the older one in the face with a beer bottle, breaking it, then dragging it down as the victim lifted up and back. The jagged glass caught his right aorta and he bled out before EMS got to the scene.

The young killer and his girlfriend were both still crying when Mark arrived. He'd do six-to-eight, be out in five, a completely changed man. Hard and ready to kill again, or Saved, or both. He'd sport more ink—not neat tats like he got at the *parlor* near campus with his girlfriend. Pin and pen stuff, Christ, skulls, and Nazis.

Since this one mattered, Mark would take everyone's statement personally. As soon as he got the call from dispatch, Mark called the command officer at the scene and told him not to let anyone leave. He got there in fifteen to find more blood than the sandwich hobos had produced together fighting with knives.

He spent the rest of the night on paperwork, entering data, and talking with the officers and the Assistant District Attorney. Mark awakened the Assistant DA at 4:00 AM when he made the call himself. The bar *slasher* was a second cousin, so the ADA would have to recuse himself. That meant his boss Arthur Kibbler would take the case.

Kibbles and Bits, they called him, because when he was done with a defendant, that's all that was left. Men he prosecuted got the harshest justice Arthur could mete out. He'd say, "They'll be happy to eat Kibbles and Bits when I let them off the stand."

Mark knew the younger Assistant DA would do what he could for his cousin; but now the kid was probably looking at more like ten-to-twelve before Kibbler was done.

Mark was glad Andy was only seven.

Chapter 4

"Andy, get your butt in here and eat, young man!"

Andy had started to climb a tree the back corner of their yard—in his pajamas. He said, "But Mama, it's Saturday."

"Nice try, kiddo," Anne said. "But it's Thursday." She gave him the raised-eyebrow Mom look and went inside to toast the Eggos. MJ had already eaten three, snuck out, and gone upstairs to the bathroom on the pretext of brushing her teeth, no doubt to text her friends.

When his mother didn't come back out right away, Andy decided to see how high he could get. His highest point until then had been the first fork, about six feet up. It took him a while to get that far. He grabbed the next nailed-on rung, stepped up, and paused—checking to see how far the ground lay below.

Mark had nailed climbing slats onto the trunk a few weeks earlier to embolden his son in the direction of greater courage. Andy said he was afraid of heights, but all his friends were climbing trees and mocking him when he wouldn't go up with them. He would watch from the ground, and they would make fun of him. One of them called him a "pussy" and Mark had to explain what that meant—though not what it was. That's when Dad decided to help his son along.

First, Mark climbed the steps, to show Andy that they were strong; then Anne went up, then MJ. Anne had to tell MJ, who was headed for the top, not to go any higher. Andy made it to the highest rung that first day with his father underneath just in case. A few weeks later, he made it to the main fork with Dad below.

Today, feeling brave, Andy was determined to get to that second fork with no one spotting him. So, with his mom inside busy at the toaster, the little towhead climbed to the main fork where he paused to look up and get a feel for how far he had to go.

He saw Everest.

Andy licked his lips and screwed up his courage. His dad had told him, "Just don't look down and you'll be fine. Keep your focus on the tree—your hands and your feet."

Andy checked his grip.

He was wearing his favorite spooky Halloween pajamas, covered in skeletons. At first, they had scared him. Now, he embraced his fear and wore them defiantly. His scheme was working.

Without looking away from the tree, Andy wrapped his hands and arms around the thick limb above and lifted himself into the main fork. Feeling stable, he grabbed up higher and, with less effort than he expected, ascended to the second fork.

***

Anne heard the blood-curdling scream from the kitchen.

A second later, the scream came crashing through the backdoor, sending it slamming into the end of the kitchen cabinets.

When Anne's feet came back down to the floor, she turned, wide-eyed. "Andy! Jeez, you scared the pants off me!" If her eyes were as big as saucers, his were blue dinner plates on his tiny towhead.

Anne knelt to face her son, who was clearly petrified.

He said, "There's red everywhere."

"I thought you fell," Anne said, checking him carefully. He didn't seem to be wounded. "Did you fall?"

Andy shook his head no, but something had obviously terrified him.

"Did you go too high, and it scared you?"

He shook no, again.

"Everywhere where? What red?" she said, like any concerned and distracted mother, trying to assess what was wrong, not sure of what her young son was trying to tell her.

Andy was shaking as if he'd seen an actual ghost. He pointed toward the neighbor's yard. "Mr. Poopy's," he said.

MJ had come down from her text chat, teeth brushed, and said, "What?"

Anne said, "Stay inside," and walked out into the backyard.

The children followed her out, MJ asking, "What is it? What'd you see? Is it cool, Andy-Fanny? Is it awesome?"

"MJ!" her mother shouted. "Stop. Sit. Now."

MJ had never heard that tone or cadence before. She stopped and sat, silent. Andy sat beside her, trembling. MJ put her arm around him and whispered, "What was it?"

Andy shook his head.

Anne asked, "Andy, were you up in the tree?"

He nodded yes rapidly without speaking.

Anne stood at the base of the tree and looked up. She took off her slippers and started climbing the rungs barefoot, as she had done as a tomboy in Iowa. When she got to the main fork, she stopped, made sure her footing was solid, then turned to look over the fence into the neighbor's yard.

She threw up all down the tree.

***

Within ten minutes, local cops, county sheriffs, EMTs, Fire & Rescue, even a few HPs were all screaming around the corners, parking in the street and on the sidewalk.

Blocking the street.

Mark wasn't far behind, having just come off shift. He got the call on his cell in his favorite bagel store. Portable blue LED on his dash, siren wailing, he narrowly missed two other incoming vehicles and found his own driveway full, so parked on his lawn by the brown hedge.

He ran out of his car and into the house to find Anne pacing in the living room alone, belting a bourbon at 7:15 AM in her bathrobe.

Mark asked her where the kids were.

"With Ailene in the bedroom." She nodded upstairs. Ailene was her sister.

Before Mark could say another word, Anne blurted, "Oh Mark, it's horrible! It's fucking horrible!" She started crying, shaking the way her son had.

Mark held her close, made her finish her drink. Then he said, "I need to go see."

"It's fucking horrible," was all she would say.

Mark guided her to a chair and made her sit. "I'll be right back, I promise."

"Is it your case?" she demanded.

"I don't know yet. I don't think so. I think because—you know—the Captain gave it to Henrickson. He's a good man."

It didn't look as if Anne heard him. She likely didn't give a good shit who got it as long as it wasn't Mark. So, he left.

Outside, Mark waded through what seemed like a hundred or more responders—more than he'd seen at that spree shooting at a high school years ago. Standard operating procedure if anything happens within a half-mile of a cop's house and his wife calls it in.

The press had begun arriving. One news van had already parked and extended its antenna to broadcast the gore "live!"

What Mark Young found in his neighbor's yard was just as Anne had described it: horrible. Worse than horrible. Worse than anything Mark had seen in his twenty-one years on the force.

The neighbors' three children hadn't just been murdered—they had been cut into small pieces and strewn around the yard. There were strips of blood-soaked cloth, probably pajamas, and clumps of bloody hair. There were little hands and feet, arms, a tiny penis.

One of the heads had been cut into two pieces and left like a freshly split cantaloupe. The killer had to have used an axe. A large one.

Mark looked and there it was: thick, sharp, heavy, bloody. There were also knives—several—and other tools. All three kids' eyes had been gouged out.

"Horrible" didn't even touch it.

"Jesus fuck," Mark said. He was stopped dead by the sights, unable to move. What if this had happened one house over? What if these body parts had belonged to MJ and Andy?

To Anne.

In his two decades of police work, Mark Young had only felt like crying once. It was stupid, a car accident in which a dog had been killed. The driver of the car had carelessly looked away for a moment, digging for a phone or a cigarette, and crashed head-on into a phone pole. The airbag saved the driver, but her dog was thrown forward from the backseat, out through the jagged windshield, skinned. Zeus died in her arms. The woman cried so hard she had to be sedated. She later killed herself.

Over a dog.

Mark understood. He'd cried that day at the accident site, for her *and* Zeus, back when he was a patrol officer and the first one on the scene. He had questioned whether he even wanted to become a detective that day.

This day, standing in a sea of children's blood and body parts, the questions came back. What was he even doing here? How could he stand to do this job?

Dead hobos were one thing, but kids, little kids...

The scene commander, an attractive larger woman named Kay Lown, said, "You ever see anything like this?"

Sergeant Kay Lown's parents had thought it cute at the time, but now everyone called her Clarabell. She went with it; every well-liked cop got a nickname. Better than Icebag the department bitch or Puddles the department weeper, neither of whom ever heard their nicknames spoken aloud.

Mark shook his head. He hadn't seen anything like this, ever. He couldn't have *imagined* seeing something like this. "Where are the parents?"

"Inside," she said. "It's pretty ugly." She asked, "Anne okay? The kids?"

"Not really," Mark answered honestly. "Henrickson's got this?"

"Yeah, he's, uh, on his way. He had a double OD over in Hilldale. Suspicious circumstances."

What was suspicious was that it didn't happen more often.

"I heard on the radio," Mark said. Most everyone around called it "Helldale" for its crack addicts, whores, and homeless people.

Clarabell nodded. She said, "So, you can feel free to..." She nodded toward the house.

"Thanks," Mark said. "They're my neighbors."

"Just, uh, share anything you get with Ted."

"I will," he promised. He was old school and good for his word.

Sergeant Lown took a last look at the carnage, then turned and walked away. Forensics were starting to measure the distance between body parts and take pictures—begin the guessing game.

What a video that would make for training.

Mark went around front, showed his badge at the door even though he didn't need to, and went inside. His neighbor sat on a couch alone while paramedics tended to his wife. She was past losing it; she was lost.

Mark approached the neighbor whom he'd never spoken to, had only seen on occasion—the last time at the receiving end of his own son's small bicycle. He said, "Detective Young. I'm your neighbor."

The man looked up. For the first time Mark thought he looked normal, this perpetually grumpy neighbor-stranger—at least, as normal as any devastated father of three murdered children could look. His eyes red, his soul hollow.

Mark said, "You're Mr. Black, Daniel Black?"

The man nodded.

"Do you go by Daniel or may I call you Dan?"

The man nodded again.

"Mind if I sit?"

The man shook his head no.

Mark sat.

Dan Black said, "I know who you are," as if to clarify that he wasn't out of his mind with grief. His voice was soft, his words accepting, even if his bearing seemed appropriately chilly.

"Yeah," Mark said, "my kids leave their stuff on your lawn all the time," trying to lighten things up—if that was possible.

Dan Black said, "Doesn't matter now." He said it as if nothing did anymore.

EMTs had strapped his wife to a gurney after giving her a shot of Ativan. As they wheeled her past, her head rolled toward her husband, her face blank from the drug and grief—no life left in her.

Dan Black gritted his teeth. He said, "You think she'll ever be the same?" But he likely knew the answer.

Mark refrained from comment. Instead, he said, "I'm sorry, but I'm going to have to ask you some questions. The detective who's handling your case is on his way. He had a double overdose on the other side of town."

"Lucky him." Dan Black stared dully at his carpet.

Mark said, "I'll just do the preliminary and pass my notes along if that's okay."

Dan Black looked at Mark Young with as much interest as he might give a dead moth in a window web, as if to say he couldn't care less what anyone in the world did at that moment—or any other moment to come.

Mark said, "If you're ready."

Dan looked away.

"Sooner is better in these cases. I'm sorry."

Dan Black said, "You're sorry a lot." He stood and walked into the dining room.

Mark took a deep, steadying breath and followed. These would not be easy questions to ask.

If the questions were hard, the answers were hell.

***

After the last police vehicle had left the scene—they'd been there most of the morning—and the clean-up team came in (paid for by an impromptu passing of the hat among the officers and through the neighborhood), Mark went home.

Next door.

Anne's sister Ailene took the kids to her house for the afternoon, and Mark went to bed. He'd been up all night, worked a double. Anne lay with him, holding his hand until he drifted off.

When Mark woke up, just after 5:00 in the afternoon, Anne had dinner ready. With nothing to do but think, she had gotten up at 2:00 and cooked for the rest of the afternoon. Mark picked at his food. Anne didn't eat. He took the night off and his captain didn't object.

They talked about checking in with their neighbor to see if he was holding it together, but no lights were on in his house. They guessed he was at the hospital with his wife—or at the morgue with his dead kids.

If he hadn't already hanged himself in his detached garage.

Chapter 5

At 10:00, Mark brushed his teeth and came to bed. Anne was sitting up, back to the headboard, twitchy. It would be his turn to stay awake. Then he realized he was exhausted—worn out—just not sleepy.

He sat next to his wife in his sleeping boxers and a loose t-shirt. She had on pajama pants and a *wifebeater* with drifting white clouds airbrushed here and there along with three happy floating cherubs—a birthday present from MJ who only knew the term *undershirt.*

Mark said, "You okay?"

Anne said, "We have to move." She sounded resolute, her decision made.

He gave her a moment to assure her that he'd heard her. Then he said, "He won't be back," with two decades' experience on the force to back up his own resolve.

"How do you know that?" she said. "You don't even know who did it."

Mark kept his cop's calm. "They don't come back." He was as certain of this as she was uncertain. "They do their awful business and move on. It's too risky to revisit a crime site. Whoever did this made it look sloppy, but—"

"Sloppy?" Anne said, and looked at her husband as if she'd never seen him before, as if they'd never met, hadn't married, hadn't been together most of those two decades.

Mark took his time. It was tough leaving work at the office when all you ever saw was death, but he knew he needed to choose his words carefully. "Careless," he amended.

"Careless?" she sounded more incredulous than before.

"Disorganized," he said finally.

Anne said, "Cop talk for brutal, insane, child murders, decapitation, and mutilation. What do you guys call chopping off a boy's penis, '*imprudent*?'"

Mark thought that if Anne been on her game and the situation less awful, she might have come up with "uncircumspect." Normally, she liked a good pun. But not on a night like this after a day like that.

Mark tried, "Honey, I'm just saying—"

"I know what you're trying to say, and I don't believe it."

"You're safe. You'll be fine," he said. "He won't come back. I promise."

"Number one," she said, "you can't promise that. You don't know. This could be the first time. There's a first time for everything, right? Maybe this is *his* first time. How do you know it isn't? How do you know, how can you promise me, that this... vicious, sociopathic *lunatic* will not come back? You can't. So don't." After a pause, she went on, "I saw what he did, Mark. This is not one of those cases, one of your cases, where you give me some vague notion of what happened, carefully leaving out the details that might worry your wife. I saw this one myself. I saw those precious little bodies chopped to pieces in our neighbor's backyard."

Used to grief and its many encumbrances, Mark listened patiently. He knew his wife had to vent, had to put events into whatever terms she needed to feel better. Still, he knew in his heart, "You'll be fine. It'll take time, but you'll get past it someday."

"It's not me I'm worried about," she said, and got up to pace, her face cold and hard, more determined than before.

Mark said, "We're safe, I promise. All of us."

"Goddammit, quit saying that! You don't fucking know!" Anne yelled. She turned away, tears forming quickly.

Mark steadied his mind as best he could. Fighting with perps and street idiots was one thing—easy to be detached—but family? Your wife? They don't teach that at the Academy. They should, but they don't.

He knew Anne felt bad about yelling at him. In their nearly eighteen years together, they had argued—seriously argued to the point of shouting—maybe three times, and always about something unimportant. A broken washing machine, an overdrawn check, braces for MJ. This was different. This was life and death. Murder on the other side of a wood fence.

The real possibility of losing MJ and Andy to a serial child killer.

Anne brushed away a fierce tear, fighting her emotions. "I feel..." she started, then stopped. She made herself finish, "I feel like everything is closing in on me."

Mark knew that was hard for her to say, to even edge near her one deep fear. He asked cautiously, "Have you had any episodes?"

Mark Young didn't like asking his wife about her claustrophobia issue, since she didn't like to admit she had one. "You haven't been up in the attic, have you?" he asked, with just enough fatherly tone to drive Anne to wide-eyed anger.

"Don't try to psychoanalyze me, you sonofabitch!" she shouted. Then she said, softer, "You're not qualified."

Mark never knew exactly where to go, verbally or emotionally, when either of them got too close to their true fears. His was control—his own. His father's lack of it had cemented Mark's doubt and concern at an early age, and that never went away.

Anne confessed, "I used the downstairs bathroom this afternoon... and I had to open the door." Mark could see the disquietude in her eyes, the disappointment with herself.

He tried to minimize her concern. "You had a stressful morning. We all did."

"Stressful," she mocked. "Try harrowingly traumatic. Insanity producing. I vomited, fell out of the tree, and drank three bourbons before nine AM."

She told him how, around 3:00 in the afternoon, she'd had to pee and used the tiny half-bath under the stairs, in lieu of going upstairs. Usually, she avoided the tight enclosure—just to be safe—but she didn't want to chance waking Mark up after their morning in hell. The other times she'd used it instead of going to their en suite bath upstairs, say when entertaining, or even working on her homework in the den, she didn't experience any panic. Hadn't in years. Until that day. In seconds, she felt the walls pushing in on her psyche and slung the door open.

"It scared me, Mark. I don't know the last time I felt that. I couldn't breathe."

Mark put his hand on his wife's arm and said, "It doesn't mean anything. It was a horrible thing to see. It was hard for me, and I see it all the time. You'll be fine in a day or two. Maybe a week. Or more. But it'll be like a distant memory at some point. That's the way our brains work."

"I'm not a cop," Anne said coldly. "And neither are the kids. We can't erase bad memories on a dime." She returned to her earlier declaration and resolve. "We're moving."

"We're not moving," Mark said with equal resolve. "There's no need."

"There is if I feel it!"

"Anne," he said, now losing patience himself. "We can't just up and move. We don't have the money, the time. Who's going to go house-shopping for something we can afford? How long is it going to take in this market? Where are we going to look? And how do you know another neighborhood will be any safer than *this* one? There's crime everywhere, you know that. There are crazy people everywhere."

"Yeah, there was one in the neighbor's yard," Anne snapped, pointing toward the Blacks' house.

"Right," Mark said. "And there could be one in the next neighbor's yard or the next or in our own house!"

"Is that supposed to make me feel *better*?" she asked with astonishment.

Mark stood quietly, walked past his wife to the bathroom and picked up his toothbrush. He took the cap off the Crest.

"You already brushed your teeth," Anne said. The chill had set in.

Mark turned and said calmly but resolutely, "I will not be intimidated by this creep, Anne. Not gonna happen."

Anne's jaw dropped. "This isn't about *you*. This is about our family, our children! Mark! Good God, what is wrong with you!" Her face was flushed. She brushed roughly at her renewed tears.

Mark put his toothbrush down and came to her, not out of compassion, but because he needed to prove that he was in control. Prove it to himself.

He said, "This is what I do. You knew that when you married me. I am not about to move because of this lowlife fuck."

Anne looked up, her eyes wide now—wide and red and wet. Pleading. "Mark, please."

"I *will* find him." The great authority that he'd invested in himself through years of training, on-the-job experience, and department demands, as well as what he felt about his own character as best he understood it, carried through.

She said, "What if he finds us first?"

Mark was past this discussion, one he'd had with countless civilians before. He knew the answer before his wife asked it. "Won't happen. He's long gone. He'd be stupid not to be." He made a confession. "Truth is, he's probably so far gone, I might not ever find him. But I'm not giving up until I know he's in custody or dead."

"It's not your case," she said, sounding thankful.

"Yeah, actually it is."

Anne stared, agape again.

"I requested it," he said. "Because it *is* you, because it *is* the kids, because he *could* have come to our yard instead of theirs. This isn't just some case on the street, some anonymous victim I didn't know. This time it's us. This time it's personal."

Which should have been the very reason his captain should have refused the request. But Captain Carter "Si-Si-Si" Corlius wasn't the refusing type. He liked anything that gave a man drive. Drive took men places they wouldn't normally go, and going to those places sometimes produced unexpected results. Results solved cases; cleared cases made the captain look good; a captain who looked good didn't get looked at too closely or too often—and that suited Carter Corlius just fine. He took Henrickson off the case and assigned Mark Young to it the moment Mark asked—*because* it was personal.

Mark went back into the bathroom to brush his teeth again. This time, he closed the door—on the discussion and his wife. What he didn't tell her, what he couldn't tell her, was that he was scared, too.

Chapter 6

The next morning, Mark slept in. Anne didn't bother him; she had other things on her mind. Normally, her husband came home from a shift, took two bites of something, occasionally drank a cup of strong coffee, then went to bed and slept until 2:00 or 3:00. This time, they'd gone to bed together—the first time in so long she couldn't remember—and didn't speak. There was no hug, no kiss, no intimacy.

No contact.

When the alarm went off at 6:30, Mark didn't budge. He made no effort to get up and help get the day going.

That's okay, Anne thought. She didn't want his help—not this morning, this morning after. She wanted to be alone, to be able to think in the light of day, to get caught up in the familiar process of family—normalcy offering a screen to the haze of recent horrors, a hopeful glimpse at clarity.

Was Mark right? Would it just go away? Or had something changed so fundamentally and profoundly, so irrevocably, that only leaving this place could make a difference in the way she felt? Could anything ever change the way she felt?

Nothing could make it un-happen. Time doesn't reverse; events aren't erased with a decision to ignore them. Was what happened next door a permanent scar on them all? How could it *not* be? Hell, Mark had said it was temporary, then took over the fucking case!

Still, Anne had to factor in that her husband was a professional—he saw this shit all the time and put it away somewhere. Some*how.* Anne had always felt as morally sound as Mark, and just as strong. She suspected that, given his job, she would and could perform and ignore exactly as he always had. His was just a career choice. She'd chosen K-12 teaching, paralegal *secretary-ing,* and real estate brokering.

Christ, she thought, *we're doomed.*

Anne watched MJ scarf her pancakes and read her vampire love book, seemingly back to normal. Andy picked at his one flapjack idly, elbow on the table, chin in his hand, mind probably in the tree.

The bloody backyard.

He had seen it, and he would never be the same. Anne didn't care what Mark thought about her process, their son's was damaged forever. MJ might get past it—she hadn't seen anything; plus, she was almost a teenager. *Teenagers can't form a sentence without forgetting halfway through what they were angry about.*

Worse than Grandmother Denise.

But maybe Andy wasn't thinking about anything. Maybe he was just being seven. Maybe—

Aw Christ, get on with it! Anne's plan was not working.

She felt around inside for the normal in her, to give her ballast. "MJ, did you remember your—"

Before Anne got to the third word, MJ held up her scarlet and gold swimsuit, without speaking or missing a word on her page.

Anne turned to her son. "Andy, eat your pancake."

Andy nodded, chin in hand, and picked a piece of pancake off the pile with his fork, but only shoved it around in the syrup.

Anne said, "All right. I think we're done here. Let's go. Get your book bags."

MJ closed her novel and ran upstairs. Andy set his fork down and lumbered away. Anne sighed heavily, certain life would never be the same in her house again, but she had no idea how to change that.

***

After Anne left to take the kids to school, Mark sat up on his side of the bed and stared out the window for twenty minutes. He could see his neighbors' house, their bedroom window, and wondered what they'd talked about last night.

Probably the same things he and Anne hadn't—or less.

He stood, went to the window, and looked down into Dan Black's backyard where the awful things had happened. The grass was still blotched with red. Humidity had kept the blood from drying completely. How could the parents be dealing with this? How could anyone?

Mark stepped away from the window to survey their house discreetly. No signs of life.

Imagine that.

After a long, hot shower—which seemed to do little good—and a shave, which did more, Mark grabbed some cold coffee from the day before (Anne had intentionally not made fresh), a stale wholewheat croissant, and a green banana.

He would go in early today. What else did he have to do?

The day passed more quickly than Mark had imagined it would. He looked over some cold files but came up with no new ideas. Since he wasn't officially on shift yet, he received no calls to go out into the field.

So, he read Dan Black's children's murder files—seven times—his own notes and those of the officer who was first on the scene. The young buck named Harold Marlin, nicknamed Buzz for his Marine-style haircut, though he'd never served, had written a mean report—lots of adjectives and pulp fiction details. He evidently took pleasure in describing the "temperament" and "apparent psychological state" of "persons involved."

Cop-speak on *SVU* steroids.

He noted that the "mother of the apparent victims appeared aggrieved to excess." Mark muttered, "Ya think?" He chose to ignore the first adjective.

Buzz wrote that Dan Black, "the father of the alleged victims, expressed no discernible emotions but rather set in one position while investigators examined the scene preliminarily."

This time Mark said, "Alleged," and shook his head. "'Set.' Jesus." Spend all that time and ink elaborating and can't get the simplest verb right.

The seventh reading didn't offer anything more than the first six, other than Mark's increased irritation with modifiers.

He ate lunch in, late—somebody had bought a pizza for Manny Spano's thirty-eighth birthday. Spano loved the four-meat special. Mark thought if Manny lived past forty it would be a miracle. After one piece, Mark ate his tasteless green banana. At least it had roughage.

He didn't call home.

Just before dark, before his shift officially began, Mark's captain Corlius—an odd cookie with several tics after thirty-two years on the force—walked through on his way home. He said, "You don't go home anymore?"

Mark said, "Not today." He figured Corlius had probably put in similar hours back when he did investigations—that brief period before his superiors had recognized his political skills and promoted him early when his predecessor was killed during an actual investigation. From then on, Corlius's job became DWO—desk work only.

"Any leads?" Corlius asked.

After one day.

Mark said, "I'm waiting on forensics."

"Everyone been interviewed?"

Only twenty-five or so to go.

"Nobody saw or heard anything."

"Ghost shit, huh?" his captain said.

Middle of the night murders with everyone asleep in insulated homes with air-conditioning blasting.

Mark said, "Ghost would've left more at the scene."

Si-Si-Si nodded and left.

Mark had seen several ghost cases over the years. Not one in ten ever came to anything.

Feeling that his day-long delve into this one had proven fruitless—or worse, pointless—Mark decided to "call in sick." That's what he told the dispatcher standing in front of him.

The woman said, "You don't look sick."

"Oh, but I am," Mark said. "You don't know the half of it."

She laughed and took him off the schedule.

At home, Anne thanked Mark for taking a second night off, and they talked about everything but what was on their minds.

***

The next day, both were back to their routines. Over the next two weeks, Mark and Anne saw each other coming and going. They hugged, they kissed, the kids giggled, and life seemed to be back to normal. The parents understood the pretense, figuring the kids didn't.

The kids did.

No one saw the neighbors, assuming they were away with family, grieving, or had moved. Mark saw it differently: the grass was mowed and the newspapers collected; garbage cans had come and gone on pickup days. Someone was home, or at least checking on the place. That was good.

Wasn't it?

Chapter 7

Mark parked his Vic with the scratched hood around the corner and walked to the crime site. Not ten minutes had passed since it happened. He asked the first uniform he saw, "Drive-by?"

The cop nodded. "Detective Bowers is..."

The young man turned to look but there was no one there, so he said, "Last time I saw him, he was over behind the ambu*lance*." He wasn't from around there.

Mark thanked him and walked that way. He was thinking how Anne was doing much better. She'd been able to talk about *the night it happened* without tearing up or showing fear. She'd dropped her demand that they move, admitting—at least agreeing—that her husband was probably right.

"He's long gone," she said, and it sounded as if she almost believed it.

She used the tiny bathroom under the stairs several times in defiance and left the door closed.

Mark wasn't usually one to say, "I told you so," but he did, and Anne smiled. She hit him in the stomach, and they had pretty good sex on the couch.

Life really had returned to normal—better than the normal of late—even if Mark still had no leads. Forensics was in, everyone had been interviewed, but no leads emerged. Nothing at all. Completely, sadly, normal.

Ghost shit.

Jerome broke his old partner's reverie. "Two dead, two on their way."

Mark turned to find Jerome returned from wherever he'd gone, smoking a Natural American Spirit cigarette from the black pack. *Kind of like his lungs,* Mark thought.

"Anyone talking?" Mark said, looking around at the hundred or more lookieloos.

Jerome said, "'Nobody saw nuthin'.'"

Mark nodded. The usual for gang violence. Nobody wanted any trouble—any *more* trouble.

***

At 10:30 PM, Anne stepped into the shower. Andy was asleep and MJ was reading past lights-out. Another high school vampire love story Anne wished she'd throw away, but MJ was hooked.

The hot water felt better than usual running over Anne's bare skin. Maybe they really were past the rough years. Maybe they could regain some of the fun and passion that had stealthily crept away one night when they weren't looking.

How many years had it been since they'd thrown abandon to the wind and gotten crazy for the hell of it? Those wild times—riding naked in his police cruiser through a county park at midnight, giggling like stoned teenagers. They might have actually *been* stoned; Anne couldn't remember.

But she couldn't forget the hilarity—and the outdoor sex after. By a bridge where anyone might have seen them and probably did.

Anne filled her hand with shampoo and massaged it into her scalp. *Heavenly*. She rinsed it out, her heavy hair hanging straight to her shoulders, dark when it was wet. She'd have to start coloring it soon, like the other women she knew. She'd been lucky so far, only having to yank out an occasional stray gray. But she knew her time was rapidly approaching.

Being thrift-conscious, Anne only used her good conditioner for special occasions—going out to eat, the rare office party or get-together with friends—or when her hair felt as if it needed the expensive stuff, when the sun had baked her by Ailene's pool or she'd taken Andy to the park and lost track of time, cheering a T-ball game and sweating like a sailor in the doldrums.

Or like tonight, when she was winding down from a particularly taxing day at work. The senior partner, Abe Lewis of Lewis, Lewis, & Llewellyn—she'd heard all the jokes—had been gracious enough to hire her on short hours after she'd finished nursing MJ, and never revoked it. He was good that way, but Anne knew the real reason he kept her. She did great work, better than any paralegal he'd ever hired.

And he liked her tits; he said so. A lawyer!

Anne felt them now. After two kids and seventeen-plus years of marriage, her breasts were holding up well. Her nipples had lost a great deal of sensitivity after Andy was born, so she was able to take Mark's intermittent rough play. He liked pinching and the occasional spank or slap.

He'd only gone too far once, and she'd let him know it, but secretly, his wanton lust had aroused her. She'd felt as though he—and the night—were close to being out of control.

Out of her control.

Even his.

The fear excited her. That's when she called a stop to it. Her desire to push sex to the edge of danger frightened her more than Mark's desire to take her there.

Before she stopped him, he had forced her, dragged and shoved her all over the house, in every room. He'd bent her over the couch and spanked her. Hard. Not just play spanking, but the real deal, the S&M kind. Her ass cheeks glowed red, with distinct Mark-sized handprints. She cried and lubricated. Plentifully.

He led her into the kitchen by her outstretched nipples. She protested and tried to pull away, but he wouldn't let go. Pain became pleasure and she became wetter than she'd ever been before.

He lifted her up onto the butcher block and fucked her so hard and deep she thought she might explode—as much from the pounding as from the lust. He had never felt so large. She had never felt so full. She had never been so electrified by intercourse. When he stopped for a moment to catch his breath, she shoved him off and ran into the den.

To escape.

He followed her. "Now I'm gonna have to punish you for that. For running away," he said in a cruel voice. *Was it real?* She'd never known for sure.

"No!" she had shouted. Had she really wanted to resist, or did she just say that because she thought she should, because she thought it was appropriate, because they were caught up in a game—a sexy, dangerous amusement with specific roles to play and lines to say?

"Stay away!" She'd wanted to laugh but was afraid that might send the wrong signal. So, she shouted, "No!" again. "I mean it. No!"

"Oh yeah," Mark said in a low and menacing way, as if he meant it as well.

"What are you going to do?" Anne asked, her eyes wide with dread and desire. He just laughed—and left the room.

He returned with a length of rope, two sets of handcuffs, and his old police baton.

They'd never played out the obvious police fantasy in the dozen years they'd been married at that point. That night, they would. It seemed like play. But was it?

Mark handcuffed Anne's right hand to the den doorknob and her left to an upright shelf column on the heavy bookcase. He shoved her feet as far apart as they would go, tying one to the open bookcase door and the other to a sturdy leg on the big sofa.

Next, he brought out his black baton, from when he'd walked a beat. He slid the side-handle into her so easily it surprised her and made her look down at the "long black cock" sticking straight out from between her firm thighs. She was a runner back then.

Mark added the verbiage—not something he normally did. It would have sounded comical if it hadn't seemed so threatening. The baton inside her, feeling *so bad and so good at the same time.*

Christ, she thought. *We've become clichés – and we're enjoying it!*

Anne had never heard Mark say anything racial, one way or another, and she had never had a serious interracial fantasy herself—at least not in years, since college—but seeing the black protrusion from between her legs, in her submissive position, made everything come alive.

When he pulled the handle out and gave her the long part, she was amazed at how much of it she took. Then he put his mouth to her. She remembered an orgasm so deep she nearly fainted. Had her wrists not been secured, she surely would have fallen over.

Mark didn't let up, telling her she gave in too quickly, too easily. "Oh, that was way too fast. I'm gonna have to punish you for *that,* now."

Anne didn't ask him what he was going to do that time. She was too scared. How much weirder could it get? Looking over her shoulder with intoxicating fear, she saw him drinking more scotch and wondered how he was maintaining such a monstrous erection—an erection at all. How many had he had already? Six? Seven?

"You want some?" He saw her looking.

She dared a tiny nod. He brought her a taste, making sure it dribbled down onto her breasts so he could lick it off—and bite each nipple a little too hard.

She cringed, but the single malt tasted better than any she'd ever had. He gave her another sip, and while she was savoring it, eyes closed...

He took a belt to her.

He was careful not to hit too hard—to leave a bruise—but he came damn close. She let go numerous barely muffled screams, not caring if the neighbors heard her. He smacked the doubled-over black leather on the inside of her thighs and on her bare, engorged labia.

The leather came away dripping.

He turned her ass crimson and worked his way down to her calves. *Slap. Slap. Slap. Slap. Slap.* The steady, even rhythm of the smacking leather working her into sex delirium.

Then he started with the pinching—inside her thighs again, down her legs, back up to her soaking wetness. Her nipples. Pulling them so hard she thought they might pop off. Twisting and wrenching them until they were as red and sore as her round, hard cheeks.

They drank more, then he fucked her standing there—fully restrained—even harder than before. She cried, and wanted more, never understanding why.

Then she told him to stop. Shouted at him. "Stop! Now! I mean it! Stop!"

She got his attention and the night's debauchery ended.

Never going there again.

Never forgetting.

In the shower now, with Mark at work and both kids asleep, Anne cried again as she rubbed herself, approaching climax. Why had she stopped him? Was she afraid he would go too far and really hurt her? Was she afraid of her own husband?

Or was she afraid of herself?

She stood in the shower, crying and rubbing her most private folds, gently at first, then harder and harder—more attacking than pleasuring herself.

It felt good. Like punishment well-deserved for letting her husband down, for telling him to stop, for doubting him, for wanting to move away, for not protecting the neighbors' kids, for not being sure she was protecting her own.

Anne rubbed harder and harder, but no release came. She pinched and twisted her red nipples that now seemed to have no feeling left in them at all. Did she have any feeling left anywhere?

Harder and harder. Fingers deeper and deeper. *Closer.* She could feel it approaching. Quicker now—

Bang!

The sound was loud and solid. Unfamiliar.

Close.

Anne stopped, frozen in the hot water, listening, muscles tensed, tight, ready.

Vulnerable.

Her breathing came hard and deep. Her heart racing. Listening with every molecule in her body.

"MJ? Andy?"

Nothing.

"MJ!"

The door opened and MJ walked in.

Good Christ, Anne had been masturbating like hell, was a mile off, and had left the door unlocked!

"What, Mom?" MJ asked sleepily, oblivious.

Anne covered herself partially as she always did, even though she knew MJ didn't care. Nudity had never been a big issue in the Young household. Mark and Anne made sure of that. They didn't want their kids growing up with *issues.*

"Did you hear anything?"

MJ rubbed her eyes. "What do you mean?"

"I thought I heard something, a bump or something."

"I didn't hear anything. Can I go to sleep now? I was asleep, I think." She held her open book at her side, but her eyes were sleep-filled.

"Sure, honey. I'm sorry to bother you. Make sure Andy didn't fall out of bed again, okay?"

MJ nodded, turned, and walked out, leaving the door open.

Anne started to object, but MJ was already turning into her room and closing the door, having already forgotten to check on Andy.

Anne stepped out of the shower and back in quickly, taking only a second to close and *lock* the door.

Then her eyes found the long, round, shampoo bottle.

Chapter 8

The medical examiner's new nighttime flunkies were taking the bodies away from the drive-by incident when Mark reached into his pants pocket and made a face.

Jerome said, "Needle in your pocket?" Old cop joke.

Mark said, "Forgot my phone again."

"You been doin' that a lot lately."

Mark didn't deny it.

Jerome said, "Annie still scared and needy and shit?" He lit up a Merit 100 and inhaled at least fifty in the first draw.

Mark thought Merits were for women, but apparently Jerome would buy anything these days, his addiction now so great he'd stopped being picky.

Now if he'd just stop asking questions about Anne.

"No," Mark said with pride and humility at the same time. "She's doing much better. *We're* doing much better."

Jerome nodded but didn't say anything. He was a cop, too. Three divorces and not yet thirty-seven. "Well, I'm done here. I'll, uh, see you back at the station."

Mark said, "Yeah," but something was off. One: Jerome was acting hinky—fake friendly or serious about something secret; and Two: they hardly ever saw each other at the station.

Mark watched Jerome go to his detective special, the silver Impala, and get in, after checking in all directions as if to see who might be watching. Then he gave a last, false smile and tip of the head and drove away—quickly—checking his phone as he steered.

Very odd.

After Jerome's Impala was out of sight, Mark reflexively reached into his pocket to call Anne. He always called at bedtime.

His pocket was still empty.

So, he walked around the corner at the end of the street, thinking how he needed to focus. Forgetting his cell was just the tip of it. He'd gotten nowhere on Dan Black's case. Three children murdered *next door* and he didn't have a clue. No one did. The press had been unrelenting, driving Mark's captain to lean on him harder.

It hadn't worked.

Mark once got so angry at his own lack of progress that he snapped at Corlius in front of two dozen officers. "Snapped" wasn't quite it. He *hollered,* "Get off my fucking back!"

To his captain.

Remarkably, Corlius didn't say anything or write him up—most likely because it wouldn't have helped the Black kid case get solved any quicker. Instead, he nodded slightly, with a stern look, and retreated to his office. Door closed.

Mark apologized to the other officers. Some muttered, "It's cool," and "Tough case, man"—two pats on the shoulder—and Mark was left to feel like shit. Reminded.

Something had to give. Soon.

***

Since Anne seemed to be over her "thing," Mark figured he could get back to work for real. *Make some fucking progress on this case!* Three weeks and still nothing.

So much for the seventy-two-hour theory. Forensics turned up less than nothing—no errant footprints, no hairs, no DNA other than the family.

Some dogs and cats. A raccoon.

Mark shook his head, wondering what the hell was happening to the world that some *vicious sociopathic lunatic*—Anne's words resonated—could walk into a man's house, take his three children out, and murder them in his own backyard.

Rage and disgust with mankind boiled in Mark's gut like carious witches' brew—a potion that leads to violence born of frustration and pent-up pain, horrors only the owner can know.

After another afternoon in the station and a few hours into his night shift, Mark again took the rest of the night off and went home. As he drove past Dan's house, he could see a few lights on inside, but no movement. They were either back from wherever they'd gone or were trying to rejoin the living. They needed to try, at least.

Mark thought it odd, though, how seeing signs of life in the death house didn't calm him. If anything, he felt more uptight—more frustration and rage, more pain and horror—as if he was letting everyone down. Doing nothing.

Fortunately, neither Dan Black nor his wife had called to ask questions like most bereaved parents did. They'd both said they would give the police ample time to do their work and not meddle. Thank someone's god for that. Of course, then they'd probably sue; but that wouldn't be Mark's concern. He'd sit for a deposition with nothing to hide. He hadn't done anything.

He hadn't *done* anything! Just spun his wheels. *Shit.*

As Mark slowed for his driveway, he remembered that he'd left his cellphone on the dresser next to his and Anne's honeymoon photo from Acapulco. What a disappointment that had been—the town, the tourists, the cost, Montezuma's Revenge, getting a ticket he couldn't talk his way out of, even with his badge.

He recalled bitching, "No professional courtesy whatsoever. Fucking Federale grifters." He hadn't taken Anne's suggestion of offering a bribe and instead had to pay a hundred-dollar fine at the station. "Fat, laughing bastard," he'd said of the happy sergeant who took the cash.

The memory made Mark chuckle as he turned into his driveway. But his chuckle ended abruptly. As his lights swept across the lawn, then down the side pavement, a man in dark sweats threw a redwood end table from the backyard through the side kitchen window.

The man raised his hand to cover his eyes from the headlights' glare—the rest of his face hidden inside the drawn hoodie—and turned to run. He wasn't waiting to get caught.

Mark slammed his Vic in Park and jumped out, drawing his duty weapon as he went. "Stop or I'll shoot!"

Screams were now coming from inside his house. He tried not to listen.

And shot.

Three loud pops in the night as the intruder swung over the rear fence in one smooth, deftly powerful leap. Just to the right of the tree Andy and Anne had climbed.

Mark dashed for the fence, firing three more rounds on the run.

Anne—wrapped in a towel with another on her wet hair—opened the back door and yelled, "Mark?! What the fuck's going on?!"

Mark hollered, "Call nine-one-one! Now!"

Anne turned back for the phone as Mark jumped the fence—not as gracefully as the man in black, but he was over it almost as fast. He snagged his pants and would have a nasty bruise, but he didn't pause to feel it.

On the run, he fired three shots—then three more—then realized he was alone.

***

The living room, kitchen and den crawled with cops. When one of their own is *directly* involved in an incident, *everybody* comes. The front yard looked like a free donut convention.

So, when Jerome walked into the house, just after 11:00 PM, smoking a Kent filtered, he said, "Someone giving away free donuts?"

"That's not even fuckin' funny, detective," Sergeant Kay Lown said, and walked out to her black-and-white with donuts on the dash.

Jerome said, "Just trying to lighten things up."

"Wrong party," Mark said.

They moved to the den where Anne was giving her statement to Detective Martin Coor, a shlumpy white guy who would have served the public better by opening a hotdog stand.

Anne was telling him, "I heard the crash and went downstairs. I saw Mark running and shooting and yelling for me to call nine-one-one, and I did." She ran a Kleenex under her nose. "I'm sorry. It all happened so fast."

Mark knew that Anne knew that was what most everyone said in those situations and that she likely felt dumb for saying it—that she was a detective's wife and should have noticed more. Retained it. But Anne Young wasn't a detective herself and it *had* happened fast. Before she could begin to understand what was happening, it was over.

Coor asked if she could give a description "of the perp" and Anne said, "No." She said she was sorry again and that she didn't see him. "Mark did."

"Right," Coor said. "Got it." He scribbled a note.

Martin Coor was two years younger than Mark Young and half as smart. What he lacked in imagination and footwork he made up for in banality and laziness. He'd be perfect for the case, leaving Mark free to look wherever he wanted with no fear of finding Martin Coor there. Unless he looked in strip clubs or adult bookstores.

Martin looked over at Mark, who nodded. He would tell Coor anything he wanted to know in detail—if he could remember. It had happened fast for him as well.

At least no one died. Dead bodies always made everything more complicated and unpleasant. *Yeah, at least no one is dead.*

That they knew of.

Detective Coor turned back to Anne, but she had begun weeping again, probably from nerves, reliving the event in her mind under questioning. Looking off, tightening up. Coor told a female uniform to take her into the kitchen and "get her something to drink."

The officer, and Anne, complied.

Mark was already on his third scotch when Jerome Bowers moved closer and said, low, "Lotta bullet holes out there."

Mark said, "That's what they say." He looked up at Martin Coor listening in, making more notes.

Jerome said, "You don't remember?"

Mark said, "Not much," and finished his scotch. It was helping his nerves—just not his memory.

Jerome said, "Some'a those holes are in your neighbors' houses. They're not too happy about that."

Mark gave him a look that said, "All right, you come home, find some guy breaking into your house where your wife and kids are asleep, two weeks after someone killed the neighbors' three kids in the worst ways possible, and you wouldn't pull down on the asshole, try to kill him where he stood? When he ran?"

Seriously?

Jerome read it right and said, "I know. But still."

Mark understood his unstated reply as well. *You've been trained not to do that crazy shit.*

Mark looked in his glass, contemplating a fourth scotch. He said, "White male, probably. Five-ten, six feet, maybe taller—one-eighty, two hundred. Maybe less. Twenty-something, thirty, wearing a dark hoodie, black or dark blue. Dark sweatpants maybe matched. Black shoes, running shoes, maybe. No shiny shit."

He was guessing at everything. The only thing clear in his head was that it was all a blur. The shithead could have been five-six and one-thirty-five the way he went over that fence so quick and easy. A high jumper maybe, college athlete. High schooler.

Probably a kid. *Jesus.* What had he been thinking?

Jerome asked, "Weapon?"

Mark knew what his answer would mean, but he wasn't going to lie. "I didn't see one."

Jerome nodded. *But you shot at him anyway, shot up the whole neighborhood. That's not going to go down well.*

Mark knew that was what Jerome was thinking, but he said, "This is why eye-witness testimony is shit. *We* can't even get it right."

He said it mostly for the benefit of Martin Coor, who gave an exaggerated nod as if he understood. Jerome always said privately that he didn't like Marty Coor, never did. Said he was "too white for his own good," and was happy never to have worked with him.

Mark nodded agreement—at spoken and unspoken sentiments—and headed for the bottle of single malt.

Jerome said, "Cap'n wants to see you first thing."

Mark said, "I'm sure he does," and emptied the bottle.

Chapter 9

The police shrink's office was nicer than Mark had imagined. This was his first time seeing one in his twenty-one years on the force. That he'd made it this far without a psych eval was remarkable. He was that good a cop.

Had been until now.

The plaque on the door read "Eileen Quarry, PsyD, DSW" So, she wasn't a *mere* psychologist; she was the real thing, a scrip-writer. Mark hoped she'd recommend something powerful and final. Double-strength *oxy-whatever.*

Sleep would be a dream from now on.

Mark sat in a chair facing her desk and observed her silently. Eileen Quarry was tallish, probably—he hadn't seen her stand yet—brunette and well dressed. Stylish, current. Attractive in a professional way. Even hot. If things hadn't been going so well with Anne until two days ago, he might have had *thoughts*.

She looked a few years younger than Mark, but she might have just been holding up well under the stress of cop-adjacent work—though he couldn't imagine how. That had to be some rough shit. Maybe better than counseling crackheads and career hookers. Or maybe not. Cops were notoriously fucked up and unwilling to admit it. Most had events in their pasts that only they knew and would never talk about with their wives or pastors, much less a department shrink. Maybe each other if they were all drunk enough.

Even then, details got left out.

After perusing the pages in Mark's file—mostly for effect, he thought, since she'd no doubt read them in detail before he arrived—the doctor put down her designer reading glasses and said, "Detective. This is a procedural interview. A weapon was discharged."

"I know. I discharged it."

Dr. Quarry smiled the way only psychiatrists and their craziest patients can and put her glasses back on the end of her nose. Looked down at the file. "Yes," she said. "I see you've been around a while."

Mark said nothing. His job at this point was to play hard-ass. Don't give away anything anyone could use at any time in any future.

His doctor looked up. "I don't mean that in any disparaging way. On the surface, you seem to be holding up quite well."

Mark still said nothing.

She carefully set her glasses on her desk pad and said pleasantly, calmly, "We don't have to go into anything personal at this point if you—"

"My wife is leaving me and taking the kids."

He looked for a reaction, as, apparently, did Dr. Quarry. Neither gave anything away.

Then, she said, "That's unfortunate. But as you know, not unusual."

Mark said with equal calm, if more intensity, "I told her I don't want to know where. Not to tell me until this is over. Which may be never."

Dr. Quarry maintained her professional demeanor. "Perhaps that's a bit premature."

He said bluntly, "The fewer people who know where my family is, the safer they are."

The doctor said nothing, so Mark gave his side of the story. "I caught the guy breaking into my house with my family inside. I gave due warning and fired. It's as simple as that."

"It's never as simple as that," she said. "This is PD. We have rules about rules."

He said, "He killed my neighbors' kids."

She said, "You don't know that."

"It's a safe assumption."

"No assumption is safe."

Their eyes had never left the other's.

After a moment, Mark stood. "Are we done here?"

Eileen Quarry leaned back in her leather chair and said, "Not by a long shot, detective. Have a seat."

Mark didn't want to sit back down, but he knew he would. He had no choice. Not this time. He knew why and he knew she knew.

"So," the attractive *mental health professional* said matter-of-factly, after Mark had retaken his seat, "you're off the case, but not suspended from duty. That's good."

"They let me keep my car."

"Even better," she said in a cheery tone, clearly meant to soothe her patient.

Mark was not soothed; but it didn't matter, and he didn't care. He was already running numerous leads in his head. He was going to *find that fucker* and he *was* going to kill him when he did. *How's that for simple?*

Of course, he wouldn't tell her that.

***

As Mark drove home from his procedural interview, his mind became cluttered with complications. Who was this doctor woman and what did she really know? What did she want from him? What might she get out of him that he didn't want known? By anyone.

What was her agenda? Did she have one? Was hers the same as his captain's? Or worse, *Interminable* Affairs? Did she even care that he was on the case of neighborhood murders that happened *next door*?

Was. Past tense. Henrickson was back on it and Mark was just a bystander headed for an ugly police divorce. He'd be lucky if a judge let him see his own kids more than once a month after shooting up three neighbors' houses.

He couldn't go looking for the *perp* who broke his window and scared his family with whatever evil intent in mind. He couldn't even go after the guy who did the dreadful deed next door, now. Drawing his duty weapon and emptying the fucking clip in a residential area—his own—obviated any more official involvement in either case, probably for good.

For good. He laughed to himself.

At some point, Mark assumed, his new shrink would ask about his childhood. Then he'd have to tell her that his state trooper father was an awful human being who mentally tortured him and his sister, physically beat Mark, and that his mother did nothing to intervene. How Albert "Al" Young had once made young Mark kill a chicken for dinner—they lived in the country, not far from town—while his sister watched from her favorite tree swing, singing the alphabet song to keep herself distracted, and his mother stared on in a psychotropic haze. When Mark couldn't murder the bird, his father did it for him—in an especially gruesome manner, disemboweling the thing first and making sure blood spattered on his son "to teach him a lesson."

The next time was easier.

Before he knew it, Mark was shooting squirrels and birds for no other reason than he could. He even killed a neighborhood feral cat with his .22 rifle once. After that, everything came easy. Becoming a homicide detective was the logical next step. Nothing bothered him—and he understood the urge to harm, to kill, to do bad things. He had wanted to do them all to his own father. Understanding criminals was light work compared to knowing himself.

What would the fetching Doctor Quarry make of all that?

Nothing good, he figured.

As he pulled around the corner, the usual way he came home, Mark saw someone standing in his driveway. Since Anne and the kids were gone, at first he thought it might be Anne's brother Smithton, the gay professor, but it was unlikely that Smithie had driven all the way down from Boston.

Mark's next guess was Jerome, but the guy in his driveway wasn't black. Next, he found himself hoping it was The Guy—that's how Mark now referred to the hooded intruder from That Night. Oh, if only he was courageous and stupid enough to come and flaunt it, to try to trick Mark into thinking he was someone else, some normal person. How sweet that would be! Mark would see through his ruse *immediately*, and this time:

He wouldn't miss.

Another few car lengths and he could see that the person in his driveway was Dan Black. Mark's momentary good mood fell, along with his vengeful spirits. What did *he* want? Was this where he started pestering Mark for details about the case? Now, when Mark was *off* the case?

Perfect.

Mark pulled into his driveway and parked. Dan leaned down to his window and said, "I was sorry to hear about your wife leaving. Mine finally got around to it yesterday."

Mark rolled up his window and shoved his door open, forcing Dan away. He said, "What? Are we gonna be divorce buddies now? Join a group? Bake cupcakes?"

Dan laughed with surprisingly good nature. "Sorry. Didn't mean to be presumptuous. Have a nice day."

The last part didn't sound entirely sincere as he turned away for his house, but what the hell? With all the fucking crazy shit going on in this fucking neighborhood, at their houses?

In their houses.

Mark watched him go a few feet and felt bad. "Wait," he said.

***

Twenty minutes later, Mark Young and Dan Black were sitting in Mark's den, drinking beer from cans, watching a football game. Neither had said much more than, "Beer?" "Sure." "Bud Light?" "Anything." "Watch a game?" "Why not?"

Now, Mark asked Dan, "Jets fan?"

Dan said, "When they're winning."

Mark chuckled gruffly. He'd been a huge Jets fan until the signal-stealing episode with the Lions. Now, he just watched the Jets because he was used to them. Knew their names and numbers. He also knew that, as the years passed and trades were made, at some point he wouldn't know any of them anymore—or at least enough of them to care. Then he could move on. Otherwise, Mark Young wouldn't let *anything* go by the way.

In the meantime, knowing who was who made watching games easier with the sound off—he could think about who had killed this neighbor's children and probably tried to kill his own. Were they the same guy? Was The Guy *that* guy? Were the events even connected? Had he shot at some lowlife trying to break into his house for food or money, prescription drugs? Guns?

Maybe just some kid out breaking shit for fun?

Fuck no. It was the same guy. *Why else would I shoot at him*? It was a gut thing. Mark felt it. *Fuck yeah,* it was The Guy—the *same* guy.

After a few downs that failed to distract Mark from his darker thoughts, he grabbed up the remote and began searching. "How about basketball?"

He found a saved Heat-Bulls game—one of those 96-95 super games—and hit play. "Last five minutes are what the game's all about."

Dan squirmed uncomfortably. Mark asked if he was okay and Dan said, "It's stupid, but I have a hard time watching basketball."

Mark busted a laugh. Then, thinking it rude said, "Sorry. Just sounded funny. I mean, *basketball*?"

"Yeah, I know." Dan stared at the floor.

Now Mark was curious. "You wanna tell me about it?"

Dan took a deep breath, "It's stupid, really."

"So?" Mark said, more curious than before. "I think I have to hear this now." He was smiling.

A guy thing.

Dan told him. "I played some sports in high school. I was tall for my age—my height now, six-one—when I was fifteen. Then I stopped growing. I mean, later on I filled out, put on muscle and all, got up to two-ten, two-fifteen. Now I stay around one-ninety. But back then I was this tall and only one-fifty. A string bean." He laughed, but it seemed to lack mirth.

Mark deduced, "So you went out for basketball."

Dan nodded.

"Were you any good?"

Dan shrugged. "All right, not great. I was quick but clumsy. No hands."

"That'll cut into your game," Mark said, already enjoying the story.

Dan said, "Yeah," sounding both humble and embarrassed. Even if it was a long time ago.

"So," Mark said, digging. "Some horrible *Carrie* thing happened at a game? Pig blood rained down on the team?" He was having fun now.

Dan laughed—his first real laugh since the murders, Mark guessed.

"No, I was just... unlucky," Dan said, and told his story.

> *Dan, six-one at fifteen, isn't the tallest boy on the court, or the heaviest, but he's substantial enough to hold his own. The gym is uncrowded as this is a mid-season game. The teams are evenly matched, the score 26-22. Dan's home team is behind.*
>
> *Feeling his oats, he sees an opening and goes for it. He gets a pass just outside the key, with no one between him and the basket, and charges for the layup.*
>
> *Every other player moves in to assist or block – whatever they must do.*
>
> *One of Dan's guards turns to block an opposing player, trips on his own big feet, and stumbles backwards just as Dan launches for the basket*
>
> *When he's midway to the dunk, his teammate's shoulders catch Dan's feet and, with the laws of motion working on both, Dan spins in midair like a pinwheel. He crashes to the floor on his head.*
>
> *Whistles blow, play halts, and everyone gathers around to see that Dan is out cold.*

"Youch," Mark said. He enjoyed a good sports injury story as much as the next guy.

"Yeah," Dan said. "They thought I'd broken my neck, but I was just knocked out."

"Concussion?"

Dan nodded. "Number one." Number two was not as glamorous.

This game has a larger crowd – students and parents cheering for the neighboring teams. Dan's teammate from before is off the court, ready to throw the ball in after an OB bounce.

Anticipating where the ball will go, several players rush that way.

Dan is looking good, playing well, running fast into the cluster as everyone leaps for the ball.

In the middle of the group, a huge guy from the other team grabs the ball, yanks it down and around into his possession – in the process elbowing Dan in the temple with the full force of his substantial weight. Young Dan Black drops to the floor, out cold again.

"Oh man, twice!" Mark said, laughing and cringing at the same time – relishing the details of Dan's demise as a player.

A woman, a mother, wouldn't see the humor; but Mark, having seen the worst sides of humanity for two decades, could only see someone getting knocked silly in a high school ball game as hilarious.

Wiping tears of laughter from his eyes, he said, "That is some rough luck."

Dan said ironically, "That was my first game back after two weeks off to recover from the first one."

"Jesus," Mark said. "They had your number." Though he knew the blows came from different sources.

Still, Dan smiled wanly and acknowledged, "It was a rough year."

Something in his voice told Mark, "It happened *again*?"

Dan nodded.

Mark laughed. "You are *not* going to tell me you got knocked out in the next game."

"No," Dan said. "I made it through the rest of the season. It was the *last* game."

Another school, the gym packed. One of Dan's teammates misses a pass, tips it, and the ball is wild, rolling down the court. Everyone going for it like the maniacal teenaged males they are.

Dan makes a diving slide on his stomach, arms outstretched, just as another kid, a wiry forward for the other team, runs in to kick the ball.

Instead, his kneecap makes direct, solid contact with Dan's cranial crown, and he's out for the third time.

"Owww! Jesus *Christ*!" Mark said, cringing again, laughing even harder. "Again? Holy Christ!" He hadn't laughed that hard in months. Maybe years. "I took some shots playing sandlot ball," he said, recalling his own sports injuries. "Some kids piled on a fumble and broke my collar bone once. You shoulda heard it. Sounded like a .22. going off. *Pow*!" He laughed at the memory.

Of course, it hadn't been funny at the time. His father whipped him for incurring the expense of a doctor's visit and some tape. His shoulder hurt for four weeks, his butt for five.

Mark said to Dan, "But nothing like you. Holy crap." He was still laughing. "Three times!"

"Third one's the charm," Dan said. "Broke the kid's knee with my head. Separated his patella so bad it ended his career." Dan's soft tone indicated that he felt bad about it.

"Happens." Mark shrugged, his laughter subsiding out of respect for the other kid. "Basketball is a full-contact sport."

Dan nodded with wry appreciation. "Not supposed to be."

"So, what happened to your head?"

"Nothing," Dan said. "Can't hurt hardwood." He clunked it like Lane Smith's dense crazy-like-a-fox Senator in *Air America*.

Mark chuckled. "But you were out of a game for the third time in a year. That's some stat."

Dan clarified, "Third time in two months. Or three, whatever it was." Apparently he was unclear in his own mind about the timespan. He said, "Three concussions," and nodded.

"Jeez," Mark said, trying to imagine the ramifications. "Ever get headaches?" It seemed like a logical question.

"I used to," Dan said. "For a year or so, maybe more." Again, he seemed uncertain of the timeline.

"But they went away?"

Dan nodded.

"You're lucky," Mark said. "Some people get one pop like that and have migraines their whole lives."

"Or worse," Dan concurred.

"For sure," Mark said. "Lucky man."

Then he realized he was talking to the unluckiest man he had probably ever known.

Dan stared at the floor.

Mark leaned toward Dan and said softly, "I'm gonna find this guy," with all the gritty determination he had in him, which was considerable.

Considering.

He reiterated, "I'm gonna find this guy, and he will pay. I will make him pay. Justice will be served."

Dan said, "Good. You should. He deserves it."

Mark nodded. Waited. Then he said, "Anything you want to tell me?"

Dan cocked his head to one side and said, "As in..."

"Anything you may have seen or thought of that you forgot—or neglected—to tell the cops. Detective Coor, Martin. He's an all right cop. Not the brightest bulb in the box, but he'll do what he can."

"I feel better already," Dan said, sullenness creeping into his voice.

Mark didn't say anything to defend Coor.

Dan apologized and said, "I thought it was a Detective Henderson or something."

"Henrickson," Mark corrected. "He was on it originally, then I asked for it. Then this shit happened here..." *The Guy, That Night. Shooting up the neighborhood.* "Marty got me, my case, and since they were related—*possibly* related—they put him on your case as well. When they took me off." His bitterness shone bright, but he didn't care.

Dan said, "So, Hendrickson's gone?"

"Henrickson," Mark corrected again. "He and Marty are tag-teaming it—whenever Ted can 'find time' to show up." He added, "He's not known for punctuality or performance."

"Sounds like a real winner," Dan said.

"Killer's probably safe as a hippopotamus in a duck pond."

Dan nodded, then asked, "Should I be talking to you about it? I mean, should you be asking me questions about my case if you're not investigating it anymore?"

"Why not?"

"Maybe it isn't, I don't know, *ethical*? Police procedure. Whatever rules you guys have for situations like this."

"There are no situations like this," Mark said.

"Yeah," Dan said, seeming to appreciate the unique nature of their neighboring problems.

Mark said, "Hell, we make it up as we go along, half the time," trying to make light of the ethical-procedural situation.

Dan didn't seem to be buying it. "I mean, I won't get in trouble for talking to you about it, about my case, my kids' case, whatever. Will I?"

Mark laughed. "In *trouble*?" He made the concept sound ridiculous.

Dan said, sounding the victim, "I don't know. Nobody tells you this stuff when you're a victim. They wait to catch you at something then all hell breaks loose." Then he turned serious. "I don't want anything to go wrong with this investigation, Mark. I want you to catch this guy." Then he corrected himself. "Well, *them*. Whoever they put on it or not. I don't really care. I just want this guy, this demon who murdered my children, caught and punished to the fullest extent possible. Whatever it takes. Whatever happens."

He didn't mention the law.

A plethora of conflicting thoughts flooded Mark's mind. Everything Dan was saying had some truth to it. He, Mark, really shouldn't be discussing this or any other case with a civilian—especially the father of the murdered kids, especially avoiding procedure and the law, etcetera, etcetera. But he wanted to stay close to the case. It was still personal. If that meant getting tight with the victims' despondent *brain-damaged* father, who might remember something, leak something, give up some clue that Marty Coor was likely to miss...

Why the fuck not?

So, Mark said, "You can trust me, Dan. I want this guy real bad. And I wouldn't say a word to anyone to jeopardize my position or yours. Just don't say anything yourself. *You* wouldn't get in trouble, but I'd be up shit's creek. Probably on full suspension. We do have rules about this stuff. I was fucking around before. I shouldn't have said what I did. They'd crack my ass good. Might even fire me. Take my pension. So no, this is between you and me, strictly. You can tell me whatever you want, and I'll look into it on my own, discreetly, without anyone ever having to know anything."

"And you'll tell me whatever you find?" Dan said.

"Absolutely," Mark said, lying through his teeth.

"You swear?" Dan said, like a high school kid.

"Cross my heart," Mark said in kind.

Then, to raise the level of the promise, Mark said something he knew he should never say to anyone, anywhere, anytime. "I want this fuckin' guy *dead*. Okay? No ifs, ands, or buts. Dead and in the ground."

He was saying: *I don't give a fuck what the rules are—I'll break every fucking one of them if I have to—because my ultimate goal is completely illegal. I'm not going to arrest this guy when I find him. I'm going to murder him in cold blood and cover it up.*

He paused a moment, then said, "Does that seal the deal for you, neighbor?"

Dan nodded and said, "Yeah, that sounds good to me. Deal. Thanks, pal."

"No problem." Mark leaned back, feeling good about the way this was going. "So? Anything?"

Dan sipped his Bud Light, looked at the television a moment, then said, "I knew he was in the house."

Just like that.

Mark sat up some. "You *saw* him? *Heard* him?" *What?*

Dan shook his head no. "It was more a feeling. In my sleep."

"Like a dream?"

Dan nodded again. "Only I couldn't wake up. I couldn't stop it." His voice quavered and his eyes reddened. That fast. He gritted his teeth, and the veins rode up on his forehead, his temples. Some deep rage flashed behind his violet-hued eyes.

And they *were* violet. Mark had just noticed. He'd never seen anyone with purple eyes before. Not in person. Not Elizabeth Taylor violet. Not a man.

Dan visibly forced his emotions down a notch and said, "I take pills. I've always been a bad sleeper, but I never took anything until maybe a year or two ago. Now, I can sleep through nuclear holocaust. Never hear a thing."

"I've been there," Mark said. His medication of choice was alcohol, but it did the same job.

Dan said, "But I dream."

"Guilt is tough on a man."

Dan bristled. "What should I feel guilty about?"

Mark softened. "What you were saying. How you sensed the guy was in the house, but you couldn't wake up to do anything about it."

"Oh yeah," Dan said, as if accepting where he was again, grateful to be back on track, for the guidance, for getting on with it. He stood up and paced the length of the den. "I've played it over and over in my head a million times or more. It comes out the same way every time." He stopped in front of Mark and finished. "They're dead."

He looked as pale and lifeless as his dead children at that moment—just in one piece.

Then he let it go just as quickly, shook it off and moved ahead. "Anyway, sorry about the bike thing and... being such a crappy neighbor. I guess I have a short fuse sometimes. Or I used to. It's different now."

Mark thought, *Now that his kids are dead and his wife left him, and he found a kindred spirit in his neighbor the cop who just promised to murder the murderer for him without telling anyone, especially his employer, the police department.*

"It was nothing personal," Dan said. "I just wanted you to know that."

Mark smiled to show his appreciation and acceptance. "It's cool, man. Sit down, watch the game. The Jets win. I Tivo'd it."

He'd forgotten all about the basketball game that was still on. He found the old Jets game and hit Play.

Dan sat down and watched the game.

Mark reached over and patted Dan on the knee—a comforting, fatherly, semi-professional gesture that said, *You're all right, you're in good hands, I'm gonna take care of this thing for you, and you'll be fine.* Just as he'd told Anne—the same sentiment—only this time he believed it a little less.

Neither man spoke another word until they said goodnight.

Chapter 10

Out of the blue, Dr. Quarry asked, "What about sex?"

Mark said, "What about it?"

"Do you like it?"

"Sure."

"Anything... unusual?"

"You mean like transvestites or hookers?"

"Transexual hookers might qualify, yes." The attractive doctor smiled. "Not that I'm shaming or casting blame. Just asking," she said. "I find most law enforcement types, males at least, tend more towards hetero-normative behaviors and tastes."

"You ask everyone if they like tranny hookers?" Mark said.

"Not everyone," she said. "And it's best to leave that term in the graveyard of time."

"Got it," he said, not really caring. "So, I'm special."

She said, "I ask everyone about sex."

"Okay." He didn't say anything else.

"So?"

"Am I gay?"

Quarry smiled. "No, detective."

"Don't you want to know if I've ever had any secret longings for sex with men? Isn't that what all you shrinks want to know? So, just ask it."

Her smile remained. "I don't need to. Being gay is not something I pegged you for. Pardon the pun."

"Ha," Mark said flatly. "Good one."

"So?" she said again.

"Sex."

"Yes."

"What about it?"

"Are you getting any?"

"Not *now*," he said with an edge.

"Okay," she said, unapologetically.

When she said nothing else, Mark said, "It's been less than a month."

"I assume you mean since your wife left."

He said nothing.

"So, you're not ready, yet," the doctor said. "To move on... or look around."

"Are you asking?"

"No."

"Then, no," Mark said.

"How are you dealing with her having left?" she asked.

"I'm sure she did the right thing given the circumstances."

"Perhaps," she said.

"Perhaps?"

"I think we're still undecided on that matter."

"You may be. I'm not."

"Okay. So...?"

"Sex."

"*Unusual* sex."

"Unusual how?"

"Unusual for *you*."

When Mark didn't reply, Dr. Quarry said, "I'm not asking you for societal judgements. I'm just trying to get at any specific sex acts you may have tried or considered that you yourself thought at the time or later might be out of your realm of interest or inappropriate."

"No."

"No?"

"No."

"Okay." She made a note, then looked up. "Any violence?"

"Only every day," Mark said.

"I meant at home," she said.

"No."

"No rough sex?" Mark said nothing, so she said, "I'll take that as a yes—not unusual for cops. So don't beat yourself up." This time she didn't pardon the pun.

"I don't plan to," he said.

Quarry took a deep breath and said, "Detective... Mark. May I call you Mark?"

"It's my name."

"Mark. What I am trying to get at—and I think you know this—is if you and your wife, or you and any other lovers—"

"There are no others."

"Fine. Then, your wife. Did you and your wife ever engage in rough sex? Did you bring violence into the bedroom?"

While he decided whether he wanted to tell her about the handcuffs and baton night, he gazed at her, trying to read her with his cop-sense. She must have felt that gaze because she looked down and pretended to make a note in his file.

Or was she giving him a chance to look? *Don't be stupid,* he told himself.

But he took the moment to see that she was wearing a sheer black blouse over a black slip or teddy over a black lacy bra. He'd noticed when he first came in that she had on a shortish black leather skirt and patterned hose.

He had also observed that her hair looked freshly styled—slightly different than before: shorter, sharper, *sexier*. She had new glasses, too, with more of those custom expensive frames. He wondered how many pairs of high-end eyewear she owned.

How many black teddies.

Dr. Quarry looked up and said again, "So..."

Mark met her look, then turned away. He said, "I used to like it a little rough, yeah. Sometimes."

"How rough?" She made another note.

"Do you have to write that down?"

Eileen Quarry looked at him. She said, "No," and scribbled the note into obliteration. "We'll see where it goes, then I'll decide whether or not to put it in my notes. But only if you agree. Okay?"

"Okay."

"So," she said, "how rough?"

Mark thought. "Compared to what I see on the internet, not bad."

"But it made you uncomfortable," she surmised.

He nodded. But, "Not at first."

"Something happened."

He nodded.

She said, "Things got out of hand, so to speak." She offered a smile.

He did not reciprocate.

"Out of control," she amended.

"You might say that," he said. "Do we have to talk about this?"

"At some point, yes," the doctor said, implying that it might as well be now. "I look for what I call instigation portals, inciting events, if you will, that might play out later in other ways. For instance, chasing an anonymous person down an alley with the intent of shooting them for breaking a window."

Mark squirmed and took a deep breath. "Fine," he said. "It was about five years ago. We always—well, not always of course—I mean to say..."

"On occasion, you liked your sex a bit spicy."

"Rough," Mark said. "There's no sugar-coating this."

Dr. Eileen Quarry leaned in. "Detective Young, I can assure you that there is nothing you can say that I have not heard before. *And* worse. Lots of couples like a little extra physicality in their sex. Cops especially. With what you guys—and women—see and have to deal with all the time, it's hardly surprising."

Mark wasn't forthcoming, so she took a different tack. "Did you try to strangle her?"

"No," he said, both shocked and a bit offended.

"Did you punch her?"

"No!" More so.

"Did you stick a gun in her pussy?"

"No!" Is this bitch fucking kidding?

Eileen Quarry sat back. "Then there you are. Nothing out of the ordinary so far. Please go ahead."

As if they were talking about sandwiches.

Mark's head was spinning. Aching. What he wouldn't give for a scotch and three Quaaludes.

He took another steadying breath and told the story of spanking Anne with the belt, handcuffing her and twisting her nipples. Penetrating her with a baton.

Eileen interrupted. "But you said she had lost some sensitivity after the second pregnancy. It's not uncommon. Some women gain sensitivity and can barely stand to be touched on their breasts. Even a light brush is painful." She demonstrated as she spoke.

Mark stared.

She seemed unfazed. "As a response to losing that sensitivity, some women simply ask for more pressure. Some ask for a lot of pressure. Some ask for what appears to be pain to the person applying the pressure, but in fact is not pain to the receiver. In fact, a woman with greatly desensitized nipples feels almost nothing. Sometimes nothing at all. Her partner can squeeze as hard as he or she likes, and the desensitized woman feels no discomfort, no pain, no sensation of any sort. Maybe slight pressure. Nothing more. But she knows she is receiving attention, knows it should—it looks like it should—hurt, but she feels nothing other than satisfaction at being noticed, at receiving attention. Sexual attention."

Thankfully, she had stopped her demonstration—a load off for Mark on several counts.

She said, "You said you handcuffed her. I'm assuming with your department-issued cuffs."

"Yeah, we, um," Mark was having a hard time. He hadn't prepared for this trajectory.

She said, "You're not accustomed to discussing your private marital sexual matters."

"No," he said.

"Not with anyone? The guys?" she said.

"No," he said.

"A brother?"

"I don't have any brothers."

"Sister?"

"We don't talk much, about anything." *Especially sex.*

"Certainly, you have friends," the doctor said.

"A few." But even that was an exaggeration. All Mark Young had was Anne, MJ, and Andy. And he liked it that way. But he said, "I don't talk about sex with my friends." He didn't talk to his friends about his wife's shoes, much less their sex.

Dr. Quarry said, "So, you've never had anyone to talk to about your sexual questions or issues."

"I never thought I had any."

"But you said you struck your wife. Slapped her and used a belt—a baton as a phallus—and that it bothered you, clearly." Though she wore no expression of judgment, her look felt harsher than any Mark had faced down before—except for Anne if she was pissed at him. Was this shrink mad at him? Already?

He tensed up. "I said she liked it rough—*we* liked it rough on occasion—and one time... I guess we went too far."

"And how do you know this?"

"She told me to stop."

"And you took this to mean that she wasn't enjoying herself?"

"Well... yeah."

Dr. Quarry laughed. "Men. You all think you know everything there is to know about pleasing women."

Mark didn't think the comment sounded very professional. *Again.*

She must have sensed that because she said, "I'm just saying: You should not feel guilty about whatever happened for a number of reasons, the greatest of which is that you really have no idea how much she was or was not enjoying the sensations of pain and fear at the time. For all you know, that moment may have been the highlight of her entire sexual life. As I said previously, she may not have been experiencing any pain at all.

"And that may have scared her. Not you per se, but the act. She got too close to the precipice and backed away, perhaps terrified. Again: not of you, but of herself, of her own needs and wants. Her deepest, darkest secret desires." The doctor leaned forward. "She was afraid of how far *she* might go. Not you."

Mark thought that could be a reasonable assumption—meant to be comforting. But it gave him little ease.

Dr. Quarry switched gears again. "What do we know about her upbringing? Anne's."

Mark knew what the doctor was going for. He divulged what he knew, reluctantly. That was Anne's business; but given the context of the current conversation, her psychological state might have had something to do with the troubling sexual event in question. So, Mark did some rationalizing. "She may have been molested when she was little. Fondled at least."

"Well, there you have it," Dr. Quarry said, sitting back. "Damaged goods. We always make the best sex partners."

"We?" Mark said.

His psychiatrist laughed and leaned forward. "'We' as in the collective—the female half of the species. We're all damaged in some way."

Mark thought two things. One: did his *doctor* mean what he thought she was saying when she said "we", or what she *said* she was saying? And Two: this whole session was weird. And one other thing.

Dr. Eileen Quarry was definitely hot.

Chapter 11

Mark woke up in his car in the parking lot around the side of a convenience store. He shook off the muddle and went inside for an energy drink. Decided to make it two extra-larges.

More kick, better value.

To get them down faster, he poured them over ice in a Thirsty-Six-Ouncer cup and had it downed in three blocks. In three more, he was buzzing.

Still thinking about his session with Eileen Quarry—how could he not think about it *repeatedly*?—Mark pulled into the public park and left his Vic among the many other law enforcement vehicles. Finding the body would be easy.

Look for the gaggle of cops.

As he sauntered that way, two stiff K-9 officers passed by with their dogs, headed back to their vehicles. They exchanged polite nods. Most uniforms deferred to plainclothes. Mark wasn't one to break tradition. His anti-social streak precluded such change.

He found Jerome by the shallow grave. Forensics had dug it out neatly to preserve the evidence and were carefully dusting the bones, hair, and nails, taking samples. Mark looked down to see summer sandals only. No clothing.

Jerome told him, "Should be one Emily Farrington, twenty-three, Caucasian, missing two years."

Mark vaguely remembered the victim's name, probably from perusing a cold case file some time back. "Who called in the tip?"

Jerome said, "Her killer."

Mark looked up.

Jerome added, "Anonymously."

"We don't have caller ID at the station anymore?"

Jerome laughed the way all the other cops laughed at cop jokes and took out a cigarette, this time a Pall Mall. "Number traced back to a teenage girl in Laughton. Sally Gibbs. Left her phone on the table at a Chili's, went to the restroom, when she came back it was gone. Nobody saw anything."

Mark said, "We get a recording?"

"He texted."

"Gotta love technology. Each advancement puts us one safe step further away from each other." Mark sniffed at the air. The stench of death was long gone; this dump site smelled only of earth.

Jerome ignored his old partner's philosophical wanderings as usual. "Said he killed Miss Farrington two years ago and buried her body here. Even gave us her dentist's name to ID her fillings."

"Nice guy. Thorough," Mark said, thinking Jerome's cigarette looked appealing—for the first time in a dozen years. He resisted the urge to ask for one. "Almost makes you like him."

Jerome laughed again. "Throw back a few cold ones, get him to tell us how we could be doing our job better."

"Hey, whatever works," Mark said. Damn, that cigarette looked good. "He say why he's so generous with his private information?"

Jerome nodded, crushed his smoke out in the fresh dirt by the grave.

A forensics woman said, "Crime scene?" She was likely no more sarcastic than anyone else in the hole—just said it first.

Jerome nodded at her but didn't apologize. That was enough between professionals. He said to Mark, "Dude sent another text. Said Miss Farrington here is just one of many he's going to tell us about 'in the near future.'"

"Even nicer," Mark said. "We should ask him to meet us in a sports bar for a beer and a Knicks game."

Jerome wasn't looking away, wasn't joking—not like him at all—so Mark said, "What?"

Jerome held back a moment, then said, "He said the most recent was your neighbors' kids."

Mark's skin tightened up all over his body, his heart flopped helplessly, his stomach rolled. But he managed to limit his remarks to, "Really?" He knew Jerome would be looking for any latent signs of improper interest, considering it wasn't his case anymore. "Anything else?"

After several moments of scrutiny that felt like minutes, Jerome finally said, "One more over in Covington Downs. We got a unit on it now."

"Don't keep me in suspense."

"Wouldn't dream of it." Jerome lit another Pall Mall. At least he was back to laughing. While putting his lighter away, he took another half-cigarette puff, then shook the butt.

"Do you mind? We're trying to work here?" came the woman's voice below.

"Just cuttin' up," Jerome said.

The woman said. "Ashes?"

"Oh yeah, sorry." Jerome moved away to flip his ashes in a benign area.

Mark stared at the skeletal remains of the twenty-three-year-old, thought about the other one over in Covington Downs, and wondered how many more there would be. He tried to imagine how he was going to break this news to Dan Black.

Or *if* he would.

***

Dan Black stared, incredulous. "He *confessed*?"

"Sorta yeah, sorta no," Mark said. He'd decided on the way over to tell Dan after all. Maybe get a reaction, a lost memory to surface. Someone he knew but forgot about.

Anything, at this point.

Dan said, "He told you where the bodies were," as if astonished that anyone, any killer, would do that. "Just like that."

"Yeah," Mark said.

"And he was right?" Dan said as a rhetorical question.

"Yep," Mark said.

"And he told you he murdered my children?" Dan said in the same way, but with something icier slipping in.

Mark had decided to tell him that part, too. See where it went. "More or less. Yeah," he said vaguely.

"So why don't you arrest him?" Dan said sharply. He hadn't moved, hadn't blinked since Mark stepped onto his porch.

Mark said, "If we knew who he was." He had an image of Jerome smoking that damn Pall Mall and could taste it. *Fuck!*

"You don't have caller ID at your station?" Dan said, driving his point.

Mark said, "I made the same joke." Then, he told Dan about the stolen cellphone, the texts, and that the killer-tipster likely destroyed the phone right after he called.

Dan paced. "This... teenage chick didn't see anything? Nothing at all?"

"Nope."

Dan said, "Fucking kids, man. Completely unaware of anything around them." He sounded disgusted.

Mark said, "She was in the ladies' room."

Dan stepped closer—too close, really. "What about the waitress, the cook? People at other tables?"

"Nada."

"Christ. So, you guys are doing nothing to stop him, right? Nothing at all. Perfect." He leaned on the sarcasm.

Mark said, "Not my case anymore—department thing—but I'm sure they're building a profile."

Dan said, "And after seventy-two hours, your chances of solving any murder go to roughly zero. What's it been now? Going on five weeks? Great. Thanks a lot, cops." *Angry* sarcasm.

Mark said, "Thirty-one days."

"Even better," Dan said nastily and sat on his porch rail. He stared across the street at the neighbor who was watching them—Milton Jenley, the neighborhood scowler.

Mark glanced over. "Mr. Jenley. Guess you get tired of that. I'll bet Mrs. Hoddeker gives you—"

"Fuck 'em," Dan said and looked away—then back with even greater ire. "Have you interviewed everyone? You couldn't have. Someone had to have seen something, come on."

Mark felt Dan's pain, if not directly; but he knew the truth. "You'd think. But it's not always that easy, not always the case. People are busy or distracted. On the phone, eating, shopping, whatever." *Shooting at someone climbing over the fence in your backyard.* "We think we see everything, but we don't. Plus, he could have been wearing a disguise."

"A *disguise*?" Dan spat it out like bad fish. "He wasn't wearing a fucking disguise."

"How do you know that?"

"That's my point," Dan argued. "Nobody saw him. You just said so. So how would you know if he was wearing a disguise or not? You don't know anything. Nobody does. This guy's just going to keep on killing and killing and there's nothing you or anyone in your *department* can do about it!"

Mark stayed silent, unsure whether what he'd just heard made sense. But overall, Dan was right. If someone didn't figure something out quickly, this guy would go on killing.

He looked across the street where he could just make out Mrs. Hoddeker watering her roses in the backyard and watching them. Her neighbor, Mr. Jenley, went back into his house, giving a last scowl before he closed the door.

"He needs to be stopped," Dan said and stood, again too close.

Because it sounded more like a threat than a request, Mark kicked into cop mode and answered with practiced chill, "You tell me how and I will."

Dan was up to the challenge. "If I knew that, I'd do it myself."

He stared a moment longer, inches away, then turned and went inside. He didn't say goodbye, didn't say good luck, didn't say good riddance.

He locked the door.

***

When the original bridge was built over the river, engineers kept the flatter spots favored by the original ferrymen. In a flood, water covered the ravine from bluff to bluff; but the town hadn't seen a flood in half a century, so the sand flats along the wide part of the river were full of life.

And death.

Mark parked his Vic with the scratched hood and worked his way down the hobos' path, through the willows and weeds to a fresh hole with old bones.

"Anna Jacobs-Crowley?" he asked Jerome. He'd heard the name over the radio and thought he'd heard it before somewhere.

"Right where he told us," Jerome said. "To the inch. He triangulated." He pointed as he spoke. "The abutment, the 'lone pine,' and the 'No Parking' sign." *Up on the bluff.*

Mark followed the directions with his eyes, turning back to see the final marker. Then he looked back in the hole.

Jerome pointed out, "Knife marks go into the bones."

Mark nodded. "He say how many more?"

Jerome shook no and started to light a cigarette, a Benson & Hedges. He stopped, looked down in the hole. The same forensics woman was waiting. He smiled thinly and stepped away, saying, "No," to Mark.

Mark was wondering where Jerome had found a Benson & Hedges, but said, "How's our probable list coming along?"

"Working on it." Jerome inhaled his cancer deeply. "We're up to two hundred. Which hundred you want? First or last? Or you wanna wait for the next two hundred?"

Mark thought a moment. "Seriously. We have that many pervs here?"

"How long you been on this force?"

"Too long."

Chapter 12

The night was quiet, thankfully. A dog barked somewhere, but it was far away. Mark sat at his desk in the bedroom in his boxers, cruising social network sites. Anne would never let him work in the bedroom, or upstairs at all. She said, "Keep your work down there. Up here is for us." Now she was gone. Upstairs was all his.

So was the mortgage.

A baseball game played on someone's TV somewhere, maybe close. Mark wasn't really listening. He was now reading a missing persons file—young women—thinking it was far too thick.

He could have accessed the files from his home computer, but this case felt different, so he stuck with paper—hard copies he'd borrowed from the office and duplicated down the street at the only remaining copy shop in town. There was a need for privacy and security. This killer's MO seemed far too efficient for just any idiot, his methods too precise, the number of bodies too high. The perp had "trained professional" smeared all over him.

Might even be a cop.

The suspect wasn't a serial killer in the normal way—if anything was normal about serial killers. No, this guy was organized and had a plan. Nothing was random. He had been working through some list—maybe only in his mind—for at least two years. Maybe five. The problem was: Where was the list and how did he come by it?

What did all the victims have in common?

So far, Mark could see no pattern, but that didn't mean there wasn't one. Neither Emily Farrington nor Anna Jacobs-Crowley had a page on Facebook or YouTube or Pinterest or Reddit or Instagram or MySpace or Omegle or ChatRoulette or anywhere else that Mark could find; but that didn't mean they never had. Getting those records would take time—and warrants.

Dan's kids hadn't been online.

Mark knew he had no time. This killer was going to strike again, and soon. Mark's job was to determine where and when. So simple. The only problem was that it wasn't his job anymore. There would be no warrants.

Except maybe for him, if he kept on.

Mark tossed the file down, helpless, and became aware of the baseball game, how it had just gotten louder. Closer.

Next door.

He turned off the light and moved to his window where he could see into Dan's upstairs bedroom above the fence, not twenty feet away. Their subdivision didn't get any points for originality or privacy. Both sets of blinds were fully open.

Mark stood in the dark in his boxers to one side of his window as Dan walked past his own window, naked. He was fit, not fat. Hung. Or maybe he'd been playing with himself.

Maybe it was just hot in his house.

Before the thought could complete itself, Dan stepped back into the frame of the window and turned to face Mark's house. To face:

Mark.

Caught, Mark chose to remain. Moving back into the dark anonymity of his room would only show weakness, admission of guilt. He put on his unconcerned cop face—which required little adjustment.

Dan didn't move for several seconds. Then he waved. Then he laughed.

Then he moved back to where he'd started and hopped onto his bed. Mark could see his stockinged feet.

Men never take their socks off, Mark thought as his hand closed the blinds and his eyes went to his own feet and brown socks.

***

Mark Young watched Eileen Quarry watching him with dispassionate interest as only a shrink can do. When neither said anything after a full minute, Mark lowered his eyes to gaze at the bottom edge of her desk, attempting to appear dispassionate and uninterested.

Trying.

Quarry leaned back in her chair but stayed fixed on him. He could feel it. He wanted desperately to tap his fingers but figured that might be a telltale sign that he was certifiable, so he forced his hands to remain still. It about killed him.

Hell of a way to spend a day off.

Finally, Dr. Quarry said, "You know..." Mark looked up and she finished, "This case fascinates me." The three kids and the two women—the connection.

The connection to Mark.

"Should I be flattered?" he asked.

She chuckled pleasantly. "If you're measured by your cases."

"It's not my case," he said. An important distinction.

"Not officially," she said, as if she knew he'd been working on it at home, in private.

In his underwear.

Mark met her gaze a moment, then looked away again. The late light of afternoon through French-paned windows made warm crosses on the carpet. Somehow, he found them soothing. He wondered if it was intentional on her part, an interior design tip she picked up from *Psychiatrist Weekly*, or merely his own religious paranoia.

Maybe his regular paranoia.

Eileen Quarry said, "I think I can help you."

Mark looked up. "I think I'm beyond help, Doctor." Twenty years of police work was enough to ruin the best.

She said, "I mean, help you find him."

Now he was interested—but more, concerned. He didn't need any outside interference from within the department—especially this part of the department. *The psycho-ward.* Still, he was curious. "You're saying... help me find him."

"Yes," she said. "Find your killer."

Your killer? Why did she say *your* killer? *I'm not dead yet, am I?*

Did she know that someone was *planning* to kill him? Is it one of her *other* patients? Another cop?

A homicide detective's mind never shuts down, not for a minute; because in that minute, he can slip.

He can die.

As these thoughts ran through Mark's mind, she added, "Though I'm not convinced it's a male."

Mark said, "Okay."

"Women are capable of such horrors," she said. "The same as men. It's not uncommon. At least not completely so." Then she added, "More so these days."

Mark eyed her the way she usually watched *him* and said, "You know this through personal experience?"

He was marginally serious, halfway joking, fully interrogating. But Quarry paled, looking like him in his chair instead of herself behind her desk.

***

It's a small house, cramped, cluttered and cheap. Trees and weeds outside the window.

A kid is screaming. He's five or six, running around as if he has ADHD or worse – but he's just a normal kid high on life and sugar. So, no excuse other than a bad prognosis.

He's kicking a ball and screaming. Screaming at the ball, screaming at kicking, screaming at life and being a boy.

He kicks the ball into the wall and it comes back on him, hits him in the head. He laughs, picks it up and throws it. Screaming again.

Glass breaks. He squeals. Then he stops and looks toward the kitchen.

He knows what's coming next, and it does.

Next, he is screaming for real, from pain, as his mother beats him senseless with a fresh, thick switch in the bathroom, bent over a peach-colored toilet. She is out of control.

She is a young Eileen Quarry.

In her office in front of Mark, Dr. Eileen Quarry looked older, tired, ashamed. Sophisticated, if guilt-ridden.

In court, a humbled younger Eileen faces the jury. The jury foreman nods. The judge slaps his gavel. Bailiffs and marshals take Eileen's son. She looks more scared than regretful. She stares at the judge.

The judge's eyes narrow.

In her office, across from Mark, Dr. Quarry looked almost as terrified as she did then, just remembering.

Women's prison – the showers. Naked women, mostly large and unattractive when they aren't addict thin. All are tough and tatted, heavily weathered. They gather in a tight circle yelling encouragement.

Showers run hot, emotions hotter. In the middle of the steamy circle, two nude women are fighting. One is a hardened prison dyke, with cropped hair, muscles and hate ink. The other woman is Eileen.

She's fighting for her life – and, for the moment, winning.

Another inmate kicks her in the ribs, knocks her off the diesel, who doesn't waste time. She's fought in these showers many times. Won nearly as many.

She climbs on top of Eileen, punching her face and breasts.

She likes punching tits. She'd gouge her enemy's cunt with a hot fire poker and fuck her in the ass with a razor-blade-encrusted dildo if she ever got the chance.

It's always been a dream. Eileen knows this because the bitch talks about it all the time.

Another female inmate tries to kick Eileen, but this time Eileen grabs the woman's ankle and bites it. Draws blood.

The dueling dyke pauses to laugh.

In that moment, Eileen punches her in the mouth, smashing the larger woman's lip in over a tooth. Blood gushes.

The screaming is fevered, insane. The women are more like wild male animals than female human beings. Mothers, with kids on the Outside. They spit on the brawlers and swear wildly, encouraging the brutality. Enjoying the diversion.

One of them pisses on the brawlers, laughing. Another joins her. Standing up, aiming with two fingers.

The bigger brawler shakes off her surprise and blood, energized. Her eyes go wide with adrenaline-fueled hatred, bred over years of incarceration. She attacks with both hard fists.

She will kill Eileen.

Clink. Something hard and sharp slides across the wet shower floor – comes to a stop against Eileen's hand.

Not everyone is rooting for the hard timer.

Both fighters see the shiv, but Eileen grabs it first, fully prepared to kill her attacker.

Guards rush in – mostly men in SWAT gear. The female inmates yell protests, hitting and kicking. They slip and fall on the wet tile.

The butch assailant doesn't stop until the clothed men drag her off, Eileen looking up with hope – until she sees the baton coming down.

The guard, a woman, smiles behind her full-face mask and cracks Eileen in the head.

Everything goes black.

Mark Young stared at Eileen Quarry, his doctor. His inquisitor. She looked up with all the rage and hate that filled her soul that remembered day.

But it had a happy ending—eventually—if loneliness and regret breed deliverance.

Years pass. Eileen has been transferred to a state mental prison where she is taking classes in psychology and doing well.

Straight As.

She's released and continues in school. The day she graduates with her Masters, her parole officer is there to shake her hand and release her into the world.

A different world.

Despite her rules of release, Eileen puts on a disguise—glasses and a scarf—and sneaks to a schoolyard to watch the shirtless older teenaged boys playing hoops at recess. One of the boys looks like her and still has scars on his back.

Eileen collapses forward, catching herself on the chain link fence.

A boy sees her and comes over. "Ma'am, are you all right?"

Fighting to stay conscious, Eileen looks up at the boy—and past him, to her son, coming over to see what's happening. He's handsome and smiling, a happy kid.

Now.

Eileen runs away before he can recognize her and report it.

***

Detective Mark Young had heard some hard stories in his time—even believed some of them. This time, he didn't know what to think.

Quarry hadn't said a word, but somehow he knew, understood every stroke. His last words to her were, "You know this—you can help me—through personal experience?"

Now she answered him. "Yes."

Mark nodded slowly, assessing her as she had been assessing him. "Okay."

She said, "Good."

She would help him, and he would let her.

***

Mark sat at his computer reading the book Eileen Quarry had given him titled *Psychology of the Criminal Mind—Studies in Deviant Behavior*. He was already a hundred pages in. Enough of it was new to hold his interest. He hadn't even logged on to his computer.

The only troubling part?

He kept reading about himself.

Mark reminded himself that cops and criminals are often just opposite sides of the same coin, psychologically speaking. Somehow, the old saw wasn't comforting.

He sensed a change in the environment that drew his attention away from the book. He looked up as if lost in thought, then reached over slowly and switched off the lamp on his desk. He turned in his chair to look across the narrow gulf between his bedroom and Dan Black's.

Dan's overhead light was off, but TV light bounced around the room like the devil's laughter. A moment later, Dan walked past his window, still nude. A moment after that, he walked back with the remote.

His cock looked longer. Maybe he'd been playing with himself again, or maybe he just gave it a tug before parading past the window, for Mark's benefit—or his own ego. After all, he was a man. A naked man who knew he had an audience.

Mark could see Dan's feet stretch out on the bed as he lay down and turned up the sound. Loud. Tonight was a movie, a police chase with squealing tires and sirens, people shouting, and lots of gunshots and screams.

Mark thought a moment, then stood and walked naked into his bathroom.

Neither man was wearing socks.

Chapter 13

Mark slept late into the morning. He hadn't fallen asleep until 4:00, after reading another fifty pages of Dr. Quarry's book. The only thing he'd learned was that he might be as crazy as anyone the author referenced. But then:

He already knew that.

In the early afternoon, Mark Young couldn't stand being locked up inside any longer. He had no idea how to fill up the days off with no one at home. So, he took a drive. Within the hour, he had found a crime scene.

He knew where to look. Didn't even need his radio.

Only two cars had been called to the smalltime robbery—some kid with a knife demanding snack cakes and soda.

Cigarettes.

The storeowner had told him where the Little Debbies were, and when the kid turned to get a few, the older man pulled a shotgun on him. The kid was still lying in his own puddle of piss and tears when the cops came to arrest him.

Mark shot the shit with the uniforms until Martin Coor showed up to take a statement from the shopkeeper. Or so he said. (One of the uniforms had slipped away to call in that *Detective Young* was *snooping around*. The Chief had apparently sent Martin to make sure it wasn't anything serious.)

"So," Martin began, "how's retirement treating you?"

Mark laughed.

Martin said, "That's good to know," seeming to appreciate that Mark *could* laugh.

Mark said, "I haven't lost my marbles yet."

"Wife gone, some guy tries to kill her and the kids—wouldn't surprise anyone." Coor shrugged. He probably meant it as an assurance, a confidence, but the underlying cop question wasn't buried too deep—not to another cop.

"What are the odds running?" Mark asked him.

"Six to one," Martin said.

Mark said, "Put me in for fifty." He handed over two twenties and a ten.

"You're in." Martin took the money. Then he looked guilty and said, "They asked me to check."

Mark said he understood. "Just a little cabin fever is all." Less than a week and he was itching to get back into the fray.

"I hear that," Coor said and started to go.

Mark stopped him. "So?"

Martin turned back. "You know you'd be the first to know."

"Yeah, I know," Mark said, knowing full well that Martin Coor was lying. "But I had to ask." He grinned, putting on his best *just being honest* face.

"Sure you did," Martin said to show that he was in on the ruse. They all did it.

The truth was that most cops never took the time to imagine what it might be like to walk in Mark Young's shoes after all that had happened to him. Even when they knew the possibility of estrangement and divorce hung Damocles-like over every one of their heads, it was always easier not to wonder about what they would do when it landed on them. Maybe it never would. If it did, so be it. You're just the newest member of the club.

Mark knew that was exactly what Marin Coor was thinking, so he changed the subject. "No new ones?" *Bodies buried in parks or on sandbars.*

Martin looked surprised. "You don't have a scanner?"

"At home? Hell no. Be too much like work." The truth was that Anne had forbidden it.

Coor suggested, "Maybe you should get one."

"Then I wouldn't get to ask you," Mark said with the same grin.

"Then they wouldn't send me out to check on you."

"Sure they would."

"Yeah, I guess they would."

Martin Coor likely knew that if their roles were reversed, Mark wouldn't tell him a damn thing either. So Mark said with mock sincerity, "But you'd tell me if anything was up."

"Sure," Coor vowed.

"Am I a suspect yet?"

Coor laughed. "Shit. What the fuck you talkin' about? With your fuckin' record? Please." His New Jersey roots showed.

Mark said, "I did try to kill the guy without much talk." *Without having any fucking idea who the fuck I was shooting at.*

"We'd all have done the same," Coor said, sounding as if he meant it.

Jerome had said the same thing—and that talk around the station was that Mark needed practice on the range so he wouldn't miss next time.

Mark told Coor, "I was out of line, I know it, but..." He didn't know how to amend the thought. Nothing came.

Coor picked it up for him. "You're seeing Quarry. The shrink."

Mark nodded.

Coor said, "She's smokin', man. I'd hit that shit with my wife in the *room.*"

Mark didn't say anything. His wife wasn't in any room he was in anymore. He didn't even know where she was.

Just the way it should be.

Coor said, "I don't know how you concentrate on talkin' to her. Those tits? That ass? I'll bet the bitch can suck the chrome off a trailer hitch."

"Who said we talk?" Mark said, playing along.

Coor laughed out loud. "Yeah, you're just fuckin' her on her desk, right?" He laughed again. "I sure as shit would be."

Mark had no response other than to shake his head, inside his head.

Coor let his joviality slide and turned serious. "What kinda shit they ask in a referral?"

Every cop feared and resented even the notion of a psych eval—took it as an insult. Usually followed by, "The shit we see? The shit we have to do? Fuck them."

One day you're doing your job when some bad shit goes down; the next day some college shithead is picking your brain for minutiae you didn't even know was there so the department can strip you of your health insurance. Some kinda fuckin' job we have.

Coor asked, "She make you spill your guts and shit—tell her how fucked up your childhood was, how your daddy was *mean* to you, and how you hate your wife and kids?"

Mark shook his head. "Not much'a that. Mostly about the case."

"What case?" Martin said, truly perplexed.

"Your case," Mark said, to annoy him.

"My case? Why my case?" Coor was now apparently worried he'd be called in next to talk about his performance on this case. Or worse, his childhood and family. His daddy.

Sex.

"Just, you know," Mark said, and then nothing else.

Coor stewed nervously, looking around at the departing patrol cars. He never was one to keep things to himself. "Because, you know, Leanne and I, we're not having the best'a times, right now. Meghan's fifteen going on forty and Bart's lost his fucking mind completely. The twins are on Adderall, but it doesn't seem to be doing a damn thing. Last night they set fire to the side of the house playing *fire*-man. Leanne's threatened to leave, *again*. Bein' a total bitch. 'Martin, take out the garbage.' 'Martin, do the dishes for a change.' 'Martin, take me to that nice new restaurant with the hundred-dollar steaks. You never take me anywhere.'" Martin Coor shook his head and said, "I'll tell you, I'm about ready to pack the whole fuckin' thing in, buddy. Then this shit with you. Christ, the whole fuckin' world's coming down around us, man." He leaned in closer. "I'll tell you a secret."

Mark said, "Yeah?"

Martin said, "Was me: I'd'a clipped that fucker before he got the chair to the window." He nodded confidently.

Mark said, "If I had reacted faster, gotten out of my car in time, had my weapon out and not been worrying about my family, I might have too."

"I *would* have," Martin said, obviously without realizing what he was saying.

The insult.

"Well," Mark said, "I'll be sure to pass all this along to my shrink. She says I need to be more forthcoming. I think she might be right."

Martin Coor looked dead-panicked.

Mark said, "Have a good day, though, Marty. And stay outa trouble. It's no fun to be in it, I can tell you that."

He walked toward his plain-wrap Vic with 220,000 miles and the dented hood.

Martin called out, "At least they let you keep that nice car."

"Full salary, too," Mark said over his shoulder. "Sure beats working for a living." He *was* working for a living; he just couldn't officially investigate the two cases he cared about most.

Some living.

He got in and drove off, leaving Martin to fume in resentment—Martin who got to work those two cases on a lesser salary. Time in.

Mark didn't dislike Martin Coor—he wasn't any worse than anyone else—but he could be a pain in the ass. Especially when he wouldn't shut the fuck up.

Mark grinned, thinking their little exchange should keep Marty Coor quiet for a while.

Chapter 14

When Dan Black came out of his front door at 7:30, the sun had sunk and evening was settling in under its veil of grey mystery and anonymity.

He drove away unaware that someone was watching him.

***

Detective Mark Young trailed Dan Black's silver Mazda family sedan several car-lengths back, enough to go unrecognized. He'd waited until Dan reached the end of the block before following and turning on his headlights. Now he stayed four cars back in traffic.

It was hardly the first time Mark had tailed someone, so he was relaxed. In his zone. He drank black coffee from a mug that read, "#1 Cop Dad" over a cartoon of a Clouseau-like detective drinking a cup of coffee while sleuthing—and about to slip on a banana skin.

Another prophetic gift from MJ.

Mark found himself daydreaming in the cool evening air that poured in his open window. He recalled Martin Coor's comments and thought about how he'd never realized what a misogynistic jerk the man was, and how Coor had made overt sexual comments about Mark's shrink.

The *department* shrink.

This was at least in poor taste, if not downright idiotic. Should Martin ever need counseling, or be sent on a procedural interview, any such previous comments would surely surface and put him in an uncomfortable position—if not a suspended one.

Still, Mark agreed that Eileen Quarry was an extremely attractive woman. She dressed well—not provocative, but intriguing, suggestive without being overt. Her hairstyle was current without being silly for her age.

What was her age? She looked to be ten years younger than Mark but could easily be ten years older. He thought, *Maybe she had surgery.* That and, *If she did, she damn sure had a good surgeon. Maybe that's why her tits are so perfect. And Marty's right: that ass! She must work out six days a week to be that tight. Those short skirts, teasing me like that. The see-through tops. That sexy lingerie. Why I'd –*

"What the fuck am I doing?" Mark said aloud and shook his thoughts away. *Christ, I sound as bad as Marty. Worse!* Jesus, before he knew it, he'd be whacking off in the car in four lanes of traffic.

At least he kept it confined to his own head, not public information. Would she make him tell her about it in their next session—his private thoughts about her? What would he say?

Yeah, this cop, this detective – he's kind of an idiot savant without the savant part – Martin Coor, Marty – you'll probably see him in here someday – he thinks you're hot and that we fuck on your desk every time I come here. So, I was thinking about all that and how you do have a great ass and...

Mark laughed, choking slightly on his last sip of coffee, and made the next right to follow Dan's Mazda onto the four-lane. Maybe he was headed for the river or the old Cloverside Mall. If he stopped at the dump site or took a stroll over the bridge, Mark would have to confront him.

Why?

Mark kept asking himself why. Why was he even following his neighbor? The poor guy was grieving, at a total loss for any explanations for such horrors against humanity. Dan Black wasn't any more of a suspect than Mark at this point.

Oh, that's why. Mark laughed and coughed again.

He was fairly certain Marty Coor was lying about Mark not being a suspect. He had to be. Didn't he? The thought made Mark shift in his driver's seat, feeling as if the seat heaters were on high—only the Vic didn't *have* seat heaters.

He wondered what Dr. Eileen Quarry would say about any of this—his *behaviors* and his *paranoia*—at the same time thinking, *She must be about a 34-C, maybe a 36-B.* Her breasts were always noticeable but not prominent; she never showed *nipplage* except for once when even Mark thought the room was cold. Maybe they *were* "aftermarket."

In their last session, she'd been asking him about his sex life with Anne again. She seemed interested in what other kinds of sexual experimentation they found exciting, interesting, or even that he'd thought about in passing.

She wanted every detail.

He told her how he and Anne liked to have sex outdoors and in unusual places. She once got him aroused in a laundromat when they were first married. They were sitting in the plastic chairs lined up against the front window—plate glass that ran the length of the store—and anyone from outside could have seen.

When he protested—worried, more—she said, "No one can see us from the back, or if they do, they won't know what we're doing." What she was doing was giving him a handjob inside his khakis.

He was hard as a rock.

Mark said, "What about her?" An older Hispanic woman folding clothes at a table in the back, past the dryers.

Anne said, "What about her?" The woman wasn't looking.

At least she didn't *appear* to be looking.

Anne said, "C'mon," and stood suddenly, pulling Mark by his hand. He hesitated, unsure. But he was so hard—and getting harder. How was that even possible?

Anne led him to the restroom and went in ahead. Only Mark saw the Hispanic woman looking at him blankly. *Was that a crucifix around her neck?* Of course it was.

Once in the bathroom, Anne turned into an animal. Mark relayed this to his police therapist.

Eileen Quarry leaned forward. "And what about you?"

Mark thought back and said, "Me too, I guess. It was kind of exciting."

"That was your first time in a strange place?"

"Probably not," he said, trying to recall. "Maybe. But I doubt it."

"Maybe your first time with her. With Anne."

"Maybe. Probably. I don't know." He was thinking they'd probably done it in his car, her car, some car, somewhere, sometime. Maybe in the woods. It was all a blur now. Except that laundromat bathroom. For some reason, that one was *painfully* clear.

His therapist said, "And it got you hot. Knowing you might get caught."

"I don't know if that was it."

"Of course that was it," she said with authority. "The possibility of getting caught doing something wrong is intoxicating for almost everyone. Especially certain personality types—ones who normally like order in their lives and try to avoid chaos or uncertainty. The disorganized emotions that result from the fear of being exposed or being caught doing what is considered wrong behavior is exciting as hell."

It was then that Mark noticed Eileen Quarry's erect nipples.

He said, "Maybe."

"Maybe, hell," she said. "You were excited."

"I guess," he admitted, staring at her breasts.

Eileen said, "Mark, I'm your therapist here. I'm only trying to get you to think about yourself in broader terms—to see where you might be, let's say... a different person than you think you are.

"We all have multiple sides—unpredictable sides—even to ourselves. *Especially* to ourselves. You were surprised at the time, which made it even more exciting." She qualified her *prying*. "I'm suggesting this solely as a practicing professional. Keep in mind I've seen and heard these things hundreds if not thousands of times, so you can rest assured nothing will surprise me or cause me to judge you in any negative way. Right?"

Mark nodded.

She said, "So, Anne gets you stimulated in public, then takes the lead, being the aggressor, which you *like...*? I'm saying at the time."

Mark nodded along.

"So, she takes the lead, drags you into a public restroom and proceeds to, I'm guessing, give you oral sex. Yes?"

Mark nodded, beginning to feel uncomfortable again. *More* uncomfortable.

Eileen said, "What else would she do, right?" and laughed. "This part isn't rocket science, I assure you. We gals know what you like, what men like—and what we like for that matter. We're generally more honest about our likes and dislikes, even if we don't express or act on them in the same guilt-free way as men."

Mark had given a soft, polite chuckle—but he'd wondered where his police doc was going with what sounded more like a confession than a probative session.

Up ahead, Dan Black turned for the bridge. Mark moved up a car length, but he was thinking how Eileen Quarry had told him in that same session, "Look, I've had those fantasies, those situations, myself. We all have. No big deal. Okay?"

Mark had nodded reluctantly. Her nipples looked like ballistic missile heads.

"I'm trying to get at a bigger truth here," his *doctor* said. "Okay?"

Baby steps.

Mark looked up, gave her the go-ahead, and she went.

"So, Anne is giving you head in the public bathroom, and it makes you a little crazy. Lust suddenly overtakes reason and care, and the next thing you know, you're fucking her—excuse me, penetrating her. Vaginally, I assume."

That was better? he thought. He nodded. Barely.

Dr. Quarry finished her thought. "But it really was *fucking* at that moment. That wasn't lovemaking. That was fucking. Hard, passionate, unrestricted fucking."

She looked to Mark for a response. He gave none.

"Okay," she had said, and seemed content that they were getting somewhere.

Where the fuck? Mark had thought then, and now—as in:

Where the fuck is he going?

Dan Black had driven onto the bridge above the dumpsite where the cops found Anna Jacobs-Crowley, and now his brake lights came on suddenly. He was stopping!

Two cars back, Mark felt for his gun. Dan sharply swerved his silver Mazda to the left, out of the right lane. Mark took up his gun. Then, the car in front of Mark did the same move—braked and swerved to the left.

Mark saw the dead dog on the bridge—almost too late—and swerved left.

Jesus. A dog.

Why the fuck was he following this man again? This grieving father? Did he have nothing better to do? That book on psycho killers? Facebook floozies? Young dumb girls with too much technology on their hands? Bending over to flash their tits or posting cellphone shots of themselves in front of the WaWa station mirror naked. Getting some guy somewhere to jack off on his computer cam for them.

And what did any of that have to do with Dan Black, for Chrissake?

Fuck if I know, Mark thought, setting his gun aside, figuring he must be bored having to stay away from the only two investigations he cared about.

But he was thinking back again.

Dr. Quarry had said, "You sort of lost your mind a little in that bathroom." She had stared holes through him as only a shrink can do.

Mark nodded slightly. He felt he was supposed to, so he did.

She nodded and bit her lip. "It's a terrific feeling, right? I mean, it's scary—because you think you might get caught and you're doing something you're not supposed to be doing—but it's exhilarating for the same reason. That's how we're wired.

"Some of us do drugs or drink too much, sometimes solely to free our wilder sides, our pent-up urges that we suppress because society tells us we're supposed to. That it's wrong to feel those things. To want them. The thrills.

"Some of us get those thrills from food—eating a bucket of ice cream on the couch when we're three hundred pounds already. Some of us get it from driving too fast, going a hundred on the freeway, knowing it's dangerous, hoping we *don't* get caught. Some of us jump off bridges on into rock pits where we don't know for sure what's under the water.

"And some of us seek those thrills from sex, taking risks with partners, or playing out seductive sex games—rough or dangerous sex games—without any regard to possible consequences. All because it excites the hell out of us and we can't stop ourselves."

Funny, Mark thought. She was running the list as if it were familiar to her—as if she had done all those things herself.

Maybe recently.

But she was a professional, wasn't she? *Yes. Sure!* So why were her nipples poking out even more? How *could* they be? They were already *out to here!*

Must be the freezing A/C, Mark had thought at the time. Even he had been cold, and he never got cold. That, or this entire line of questioning was causing him to freeze up inside. Either way, *I have to stop staring at her tits!*

When Eileen Quarry then leaned forward even further, Mark wondered where she was finding the room behind her desk.

At least he could see her hands.

She said, "The details of what happened next are not important."

Thank god!

But she ran over them anyway. "You didn't last long—maybe a minute or two, maybe thirty seconds—then you had one of the most intense orgasms you've ever had. As did she."

She stared at him, piercing him with her sex-inquisition eyes, forcing him to remember that night in the laundromat that he'd long since forgotten, how the experience had been every bit as intense as his psychiatrist described it, and then some.

He nodded.

Dr. Eileen said, "Extremely intense. Then it was over." She never stopped looking at him as if trying to see into his soul. His libido.

Mark had thought, *Why did she wear that silk top today, and what is she wearing under it that I can see her nipples so plainly? They must be an inch long! At least half an inch—of pure titanium! Carbon steel! Some indestructibly case-hardened material!*

In the dented Crown Vic, Mark laughed at his own joke. *Case-hardened. Ha.* He wasn't even a breast man. Or was he? Had he been all along and just didn't realize it? Had his *sexy-as-fuck* police shrink brought it out of him? Made him stare as part of some sneaky psychological *test*?

Mark remembered being unable to look away, as if spellbound by something he'd never encountered in his life before. Magellan seeing the Pacific Ocean for the first time. If he felt silly, he also felt embarrassed. Surely, she had to have realized he was staring, never taking his eyes away like a twelve-year-old with his first hot substitute teacher.

At that point, Eileen Quarry had thankfully sat back, and her nipples receded. Mark wasn't sure whether his sigh of relief was audible, only that he had heaved it.

Sitting in the Vic, he sighed again and made himself refocus on his tailing project.

He looked up ahead as, two miles past the bridge, Dan drifted into the bike lane—then whipped left across two lanes into a long, double left turn pocket made for thirty cars.

"Shit!" Mark said aloud. He yanked the Vic right onto a short side street, then right again into the alley, racing back the other way, *away* from Dan. How long before the red light ahead turned green and Dan was gone?

What did it matter? The guy lived next door and wasn't likely to move away tonight. But Mark wasn't thinking about that problem; he was thinking about *this* problem. *Catch up!*

At the end of the alley, Mark slammed the brakes, turned right, and sped a short quarter-block back to the main road. He gave a cursory look to his left and drove straight out into traffic.

Horns blew, brakes locked up and tires squealed.

"Sorry," Mark said courteously to no one in particular. He crossed into the left lane, almost clipping a dump truck, then whipped left into the turn pocket and—

Eyes wide, slammed his own brakes—almost plowing into the back of a silver car—Dan Black's silver Mazda, waiting for the light to change.

"Goddammit!" Mark said as he slid down into his seat. Had Dan seen him? He would, that was for sure, if he happened to glance in his rear-view mirror.

Mark looked left and saw a clear path across the other lanes to the last side street before the intersection. He went for it. Still slumped down in his seat, he cranked left and floored his Ford, being careful not to chirp the tires and draw attention. Luckily, there was no curb, just flat, lined pavement.

If Dan happened to look back in his mirror, he would only see the side of a car with a driver who would probably appear to be an old person barely tall enough see above the steering wheel.

That was what Mark hoped as he crossed the vacant opposing lanes gratefully, departed the main highway on the far side, and flew down the narrow one-lane dark side street with *nowhere to turn around, no other side streets and no streetlights!*

"Fuck!"

The first turn that appeared too quickly in Mark's headlights was a right. He hit the brakes as hard as he could, locked the tires up and drifted the corner. He thought this street would put him out on the next four-lane road onto which Dan would be turning in a moment, if he hadn't already, and that that wouldn't be bad. Mark would be ahead of him, unless—

The street ended. "No Outlet."

"Motherfucker!"

Mark slid to a stop. There was no room for a three-point turn; six would be needed. He threw the Ford into Reverse and floored it back toward the first dark side street, not bothering to pause at the stop sign.

The drunk in the pickup missed Mark's Crown Vic by inches, ran off the road on the left, and saved it by running back across and off the street on his right—then wobbling back to center and blowing his horn. *Sure, now.*

He never slowed down.

Neither did Mark. He cranked the wheel to his left into the center of the street and had the car in Drive before the big sedan was fully stopped. The transmission ground and complained but complied. His tires threw blue smoke into the red taillight glow.

He sped back for the main drag, getting up to ninety on the side street. Then stopping—more or less—watching, timing it... timing it... quick looks left and right, and...

Going for it.

Among the usual negative loud fanfare from angry drivers for his maneuvers, Mark plowed into oncoming traffic coming from his left. At least they swerved out of his way—not much of an opening, but enough to get him back on the right side of the road. Then, he saw:

The light was yellow. Dan was gone.

"Where are you?"

Mark sped up in the left turn lane—the light would be red before he got there—wishing he could whip out his *fucking blue light* and blast his siren.

But no. This one was a grit-n-go, traffic-be-damned deal. Hopefully no one would pre-run their green from either side.

As he sped through the intersection in a controlled left drift, Mark checked cursorily both ways and saw no imminent moving objects. He heard them, though; they let him know what they thought of his vehicular operation *skills*.

When he was free of the danger—no other cops around, thankfully (how would he explain *that* one to Captain Corlius?)—Mark was on the lookout again.

"Where are you, dammit?" he asked again into the night void.

No answer came for two blocks. Then, glancing right, he caught a glimpse of Dan's silver Mazda, parked at the mall near the street. Dan was walking toward the main entrance.

Mark cut off some poor family in a van to jump a lane and turn right into the mall lot. The mother didn't have time to honk, but he could almost hear the family's screams.

He parked two rows over, jumped out of his plain-wrap and ran for the front doors.

Chapter 15

Mark burst through the mall doors—old school, not automatic—knocking a late-middle-aged black woman on her broad butt, packages flying everywhere. Mark thought he really didn't need to draw attention to himself right now—*right away!*—as the woman was saying, "I'm so sorry. I wasn't looking."

"No, no, no. All my fault. I came in too fast. Are you okay?" He offered her a hand up.

She was a large woman, so it took some doing. But she got to her feet with a shaking head.

"Are *you* okay?" she said. "Usually, anyone running into me is the one needing a body shop." She laughed and handed Mark a card. "Grace Patterson. I'm running for county commissioner."

That's why she's being so nice! Mark picked up one of the packages and handed it to her. He started to say his usual, *I'm a public servant, I'm not allowed to participate in any campaigning of any sort, sorry.* But in the interest of speed and brevity, he went with, "Well, you earned my vote just by surviving the impact."

She said, "Thank you," and started to outline her plans in office as she gathered up her last package. Mark took the opportunity to slip away.

Searching.

He scurried off, scanned this way and that, still wondering what the hell he was doing here—why he was even interested in Dan Black's comings and goings and—

"Mark! What're you doing here?"

Mark spun to find that Dan had walked up behind him and was standing not two feet away. Where the hell had he come from? Was he waiting, watching? Were Mark's detective skills diminished from lack of practice or personal involvement? He would never have stopped for the woman before. Was he losing his edge?

Mark forced himself to stop thinking and say, "I was about to ask you the same thing."

The part of him that allowed him to regain his composure—his cop's attitude and experience—was at once the same thing that made him sound like an interrogator.

At least an asshole.

Dan seemed not to notice. He said, "Going for ice cream. Want some?"

He nodded to one side to indicate the way and started walking.

Mark fell in behind like a trained mule as they passed the inside entrance to Pete's Pizza, Pub & Keg. He said, "Kind of a long way to come for an ice cream cone."

"You haven't tasted it," Dan said as Mark caught up. "I used to bring my kids here all the time."

Some melancholy snuck into his voice. Understandable.

Before Mark could apologize or explain what *he* was doing here, Dan said, "What brings you all the way out to Cloverdale? To the mall."

The Mall.

Cloverdale had been the first mall in the city and was notoriously downscale, old school, and just plain old and plain.

Mark opted for the truth. He wasn't sure why, but he said, "Following you."

Dan stopped. "Me? Why me? What'd I do?"

"I don't know. Just a hunch."

"A hunch?" Dan said. "About what?

Mark went for honesty again. "You."

"Me."

"Yeah."

Dan went silent and looked Mark over as if trying to figure him out—what this was all about. Finally, he said, "Should I be worried?"

Mark said, "I don't know. Should you?"

Dan eyed Mark some more. "What is it you think I've done?"

"I didn't say you did anything. Did you do something? Something I should know about?"

"You?"

"Or Martin Coor, your detective."

Dan said, "He's my detective?"

"Yeah, you have your own detective."

"On my case."

Mark agreed. "On your case. You knew that. Martin Coor."

"My *kids'* case," Dan said.

"Your kids, yeah. The detective..."

Mark realized just how bad this was sounding—following his neighbor who had recently lost his three children to a psychopathic murderer and his wife to the effect of those murders. Dogging him to a mall in the hinterlands for no other reason than he was bored and had no cases he cared about except this one that was personal, even though he had no jurisdiction over the matter and *what the fuck was he doing!*

No answer came.

Dan said with mild suspicion, "So you followed me. What? From home?"

Mark nodded, feeling worse about his choice to do so with each moment. He sensed a lawsuit.

Dan said, "On a hunch."

Mark nodded again, feeling the need for a Tums—or ten. Lawsuit for sure.

A quiet moment passed, then Dan laughed out loud like a jolly mall Santa, shook his head, and walked off.

Easy as that, it was over.

Mark sighed heavily. *Jesus*. What had he been thinking?

Mark caught up as Dan walked into the Ice Cream Circus. "All the flavors of the Big Top!" it read. Mark didn't think that really made sense, but he followed Dan inside.

The ceiling was draped with a fake red-and-white striped tent running up to center on a fake pole that was not holding it up. Around the sides were circus murals—clowns, tigers in cages, elephants in rings. The usual.

Irritating circus music.

The place seemed to be doing good business—parents and kids, some adults without kids, some kids without parents. With a possible serial killer on the loose, Mark thought, *What the hell are these people thinking!*

The man making cones for the kids was in his late forties, average height but wide in the middle—a jovial ice cream vendor with a big circusy moustache—squatting down in his apron talking to a little redheaded girl of about nine.

When he looked around and saw "Dan-o!" he stood up, patted the little girl on her head, told her that her flavor was his favorite too and walked back behind his counter. He put his floppy striped "circus" hat on his thick mane of curly black hair and said to Dan Black, "What'll it be tonight? The usual?"

Dan said, "Yep. Plain ol' vanilla."

"Yoooouuuu got it!" the gelato barker said and started dipping. Then he looked up at Mark and said, "Yer friend, too?"

Dan turned to look at Mark, who only now realized they both knew he was there.

The ice cream clown said, "Vanilla for you too, amigo?" He didn't look Spanish, more Greek—from Detroit.

Mark said, "Chocolate chocolate-chip, if you have it."

"Oh, do I have it!" the striped scooper said exuberantly. "Chocolate chocolate-chip it is! My little friend here's favorite flavor, too! Right, honey?"

He grinned down at the little ginger girl and winked. She nodded with enthusiasm and licked at her cone as aggressively as she could with braces.

Dan said, "Best damn ice cream in the city."

The clownish vendor behind the counter grinned, tipped his head jauntily, and handed Dan's vanilla cone to him. He said, "Frozen love from Chuck Love."

Dan chuckled. "Says that with every cone. He's something else."

Mark thought, *Something else, all right.* Something that defied description in a civil society.

The little girl said, with a lisp, "The chipth get thtuck in my brathes, but I don't care. Ithz yummy!" She licked some more, from bottom to top, then twisted the cone and did it again. A chip got stuck in her braces and she sucked it out loudly. She was a corker.

Mark moved closer to her and said, "Where are your parents, sweetheart?"

Always the cop.

She nodded her head toward the doors, the mall, and said between licks, "Out there, thumwhere. Sthopping for sthkool thupplies." Definitely a corker.

Mark looked out into the mall. Dan looked at Mark. Mark looked back to see that Dan and the ice cream dummy were both looking at him.

Mark turned back to the little girl. "They shouldn't leave you alone."

"Itth okay. I'm a big girl." She licked her way around the cone, quick and playful.

Dan Black bent down to her and said, "You should listen to this man. He's a policeman. He knows best."

She stopped eating and listened intently as if to Svengali himself.

Dan finished, "You can trust him. You *should* trust him."

The girl stared back as long as Dan stared at her. She said, "Okay. I will."

Dan stood away and the little redhead started licking her cone again, out of her momentary trance. She turned and walked off to sit in a chair by herself in the corner, licking and swinging her legs, her little feet not reaching the floor. Dan and the creamery weirdo watched her while Mark watched the clown, thinking there was something skeevy about him, a dairy nerd/used car salesman who was better at hawking ice cream than old Pontiacs.

Dan said to Mark, "I guess we know better, huh?" Back to the melancholy.

The grief.

The ice cream goof handed Mark's double chocolate chocolate-chip cone to him. Mark reached for his wallet.

Dan stopped him. "I insist." He explained, even though he didn't have to—it was only an ice cream cone, after all—"It is my pleasure to introduce you to Chuck's incredible ice cream. He makes it himself in the back. Sometimes all night long, then works all day. He's a champ. A frozen dessert gold medalist."

He pointed at the wall where a certificate proclaimed such.

Mark didn't think the document looked real and wondered who would make up such a thing or give out such an award. *Chuck!* he thought. *Of course. Chuckie!*

Chuck the ice cream Love god.

The faux circus dweeb smiled, said, "Long as everybody's happy, Chuckles is happy!" and went to help the next parents in line.

Chuckles. Mark visibly cringed.

Dan licked then bit into his ice cream. Mark did the same to his.

Dan said, "Damn good ice cream, isn't it?"

Mark nodded. He didn't think it was *outstanding,* but said, "Yeah. It's good."

Dan took another bite and said around it, "So, what'd you think I was doing? Really."

Mark stopped eating. He looked at Dan, then at Chuckles, and said, "I don't know. Really."

Dan said, "Hmmp," unperturbed, and ate his vanilla. He said, "You look tired. Are you okay? Holding up? 'Cause you look beat."

Mark stared at Dan a moment, feeling beat, thinking Dan looked positively perky, then said, "Thanks for the cone," and walked off.

"My pleasure," Dan said, watching him go as Chuck came back over.

"What gives, Dan-o?" he said.

Mark heard the ice cream *fruitcake* and looked back to see him grinning and waving goodbye, Dan raising his cone in a goodbye toast.

Mark nodded goodbye and strolled away, continuing to eat his chocolate cone, thinking it really was pretty good ice cream—better than he'd thought now he was actually tasting it. He turned the corner out of their sight.

Then he doubled back, peered from around a concrete column through the windows of a jewelry store and watched, unseen, as Dan shrugged a goodbye to his ice cream buddy and walked out the other way, licking and eating casually.

Chuck served the next customer with theatrical good nature, doing his job.

When Mark got back to his car, the ice cream wasn't tasting so good anymore. He threw the remainder on the ground, opened his door, and got in the Vic.

Before he knew it—literally, as he got lost in thoughts that overpowered recognition of his own motions—Mark was speeding out of the parking lot and through the light as it turned red.

This time, he didn't apologize to anyone.

Chapter 16

Mark Young sat upstairs in the dark, nude, and thought about how he and Anne would get back at each other when they were miffed, usually over something insignificant—he'd drink the last of her favorite fruit punch intentionally, she wouldn't wash his underwear when she knew he was on his last pair.

How irritated it made them both.

They knew the other's buttons. Such was the cost of long-term relationships, going on twenty years of pent-up frustrations with the other person's annoying isms.

Mark didn't miss that part.

Sitting in the flashing blue glow of his laptop, Mark cruised the pages of social networks, focusing irately on *girlie* blogs—young women telling the world where they'd be and when, where there were right now. His telepathic thoughts, warning them, had had no effect at all.

Mark shook his head in the dark room, but the pain inside wouldn't go away. The aching hurt he couldn't describe or pinpoint.

The reason.

He turned to a photo on the nightstand of Anne and the kids at last year's July Fourth fireworks interoffice party. Eight-thirty and the sky still light—fireworks wouldn't start for another hour.

Andy was chasing and being chased by Martin Coor's twin boys, who were a year younger, and their chocolate lab Callie. Martin's older daughter Meghan, from a previous marriage, had just turned fifteen. In a show of teen defiance, she wore an outfit entirely inappropriate for public-police consumption. It read, "Just say No to D.A.R.E."

Looking back a year later, Mark chuckled. He remembered the scene clearly.

Martin was chewing Meghan out, but she wasn't listening. She was flirting with a nineteen-year-old rookie, pulling him in with her downturned eyes and upturned breasts.

Martin lost it.

The younger cop almost got the better of him, until the older detective got in a wild left hook and almost knocked the kid out before anyone was able to break it up.

Martin yelled at Meghan, "You see! You see what that type of behavior causes!"

His daughter swore she'd never talk to him again and called her mother to come pick her up. Her mother, a smart lady, had *advised* their daughter not to wear the Daisy Dukes and politically incorrect micro-top.

As Mark learned later, after Mom had lost the debate, she wisely didn't drive too far from the playing fields. So, when the call came, she was neither surprised nor too far away—three blocks, parked outside a wine café, talking to their eldest, Bart, who had definitely lost his mind because he was threatening to join the Marines unless his father bought him a Corvette.

Bart who was colorblind and had asthma.

While the chief chewed out Martin and the rookie, Martin's ex-wife picked up their trashy daughter. She made brief eye contact with Martin—enough to say, *I tried and she wouldn't listen, but this is equally your fault*—then drove home. Mark saw it all and was amused.

Neither cop got a suspension, or even a write-up; but neither enjoyed the fireworks.

The young cop later apologized. Martin threatened to kill him if he ever looked at his daughter again. The younger man agreed, apologized again, said he hadn't known Meghan was Martin's daughter, and they shook hands. He said he honestly thought she was at least eighteen, if not twenty. Martin himself had said Meghan was fifteen going on forty.

Martin could only groan and apologize in return. He might have to depend on this young cop to back him up someday. "No hard feelings," he said—hard to tell if he meant it. "It's rough when it's your kid," he added.

The young cop said, "I know what you mean," though this was doubtful since he had none yet.

Martin then groused about it all to Mark and Mark said he could sympathize. MJ had only been ten at the time, but she would soon be eleven, then twelve, then fifteen and thinking she should have the same rules as any adult young woman, posting her life on the internet.

Sitting at his computer now, Mark tried not to think about those coming years. But he had logged on to and was now a "guest" on a social sex site. A headless man with shaved private parts and an enormous erection jacked off for a college girl in another window, who was playing titty-rub with her half-naked roommate. Then they hopped up, stripped off, and started kissing—putting on a real show, holding each other and pulling their buns apart.

The lonely stud blew his load.

Mark stood, nude, enraged—not engorged—and threw his laptop at the dresser on the far wall. The dresser survived; the laptop did not.

He didn't know what came over him so suddenly, but he felt dirty.

Alcohol helped.

Minutes later, hot water cascaded over his body like a cleansing summer rain. So why didn't he feel any cleaner?

Why? Because he knew he was stalling, putting off the inevitable.

An hour later, shortly before 2:00 AM, Mark sat in his Vic in The Mall parking lot. Very few cars remained at that time of night. The only place still open was Pete's Pizza, Pub & Keg, or as the locals called it, Pete's-a-Pubber.

At 2:00, Pete closed for the night.

Mark thought about the July Fourth picnic, Callie the chocolate lab biting little Andy because the dog didn't know they were playing—he thought Andy was attacking his twin wards—because a dog doesn't know what it's doing.

A dog operates solely on instinct. Like Mark had in his prime.

Was his prime past? Already? He took a deep breath, held it, then popped the air out and sighed as heavily as a police widow at another cop's funeral.

Then, he saw her, looking just like her Facebook post. Same outfit, same purse, same 'do—smoking one of those long, black, nasty clove things.

Mark wished he had a cigarette, for later—a real one—a Marlboro or a Camel.

He watched her smoking and digging in her purse, oblivious as the side door of the mall closed behind her, paying no attention to anything at all. No one around.

He started his car.

***

Walking unsteadily, weaving slightly, she couldn't find what she was looking for.

Before she realized anyone else was there, anything was moving, an old crappy car had fallen in behind her, creeping along, shadowing her.

When she heard car tires run over a go-cup with a crackle and a pop, she looked back. She'd finally found her bubblegum in her purse and now dropped the pack on the ground along with her clove *ciggie*.

The vast lot was lit, but the lights stood far apart. She couldn't see into the plain sedan to tell if it was anyone she knew—but she knew it wasn't.

Without moving, she turned to see where her car was parked—a hundred feet away, at least.

She looked back. The big, dark car was still creeping toward her with predatory intent, As if it was alive and hunting, and she was the prey.

She picked up her pace, trying not to look frightened or in a hurry, but her steps fell unevenly, her heels too stylishly difficult for making good time.

For escape.

She was more than a little drunk. More than a buzz. "Happily plastered," she'd told Jeremy, her gay friend from high school who posed no threat to her body. She wanted to fuck Terrance from England. *Bad*. She thought he looked like John Lennon, only not old or dead. Like a young John Lennon today might look, with the long hair and round glasses and a wild accent. The deep thoughts and tight pants.

The only one who wanted to fuck him more was Jeremy.

When she looked back to check, a slit of light crossed severe eyes. Now she knew for sure that she didn't know him, and that he had a purpose—her.

She ran.

He put the accelerator to the floor. The engine growled and the tires squealed, but no one was around to notice.

She ran as fast she could without falling, which wasn't fast enough as her pursuer swung wide and cut hard, screeching to a stop between her and her car, his engine idling, his windows up, making no move.

She stopped running and started crying. She had no idea what to do—no exit strategy, no emergency preparedness. All she had was a brain addled with alcohol and music, good times and laughter, fun lust and dance memories, carefree middle-of-the-week abandonment of work and life. How could she have known she'd end up here?

With him.

This man.

In his car.

Blocking.

Waiting.

She looked around slowly, careful not to let his car out of her peripheral vision. No one was anywhere—no one to hear her scream, no one to intervene, no one to help.

No one to stop this.

Leaving the car running, he opened his door and stepped out.

She could see him clearly now. He was old and looked mean, careless and cruel. His was not a kind face. Not a nice man. She could tell that at a glance.

She fought her tears as hard as she could. *Don't show him you're afraid. That'll only make things worse.* She thought her father may have told her that once—or she saw it on a TV show.

She yelled because she couldn't stop herself. "Don't you fucking come near me!"

The man opened his jacket just enough for her to see his gun and part of his badge.

She didn't move. She didn't dare.

He said, "Do you know what happened here a month ago?"

She said, "No."

"A girl was kidnapped. Murdered."

"She was like, twelve."

"I thought you said you didn't know."

"It was on the other side." She glanced at the badge and hoped. "Are you going to arrest me?"

"For what." He said it not as a question. Like a cop would.

She said carefully, "I don't know. Drinking, I guess."

"Have you been drinking?" When she didn't answer, he said, "Good answer."

She had no idea what to think, other than what the fuck she was doing here this night, how this night had turned into this, and what *this* might turn into.

He moved closer.

She braced.

He said, "That your car? Over there?" He nodded to indicate that her car was too far away to be of any help to her.

She understood and nodded.

He said, "Too bad. You almost would have made it."

She started to shake. She could feel it in her fingers, her teeth. She said, "Almost," but it was almost a whisper, almost a question.

The man nodded.

She said, even softer, "Would have?"

He nodded again.

The shaking was getting worse. She tried as hard as she could not to show it.

The cruel-looking man glanced at her trembling hands, then back into her eyes. He showed no emotion. That scared her more than anything.

He said, "If I wanted to, you'd already be mine. You'd be gone. *Poof.*"

The sound was somehow more frightening than the idea. She trembled more.

He said, "In a few hours, maybe a day or two, maybe after weeks of torture and rape, rape and torture, sodomy. You know what that is?" Before she could answer, he said, "Of course you do. You're the information generation. Everything is at your fingertips. Click a button and you know the answer to everything." He paused before concluding, "Except how to get out of this."

At the sound of water running, they both looked to see that she was no longer able to hold hers. Clear urine ran down her legs, spraying between them, splashing onto the ground, her mesh micro-thong offering no resistance.

Before she was fully drained, the man said, "After all of that—whatever I wanted, really—after all that time being alone and scared, helpless, a complete victim of my sick and twisted imagination, my perversions—you'd be dead."

He talked to her while she was peeing, as if she wasn't peeing at all, as if she wasn't standing in the middle of a public parking lot—with no public—peeing through her panties and skirt, onto her hundred-and-thirty-dollar open-toed shoes, splattering her ankles. It made the lecture that much more humiliating and terrifying.

Finally, her bladder was empty—her brain full of his words and the fear they generated. Her eyes red and wet.

He said, "Is that what you want?" as if it was a choice—as if *she* had a choice in these matters.

To be certain, to make sure he was saying what she thought he was saying, she said, "To die?"

He said, "And the rest."

"No."

That wasn't what she wanted at all.

She looked in his eyes but saw no life. She looked at his chest but saw no movement. Was he even alive? Was he some kind of cop zombie come to kill and eat her? She'd seen that on TV, in the movies, online and in video games. On her iPhone. That shit followed her everywhere. She *loved* slavering zombies.

Now this.

The man held out his hand for her to take. She didn't want to, but he didn't retract it. She figured she had no choice, so she took his hand, so much larger and stronger than hers. He squeezed—not enough to hurt her, just enough to make it abundantly clear who was in charge.

She hadn't stopped shaking.

He nodded to one side, towards his car—his long, dark car with the engine running—in control of the situation.

Detective Mark Young—the name on his badge, which she could now glimpse under his jacket and would never, ever forget. *Mark Young.* She would remember that name up until the moment he killed her, or the rest of her life if she got away.

She had little hope for the latter as he led her toward the plain sedan with the license plate turned away, but she kept saying the name over and over and over and over in her head so as not to let it slip away to terror.

She wanted to pull away and run. As if on cue, he tightened his grip. Tremors had gotten the best of her. Her head was shaking on her neck now, turning her into a bobble-headed *victim* bathed in cool costume jewelry, about to die.

Helpless.

Closer to his car.

Waiting like a hungry animal.

And closer.

The door open, the engine running, ready to take her away.

Closer.

She could feel the heat coming off the idling engine, under the wide, scratched and dented hood. Then...

He continued past it to stop just short of her car, the little Scion box she loved so much. Her father had given her the car for graduation, winking and telling her to, "Stay outa trouble."

She only wished.

Detective Mark Young reached across with his other hand and took her keys from her. She looked down, confused. She didn't remember retrieving them from her purse, but there they were.

In his hand.

Mark let the tiniest grin slip—a mean, evil smile, she thought—and he hit the open-locks button. Her car chirped happily, the lights came on inside, and power locks popped up for her entry.

Her escape.

Mark said, "Or," and hit the lock button.

Her car chirped, just as joyous to deny access.

She looked at him, then at his car. He looked at his car too—still idling, still waiting.

He then held up her key fob and pressed the alarm button. The lights flashed angrily on her little Scion, the alarm screamed for help, for attention, but...

No one came. Mark looked at her and together they looked around the expansive lot. There was no one *to* come. He hit the alarm button and silence returned.

Darkness.

He said, "It would have been better than nothing."

She peed again, just a little, but that was all she had left. She never could hold her liquor or control her bladder—always spread-legged and squatting over the club toilets, spraying the seat like all the other girls, but ten times a night, fifteen sometimes.

"Tiny bladder," she always said with a giggle before stumbling to the ladies' room *again*. On a dare once, she'd gone in the men's room, peed in a urinal standing up to prove she could do it. Now she did it routinely even if there wasn't a line for the ladies'. She was a brave one, all right, a thrill seeker.

Nothing thrills like real life—her legs wet again.

Mark looked down briefly, understanding, then he hit "unlock." The car chirped, the lights went on, the locks popped.

He opened her door.

She eyed him with caution, suppressing hope as best she could—to little effect—and said, "Are you going to let me go home now?"

"Is that what you want?"

She thought something had changed in his voice, his demeanor, so she said, "Yes." Then she asked, "Why?"

Mark said, "Because I really am a cop. But if I wasn't..."

He held her keys up—then dropped them on the ground.

She stared at him full of doubt. A look down at the keys, then back up at him. He was still showing nothing. He was waiting. Again!

She was supposed to pick those keys up. She understood this, did not want to, but knew she had to. She bent down and took hold of her keys—very aware that her face was even with his crotch. Not somewhere she wanted to be.

Or worse, in that awful picture he had painted of their potential, short future together.

She started to stand up, but Mark reached down and stopped her, forcing her to look up at him. She saw that face again, cold, dispassionate.

But something was different this time. The cruelty was gone—she couldn't say it was replaced by kindness—but he said, "Don't be stupid again."

She looked back at the side door of the mall. No, she would not be doing this again. Ever!

That wasn't what *Mark Young* was saying to her. What he now said was, "Don't tell the world where you're going to be at two in the morning. Alone."

She thought back to her happy posts about where she was going, whom she was going to be with, what they were going to do—and the mobile posts from her phone while they were doing it all. How stupid she had been!

"Had a grt time at Pte's-a-Pubbr 2night! Time 2 hd home. Closing time! Woohoo!"

Fucking Instagram.

Detective Mark Young said, "Okay?"

She nodded quickly, passionately, seriously.

Mark nodded in return, as if they'd made a pact. He smiled briefly—it almost looked like a real smile, a kind smile, an honest smile—then he walked to his car, got in, and rolled away slowly.

She was alone. She was alive! She was *safe*.

For the moment.

This young woman—who felt like a little girl—scrambled into her car, slammed the door, threw the locks, and dropped her keys. Afraid to reach for them without keeping her eyes on the entire lot, she bent without looking, felt around, found the keys, stabbed them into the ignition, started her car, and tore off.

Now she was safe; but she would never feel safe again.

Chapter 17

The next morning, Mark Young walked into the station, knowing what was about to happen. He'd hoped it wouldn't come to this but knew it probably would.

Jerome met him and said, "You really stepped in it this time."

Jerome with a half-smoked pack of Lucky Strikes on his desk.

Every cop in the building stared when Mark passed. They all knew. Cop World is small. Rumors fly faster than in a nursing home.

When the muted yelling started in the Captain's office, they all hung their heads and went to find something else to do.

Anything else.

Mark was officially on suspension until further notice.

***

At their scheduled appointment, Dr. Quarry said, "They took your badge." She showed no compassion or disagreement with the decision, but no judgment, either.

Mark said, "But I still get to come here," and he almost smiled.

Eileen Quarry was no patsy. She said, "It could be worse."

Mark said, "I doubt it." That badge meant everything to him—always had. More so lately because it was all he had left. Now, it too was gone.

She assured him, "You'll get it back."

"Not soon enough."

"You're a cop through and through," she said.

"And then some."

She nodded. "What you did was pretty stupid."

He shrugged it off. "I care about people. I just have a poor way of demonstrating it."

"At least you understand that," the doctor said.

Mark shrugged again. He would live with his actions. What choice did he have?

Eileen Quarry said, "What were you doing there anyway?"

"Pointing out the obvious."

"If it was so obvious, why did it need pointing out?"

"Because people don't always see it."

She chuckled. "People *rarely* see it."

"On that we agree."

He thought that if the opposite were true, Dr. Quarry would have no patients.

She *pretended* to look over Mark's PD file a moment, then said, "You're not going vigilante on us, are you?"

He hadn't noticed her looking up, but there she was staring straight at him—cutting through him, *per the usual.*

He said, "No. There are laws." He grinned.

She said, "I have to ask, you understand."

"Sure," Mark said. "I'm fair game."

Eileen leaned forward. "I don't care for the hunting analogy. I'm not hunting you, in any sense, and you are not my prey. As for fair, I try to be, but ultimately the decision is not mine and therefore not entirely fair in the end. So, following on that note: this is *not* a game."

Mark wanted to say, *Sure it is, it's all a game. They hide, we seek. They hope they win, we hope we win*. But he said, "Depends on your perspective."

"I was talking about us, in here. What we do in this room."

"What we talk about," he said.

"That too," she said.

Now he was thinking, *Oh yeah, your assessment of me – whether I'm fit for duty or a schizophrenic nutcase headed for permanent suspension or firing.* But he said, "Our work."

Dr. Quarry didn't agree, didn't disagree. Instead, she said, "I'm leaning towards a male."

At first, Mark thought she was talking about herself. Then he realized she didn't do that, couldn't do that (not professional), and her dating situation was none of his business (*very* unprofessional). She was talking about helping with this case that wasn't his case (*completely* unprofessional—which instantly broadened his respect for her), the case that now was so off-limits he would be allowed to discuss it with no one at all in any professional capacity (except his mental health *professional*?).

Wow.

Mark was game; anyone was better than no one. So, he said, "Anyone I know?"

She said, "Maybe," and didn't look away from him.

After a beat, he said, "Oh, I see. That was a joke."

Quarry said, "Or not. Sometimes they're closer than we think. Sometimes they're us. We don't even know it."

Was she was speaking from personal experience again—or was she implying something different, something new? Was she suggesting that Mark should consider a suspect he hadn't considered:

Himself.

Once she'd apparently gleaned that Mark understood her implication—*professionals* can tell when a patient has heard, if not accepted, their point—Eileen Quarry said, "I'd say your suspect is at least partly schizophrenic."

Mark shifted in his seat again—he had that unsettling feeling of being analyzed beyond the norm for a PE—and said, "Partly?"

She said, "There are degrees. Essentially, the important factor is whether or not he or she knows it. In this case, I'm guessing he doesn't."

"He's undiagnosed," Mark said.

"Untreated," his doctor said, pointing out the important difference.

Mark was relieved he'd been let off the hook, so he said, "You're saying we might be looking for someone who has been diagnosed, may have received some treatment, but at the current time—"

Dr. Quarry interrupted. "Or the times of the murders. During those periods or lapses."

"Right," Mark said. "He might be receiving treatment from time to time—in the meantime. Between."

Maybe he wasn't off the hook.

She said, "It's unlikely, but it can't be eliminated as a possibility."

Sensing he was *not* off her hook, Mark said, "Could he be receiving treatment, but still be as out of touch as a politician or movie star who believes his own press?"

Eileen laughed and said, "Correct."

Mark appreciated that she appreciated his joke. Cops and politicians mixed like Sunnis and Sikhs—only with less respect for each other.

He said, "But you're saying it's more likely he has been diagnosed—"

"Or not," she said.

"Or not," he said, trying to understand her remote-viewing diagnosis without relating it to himself and his fears about his own erratic behaviors of late.

"Whatever," he said, "he's probably not receiving treatment now, so he may or may not even realize he's crazy."

Fuck. Entirely too close to home. Next, she'd be asking him if he ever walked around naked or took showers that did no good, or pissed in the backyard—or continued to stalk young women on the internet.

Stalk. It had a bad ring. Made *him* sound crazy.

Dr. Quarry clearly didn't care for *that word.* "I prefer not to use that term. I don't find it particularly accurate or helpful in any way. And on this I *do* speak from personal experience. If we are trying to better understand ourselves, pejoratives only serve to get in the way of self-realization. Categorizing ourselves or others in derogatory ways does nothing but throw us off course and impede progress."

Mark said, "Okay."

She moved on. "I think the main thread of what I'm hinting at here is that he, or she— granted it still could be a woman—may or may not know he's doing these murders. He may think he is and not be sure, or he may even think someone else is. Either way, he can't be sure when he looks in the mirror."

"These guys look in the mirror?"

"All the time."

"What do they see?"

"Nothing and no one."

***

After driving around for what seemed like days but was less than three hours, Mark went home, had several drinks, pissed in the backyard, stripped off his clothes, took another non-absolving shower, then stared at himself in the mirror for twenty minutes.

He didn't see a damn thing.

Chapter 18

Mark parked his thrashed Crown Vic by the other law enforcement vehicles and med services and walked toward the woods. The hiking trail appeared well used and clearly marked, snaking through a dense copse of oaks, then thick brush, where it opened up and climbed the low ridge. At the top of the hill, Mark found Jerome Bowers—not smoking!

"How's retirement?" his old partner asked.

"Fuck you," Mark said, and wiped away some sweat.

Jerome pulled out a Marlboro.

Mark said, "Kind of dry for that up here, don't you think? Humidity's low and all."

Jerome said, "Yeah," and lit up. He nodded ahead to the mob of cops just over the ridge and started walking that way. "They let you keep the car." He sounded neither surprised nor envious.

"For now," Mark said, following along. "Did a hiker find the body?"

Jerome's Marlboro smelled so good Mark could almost taste it. He was thinking, *Why now?* Cigarettes had smelled nothing but revolting for at least ten years.

Jerome shook his head no and said, "Lady walking her dogs."

"Dogs found it?"

"Dragged her over and she almost fell on the body."

The responding officer had sat the woman down on what had to be the only bench on this mountain, where she was now giving her statement. Her dogs lay under the bench, panting in the heat.

Mark asked Jerome how fresh the body was, and Jerome said, "Last night." That was according to forensics on the scene. "No coyotes, no other scavengers. No bugs."

Mark said, "Lucky break," and Jerome agreed.

Jerome was looking at his watch and fidgeting a lot, so Mark asked him, "You okay, Jerry? You seem like you're under a lot of stress." *More so than usual,* Mark thought—more than the job called for.

Jerome said he was okay, just tired, and nodded Mark over to the bushes, behind which a nude body lay partly obscured.

It looked small.

Mark put on his cop-face of indifference and experience and stepped around the bush where a forensics team was packing up their gear, telling the coroner's people they were done and the body could be moved.

"Holy fuck," Mark said, low and eerie, his cop's aloof coolness dissipating like a cat's on seeing an unleashed Doberman.

Everyone turned around to stare, surprised to see Mark Young, suspended veteran homicide detective and all-round tough guy staring, surprised. Even shocked.

Jerome came to look. "You know her?"

Mark turned and violently pushed through the brush, back to his car.

"Mark! Do you know her? Hey! Hold up!"

Mark didn't stop. His head felt ready to explode. He hadn't been prepared to see the wide-open pale blues eyes on the small, pale, nude corpse with orange freckles and braces whom he'd last seen eating *chocklit chipth* alone.

***

Dan Black opened his front door dressed only in loose-fitting boxers.

Mark said, red-faced, "Wake you up? It's ten-thirty." *You should be awake. Anyone normal should be awake.* He walked right in.

Dan said, "Yeah," and "come on in," with dry displeasure, then shut the door.

Mark started pacing the living room. He said, "Rough night?"

Dan said, "Huh?" then, "Yeah. New job."

Mark came closer. "Doing what?"

Dan's brow furrowed. "Security. I'm a vet."

Mark realized he didn't know either of those facts and it bothered him that he didn't. He nodded in short bursts and said, "Night watchman?"

Dan nodded.

Mark said, "I thought you were in sales."

Dan snorted. "Where'd you get that?" When Mark didn't say, Dan said, "I never told you that, or anyone else. Sales, shit. I couldn't sell atomic bombs to Al Qaeda." He frowned and went into the kitchen.

Mark followed, not appreciating Dan's blithe dismissal or his alliteration.

Dan opened the refrigerator and poked around, the front flap on his boxers opening to reveal more than Mark wanted to see. Taking out a carton of Minute Maid, Dan asked, "Lemonade?" and went for a glass.

Mark said, "No thanks. That little girl is dead."

Dan stopped moving. "What little girl?"

"From the ice cream store. Little ginger girl with braces? Liked her chocolate chip? Raped, sodomized, and strangled. Then raped again, apparently."

Dan set his glass down on the counter, his hands shaking slightly—as if he could see his own children dead again in the backyard. "Jesus," he said. Tears came to his eyes.

"Yeah," Mark said, feeling no guilt for laying it on so hard. "So. You were working."

Dan nodded—then it apparently hit him what Mark was saying. "Now, wait a minute," he said.

Mark had laid the trap, now moved closer to examine what he'd caught. "What time?"

"What time what?" Dan said, ignoring his breakfast lemonade.

"What time did you work?" Mark said.

"Midnight to nine." Dan's pallor was gone, replaced by rising pink ire.

Mark said, "Time of death was between ten and eleven o'clock last night."

Dan bristled. "I was *asleep*. I got up at eleven."

"Witnesses?" Mark said without hesitation.

"To me sleeping? No." Dan had gone from sleepy to edgy to deeply agitated in seconds. He paced away, then stopped and came back. "I didn't kill that kid. Why do you have such a hard-on for me?"

Mark shrugged. "It's a hunch. I told you."

"Yeah," Dan said, "and you caught me eating ice cream."

"With a little girl who ended up dead a few hours later."

"I wasn't 'with' her," Dan said angrily. "She was just some kid in the store. Hell, you're the one who started talking to her. Maybe *you* killed her."

"That's not funny," Mark said.

He twitched, and it made him feel prickly inside, made his bones itch and his organs ache. He felt dishonest in his pursuit of his grieving neighbor, but he didn't know why. This is what he did. What he always did. He had hunches and he followed them, and sometimes they led him nowhere and sometimes they led him to some truth.

But he never questioned them. Not until now. This time, he wasn't sure where his gut was leading him or why he was even here. That bothered him, and he didn't know why.

Dan must have sensed it because he said, "Doesn't feel so good when it's flipped around on you, does it, friend? Where were *you* between... whatever, whenever—nine and ten."

"Ten and eleven."

"Ten and eleven, fine. Where were you?" Dan was now pushing, moving closer, getting into Mark's space.

"Where I was doesn't matter," Mark said icily.

Dan said, "It might matter to that little dead girl." He was snarling mad and not backing down.

"I'm a cop," Mark said.

"Oh yeah," Dan said, spitting out his sarcasm like raw, rancid meat. "Cops are always good guys. They never kill anyone. They're always in *control*. They never break the law. That's right, now I remember. They never shoot anyone in anger, never kill someone just because, never murder to cover up *the bad thing they did* because they're good cops and 'didn't do it'! Good cops. Good people. Good neighbors. Well hey, I've got news for you, Mark. Good neighbors kill people, too."

Now Mark was the crimson one. He growled, "She was raped, strangled, sodomized—"

"Yeah, you said. I heard that part," Dan said. "Thing is: In this world, this world today, we don't know shit. We don't know who does what or why they do it. We can only guess. Go on our *hunches*, right?

"We're *all* fucked up, Mark—every one of us. You, me, the freaks next door and across the street. Down the way. Across town!" Dan was really putting the drama to it, but now he pulled it back some. "There are plenty of bad cops, Mark, and you know it. Sick fuckers who do all kinds of twisted, awful things. To kids, too. Their *own* kids. Look what someone did in my house—in my goddam backyard. And you cops, you *good* cops, don't have a fucking clue. Not one!"

Dan took some tight steps away, then turned back, hateful. "So, your little ginger girl, your *one* dead little ginger girl you didn't even *know*? Don't tell me anything, don't ride my ass with your pointless, clueless, *baseless* cop hunches. And don't tell me no cop could have done that. Anyone could have done that. Any man, woman, or child. Any neighbor, any lawyer, any judge, any politician, *anyone*. Any *cop*."

"Not this cop." Mark gave it back to him, regathering his steadiness.

Dan said, "Your hunch was wrong before and it's wrong now. I did not kill that little girl. I didn't even *remember* her until you brought it up. Now get the *fuck* outa my house."

The face he put on was Trojan-like—fierce, meant to instill terror and doubt. To intimidate. To threaten with something terrible deep inside him, dying to be released.

Mark had seen it countless times on the street. Cornered criminals were renowned for feigning a pronounced lack of fear. Some truly had none—no moral compass, no compassion, no feelings of any kind; but most were afraid—and most of *them* were afraid all the time.

Afraid to show it.

Anger and intimidation never worked on Mark Young, never bothered him at all. If anything, it had the opposite effect, making him calmer and cooler, his thought processes sharper and faster. He smiled and said, "Kind of overreacting aren't we, Dan?"

His practiced act did its intended work.

Dan went jumpy, almost wild. "We? What's this 'we' shit? I thought we were friends, and if I'm not mistaken, you're accusing me of murdering a nine-year-old girl!"

"How'd you know she was nine?" Mark said without even thinking. He'd done this so many times, thought about this case so much and so often, everything was already there for him. The words arrived synchronous with the thought.

Dan seemed genuinely stumped by the question. He looked around as if searching for the answer in his kitchen. It apparently wasn't there, because he said, "I don't know, honestly. Lucky guess. Maybe I remembered from the ice cream parlor."

"She didn't say," Mark said, though he wasn't sure she hadn't.

Dan seemed flummoxed. "I *don't know*. It's in there somewhere, I can't tell you why. Maybe Chuck said it. Maybe it was just a wild guess based on what she looked like. Picked it out of thin air. How do *you* know?"

1"I just came from the crime scene. Put on your pants."

"Why?" Dan said. "I'm not going anywhere."

Mark said, slower, "Put on your pants. You're coming with me."

Dan grunted a laugh. "I'm not going anywhere with you. You're not even a cop anymore."

"I'm on suspension. I'm still a cop."

"Yeah," Dan said, "but you're on suspension. You have no authority—certainly not over me. Besides, how do I even know where you're wanting to take me?" He mocked, "*Downtown*?" Then he said nastily, "Out in a field somewhere quiet? Out behind the barn maybe?" He nodded, then chided, "Did they let you keep your *gun*?"

Mark went quiet.

Dan said, "Thanks, but I'll stay here."

Mark said, "I think you better come with me. To the station. How's that? Okay?" Not that it was a real question, but he put it that way as a tool, some more bait.

Dan didn't take it. "No, it's not okay. You're not on active duty and I don't have to go anywhere with you." He was clear and defiant.

So, Mark agreed. "No, you don't."

***

Fifteen minutes later, Dan was in handcuffs—still in his loose boxers—and two uniform cops were leading him out to a black-and-white.

Jerome stood close by, Mark at his side with a smirk of civic pride.

Jerome said, "You better be right on this."

Mark said, without hesitation, "Oh, I am. I know the look. *You* know the look. The reactions, the slips. It was all there, Jerry. Every bit of it. You would've done the same thing."

Jerome looked his old partner over, sighed heavily, and turned for his detective special Impala.

Mark said, "Do I at least get to watch?"

Chapter 19

Jerome gave Dan Black a tough grilling. Martin Coor came in to help as he had a few questions himself. Even Ted Henrickson put in an appearance. No one had seen much of him lately—he always claimed he had "other things to attend to."

Captain Corlius had re-assigned most of Henrickson's cases to other detectives, so everyone figured his days were numbered. Whether he was cracking up from the pressure or had some secret no one wanted to know, either one got you a referral; and, with so many departmental budget cuts, a referral usually got you fired.

Henrickson only asked a few questions, all of them having to do with his case—the only one he seemed to be spending any time on at all, involving the murders of a crack dealer, his wife and teenage daughter in Helldale.

Mark knew about it only because the dead family had reportedly lived in his hometown, a small farming area just outside the city limits. There they had cooked meth as a family for two years before moving to town, where they were murdered within a week.

"You know anyone named Kelsridge?" Henrickson asked Dan Black.

Dan said he didn't.

"What about Dougherty. Carla Dougherty?"

Dan said he didn't.

"Eirena Kelsridge. You're sure?"

Dan said he was sure.

"You ever been to Paducah or Poughkeepsie?"

Dan said, "Is that a joke?"

Henrickson said it wasn't and left.

Jerome and Martin Coor shared a look of befuddlement and doom for Henrickson and went back to grilling Dan. Mark watched from behind the two-way mirror.

Looking for signs.

Dan was rattled, clearly, but he kept to his story. He was also clearly worried about losing his job. "I'm a vet, man," he told Jerome.

"They watch us—like they watch you." His face said, *You know what I mean.*

Jerome said, "You sayin' I'm black?" stating the obvious and maybe looking to tussle.

Dan said, "I'm saying they watch you in a different way. And believe me, they watch us in the same way."

"I doubt it's the same way," Jerome said and turned away for a cigarette, this time a Tareyton. *Where the hell does he find these things?*

Martin took over as good cop. He said to Dan, "I know what you're sayin', man. Vets coming back these days do some pretty crazy shit." His attempt to be sly. "Have you been doing some pretty crazy shit, Dan? Since you got back?"

Dan stared up ruefully—not at his situation, it appeared, but at Martin Coor's lack of finesse or creativity. He said, "No. What I'm telling you is there's no way I could have killed that little girl and gotten to work on time. It's all the way across town. How many times do I have to *say this*!" He all but shouted at the detectives.

"Easy, dude," Martin said. "We're just asking some questions, here. Nothing official. You want a lawyer? You think you need one?"

Dan shook his head in frustration. "No. I do not. I didn't do anything."

Martin laughed. "Good, 'cause we've never heard that one before."

Dan gritted his teeth.

Mark watched closely.

In the interrogation room, Jerome turned back with his lit Tareyton filtered. "Aw, go easy on him. Mark dragged him outa bed and into this hole in his underwear." He turned toward the mirrored glass and inhaled intentionally.

Mark knew Jerome was looking at him—and why. He muttered, "Ask him about the girl, Jerome."

A voice came, "Huh?"

Mark had forgotten his captain, Corlius, was in the room with him. He'd seemed distracted, disinterested—so silent that Mark forgot he was there.

"Nothing," Mark said. "Just thinking out loud."

His captain said, "Uhm," and went back to his private thoughts.

In the interrogation room, Dan said, "Have you asked Weatherly?" His boss.

Jerome said, "We got the impression you didn't want us to—with him watchin' you so close and all." No apparent sincerity or sympathy.

Dan hemmed and hawed and eventually said, "What else am I gonna do? You won't take my word for it. You're gonna have to ask him."

Martin said, "What are we gonna ask him?"

"If I've been late for work *once*."

They waited.

Dan said, "I haven't. I've been on time every single night since I started there a month ago. Haven't missed one. Last night was no different."

"So, you were on time," Jerome said. *Big deal.*

Dan looked up as if he realized, "You already checked with him."

Neither Martin nor Jerome revealed anything.

Dan said, "Nice. Thanks for that."

Martin said, "Just doin' what we get paid to do."

"I thought you were getting paid to find out who killed *my* children," Dan said sourly.

"I guess I am," Martin said.

"And how's that going? Any leads yet?" Dan snarled.

Martin said, "I'll let you know, later."

Dan shook his head, indicating his displeasure with them, and Jerome looked at the mirror with Mark behind it.

Mark said quietly, "Stay with him, Jer'. He's close."

Captain Corlius said, "Huh?" again.

Mark told him it was nothing again and tried to see what Dan was hiding, what he wasn't remembering. He saw Dan's eyes light up.

There it is.

Dan said, "Wait. I have a witness."

Martin said, "A witness. To the murder?"

Dan said, "That's not even a little bit funny. A witness who saw me go to work, who saw me leave my house at 11:15 last night."

"Yeah?" Jerome said, as if completely uninterested and not believing this sudden shift at all. "Who?"

Dan looked at the mirrored wall, nodded toward it and said, "Him. Mark Young. Detective Mark Young. He's on suspension, so he was home, drinking." Dan glared at Mark through the glass, his words getting bitter toward the end of his accusation.

Now Jerome and Martin Coor turned toward the mirror.

Apparently sensing something was wrong, Captain Corlius looked up and said, "What the fuck just happened?"

Mark remembered.

Mark is nude. He's been staring into his mirror for what feels like days, an empty rock glass in his hand—his third scotch in thirty minutes—and he's decided there's nothing to see. He's tried and he's done trying. He's not even sure what he's supposed to be looking for.

He turns off the light and walks back into his dark bedroom with only the blue light from the monitor of the desktop PC he brought up from downstairs.

He crosses the room for the almost-empty liquor bottle on top of the tall dresser. Passing the window, he glances down to where he sees Dan Black getting into his silver car in his security uniform.

Thinking nothing of it—focused on the bottle and getting to it—Mark sways as he pours the last few ounces, the last drops, of blended scotch into his glass. He sets the empty bottle down by the computer, which reads "11:15 PM."

In the observation room, Mark felt as if he'd seen a ghost.

His own.

Captain Corlius went back to his office without a word—and slammed the door loud enough to send cops scattering, just in case.

Minutes later, out front in the parking lot, Jerome stood with Mark off to one side. Mark hung his head in disbelief at his own stupidity.

Jerome smoked another Tareyton furiously, like a laboring locomotive. "You forgot? You fucking for*got*?! What the fuck is wrong with you, Mark? You smokin' crack now?"

"I don't know," Mark muttered, still dumfounded at his mistake.

"You don't know if you're smoking *crack*!"

"No!" Mark said. "I may have had a few drinks."

"May have? A few? Ten? Twenty? A whole fifth?"

"Maybe."

"Christ, Mark! You're still a cop. You're on suspension is all."

"What, cops don't drink now?"

Jerome smoked faster. "That's not what I'm saying and you know it." He threw his cigarette away and immediately lit another as he spoke. "You accuse the man of murdering a child, demand he produce a witness and he produces *you*? You *forgot*? How the fuck hammered were you, man!"

"That's none of your business."

"None of my business?! You called me to *arrest* him! I'd say it's completely my business—unless *you're* gonna go in there and tangle with the captain and his lawyers."

Mark remained silent.

"Hell, this fuckin' guy is probably gonna sue me personally!" Jerome said, smoking faster and faster. "I can't afford this shit right now, Mark. I mean it."

"I'm sorry."

"Yeah, you are. You are one sorry motherfucker, I'll tell you." Smoke billowed above him like a coal-powered power plant. He said mockingly to his old partner, "So, what? You're gonna tell me you're under a lot of stress?"

Mark looked away and Jerome went on the attack. "Maybe this hot shrink you're seeing has your head all twisted in knots. Maybe you're thinking you'd like to fuck her and it's making your head go all crazy."

Everyone knew who Dr. Eileen Quarry was—what she looked like. But how could Jerome make that *insane* leap? Mark looked up but bit his tongue. He went with, "It's not like that, Jerry. Come on."

Jerome wasn't having it. "Maybe she's got your head so spun around you don't know which way is up anymore. Maybe you miss Anne and the kids. Maybe you're not crazy about being on suspensions because you *shot* at someone in your own backyard and pumped a dozen rounds into your neighbors' houses! Maybe you're all confused about what's been happening!"

Mark looked at his old partner as if to confirm some part of that but said, "It was only nine."

"*Only* nine," Jerome spat, puffing hard on his dwindling cancer stick. "Well, I don't give a motherfucking *fuck* of a fuck! You deal with it, motherfucker. And you deal with it on your own motherfucking time. Not mine!" He was so angry he stopped smoking to poke the glowing butt at Mark's face. *Then* he took a mean puff.

Mark said, "Yeah. That wasn't good, in there."

Jerome's eyes flew wide. He flipped the Tareyton filter at a passing squad car and took out a half-gone pack of Salems. He said, "Lemme tell you somethin', old friend. That shit in there? That made me look bad. Not as bad as you, but bad enough. I went out on a limb for you and you cut the goddam limb off! And that's just the beginning of the shit I'm gonna have to put up with from our esteemed Captain Tightass. This shit's gonna go down like elephant shit in a carnival."

It didn't wholly make sense, but the picture was graphic and effective.

"And I'm tellin' you," Jerome reiterated, "I ain't got time for this shit right now. You understand?"

"Yeah," Mark said. He started to say he was sorry again, but Jerome got there first.

"I don't think you do!" Jerome hollered. "I don't think you understand one micro-iota of what the fuck just went down in there!"

"I didn't mean I understood what it means for you personally," Mark said. "Whatever's going on in your life—"

Jerome blurted, "Fuck that! Fuck my life! You know why? 'Cause it's only your goddam motherfucking life that you care about! Narcissistic motherfucker. All your goddam 'stress'!" Jerome looked about to explode from his own stress. He turned away. "White man's burden, my ass."

Mark said, "Jerome, I'm really sorry. I was so sure." He still couldn't figure out what had gone so wrong, how he could have *been* so wrong. How could he have forgotten seeing Dan—and did that even matter? Dan could have killed the girl, gone home, gone to bed, gotten up, showered, dressed...

Fuck, it mattered all to hell.

Jerome pulled a Salem menthol from the pack, but he was so angry he didn't even light it. He said, "Yeah, and about that." *In there*. "I don't know why you got such a hard-on for this sad motherfucker. His children were slaughtered in his own backyard while he slept. Your kids are alive because you got lucky and forgot your goddam cellphone. Now cut this poor bastard some slack. And don't call me unless you have the killer locked in your basement with a signed confession and *ten goddam witnesses to every murder*!"

Mark knew he didn't have to say anything for Jerome to know he agreed—even if he didn't have a basement. Jerome lit his Salem, glared, and walked off. Then he turned back.

"And don't show up at another one of my goddam *incidences* unless I personally invite you. You understand me? I ain't fuckin' around. I don't want to even see your sorry ass lingering around one of my investigations, hanging out with the losers and winos on the corner. I see you anywhere *near* me, anywhere near anything I'm investigating or even just doing because I *want* to do it—and I'm going straight to the captain for a got-damn restraining order on your ass!"

He went back to his chimney impersonation and headed inside.

Just as he got to the door and reached for the handle to pull it open, the door swung open into Jerome's fingers. "Goddammit! Watch what the fuck—"

He stopped himself. It was Dan Black. Someone had given him a t-shirt and khaki shorts to wear home. For a moment, it looked as if he might cuss him right back, until he saw it was Jerome—and Mark behind him.

Watching.

Dan's face was hard, cold, done with it all. He looked at Jerome and said, "Sorry, man. I didn't see you coming."

Jerome looked at the full glass doors, massaged his aching fingers, and threw his just-lit cigarette away. "It's cool," he said.

Even if it wasn't—for any of them.

Jerome went inside and let the door close behind him, leaving Dan and Mark to face off. Dan said nothing, his look impenetrable, unrepentant, and full of bald abhorrence.

Mark met his gaze and said, "I'm sorry, Dan. I fucked up."

He expected a tirade more potent than Jerome's, but nothing changed in Dan's eyes—as if he wasn't seeing Mark at all. At least not as another human being.

Mark held his ground, his gaze. He had met and mastered worse.

Finally, Dan said, "My. Kids."

Mark looked away.

Chapter 20

Mark Young opened his front door wearing maroon LSU track shorts and a grey USC t-shirt, beer in hand, to find Dan wearing old, loose USMC sweats.

Dan said, "I think I can help you."

Since he didn't appear still angry, Mark said, "I've heard that before." He was thinking of Dr. Quarry—had just *been* thinking about Dr. Quarry.

In a personal way.

Dan Black said, "You haven't heard it from me."

Mark considered the offer—and where they had left their *friendship*—and nodded Dan past.

As he entered, Dan asked, "What happened to your hedge?"

"It died. Some beetle or something." Mark closed the door behind them. As if he gave a fuck, had time to give a fuck, about fucking *flora*. "Shouldn't you be resting for work tonight?"

"I called in sick. Told the boss man the cops held me for six hours for nothing. Turns out, he'd heard."

"Yeah," Mark said, chagrined. "Beer?"

"Sure."

Mark got Dan a beer—a local microbrew for a change, though he didn't usually care for seasonals—and sat in his favorite chair while Dan paced and sipped.

"This isn't bad," he said. "I'll have to get some."

Mark said it had more whang than he liked. "It's like a double IPA. I think it's the pumpkin."

Dan said it was too early for "Halloween brew" and paced more.

Mark waited him out.

When half his beer was gone, Dan said, "This isn't easy for me."

"Drinking beer, sharing man-moments, or pacing in my house while I stare at you and wonder what the hell ever brought you over here to begin with?"

Dan said, "All of that and more."

Mark said, "Fair enough."

They drank the rest of their beers and Mark got two more—Pabst this time. Old Reliable.

Dan set his down on a coaster on the end table and said, "Here's the thing: What I'm about to tell you, in confidence, is going to be very difficult for me."

Mark said blithely, "Confessions always are."

Dan said, without skipping a beat, "Especially when you're confessing for someone else."

Mark took a long slug of his PBR and asked, "Who're we talking about?"

Dan appeared nervous, impatient. "You know I really don't like that 'we' thing."

"Yeah. You said."

Dan went for his Pabst, emptied half the can, and sat where he usually sat, ninety degrees to Mark. He only seemed now to notice the TV was on—without sound as usual—and said, "Last night's game?"

Mark said, "I don't know. Maybe." *Go on. Tell me what you have to tell me. Then we can talk sports.*

Dan took another steadying breath and said, "Chuck. From the Mall?" Dan made sure Mark was listening, then finished, "That girl. The dead one."

Mark said, "The ice cream guy and the ginger?"

Dan nodded.

Mark stood bolt straight out of his chair. "What about it?"

Dan seemed taken aback by Mark's sudden movement and intensity. He leaned back.

Mark yelled, "What do you know about it!"

"Nothing!" Dan shouted back.

"Then what the fuck are you doing here talking about it!" Mark yelled again.

After all that went down today!

"Calm down, bro," Dan said.

"'Bro'?" Mark said with deep incredulity.

"Just calm down," Dan said. "Jeez. I told you this was difficult for me."

Mark continued to hover and yell. "So what! If you know something, goddammit you tell me! If you don't, don't come over here saying shit like you know something if you don't!"

"Okay!" Dan said.

"So, do you?!" Mark's eyes were as wide as Anne's had been that night.

"Maybe! I'm not sure!" Dan seemed to cow some. "I wanted to... to run it past you," he said, as if fighting internal demons. "To see if I'm on the right track, on... any track at all. To see if... I'm going crazy." He slumped—whined with his body language.

Then he said, "I know something. I mean, I *may* know something. I just don't know if it's anything... important." He looked up cautiously and added, to clarify. "It's not about me, okay? I didn't do anything. I swear. I did *not* kill that little girl." He got quieter. "I need to know that you believe me about that."

Mark was finding his calm place again, but he wasn't ready to make deals. He tried to guess, "So. It's about Chuck. Chuck did something."

"I don't know. Maybe not."

Mark was yelling again. "Did he kill her! Did he say something! What!"

"No!" Dan protested. "Well, yes—"

"Yes or no!"

"In the past!" Dan was yelling back now. "Not about this! Not about this girl!"

"Then what the *fuck*!" Mark poured down his beer and went for another.

He did not bring one back for Dan.

Dan said, "Look, I'm trying to tell you. You don't make a guy feel very comfortable, dude."

"Not part of my job description to make people feel comfortable, *dude*," Mark said bitterly. He sat, almost draining the entire PBR in one slug.

Dan watched it and said, "Mind if I get another?"

Mark looked at him, grabbed Dan's beer and shook the can. It was empty. When had he drunk it? More important: Who cared? He nodded Dan toward the kitchen.

Dan stood, went into the kitchen, and returned with a cold PBR, *schwipped* the tab and took a long sip. He said, "Really. You don't do much to instill confidence."

"Not my style," Mark said without regret.

"You don't have a style. You have a presence."

"I'll take that as a compliment." Mark finished his beer and opted to take a breather. He was feeling his beer buzz and didn't want to miss anything important—*again*.

Dan said, "He talks about kids— "

"Chuck does," Mark interrupted immediately.

"Yes! Let me tell the damn story!" Dan said, irritable.

"Go ahead," Mark said, but he was champing at the bit.

Dan said, "He talks about kids. And women. How he loves them and hates them. How they need to be taught a lesson now and then. A hard one. Shit like that." Dan half-shuddered. "It's creepy."

Mark waited, but Dan said nothing else. So, Mark said, "That's it?"

Dan was quiet.

Mark said, "What else?"

Dan looked increasingly squirrely.

Mark's voice raised again, along with his ire. If there was one thing he hated more than perps lying to him, it was perps holding out on other perps. He stood—face to face with Dan who hadn't sat—and started yelling again. "What else! What are you not telling me! You know something! Tell me what it is, goddammit!"

"He's a *friend*!" Dan protested.

Marked yelled back, "Some fucking friend! Probably killed your kids, too—and wanted to kill mine! You're gonna protect him from *that*? What kind of fuckin' friends you *got*!"

Dan met Mark's look uneasily, as if trying to back him down, only his heart wasn't really in it. He finally turned away, pacing again, as if trying his best to summon the strength to say whatever awful truth had to be said.

Finally, he turned back. "Okay," he said. "He had a party once. At his house. All these creepy guys hanging out. Older guys, youngers guys. All freaks, man." Dan nodded as if he remembered it all vividly—how disturbing he had found it. "He shows us this website—I didn't even know shit like that existed." Dan appeared greatly troubled by what he'd seen. "Sick shit, man. Dead kids. Women."

Mark said, "You mean like a snuff site?"

"What's that?" Dan asked.

Mark said, softer, "You know, they uh, sexually molest a woman or a kid—then kill them. On camera."

"No." Dan shook his head. "It wasn't like that. They were already dead."

Mark said, "Like *Faces of Death*."

"What's that?"

"Jesus, Dan. Get out much?"

"No," Dan said. "Not really."

"They're like uh, videos of dead people killed in car crashes or shot or in weird accidents. Electrocuted, drowned. Whatever. Just dead people. Dead people to look at and see what they look like dead."

"Yeah," Dan said. "Like that." He thought a moment and said, "But only kids. Kids and women. Mostly kids. Dead kids." He thought some more. "It was fuckin' sick, man."

"You didn't say anything?"

"Like what? What am I supposed to say? The guy invites me to his house for a bar-b-cue and the next thing, there's this bunch of weirdos hanging around his computer watching videos of a dead kids and women... and they're fucking... laughing and shit. It was *sick*. Turned my fucking stomach."

"Again," Mark said. "You didn't say anything?"

Dan snapped, "What was I going to *say*? It was his house!"

"Tell him it's fucked up and you're leaving," Mark said. Seemed obvious to him.

Dan sat, his troubled memories apparently getting the better of him. He said, "I did. I left and never went back." To preempt anything Mark might have to say about that, he added, "And I never brought it up again."

"Why not?"

"I just pushed it out of my mind, man, c'mon! I didn't want that shit in my head! Don't you ever do that? See something you didn't want to see, do something you didn't want to do, you regret doing it or seeing or hearing about it, so you push it out of your mind so you don't have to keep seeing it over and over again. You're a cop. You must do that all the time."

That one struck home. Mark said, "I try." Then he said, "Doesn't work too well."

Dan said, "Well, yeah. When you told me about... about that girl with the red hair, and her little ice cream cone and her braces, I... I just... It all came back—I mean later, after—and I couldn't get it out of my head."

He didn't say it with guilt, but guilt was layered on top of his words when he added, "After today, after they... rode me so hard, asking me all those questions about her and... what happened. It... it all just came back in a flood, in the taxi on the way home."

Mark thought Dan seemed to be linking the guilt he felt for not remembering the ginger girl to the guilt he felt for the deaths of his three children. But he wasn't sure, so he didn't say anything. He didn't want to show his ass again—not twice in one day.

Dan looked up, eyes reddening. "I had to tell you." His voice was a raspy whisper.

Mark thought Dan was going to cry, but he didn't. He looked down at the floor and shook his head. Then he looked up and said, "You have to get in his house, man. There's evidence in there, I just know it. You gotta get in there before he gets rid of it. Before he gets rid of everything."

Dan shook his head from side to side, looking worried. Then his face came up with a look of deep desperation.

If Mark was shocked, he didn't show it. Cops don't work that way—especially suspended cops. And had the presence of mind to say, "I can't do that."

Dan nodded and said, "No, I guess not. Not after what you did to me today."

No one in the department would listen to Mark—maybe ever again. To make the point that he understood that fact, Dan added, "Who would listen to you *now*?"

Mark heard something he didn't like in those words, an accusation—but mainly, another confession. He started yelling again. "Oh fuck. You didn't tell him, did you!"

"Tell who? What?" Dan said.

"Chuck! You didn't tip him off, did you!"

"No!" Dan shouted back, standing to defend his non-action. "What do you think I am!" Then he remembered with hard cynicism, "Oh yeah, that's right. You think I'm a child murderer!"

Mark softened. "I said I was sorry about that, and I am. Sorry as hell."

Dan took a deep breath. All of this was very difficult for him, obviously. And he was worried. "If Chuck hears that they had me in for interrogation, he's gonna put two and two together, remember I was there that night with those freaks and their videos, and he's gonna get rid of everything, every shred of evidence in the house—on his computers and in his closets. I'm telling you, Mark, it's there. I know it. I can feel it. Like one of your hunches. This one's mine. I just know it."

Understanding that feeling, Mark said, "Okay," but nothing more. No commitment.

Dan said definitively, "He killed that girl, and the evidence is in his house right now. He's holding onto it, savoring it, man. He's so fucking cocksure he got away with it that he's keeping it and whacking off on it while he watches those goddam sick videos." He again shook his head to indicate his deep disgust.

Then he looked up and said, "You could make an anonymous call."

Mark was already thinking past that. "No, that's not good enough." He calculated that the department was probably getting a hundred "tips" a day, if not a thousand—with not one of them leading to any real evidence. They would have to sift through it all, decide whether this tip was worth pursuing. That would take time, then—

"Or I could make the call," Dan said.

"No way," Mark said, again knowing how his department worked. "You were just questioned in that case. If they ever found out you called it in, they'd figure you were trying to lay the blame off on someone else, and they'd never leave you alone."

Dan looked up and smiled for the first time, realizing what Mark was saying—and doing for him. "Thanks for that."

"My pleasure," Mark said. One of the few pleasures he'd had recently. Being off active duty wasn't Mark's idea of fun. Being in the battle of good versus evil day to day was his one true pleasure in life—and he had effectively taken it away from himself by lighting his own blue flame.

That didn't mean he didn't still think like an active-duty cop. He said, "There *is* one way to get the cops there."

Dan looked up.

"You remember where he lives?"

***

It took Mark only a few minutes to gather what he needed and throw it in his trunk. He was waiting in the idling Crown Vic when Dan came back from changing his clothes. They drove off and, twenty minutes later, Dan showed Mark the old frame house, sitting up on low pilings.

Mark pulled to the curb, parking two houses down. He hopped out, went back, popped the trunk, and removed an old canvas tote bag.

No one was out in the dodgy neighborhood, so Dan and Mark were able to walk unnoticed into Chuck's yard. They could see him inside, sitting in a La-Z-Boy in his underwear, watching a rerun of *F Troop*, laughing like a loon, kicked back with a large bag of crispy cheese snacks and a cold twenty-ounce. Old Milwaukee.

Mark whispered, "So, he's a cheap killer."

Dan whispered back, "Yeah, you splurged on PBRs."

Mark laughed quietly, his mood elevated. He loved his work—especially when he was skirting into the gray areas to get something done that involved pushing boundaries.

Every cop loves a good workaround.

They crept low, below the level of the untended hedges, around the side to the phone box. Fortunately, Chuck still had a landline.

Mark muttered to himself, "Hadn't thought of that." What they would have done if Chuck had gone strictly mobile.

Dan said, "What?"

Embarrassed to admit it, Mark said, "Nothing," and reached into his old lineman's bag. He took out a push-button phone unit with wires hanging, each with an alligator clip on the end. He said, "I clip this into his line, dial nine-one-one, and hang up."

Dan said, "They'll just call back. They have to."

Mark grinned. "Not if I cut the line before they can." He held up his wire cutters, ready for the job. "Then they have to come and investigate. It's the *law*."

Whispered glee.

He pulled out a small screwdriver and removed the center screw from the junction box, then the cover, revealing the wires into the house. Holding a tiny flashlight in his teeth, he found the wires he wanted and attached his alligator clips to the terminals.

Dan asked, "Where'd you get all this shit?"

"Where does a cop get anything?"

Dan rolled his eyes in the dark, but Mark saw and grinned wider.

He loved this shit.

He punched in 9-1-1. A voice came over the line. "Nine-one-one operator. What's the nature of your emergency?" Some of them had to sound more important—as if saving lives wasn't important enough.

Mark cut the wires.

They scurried back to the street and down to the beater. As he and Dan climbed back into the Vic, Mark said, "Now we watch the fireworks."

A squad car turned the corner within five minutes. "Damn," Mark said. "Call times are low around here. I would've finished my lunch and ordered another coffee before checking on a dropped nine-eleven call. Get down."

He slumped down in his seat, so Dan did as well. They peeked over the dash just enough to see as the patrol car stopped in the street in front of Chuck's house. Both cops got out, adjusted their belts as only patrolmen can do—they were both men—and strolled for the door as if nothing unusual was going to happen.

They left their car running in case something did.

Mark said to them, from this distance, "Remember your training, boys. Go by the book."

They were young—barely twenty, it looked—both built solid as a cement bunker with arms like the Guns of Navarone. If Chuck bolted, he was in for it.

The thought made Mark giggle.

Dan stayed quiet, watching every move and moment as the cops stepped onto the porch, each with a hand on their duty weapons.

One officer stood off to one side, where he could look in the front window, and the other pulled the screen door open. He knocked and announced, "Police. Open the door, please."

From two doors down, Mark and Dan could see Chuck jump up out of his Barco-coma.

The cop at the window shouted, "We got a runner!" and leapt off the porch, clean over the hedge, headed for the back door, calling for backup on the run. "Unit Seven-Three-Two Baker requesting..."

He ran around the side of the house, holding his belt as the uniform at the door yelled, "Police! Open the door or we're kicking it in! Police! *Open the door motherfucker*!"

He was already kicking it in.

Mark giggled louder. "'Motherfucker.' Listen to this. This is gonna be good."

Dan didn't look so sure.

Mark turned to him with a grin that showed more teeth than cheek and said, "Don't you just love to see police work executed properly."

Dan nodded wanly. He looked scared.

Mark said, "It's gonna work just fine. Don't worry."

"Yeah," Dan said. But he didn't sound convinced.

Mark looked back to check on the action, saw something, and said, "Shit! Stay here, don't move!" He was out of the Vic before Dan could say okay.

What Mark had seen was Chuck getting away.

Cop #1 got slowed down scaling a fence into the backyard, then fending off Chuck's attack dog. Cop #2 had cracked his ankle bone kicking the triple-bolted door in and was now hobbling through the house, room to room, gun extended, yelling, "Police! Get down on the floor and don't move! Police! Get down on the floor and don't move!" as Chuck ran—swiftly for a fat ice cream jerk—through the next-door neighbor's yard for freedom, having climbed out a side window.

Mark was waiting behind a bush and clotheslined him. Chuckles went down like a sand-weighted tip-over punching clown. To make sure he stayed there, Mark threw a full body-weighted punch to Chuck's temple.

Chuck's lights went out.

Mark could just see Cop #1 trying to kick in Chuck's reinforced back door, about to break his ankle. Mark shook his head and called out—in his very worst old-lady impression, "Officers! Over heeere! Here he is, officers! Help!"

Then he ran like hell.

Before the cop got to Chuck, Mark had reached the Vic, saying as he climbed in, "That was sweet." Then he saw—

No one in the Vic. Dan was gone.

"Fuck."

Mark looked everywhere. Not in the front seat. Not in the back east. Not outside the car.

"Fuck!"

Mark started the car—and sat.

"Fuck!!"

It had been going so well, too.

"Fuck!!!"

Mark's only choice was to drive and hope Dan was close enough to see or hear and *come get in the goddam car* before either of the cops—or the backup officers whose sirens were coming fast—saw them.

Keeping his head low, Mark hazarded a glance and caught the backyard cop cuffing Chuck—who was still out cold—and calling it in.

"Seven-Two-Three Baker. We have a suspect in custody for that kid's One-Eighty-Seven."

Mark nodded, happy, spiteful. Fucking child killer. He was glad to see Chuckles in custody, but he'd kind of been hoping they'd shoot him before—or just after—cuffing him.

He looked ahead again and slammed on the brakes. Dan was standing dead ahead like a startled deer with hands—held out straight to stop the four-thousand-pound Ford.

As Dan ran around to get in, Mark snuck a look to see if the uniforms had noticed his car. The cops were busy kicking Chuck, so they didn't notice.

Resisting arrest was a beautiful thing sometimes. So what if the molester was unconscious?

Dan climbed in the car asking, "Where the fuck did you go?"

Mark said, "Where did I go? Where the fuck did *you* go!"

Dan said, "I had to piss." When Mark looked at him as if to say, *What the hell is wrong with you? Now? Here?!* Dan said, "I was nervous! I'm not used to this!"

Mark rolled his eyes and drove ahead, past two marked units screaming in from the west. Two more were coming from the other end of the street. He grinned.

Yeah. This had gone perfectly, after all.

Chapter 21

Mark Young was awakened by soft knocking on his front door. He squinted into the light and looked for his nightstand clock, only to realize he was on the couch in the living room where he'd fallen asleep in his clothes, his mind numbed from a few boilermakers. He checked his watch: noon.

The knocking came again.

Mark made his uncooperative body uncoil and stand, shaking off as much of his one-position sleep as he could, and walked to the door. It was Dan.

"Hey, buddy. Awake?" he said. Then he looked Mark over and asked, "You all right?"

"Rough dreams," Mark said. Mainly, the one he'd had since he left home at eighteen—his sister singing the alphabet song in her tree swing next to the old home while Mark's father kills a chicken and his uncle commits suicide with a gun to the back of his head again and again.

"You look like shit," Dan said.

Mark said, "Thanks," and explained as best he remembered. "I fell asleep in the driveway. Had no idea where I was when I woke up."

"That's bizarre," Dan said.

"I just closed my eyes for a second and woke up three hours later in my car."

"Oh, in your *car*. I've done that," Dan said with a chuckle. "Happens to me all the time, all over the place." He walked in and looked at the sofa pillows askew on the floor, coffee table shoved out, Anne's Afghan crumpled on the bottom cushions, Mark's similarly crumpled clothes. He said, "Looks like you made it onto the couch."

Mark yawned. "Yeah. At some point. The sun was coming up, I think."

"Then the dreams started."

Mark said, "I guess, yeah." Groggy dullness filled his head like a wet blanket.

"Anything prophetic?" Dan squatted some, like a sleuthing cartoon cat, his arms feeling around for, "Any *clues* about my case from the Jungian beyond?"

For an aggrieved father, he seemed awfully chipper.

Mark said, "No," with intentional irritability. He didn't feel like going into the details of the chicken killing, the awkward suicide, or his dead mother watching passively.

Dan *chirped*, "Can I make you some breakfast?" and headed for the kitchen.

"No," Mark said grumpily, and followed. "I think I have half a Subway in the fridge." When he looked, it was gone. Instead, he found leftover pierogies from Lucassic's and was happier for it.

Dan said, "I've been up since six. Slept like a rock. Man, that was nice. I'd almost forgotten what it was like to sleep like the dead."

"Tell me about it," Mark said. He hadn't slept well in years. "Pierogi?" He offered to share his sauerkraut and potato treats, swimming in butter and onions. Perfect for breakfast. If only he had some coffee. He considered making some but just didn't have the interest or energy.

Dan said, "No thanks. I had a big breakfast at nine. That was some night last night. Have you seen the news?"

Mark woke up as if from a line of white powder. Last night! That was why Dan was so awake and perky. In his bleary, post-nightmarish sofa doze, Mark had forgotten. He rushed to the den and turned on the television.

As the screen came to life, Dan said, "This is some awesome shit," and sat like a little kid on the edge of the couch ready for Saturday cartoons. "Look, look, look," he said. The bottom scroll read, "Ice cream vendor arrested, charged with multiple homicides."

Mark found the remote and turned up the sound as his captain Corlius was saying to a reporter, "... significant evidence to suggest that he is responsible for several child murders in the metro area. I have nothing else to say at this time."

He left the mic' array and the shot went in-studio where one talking head said to the other, "Well, Carol, it looks like we might finally have an end to these awful killings of innocent children."

Carol said, "That's right, Ted. And coming up, animal *pirates* take over the mall for a day—and they're *nude*!"

Her joy at changing the subject was only slightly stranger than the screen image—pixelated private parts of a dog dancing on his hind legs while wearing a peg leg on his front paw and a Jack Sparrow hat.

Mark muted the TV.

Dan said, "This deserves a toast." Then he thought better of it. "If it's not too early. I mean, you just got up."

Mark thanked him for his concern as he went back into the kitchen. He grabbed two of the micro-brewery pumpkin/wheat ales from the fridge—his last—popped the caps, and handed one over.

Dan raised his bottle and said, "Cheers, pal. To law enforcement!"

They clinked their bottles and Dan said, "Let's sit outside. It's a *beautiful* day." He added why. "They caught the bastard."

Mark said, "With your help, buddy."

"I just tagged along. You did all the heavy lifting."

As they stepped out into the warm sunshine—the air comfortably cool—Dan said, "Maybe you can get your badge back now."

Mark said, "If I even want it."

Dan stopped with a look of shock. "Don't talk like that, bud. Law enforcement is your whole life."

Mark said, "Maybe that was the problem."

He looked at the back fence—the bullet holes. What the hell had he been thinking? What if a neighbor was walking past, or someone on the far side of the alley was out in his yard, minding his own business? What if someone's wife or mother had been in the line of fire?

Someone's kids.

Mark was now thinking he was no better than Chuck.

He had run his own family away with his narrow focus. First, he almost got them killed, then he drove them away. Chuck couldn't have done a better job himself.

At least they were all still alive—even if Mark didn't know where.

Dan intuited Mark's thoughts. "You'll find them again. No one can stay hidden forever." When Mark didn't respond, Dan guessed right again. "No word yet?"

Mark said, "I don't want to know." Besides, "They're better off without me."

"Don't say that. And look, they got the guy," Dan said. "Anne and the kids can come back now. They're safe."

Mark shook his head. "They're not safe as long as I'm here."

"What's that supposed to mean?"

Mark shrugged. "Until I get my shit together."

"You're a cop, man," Dan said. "You'll be fine once you get back on the job." He went all cheery. "Cases to crack, bad guys to bust. Heads to roll!" Then he added, "Call them back home. You'll be fine."

Mark gave a lackluster chuckle. "I don't know where they are to call them."

"You want me to look into it? See if I can find them for you?" Dan offered.

Mark looked at him as if he was insane.

Dan laughed and said, "That was dumb. You're the cop. If you can't find 'em, what could *I* do?" He laughed again and rolled his eyes comically. "Stupid," he added. "Sorry."

"No biggie," Mark said, somewhat out of character; but he was starting to feel more positive, even chummy.

Then Dan said, darker, "At least you've still *got* a family." He sat heavily on a plastic deck chair and stared at the ground.

Mark felt selfish. "I'm sorry, man," he said. "I wasn't thinking. That was insensitive of me. Entirely inappropriate."

"Hey," Dan said, "you miss them." He looked like a beaten puppy.

"Yeah, but..." Mark couldn't find the words for a moment. Then he said, "I have no right. Not with your situation. I'm sorry. I wasn't thinking."

Dan said, "Yeah, you said that, but..." He shook his head. "They need you, man. You're their father, Anne's husband. You're Daddy."

Those words cut deep. "Maybe you're right. In time." Mark took the other chair, sipping at his ale rather than sucking it down. It felt better that way today. Taking his time.

Dan said, "In the meantime..." He nodded his head with bitter determination. "Chuckie is gonna fry for all of them. Every one."

"What do you mean?" Mark said. "You think... your kids?" He thought it was too early for such a conclusion.

"Especially my kids."

Mark stood up. He knew to be nervous with that kind of talk—it always meant something.

Something else.

He said, "What did you do?" Another hunch—maybe this one would be right for a change.

Dan looked away.

Shit. Mark didn't want to be right.

"What did you *do*?"

Dan stared at nothing a few moments, his eyes glassed over as if he was trying to decide whether to tell Mark anything or just let things ride.

Mark persisted, *insisted*. "Goddammit, Dan. What did you do? If you did something, anything at all having to do with this shit, I need to know about it, and I need to know about it now before it goes any farther."

Dan sighed heavily and confessed. "I took some of little Dan's clothes and Melissa's nighties, and Billy's, last night—their underwear—and I left them in the sick bastard's yard. That's where I was when you got back in the car. I wasn't really taking a leak."

Mark stared in disbelief. "You fucking *what*?!"

Dan looked more shocked than remorseful.

Mark shouted, "Are you that fucking stupid?!"

Dan got to his feet. "Don't talk to me like that, man."

Mark was incredulous. "Are you out of your fucking *mind*?!"

"He *killed*. My kids!" Dan shouted, louder than Mark.

It knocked Mark's fervor down a notch. "You don't know that."

"So what?" Dan spat and turned away.

"So *what*?" Mark said, sarcastically. "You could jeopardize the whole case against him! That's what! Jesus fucking Christ!" He turned away.

Dan said defensively, "You cut his phone line."

"They don't know that!" Mark countered.

Dan said, "So how are they gonna know—"

"That your kids' clothes just *happened* to be scattered around his backyard when all of the other evidence was carefully hidden *inside*? What the hell were you thinking?!"

Dan said, focused, "That the motherfucker who did this needs to *pay* for it!"

Mark continued to shout. "And he *will*! For what he *did*! Not for what he *may* have done! What you may *think* he did. And if he didn't, they might just throw the whole fucking case out, now! All that work for nothing!" Mark paced his deck, angry at himself as much as Dan. "Fucking amateurs. Civilians. What was *I* thinking? Jesus, I'm the one losing my fucking mind."

Dan said, "C'mon, bro. It's not that bad. They'll never put it together."

Mark spun on him. "Are you really that dumb?"

Dan looked hurt and confused.

Mark said, "Forensics? Ever heard'a that? Fingerprints? DNA?"

"That stuff would already be all over them. I'm their father."

"Right," Mark said, even more sarcastically. "Good thinking."

Dan looked away again.

Mark said, "And *his* DNA?"

Dan didn't look as if he understood, so Mark said, "Where is it?"

Dan definitely didn't seem to understand. He shrugged.

Mark said, "It isn't. There is none. There will *be* none. They will find none because it won't *be* there! Unless you had Chuck over at your house and he went through your kids' drawers and touched their clothes, drooled on them? Their *underwear*!"

Dan slumped, seeming to finally understand. "Oh, shit," he said.

Mark spun and threw his half-full seasonal beer bottle against the far wall. It exploded in brown, then white. He said, "Shit indeed, my friend," purely for effect, and went inside, slamming the door behind him.

Inside, Mark turned angrily to look out. Dan glared at the shut back door a moment, then threw his bottle at the wall with equal defiance.

His was empty. He stormed off for home.

Mark stormed upstairs, threw his clothes off, and took a shower. Again, he didn't feel better at all. He dried off, closed all the blinds, drapes and shades, and sulked the rest of the day, nude.

A steady stream of alcohol helped.

***

Around 5:30, the doorbell rang. It couldn't be Dan—he always knocked.

Mark peered out from behind a curtain and saw Jerome on his porch, a manilla envelope in his hand. Considering their last exchange—and his current, steady stream of alcohol—Mark decided Jerome didn't warrant getting dressed up for and opened the door naked.

Jerome stared a moment. He looked down and said, "Hmmp. You borrow that tiny thing from the captain? I thought you had an actual dick."

Mark said, "Yeah, that's pretty funny. What do you want?"

Jerome sniffed, just to show he was unperturbed, then handed the large envelope to Mark. He said, "You didn't get this from me."

A car drove past slowly. The occupants stared, their heads turning in unison.

Mark looked at them, then opened the envelope and glanced at the cover page. He looked at Jerome, glanced back down at a few other pages and said, "Where did *you* get it?"

"Old friend at the VA in San Francisco." He gave his old partner the once-over, then turned to walk away, saying over his shoulder, "Interesting read."

He got in his Impala and left. He hadn't even lit a cigarette.

Then Mark noticed the empty, crumpled Vantage Lights pack on his lawn by the dead hedge—and the neighbor across the street, Mrs. Hoddeker, standing stock still, staring.

Mark waved. "Hello, Mrs. Hoddeker. I was in the shower when the doorbell rang. Department business. Didn't have time. Sorry."

Mrs. Hoddeker gave a sallow wave and matching smile, then went back to her watering.

In the *back*yard.

Mark went inside to pore over Dan Black's military service record.

Chapter 22

At their scheduled time the next day, Mark gave Dan's file to Dr. Quarry, and she pored over it in much the same way that Mark had—only with more intensity and clothing. She finally looked up and said, "You didn't give me this."

Mark said, "I don't even know that *I* have it."

Eileen Quarry laughed. "I'm surprised it even exists. The Army is notorious for disappearing files they don't want out there—especially head injuries." She glanced down again as if to make sure she'd read it right.

Mark said, "He was deployed twice. Iraq and Afghanistan. It says he was injured, but it doesn't say how."

She read. "Or where, specifically. Just 'head.'"

Mark said, "So what does that tell us?"

"Maybe nothing."

She closed the file, stood up, smoothed out her smart suit, took a cigarette out of her drawer, moved to the window, opened it, and lit her Virginia Slim.

She must have felt Mark's eyes on her because she said, "Filthy habit. But it's better than the alternative."

Mark gave her a quizzical glance.

She said, "Booze, anonymous sex, road rage."

Mark nodded. He understood well.

She began to pace and said, "TBIs—Traumatic Brain Injuries—and PTSD—"

"That's what they say I have."

Quarry stopped pacing. "Actually, that's my call. But, yes, probably. Minimally. Sure. Some. Hard to tell. We'll ferret that out over time."

Mark looked at her as if to say, *What the fuck kind of diagnosis is that?*

She said, "At any rate, TBIs and PTSD have gone largely unreported by the military, as you probably know. No surprise there. But unofficial estimates are well over four hundred thousand cases since the year two thousand. Probably more. There have also been stories of higher-ups ordering files burned—hundreds at a time. So, who knows?"

Mark said, "Why would they burn files? You're talking about soldiers' official records here, right?"

"Both conditions are difficult to pin down and usually end up costing the military a shit-ton of money down the line. That's a technical term by the way." She laughed and went on without waiting for Mark to catch up. "The point is, TBIs and PTSD usually result in years of costly treatment, so the military pretends they don't exist and buries the studies and reports—individual files."

Mark hadn't heard that before and found it disturbing. He wondered what would happen to him if he ever took a bad shot to the head. With his recent record, they'd probably burn him along *with* his file.

Anne and the kids would get nothing.

Dr. Quarry took a long drag off her Virginia Slim, blew the smoke out the window like a movie star, and said, "I did some pro bono work for a Vets' org' in Seattle. Saw a lot of both. Lotta kids don't make it." She said it with professional detachment, but it was evident that the experience had affected her.

Mark wanted to get back on point. "So, all of that tells us exactly what about my neighbor?"

"All? Exactly? Tells us?" She grunted and put her cigarette out on the sill—after a long, last draw on the butt. She could be an odd one.

That was Mark's *professional* opinion.

She closed the window and said, "What it tells us 'exactly' is not much at all, unfortunately, since a lot of the file has been redacted. But in short, if he does or did suffer from either—"

"He could be our killer."

Eileen said, "Mmm," as a corrective *No*. "I was going to say that if he suffered such injuries from this head wound, he might also suffer some kind of disconnect. A lack of empathy, perhaps. It's not uncommon."

"So," Mark deduced, "he could—might be able to—kill without feeling it."

"It's a leap," she cautioned. "TBIs and PTSD do not a sociopath make. Inappropriate, even irrational behavior, yes. Being nude in public, for instance."

Mark first thought of Dan walking past his windows nude—then he remembered standing in his own doorway with Jerome just the day before.

Waving at Mrs. Hoddeker across the street.

He realized his doctor was now watching him closely. He shifted in his seat.

She said, "Ring any bells?" almost as if she knew exactly what he was thinking—what he was seeing in his mind's eye.

Himself, naked.

"Maybe," he said. "What else?"

He figured Dr. Quarry intuitively knew when a patient was holding back, but she said, "In extreme cases, we might see more violent behavior—suicide attempts, attacks on their own families—"

"Bingo," Mark said with certainty.

Dr. Quarry cautioned, "Not so fast. It's rare. We see fits of rage, mainly—yelling, punching a wall, breaking things—mostly acting out due to an inability to re-adapt to normal civilian life. Occasional blackouts, bar fights, maybe a car accident. Alcohol and drug abuse, often. Overdoing the prescription drug combos, which further fuels the outbursts and violent behavior. Suicide is much more common than homicide.

"Mostly, it's just minor behavioral issues like forgetting to tend the grill, leaving the shower running, the dog outside, that sort of thing. Chores undone. Forgetting social norms, manners—inappropriate behavior."

She let that one hang a moment, then added, "Maybe planting evidence without considering the consequences. But what you're suggesting does happen, maybe more than we know."

Mark bookended, "Not everything is reported."

"It never is."

***

Mark sat in his car at a park for most of the rest of the day, watching kids play—and their parents watching them. He thought about his own kids, and Anne—specifically, what he'd found on her PC earlier.

While he was setting it up upstairs, Mark ran across her "My Pictures" folder and opened it. He found much of what he'd expected—digital photos of the kids' lives, Mark and Anne as proud parents, one or both of them with MJ and Andy as they grew up, then more and more without Mark. Then none.

And a few pictures he didn't expect.

When Mark and Anne were still dating, she was also dating a guy named Floyd Matson, from Georgia. They had known each other briefly at college, then ran into each other at a produce stand over some fresh corn. They chatted about vegetables and ended up in bed.

Apparently—as Anne later told Mark—they spent a blissful four months together before she met Mark and fell in love. She stopped dating Floyd a few weeks later, but continued sleeping with him up to that moment.

Mark had understood completely. There was no commitment at that point. He would have continued screwing the girl he was seeing (what the hell was her name? Ashley, Ashton— some college chick) but she had gone home for the summer after her senior year, in the break before grad school, so he had no one to fuck while Anne was fucking Floyd and him, doing double duty.

That's the way the argument sounded years later.

It had started out as a disagreement about who was supposed to buy the chicken for an office bar-b-cue and Mark just threw Floyd in to be mean. He was drinking heavily at the time. Anne was defensive as hell, he thought, and overly protective—why wouldn't she be?—but he had a hunch.

And he had an acquaintance from work, a private eye who occasionally turned up in the station with questions about a missing person or a felon on the lam—anyone with a reward on his or her head. Mark had him follow Floyd around for a month.

The PI came back with nothing. Floyd was seeing a woman named Eve that he would marry soon after; so, Mark never thought another thing about it.

Then he found a recent photo of Floyd on Anne's hard drive. He knew it was recent because when he enlarged it as far as it would go, he could read the dates of beer discounts in the store window behind him. "Busch Ice $5.99 thru—"

Four months ago.

Now, Anne was gone with the kids, who knew where, and everything was better that way. Mark didn't figure he'd ever see her again, after all that went down and how he was such a jerk about it, but he missed her, and he missed his kids.

Seeing Floyd's photo stirred unhappy memories and questions of infidelity.

After hunting briefly for other photos and clues as to what might have transpired between them, Mark removed *all* the pictures and never looked at them again.

Ancient history—made so instantly with the push of a delete button.

As Mark sat there in the park in his plain sedan, looking at all the happy families, it hurt to think about all the happy times he had missed by being too involved in his work.

He hurt for Dan Black as well and went to see him, wondering if Dan would even answer the door after their last spat about planting evidence in Chuck the Clown's backyard.

***

Dan opened his front door and Mark said, "Got a minute?"

Dan said, "Always for you, neighbor." He turned away and went inside, leaving Mark to let himself in.

Mark allowed him his distance and poisoned memory—then showed him the files Jerome had procured from his friend at the VA.

Dan sat at his dining room table, flipping the pages with disbelief. Pale.

Mark said, "Want to tell me about it?"

Dan shifted in his chair, glanced at another page, then closed the file angrily. "I don't like to think about this," he said. He didn't mention how much he probably didn't want to think about how his classified military files ended up in his neighbor the cop's hands.

Now it was time for Mark to be distant, to allow his own poisoned memories. "Make an exception. Neighbor," he said.

Dan stared back a moment, then replayed a prior moment by getting up, getting only one beer, and sitting back down.

He said, "We were on routine patrol. As much as anything over there was ever routine."

> *The desert tan Humvee is rolling quickly through the streets around Kabul that have been decimated by drone strikes, mortar hits, and hatred – inborn and imported.*
>
> *There are four of them: the Driver, a soldier riding Shotgun, a Gunner up top on the .50, standing through a hole in the roof, and Dan in the backseat.*
>
> *Full Kevlar.*
>
> *It's wartime – but they're cutting up, having a good time passing around a girlie mag. Shotgun shows it to the Driver who whistles and says, "She is* smokin'*."*
>
> *Shotgun agrees and says, "Check out that greasy EBGB, dude." He air-humps in the passenger seat.*

The Driver shows the page to Dan, who laughs. Shotgun passes it up to the Gunner, the Driver shouting up, "Just your type, Gunny!"

Gunner takes the magazine, lifts it up for a look and says, "Fuck, man! She's got a dick!"

The three other men laugh so hard they would cry if it weren't for the sudden explosion under the front axle.

The IED is powerful. Flames, smoke, and debris pour out as the Humvee is blown up and over, backwards. It ends up on its top, tucked under itself, sliding fifty feet before coming to a rest.

The soldiers inside are tossed around like mannequins. Dan's helmeted head hits the B-pillar and the roof with the approximate equivalent of a sledgehammer hitting concrete. Then everything is quiet.

Except for the moaning.

Reflexes kick in and the three from inside stumble out – Dan, the Driver and Shotgun – disoriented. Shotgun's knee is bleeding, his patella exposed.

*"*Fuck*!" he yells, buckling, then lifting himself back up. The Driver has a broken shoulder for sure, and blood is running from Dan's left ear. He looks dazed. Lost.*

They all do.

Shotgun is now yelling, "Dougie! Gunner! Gunny! Doug, man!"

They now see their gunner – underneath the Humvee, his skull crushed like a melon dropped from a high-rise.

A slight breeze kicks up dust; everything else is still.

*Shotgun howls, "*Aaauuuggghhh*!" and empties a clip into the air. His best friend is dead.*

His Lieutenant, the driver, says, "Easy, Soldier. Stand down."

Shotgun yells, reloads, and shoots again, cursing God.

"Soldier, I'm talking to you. Stand down!" his Lieutenant says.

"Fuck you, Lieutenant!"

Dan tries to intercede, but no words come. It's as if his mouth is no longer connected to his brain. He reaches up, feels something wet and sticky – pulls his fingers down to see the blood.

It makes him woozier.

Shotgun is still yelling. "Fuckin' Hadjis killed him, motherfucker! Motherfuckers!"

He digs in the vehicle for another clip.

His Lieutenant is yelling, "Goddammit, Luther! Stand the fuck down! *Get a grip, goddammit!" He moves too quickly and pain shoots through his shoulder. "Fuck!"*

Fresh magazine in hand, Shotgun looks for who did it – someone to take it out on – anyone...

A small cluster of Afghani kids stand not fifty meters away, staring, silent. Afraid.

Shotgun sees them.

He swings his assault weapon around and mutters, "Little fuckin' towelhead motherfuckers. Did you do this? Huh? Did you do this?!" He slams the magazine in, muttering, "Well, you won't grow up to do it again."

Now, Dan can speak. "Luther, no. Don't do it, man."

Luther does it. Unloads his entire clip at them, yelling, "You did this! Fuckin' little Hadji motherfuckers!"

By the time he's done cursing them, the clip is empty, and they're all dead.

Dan falls to his knees, crying – wailing in the desert sun and dirt. Crying for the children.

The pile of dead children.

In his kitchen, Dan's eyes had gotten red and watery. He wasn't touching his beer. He said, "I had a headache for three days, maybe... four, five. I don't know. They gave me some aspirin, said I was okay, and sent me back out."

Mark said, "This guy Luther—Shotgun—he got punished?"

Dan looked vacantly at Mark and said, "Yeah."

Gunny and the children are dead – but the three soldiers who survived are not alone. A single old man, an Afghani in robes, has seen it all, and now just stands frozen, afraid for his life.

The three soldiers see him. The Driver, the Lieutenant, makes a command decision. He grabs a fresh thirty-round box magazine, tosses it to Shotgun, and says, "Luther. Pack up. Lock and load."

His implication: It's going to be okay. They're going to track the old man down – the witness – and kill him.

Shotgun grins, drops his spent magazine on the ground and looks down to slam in the fresh mag. In that instant –

The Driver, his Lieutenant, steps over quickly with his handgun and shoots Shotgun in the head.

Luther drops like a sack of wet sand in the desert. Dead.

Blood forms a puddle in the dust.

Dan looks over. He can't begin to understand what has just happened—and he likely never will. He cries more. Wails. He can't help himself.

His Lieutenant says, "Fuckin' war is hell, man."

He turns the gun on himself and fires.

Dan is alone.

At his kitchen table, Dan was no longer crying. He was pale, still, shaken—permanently affected, never to look at the world in the same naïve way again. Obviously.

This wasn't another funny story about Dan falling on his head in a meaningless high school basketball game. This was the true horror of war, the real *Faces of Death*.

This was Dan's turning point—that much he was making clear. Nothing else mattered; nothing had mattered since that day in the desert.

Mark had seen bad things on the force, over the years, but nothing like that. He said with deep sympathy, "Thing like that stays with a man a long time."

Dan corrected him, "Thing like that never leaves." He sounded as if he had as much life in him as Shotgun and the dead kids.

His own dead kids.

He stood, leaving his untouched beer and his military records, and walked out of his dining room. Mark could hear him plodding up the stairs.

Mark sat still a moment, thinking, empathizing—then picked up the files and the beer and headed for the front door.

Dan's clothes were strewn on the floor and stairs where he left them.

Chapter 23

The next day, police announced that they would walk Charles "Chuck" Love up the courthouse steps for his arraignment hearing sometime after noon. It was hot. Blazing hot. A mini heatwave had swept in overnight and the temperature had crept over a hundred by 10:00 AM. On the steps, the heat index had to be pushing one-twenty.

A mixed crowd assembled to see the child killer in person. Most were there to encourage Chuck's immediate execution. A few against the death penalty carried placards and chanted.

Take one life, then take the other;

It's wrong I say to take another!

Their kids carried signs (made under their parents' supervision) with hanging stickmen (even though the state hadn't hanged anyone in decades). Signs on the other side read "Hang him now!" (they had just come from a Pro-Life rally).

A scuffle broke out between the two warring factions but died just as quickly when a woman fainted from the heat and everyone came to her aid, united.

News reporters from far and wide sat in their air-conditioned news vans awaiting the perp walk, antennas poking up in a cluster like a giant alien pole barn under construction.

Inside the courthouse, in the main courtroom, old Kibbles and Bits himself stood at the ready, his dark blue suit freshly dry-cleaned for the occasion. He fingered the charges eagerly: seven counts of murder (more to be added later); nine counts of aggravated assault; two counts of resisting arrest; two counts of fleeing a police officer while being arrested; eight counts of threatening (two) police officer(s) with physical violence; ten counts of attacking (the same two) police officer(s) while being arrested...

The list went on.

Outside in the savage heat, an ambitious young black man sold "Cold water!" for "One dollar!" A sad old white man did the same on the opposite end of the crowd. "Cold water! One dollar!" Lots of folks bought cold water from the men. No one knew they were both convicted felons out on parole—the black man for robbery, the white one for murder.

At 2:00 PM sharp—in the peak heat of the day—a buzz went through the crowd. "He's coming!" "He's coming!" "They're bringing him!" "He's coming!"

They knew because the reporters, who'd been alerted moments before, scrambled out into the heat with their microphones and cameras. They took their positions and started chattering:

"Mike, I'm here at the county courthouse where we have just received word..."

"... child murderer Charles Richard Love..."

"... is being transported at this very moment..."

"... and will arrive here..."

"... momentarily."

Any one of them could have been exchanged for any other and the news would not have suffered.

At the sound of squealing tires—the cops knew how to make an entrance—all the cameras swung for the corner. A plain white police van—flanked, led, and followed by what seemed a small army of motorcycle officers and black Tahoes—made the turn onto Cliburn Avenue. Seconds later, they screeched to a stop at the curb.

Police officers in full body armor appeared from nowhere and shoved the crowd back, forming a path for the accused child killer and his armed handlers. Headsets buzzed. Dark glasses scanned slowly and evenly in every direction.

Someone gave the word: a silent nod.

A cop opened the van's side door—they always used this van for The Walk of Shame—and Chuck was nudged out. He wore a white county jail jumper with wrist, waist, and ankle chains. Neither the cops nor District Attorney Arthur Kibbler were taking any chances that anyone might like the guy or feel sorry for him.

Their thinking proved correct. A roar of condemnation rose from the crowd that would befit the Coliseum. Only the lions were missing as an abundance of Christians yelled "Kill him!" "Kill him!" "Kill him!"

Some moderates put down their hotdogs long enough to yell, "Child butcher!" "Murderer!" and "Kid killer!" while foaming mustard at the mouth. Some country cousins hollered, "Kill that-thur muthurfuhckur!" alongside some black militants, who said it right.

A bearded man in a heavy brown robe looked ready to pass out but managed to holler the same slogan as on the large sign he carried. "Repent before it's too late!"

A girl with purple hair said, "Dude, I think *you're* too late."

The savior ranted on, undeterred.

The few protesters continued their "other/another" chant off to one side, but they were easily drowned out. Their kids had dropped their stickman signs to come see the Child Killer up close—as if he were a movie star rather than someone who might want to slay them as well. But they had never seen an actual murderer before, and it was exciting! They would remember this day forever.

Chuck looked terrified, probably thinking he'd be lucky to make it halfway up the steps before the crowd swarmed in and beat him to death under the granite scales-of-justice wreath above.

"Let's go." The cop who'd opened the door took Chuck by the arm. Another beefy, Kevlar'd cop took his other arm and they started up the steps.

Chuck hesitated, eyes wide with terror.

"You'll be fine," the cop said in a calm, soothing voice. Obviously, he'd done this many times before and had no intention of anything bad happening to his charge.

Not on the courthouse steps.

"Stay back!" other cops shouted. "Stay back!" "Make room!" "Stay back!"

They only pushed and shoved when they had to, when some asshole civilian thought that yelling, "Fuck you! Die Child Killer!" was his constitutionally protected right.

The other honor guard members—and perp walks *were* an honor—had spread out to keep a wide eye on the agitated, overheated crowd of Chuck haters.

So, they didn't see the quiet, cool, redheaded man with the gun.

He put a bullet in the back of Chuck's head before anyone noticed him. He just waited for the cop on his side to pass, then stepped out. The bullet was in the chamber and the hammer pulled back.

He was ready, willing, and enabled.

Chuck was dead before the calm cop and his partner dropped him to the ground so they could wrestle the man with the gun down and cuff him.

"Shooter down!" seemed anti-climactic, but people screamed and ran because they'd seen other people do that in movies. The cops on the outer ring abandoned crowd control in favor of securing the area in case there were others. There were not.

Most of the folks who wanted Chuck dead were halfway down the block. Still screaming. Everyone else was running for the courthouse doors, their cars, the safety of the tall Doric columns. The panic that instantly overtook all reason was exactly what every policeman there had been taught to expect—and dread. The public didn't let them down. It didn't mean their hearts weren't beating as hard as anyone else's.

The chaos was so complete, so overwhelming, that no one heard the redheaded father say to Chuck's corpse, "That was for my little girl."

He obviously didn't care that his own life was ruined. He'd done what he came to do, and all was right in his heart.

Mark Young watched the spectacle on TV at home, in his den. The images bobbed as camera operators decided whether to record their reporters, the body, the shooter, the cops—or just run away to safety themselves.

Mark hung his head and shook it at the floor.

***

Downtown, Jerome, Captain Corlius and several other cops, plain-clothed and uniform, watched the debacle on their station TV. Corlius threw a sheaf of papers at the wall and shouted, "Fuck, fuck, fuck, fuck, fuck!"

The prospect of a clean conviction had evaporated, making the department look inept. The Chief would be in a foul mood for months—and it had all happened in three seconds. So much for extra time off.

"You *fucker*! You *rotten fucker*!" Corlius said of the avenging father—not Chuck the killer—and threw more papers, startling the assembled officers. They'd never seen him lose his cool like that. He was usually as cold and quiet as a child molester.

Someone turned the TV off before other cops could join in and the place looked like a raid at a political convention.

Jerome said, "At least it wasn't Mark."

A few cops wanted to laugh but knew they shouldn't—at least until they left the room and went outside the building for a smoke.

Jerome turned to their captain. "I guess he can have his badge back now, huh?"

Corlius was back to his old self—silent, detached, spooky—and just turned away. He went into his office and quietly closed the door.

Jerome grabbed a half-empty pack of Bristol Full Flavor 100s and went out for a smoke. He wouldn't be laughing with the others, and they'd all clam up when they saw him. He was, after all, Mark Young's ex-partner.

They might still have a connection.

***

Mark Young heard a knock at his door a short while later and found Dan Black on his porch. He wore a look of contrition and guilt. Mark decided to cut him a break.

He said, "At least it wasn't you."

***

Dr. Eileen Quarry met Detective Mark Young at her office door—something she hadn't done once since they started their sessions.

"Big day," she said with a big smile, and let him in.

She closed the door.

Mark said, "Why's that?"

Dr. Quarry said, "I've recommended they return you to full active duty and they agreed." She seemed pleased. Then she asked him, "Are you still having the blackouts?"

"I wouldn't call them blackouts."

"Waking up in a strange place, having no idea where you are."

Mark squirmed. "Once or twice."

She nodded. "Well, I'm writing it off to working too hard."

Mark nodded and said, "So. What now?"

Eileen smiled.

***

They sat outside Chez Noir in the smoking area. Though it was not yet evening, Eileen ordered and paid for their drinks. Mark had a "scotch rocks," and she had a "double Tanquerini with extra olives." She speared them, ate them with exuberance, and smoked like a movie star again—posing with her head tilted back to blow smoke at the overhang.

My close-up, Mr. DeMille.

Mark wasn't wholly comfortable with the arrangement and said, "Are we sure this is legal?"

Eileen Quarry said, "In almost every state," and laughed heartily. She finished her drink, ordered another round, and said, "You're not my patient anymore. I officially released you and closed out your file."

Mark asked if there wasn't "some statute of limitations or something on patient-doctor relationships?"

She said, "We aren't having a relationship. It's not like we're trying to commit sodomy in Mississippi." Then she added, as if asking a genuine question of great pique to her, "Have you ever been to Natchez? Lotta fun things you're not supposed to do down there." And there was that hearty laugh again.

The waiter brought their next round and left. Eileen nodded for Mark to finish his first Glenfiddich 21. (She had insisted.) He did. She then raised her second double for a toast. Mark obliged and they clinked glasses.

He said, "You certainly know how to go out in style."

And she said, "I haven't even gotten started yet."

***

Two hours and four more rounds later, Dr. Eileen Quarry was taking it doggy style on her couch—one red high heel on the floor, one stockinged, black-gartered knee on the tan Italian leather. Her ass was tight, her muscles toned, her voice loud and growly.

"Almost... almost... don't stop... almost... right there. Yes! Yes! Don't stop! *Yes!*"

Her entire body shook, she squealed, and a low giggle became a full-on delight.

She was a laugher.

She shook some more, gripping the pleasure deep inside, riding her orgasm to its stunning end. Then she let go.

Mark fell to the floor, pants around his ankles, shirt over his head, sweat pouring from every pore like a marathon runner in August.

In Miami.

She laughed some more—Mark had the presence of mind to note how it tinkled—and rolled off the couch onto him. She held him surprisingly tight and said seriously, "I was worried there for a while."

"That I wouldn't make it?"

"That you'd find me out." She held him desperately close.

She was drunk, he was drunk; he was confused, she was somber.

He said, "Is there something else I should know?"

Without letting go, she moved her head just enough so he could almost see her eyes and said, "When I know I can trust you."

"When will that be?"

"Maybe never. Do you ever stop being a cop? Even for a few minutes?"

"Maybe a few, here and there," he said.

"Yeah, right.," She reached down and squeezed his spent balls much harder than he would have liked. "Real lady killer, you," she said. "I know your secrets. You'll have to mine mine." She laughed. "Get it? Mine mine?"

She leapt up, wiped a tear from her cheek—a tear he hadn't noticed—and said jubilantly, "Port time!" and staggered off to get it. Mark said he was more of beer guy and she said, "I hope imported isn't too fancy."

She laughed that special laugh again and Mark couldn't help thinking it was delightful. Nor could he help placing the same superlative on her figure. From the back—nude except for her lacy garter belt and net stockings, as she now kicked off her red pumps in opposite directions—she looked fifteen years younger than she probably was. Even her back was toned and defined, her butt and legs remarkable.

She turned around to walk backwards, playfully teasing him with her hands on and off her breasts, swaying them intentionally at him while laughingly enjoying her own show and freedom.

Mark thought, *What the fuck am I doing here?*

And why was he enjoying himself so damn much?

After two more hours of fun, they kissed and Mark left to go home. He had just opened the door of his Crown Vic when Eileen Quarry, his former police psychiatrist, came running out in a full-length mink coat.

She pulled it open to reveal no more lingerie and said, "Just in case. Men have such short memories."

Mark said, "I don't think I could ever forget *that.*"

She thanked him.

He said, "Thank *you.*"

"No, I mean it. Thank you for... not judging me." She forced a sad smile and held out her arms.

Mark took her into his and said, "Why would I do that?"

Holding him tightly, Eileen Quarry confessed, "I'm not a good person, Mark. I'm a very bad person. I... this..." She choked back some nameless emotion. "It must end, tonight." She forced a wan smile. "Or maybe tomorrow." Then she pulled away some, put on her best big-about-it face, and said, "It's been fun. Really."

Her words and conflicting emotions only confused Mark that much more. He had to ask her, "What are you saying? What does that mean? End what?"

Dr. Quarry checked around them, looking like a paranoid conspiracy nut, then held him even tighter and whispered in his ear. "When you're going over your list of suspects... don't forget me. Think of *us*."

He said quietly, "Why would I—"

She put her finger on his lips and said, even softer, "Think of me—and you. What I've told you—and what I haven't. Think of what it means. What you've intuited and understood."

"I don't think I've understood anything of what you're saying—now *or* then."

"I think you do. I *know* you do. Inside... you do. So, play it out. Let it go where it will. You'll find who you're looking for. I promise you. I know it for a fact."

There was a *but* coming.

She said, "When you do, when you learn the truth, know that I tried to help you, I tried to make you see inside and understand. I tried to explain myself. I tried. I really did. To help you see. But these are dark areas, enigmatic half-truths. They hide like invisible cave monsters in your soul. You can survive it—*this*—but it will take everything you have. And you will be hurt by it. I'm sorry, but you will be hurt."

Any buoyancy Mark Young had seen in Eileen Quarry evaporated like a match flame in a cyclone. He pushed her away just enough to see her face, her eyes.

She said again, "I am not a good person, Mark Young. I'm just not."

A second later, she pulled away as sharply as she had inside, and put on the same jovial—if false—smile. "But, like I said," she said, "it was fun. While it lasted!" She made it sound sunny and trivial.

Maybe sensing that, she added, "My door is always open—professionally and privately." She looked back at her house.

He looked over. Her door *was* open; she had left it open. Had she planned this entire exchange? And what the hell did any of it mean? It sounded like psycho-babble gibberish in his head.

Sensing her growing discomfort—if not understanding what it was or where it was coming from—Mark took out his wallet and a business card. He said, "And you can call me if you need anything. My cell's on there. Anytime."

Eileen wiped a tear, exactly the way she had before—as if it was a performance, a rehearsed move—and said, "I'll understand if you don't pick up."

"Why wouldn't I?"

"Life is complicated. Death is a mystery by necessity—even to professionals."

Did she mean professionals as in psychiatrists and cops—or killers?

Mark knew how a bad past never really leaves you, even an ancient bad past. It lingers and haunts, rubs at your soul like heavyweight sandpaper applied directly to your brain. Tough grit. The tougher, the grittier—the deeper it cuts and the faster it wears you down.

The faster it wins.

Mark thought how it was good that brains have no nerve endings; otherwise, he was certain he couldn't have stood the pain of the past few weeks.

This night!

He heard her saying, "This is hard, I know. *You* were hard. My *god* you were hard!" And the tinkling laugh which faded as quickly as it arose. "I'm really not," she went on, stumbling over her emotions. "Not hard. Not a good person. I'm... sorry."

Why did she keep saying that?

Before Mark could ask her, Dr. Eileen Quarry ran into her house, holding the coat tightly around her naked body.

He watched the house as she turned off the lights in each room until the house, and Mark, were left completely in the dark.

Chapter 24

Corlius called Mark into the station the next morning and told him, in his captain's office, "Be smart. And if you can't, at least don't be stupid."

He shoved Mark's badge back across the table. His duty weapon.

Mark said, "I'll try," took his things, and turned away. But before he got all the way out the door, his cell buzzed—a text message.

"Have confess 2 make. My house ASAP. Last nite was GR8!!! Luv, E."

Corlius looked up at Mark standing in his open door and asked, "Everything all right?"

"Huh?" Mark turned back to see the irritation on his captain's face. He said, "Oh. Yeah. Neighbor. Wants me to bring in his garbage cans for him. He's on vacation, I guess."

Captain Corlius said, "Neighbor as in Dan Black?"

Mark wondered why his Captain was asking that in that way, but said, "No. Other side. Belton. Pain in the ass, but whattaya gonna do? He watches for us when we're gone." Then he reconsidered. "Well, when we were." *A family.*

Corlius nodded. "I got one'a those." Then he asked, "Heard from Anne yet?"

"No."

His captain said, "Probably better that way."

Mark said, "Probably the only way it is," and left.

He didn't get two feet before Jerome was on him, looking over his shoulder at the text message. "Crime don't take a holiday just 'cause you're playin' doctor, *pardner*."

Mark said, "Fuck you," with no emotion and closed the phone.

Jerome laughed and said, "You comin', or you busy?"

"What've we got?" Mark asked him.

"Sinker on a tip."

Mark stopped. "Our guy?"

"Looks that way."

***

What it looked like at the site was grisly. A woman's blue, nude body being dragged into a skiff by police divers. One of them slipped, his grip faltered, and he left half the woman's skin on the rough gunwale of the boat.

"C'mon guys, Jesus Christ," Frank Hitchens bitched. He was a round guy with a forever dour puss form the coroner's office.

The cops were blithe about it. "She slipped." What could they do?

Hitchens was not impressed. "You wanna leave me a *little* evidence, maybe?"

The other diver-cop said, "She's got fuckin' chains wrapped around her, Frank. You wanna get in here and lift her out?" He added, "The water's nice."

"Yeah," his diving buddy said. "Come on in!"

They both laughed and slid the naked dead woman's body onto the deck of the small boat as if she were a large fish.

Hitchens said to Mark and Jerome, "Fuckin' clowns. I got a job to do. I don't do this shit for the giggles."

He walked toward his black van.

Jerome looked at Mark and they shared a snorted chuckle. Then Jerome gibed, "First day back three-to-midnight. Not bad. Who'd you blow?"

Mark said, "Didn't catch his name. Got him off your list. He said I wasn't near as good as you."

"Still makes you a cocksucker."

Jerome's phone rang—Parliament's "Give Up the Funk" ringtone. He checked the caller ID, and his great mood went south. "I gotta make a call," he said, and walked away behind a tall stand of bushes.

Mark thought nothing of it. Jerome was always changing his temperament on a dime—one of the reasons he'd never missed him as a partner

Mark walked over to the divers. "What's up, guys?" he said, sounding more like a normal person than himself.

The divers were busy trying to get the chains off their sinker without removing any more of her skin. One asked, "Frank gone yet?"

Mark, who was higher up the bank, looked back over his shoulder at the black van where Frank was suiting up for the messy work ahead. He'd dropped his protective splash-glasses and was cussing at the dirt.

Mark turned back to the divers. "I think he'll be over in a minute."

The other diver said, "If I come back in another life, I'm coming back as a stiff fulla gas and ready to blow on Frank's shift." His buddy thought that was hilarious.

Mark smiled politely and went looking for the officer in charge of the scene.

"Same drill?" he asked the woman when he found her.

Lieutenant Nann—Nancy Nann; she had cruel parents, too—said, "Texted on a dead cell. Said her name's Lydia Hamilberg. Been missing a couple weeks." Lieutenant Nann never looked up from the computer screen in her squad car as she continued to enter her report.

Once again, Mark thought he recognized the name from some time in the past. He glanced back toward the boat and the body but now couldn't see either. He said, "Body was in pretty good shape." *Until Frick-n-Frack got ahold of her – and let go.*

Nann said, "She was down pretty deep, they said—eighty feet, maybe."

Mark said, "Cold down there."

"Must be." Nann continued to type, never looking up.

Mark wandered off.

He didn't get ten feet before his phone was vibrating again. Another text. "Please hurry. Important stuff 4 U 2 C. MAJOR break in ur case! E! Can't wait for you to C ME!" Several emojis followed—hearts, puckered lips, eggplants, and peaches.

Mark looked at the time—4:30—and sighed. His shift had just started. He had a long night ahead. She'd just have to wait, as would he.

That was fine with him. He was having serious doubts about their liaison. He kept seeing his erection going in and out of her—while thinking of Anne.

He thought about Anne cheating on him with Floyd Matson but knew he was just trying to rationalize his own bad behavior. On the other hand, Eileen was hot—if weird—and last night was some of the best, raw sex he'd ever had, other than that one wild time with his wife. And the laundromat, and under the bridge in his patrol car. The park.

But it was different with Eileen Quarry, and not just because she was "new." Mark had never yearned for *strange*. Cops were notorious cheaters, and he'd had plenty of offers—from women officers, grateful citizens, even female perps.

Still, he'd never cheated on Anne, even if *she* had—

"Cutting out early?" Jerome asked as he walked back from the bushes pulling up his zipper. His mood seemed to have re-elevated.

Pissing must agree with him.

Mark said, "I think you flipped a little aggressively, there." He nodded at the droplet marks on Jerome's pants.

"Shit." Jerome wiped futilely at them.

Mark knew he didn't have to say anything but decided to anyway. "I don't feel so good." He nodded toward the water.

Jerome looked over at the side of the lake where the divers were laying the nude dead woman on a body bag for Frank, the coroner's assistant, who was already waving them away.

Jerome said, "You went soft in three weeks? Must be some sort of record."

Mark said, "As I mentioned before..."

"Yeah, fuck me," Jerome finished for him.

Mark threw a polite smile at his old partner, got in his car, and drove off.

Jerome yelled after him, "I hope you feel better and come back real soon!"

Mark stuck a bird finger out the window and kept going.

***

Since it was a slow night in the city, Mark managed to piddle around doing nothing until sunset. He put in an appearance at the station, but no one was there. Corlius had gone home early for the day.

After dark, Mark drove past his house. No lights were on because he wasn't home. Next door, all the lights were on, but all the shades were drawn. Dan's car was in the driveway, but there was no sign of movement in the house.

Mark drove on.

He rode past The Mall where he had scared the girl—the same mall where two children had gone missing. The Ice Cream Circus sign was still up but partially covered in black plastic. Mark could see where people had thrown rocks through it.

Shot it.

***

In the nicer Splinter Heights subdivision, Captain Corlius was just getting home. He had left work just after 3:00 in the afternoon. Now it was 10:30. His wife's car wasn't in the driveway and no lights were on inside. He closed and locked his car, a new Explorer the department had provided, and went inside.

***

Out by the interstate, a plain-wrap sedan with a flashing blue light on the dash was pulling off the access road behind a long-bodied white Ford van with no rear windows.

No plates.

Jerome Bowers climbed out of his Impala, Glock in hand. He flipped his Lark King onto the pavement where it slid and sparked in the darkness as he walked toward the van with his duty weapon held in front.

He eased up to the driver's window—checking in the side mirror to make sure he was alone—then stuck his Glock in the driver's face.

Jerome said, "Hola, amigo. Esta solo? Are you alone?"

The terrified Salvadoran in the driver's seat nodded rapidly and said, "Si. Yes. Alone. Yes. Solo." He had a heavy accent and wasn't anyone Jerome recognized as local.

Detective Bowers regarded the Latino suspiciously and opened the door with his free hand. He waved the gun to enunciate his request. "Get outa the vehicle, sir. Salida."

"Si," the man said compliantly. Nervously.

He acted as if he wanted to look in the back of the van but checked himself. He raised his hands and stepped onto the pavement. He wore blue jeans and a red t-shirt advertising a carpet company called "Spread 'Em!" It showed a cartoon woman with her legs spread and big bush.

So, it wasn't a real business.

Jerome pointed his gun at the girl's crotch and said, "That's disgusting. Malo."

The smallish man looked down and said, "Si. I'm sorry. I know. Is my brother's. I didn't have a clean shirt to—"

"Shut up." Jerome waved him aside with the Glock. "Turn around, put your hands on your head and don't move or I'll cap your ass. You understand 'cap your ass'? Shoot you?"

"Si. I no move."

He put his hands on his head as instructed and Jerome patted him down. Then Jerome said, "Now stay that way and don't move or I *will* cap your mangy ass. No muevo!"

"Si, I don't move," the small man said again and stared at the passing cars on the freeway—too far away to help him if he needed it. They wouldn't be able to see him in the dark, anyway.

Keeping the gun trained on the driver's shoulder blades, Jerome backed up to the rear of the van where he pulled out a small but powerful LED flashlight. "No muevo!" he warned again.

"No, si! No!" the man said. He looked as if he meant it—or he'd just messed his pants.

Jerome quickly opened the unlocked rear doors of the long van. It was dark inside because the dome lights had been disabled. Using his flashlight, he made a hasty assessment of the contents, then moved quickly back to the driver.

"Okay, let's go," he said.

The short Salvadoran looked scared shitless—not without reason, out here in the middle of nowhere with this tall, lanky black American cop holding a 22-round Glock to the back of his head.

He said, "Jefe, *sir*. I don't know nothing—"

"Shut up," Jerome said.

"They jus' say to drive. Don' tell me where."

"Shut. Up!"

"Si, lo siento. Don't shoot!"

"Just go. Walk! No talking. No siento."

Jerome shoved the man ahead with his gun and followed. When they were a hundred feet from the van, in the headlights, Jerome said, "Okay. Stop. Halto, aqui."

The man stopped. He was shaking.

Jerome said, "Now I like 'em where I can see 'em. Your hands. Los manos? Comprende? Los manos!"

The man held up his hands. Frozen.

"Bueno," Jerome said. "Like that. Don't move."

The man said, "No muevo."

"Si," Jerome said. Then he turned and walked back to the van, leaving the man alone, a hundred feet away, headlights showing enough of the surroundings to indicate a field of high grass and low brush to the side away from the freeway.

As he walked away, Jerome spoke into his wrist. "This is unit six-four-eight Alpha. I've got a van full of contraband drugs out here on Old Highway Forty-One, the frontage road. We're about six miles out, maybe around marker two-eighty on the Interstate. Suspect in custody."

As he passed the van, Jerome reached in and turned off the Ford's headlights.

Jerome shouted over his shoulder, without looking, "No muevo. Okay?"

"Si, okay," the man shouted back and stood very still.

Jerome continued to his plain, silver Impala behind the big van and got in. From where he sat, he couldn't see his drug suspect.

Fernando Flores-Peña broke for the bushes.

After a long minute, Jerome got out of his car, opened the left back door of his Impala, and returned to the rear end of the van. With his small flashlight held between his teeth, he grabbed four large, full black garbage bags—all he could carry—and dragged them over to his car where he threw them in the backseat and closed the door. He hopped back in front, started the car, whipped a U-turn and sped off in the other direction—westbound.

This time he held the transmit button down on his police radio and called into the station. "Two-four-three Delta. I am in pursuit of a suspect on Old Highway Forty-One, eastbound."

The dispatcher confirmed his call and location and Jerome said, "Suspect is a black male, approximately six-three, two hundred and twenty-five pounds. He's wearing a grey sweat suit and hoody, possibly a hat under. Believed to be driver of the white Ford van parked near exit one-two-six on the access road. I repeat Old Highway Forty-One, eastbound, near exit one-two-six, frontage road. Black male, six-two to six-four, weight approximately two-twenty-five to two-forty. Grey sweat suit with an orange or red stripe down the sides." As an afterthought, he added, "He may be wearing a blue ball cap. Dodgers blue, unless he threw it away."

The dispatcher confirmed everything Jerome told her.

***

In his well-appointed Splinter Heights home, Captain Corlius sat watching hockey. Being from Minnesota, he was a fan. He dialed his wife's cellphone for the second time in an hour. The first time, she hadn't answered. This was her night out with the girls, so that didn't surprise him.

When she didn't answer again, he thought, *Good,* and left the den. He poured himself a bourbon and Seven and retired to his home office and his laptop to pore over some old pictures of their daughter.

***

Mark Young parked his Vic across the street and three houses down from Eileen Quarry's. Her Lexus was in the driveway and lights were on in the house. Otherwise, there were no signs of life.

So, he waited.

A few cars drove past in the next hour—one very slowly. But it pulled into the driveway of the last house on the block, and the old man went inside his house. No one had come or gone from Eileen's and Mark hadn't seen movement inside.

He checked his phone to see if he had any dropped or missed calls, but he'd received no more texts from his former psychiatrist, recent lover, and *case advisor*.

What the fuck was he even doing here?

***

Out by the freeway, on Old Highway 41, a phalanx of county sheriffs and highway patrol cars had gathered around the abandoned van. Even ATF made an appearance. Forensics was dusting for prints. DEA was on the way, having been delayed by what seemed to be three completely random crack lab informant reports. (All three would prove accurate, called in by the same disgruntled employee who would later be found decapitated in his baby's bedroom, his infant daughter and wife having slept through the *deposit*. Calling all three in at the same time—even from different cold phones—left little doubt in his employers' minds as to who had dimed them.)

Six large, black garbage bags full of pot remained in the van. A tall black man in a gray running suit was arrested less than a mile away. He claimed to be out jogging, which turned out to be true and without question when he turned out to be a prominent defense attorney married to the Assistant Mayor, who vouched for his earlier whereabouts, as did their four kids.

Jerome knew which brothers ran when and where.

***

In his den, his bourbon and Seven dry, Captain Corlius sat behind his desk, laptop open and pants around his ankles, when his wife returned home unexpectedly and caught him. She had come in silently in case her husband was sleeping and wasn't suspicious.

Until she was.

"What are you doing?" she said.

She was already around the desk, looking at the computer screen before he could figure out what to do other than yell angrily, "Get the hell outa here!"

He didn't stand.

As he bellowed and swatted his left hand to wave her off, she registered the sight of their daughter at age ten, standing nude in front of a plain wall, looking directly into the camera. In another shot, in a separate window, she was bending over away from the camera, her ankles straddling two short stacks of paperback books placed on the floor three feet apart.

Her husband had several other windows open.

He had been unable to suppress his just-arriving orgasm; semen covered the purple mushroom cap of his erection and made his fingers white from index to pinkie.

She slapped him across the face, then yanked the laptop off the desk and threw it into the bookshelf. She glared at him with more hatred than she had ever felt for anyone, anytime in her life—even the drunk driver who had killed her parents.

She stormed out of the room.

Corlius stood, his erection withering quickly as he jerked up his pants, cleaned off his hand with a tissue, and grabbed his gun from his desk. He shouted to the other room, "What are you doing? Where are you going? You can't tell anyone about this!" He staggered out into the great room, buckling his belt.

She had the phone in her hand. She had already dialed. She hissed, "Our *daughter*? You *disgust* me!"

Captain Corlius threw up.

His wife saw the Smith & Wesson Chiefs Special in his hand and said, "Don't you dare go back in there and kill yourself. I will *not* settle for insurance!"

She was a tough woman when she had to be—one of the things that had attracted him to her in the first place. That, and, when they'd met at seventeen, she'd looked twelve—something she remembered now.

Someone answered at the station. The Captain's wife said, "I'd like to report a crime. A pedophile. Living in *my own house*!"

Captain Corlius reacted quickly. He dropped the gun, ran into the den, grabbed his laptop, and ran out the front door.

Margaret screamed after him, "Come back here, goddammit! You will not get away with this! You will not defile this house and this family with your goddam sickness!"

She had suspected for years, but he had been careful. Now every horrible notion she had ever entertained rushed into her being like so much raw sewage. She could taste it in her mouth.

The police operator calmly asked her name.

Margaret said equally calmly, "This is Margaret Corlius, Captain Carter Corlius's wife, and I want to speak to Mitch Farmingham immediately." Mitch was old school Internal Affairs. He played rough. "Yes, I know he's not in. I want you to call his cell number and patch me through immediately. I have an internal affairs criminal matter to report that can't wait."

Margaret heard her husband's department Explorer start and she yelled out the still open front door, "Fucking *pervert*!"

She reconsidered her hesitancy to him killing himself.

Chapter 25

Jerome parked his plain-wrap Impala on a lonely dirt road in a spot that couldn't be seen from anywhere, but from which he could see a half-mile both ways into the night. Nervous but confident, he smoked an L&M and fidgeted, his dashboard littered with a dozen partially empty cigarette packs, all different brands. He threw the butt out when he inhaled burnt cotton and grabbed another pack, fishing out a fresh cigarette—fresh being relative.

Before he was halfway through his Newport 100, a pair of high beams came around the far bend, dimmed, then went out. The black Escalade on big rims stopped fifty yards ahead.

Jerome looked to his right, into the broad field of low weeds, and saw the flashlight signal—three blips, a pause, and two more.

The Escalade pulled forward. Jerome started his car and rolled up to meet it, window to window.

When he was even with the Cadillac, the left rear smoked window glided down silently and a brown hand reached out holding a thick envelope. Jerome took the envelope, without stopping, and drove off into the night.

Moments later, two young black men came hurrying out of the field with the four large black garbage bags of weed. They put them in the back of the Escalade and got in the other side. The Escalade pulled away, turning the headlights back on before the bend.

***

Mark Young approached Eileen Quarry's front door with his duty weapon extended in front of him. He stopped, listened, heard nothing, and knocked gently. The door fell open, unlatched.

He went in.

Nothing was out of place, nothing any different than he'd last seen it when he left her on the couch, sipping her Port in the nude, before she followed him outside in the mink. He could still see her opening the coat, her stark nakedness—all of it making him feel more discomposed by the moment.

He walked softly, quietly, choosing not to call out Eileen's name. Instead, he peered around the first corner of the living room into the den to see that she was back on the couch, wearing the lingerie again, only now...

She was dead.

Her wrists had been slashed, blood was everywhere, and there was a message on the wall—most likely written in her blood—in neat block letters which anyone might use. It read: "Not if I get there first."

Mark felt that ten-grit sandpaper in his skull, scrubbing his brain. But this time it hurt like hell, as if his brain had grown nerve endings. He felt that queasiness again as well, deep in his stomach, and thought he might throw up, but he didn't. He was too busy considering how to explain this.

Any of it.

***

When the usual phalanx arrived, Mark was lost in thought—grief, confusion, self-doubt—but he was able to dredge up some professional *attitude* for Martin Coor's detailed questions.

Martin seemed particularly interested in the sex, of course. "Details, man. I need details."

Pen poised.

Mark said, "No, you don't."

Martin said, "Dude, you were fucking her. I want to know every last little detail about you fucking her, to go into my detailed report about someone murdering her."

"Is it murder? Are we sure of that already?" He was thinking it looked like a possible suicide.

Hoping.

"Pretty sure," Martin said. "The puncture wound at the base of her skull, administered from a low angle, as it appears to be—and quite deep—which would be virtually impossible for a person to self-inflict, would seem to indicate—"

"I get it," Mark said. He hadn't inspected the body. He hadn't been able to—for practical reasons of disturbing the body, and because the thought of touching her brought the nausea back, powerfully.

Coor said, "Probably an icepick, though there's no sign of a weapon or razor blades—"

"Am I a suspect?" Mark asked directly.

Martin looked shocked. "What? Of course not. You discovered the body."

"So, I'm not a suspect."

"No. Not yet. Should I be looking at you? Where were you last night?"

"I was here."

"After you were here."

"Home, I guess."

"You guess? What do you mean 'you guess?' You don't know where you were after you were here fucking her and she ends up dead?" Coor never was subtle.

"She was alive when I left, Marty. But she was acting pretty hinky—"

"Who wouldn't be after being fucked by you?" Martin said with no trace of amusement or awareness.

Mark said, low through lightly clenched teeth, "I had some drinks—here—and drove home." He left it at that.

Coor said, "So, you don't remember driving home." When Mark didn't disagree, Coor said, "What else don't you remember?"

Mark stared Martin Coor down until he looked away. Then Mark said, "I didn't kill her, Marty. I can guarantee you, I did not kill her."

"Is that because you know who did?" Martin said, poised and ready to scribble something with the "First Federal Wants Your Interest!" ballpoint he'd pinched from the bank.

Mark said, "No, it is not. I have no clue who did this. If I did, I would be telling you. No, I would already have told you. I might even have already taken care of it myself."

"I didn't hear that," Martin said needlessly, and didn't write it down. "Look, Mark—"

"No, you look," Mark said, standing and getting in Martin Coor's face. "What I did with her may have been inappropriate—"

"*May* have been? Shit. You got different definitions of shit than I do." Coor scoffed. "You were fucking her, man. Fucking your department shrink."

"She wasn't my shrink anymore."

"Is that legal?" Coor asked, sounding genuine. Apparently, he didn't know the answer either.

"Marty," Mark said with an edge, as he pulled his peer to one side, where no one could hear them. "Don't think I don't know what's going on here. You all but drooled on your hard-on when you talked about her to me. Do you remember telling me how you'd like to 'hit that shit' in that conversation?"

Martin's eyes went shifty.

Mark didn't let up. "Did you get a hard-on when you went in there and saw that 'fine ass' on the couch, covered in blood? Did you have to excuse yourself to go whack off in her bathroom? Should I have the forensics gal go in there and scrape for semen samples?"

Martin went red and he almost yelled, "What the fuck are you talking about!" He glanced around as if to check no one was looking. One uniformed officer, a female, was looking—but she kept walking, at least acting as if she wasn't interested.

Or knowing better than to show that she was.

When Martin looked back, Mark said, "I had sex with her once, last night. It was inappropriate, maybe, *probably*, but it happened. That's that."

Martin glanced up, then started to write.

Mark grabbed his hand and said, "Let me finish. Then you can write your notes."

Martin Coor glowered and waited for Mark to remove his hand from the pilfered pen.

Mark did and said, "I didn't feel good about it—*certain*. But let me tell you, that woman knows what to do. Knew. It was probably some of the best sex I've ever had in my life, and I can't tell you why, except that maybe it was one of those chemistry things. We hit it off, physically."

Martin was staring, *maybe-probably* envious.

Mark said, "But I left, and I knew I wouldn't go back. I'm married—there's more to that than I'm going to go into with you. It's none of your business. But that wasn't the issue. She had been my shrink and something about that just felt wrong."

Martin said, snidely, "She knew too much about you and could tell tales out of school."

Mark told the truth. "Maybe that, too—although to be honest, I don't know that I ever said anything to be worried about. It was mostly about the shooting incident, and we dealt with it."

"What else?" Martin asked. At least he wasn't writing now.

"Well," Mark said, "that's what I was going to mention, what I was trying to tell you. She was helping me with this case. Dan Black's kids."

Martin bristled. "*My* case."

"I know," Mark said. "But it was my neighbor, my wife and kids who had to leave. So, I had—have—a personal interest in it."

"I'm sure you do," Martin said, being snarky. "Especially now." Especially snarky.

"Marty, for Chrissake stop with that shit. I'm trying to help you out here." Something occurred to Mark that he hadn't considered, hadn't asked. "Is this even still your case?"

Martin went shifty again.

"Aw, Jesus Christ, Marty."

Martin said, "It's Bowers'."

Jerome Bowers, Mark's old partner—who wasn't there.

"So, where is he?" Mark asked.

Martin shrugged. "Said he had something to do, something he was busy with and would be here as soon as he could."

At that precise moment, they heard squealing tires and turned to see Jerome—blue light flashing on his dash—speed up and stop on a dime in the middle of the street. He was out of the Impala, lighting up a Viceroy, and walking toward them before they had a chance to continue.

"Sorry about that," Jerome said to Martin, with a glance to Mark. "I had a thing with a college recruiter for the kids. It was the only time he could meet."

"All right," Martin said, putting away his unenhanced notebook. "He's all yours." He looked at Mark and walked away.

Jerome called out, "Thanks for covering, man."

Martin waved without looking.

Jerome shouted, "I'll get up with you on your notes later."

Martin went back in the house—then, apparently thinking better of it, came right back out, glanced over at Mark and Jerome, went to his car, and left.

Jerome looked at Mark for an explanation.

Mark said, "He thought she was hot, but I was fucking her."

Jerome raised his eyebrows.

Mark said, "College recruiter at ten o'clock at night?"

"Yeah, he's busy," Jerome said. "It's that time of year. I know the kids are still young, but I have to take the opportunity when it knocks." He looked at Eileen's open door and said, "Anything I need to know?"

Mark said, "No. You?"

"No."

"Good. See you tomorrow."

Jerome said, "Yeah." He headed for the open door and the fresh corpse of the attractive but obviously troubled dead police psychiatrist.

Mark got in his car to go home early. He figured he deserved it.

All he could think about, for some reason, was getting in the shower when he got there. But he knew it wouldn't help. Same shower, same water, same temperature. How come it never helped at all anymore?

He knew how it would play out. He would stand in the fresh, purifying flow, tapping his forehead against the tile, and he would not feel one iota better.

If anything, he would feel worse.

So, he stopped in a convenience store to buy some beer—the fancy imported stuff—and went in the store bathroom to stare at himself in the mirror.

He still didn't see anything.

Chapter 26

The next morning, Mark woke up feeling refreshed. He felt so good it startled him. He had drunk the entire six-pack—three before his shower, three after—and crashed.

As predicted, the shower didn't help much. He still felt dirty—that wasn't going away—and he still couldn't see anything in his home mirror, either. But for some reason unknown to him, for the first night since any of this began, he slept like a tired baby and felt fabulous.

The clock said it wasn't noon yet, so he cooked breakfast. Three eggs, toast, and frozen hash browns, crispy the way Anne always made them. They tasted almost as good as hers. He went so far as to get out the pancake mix, then decided that was overkill and put it away. He put extra butter on his seven-grain toast and ate strawberry jam from the jar with a spoon.

He called Dan Black to see if he wanted to share breakfast but got no answer, not even voicemail. Mark peeked around the curtain over the side window. It had been replaced by a shifty gypsy type who asked for half the money up front, then recanted when Mark (intentionally) flashed his badge when getting the cash from his wallet.

Dan's car was gone.

Probably at work, Mark surmised. Security was a shitty business—long hours, usually at night, in lonely places with no one to talk to, nothing to do but walk around and pretend to be interested though not interested enough to steal anything. Mark laughed. At least police work involved real criminals.

Mainly, Mark was starting to feel like a cop again. A real cop—a better cop.

He wondered how the press was characterizing Dr. Eileen Quarry's murder. Eschewing yammering bubbleheads on TV, Mark slipped out and stole his neighbor Belton's paper; he was probably still on vacation. To be safe, Mark planned on returning it when he was done reading.

At least he had his boxers on when Mrs. Hoddeker saw him this time. He waved as he stole Belton's paper. She waved—again without smiling—and went to water her zinnias in the back, probably thinking it might be time she and Mr. Hoddeker moved. Though they'd been married fifty-two years, she still called him Mr. Hoddeker when referring to him in conversation.

Mark read the detailed article titled "Psychiatrist Found Dead at Home—Murder Suspected."

He said, "So now it's only 'suspected.'" There was no mention of the icepick hole in the nape of her lovely neck. Mark *suspected* Jerome had something to do with that.

He was also surprised at how detached he was from feeling any pain, guilt, remorse, or even sorrow. And he was thrilled not to see his name mentioned anywhere. Jerome Bowers was mentioned as the detective in charge of the case, but the reporter reported that, "Det. Bowers has not yet issued a further statement."

He wouldn't, was Mark's guess. Jerome hated reporters more than he hated not smoking.

Mark stopped reading to ponder his old partner's odd behavior of late, then let it go just as quickly. All cops have secrets.

All *people* do.

He got up, made bacon, read the funnies, and actually laughed at two.

***

That afternoon, Mark's good mood elicited a cold glare from the silent policemen stationed at the captain's open door. The empty office.

Mark said, "Where is he?"

He hadn't heard yet, and there'd been no mention in the paper of anything amiss ae the station. Of course, there wouldn't be, not until someone found Corlius and formal charges were filed. But Mark didn't know what they weren't commenting on yet, either. He never called the station unless they called him.

He'd learned that lesson long ago. Nothing good ever came of checking in without being summoned. Someone always found something for him to do, usually something he didn't *want* to do. So, he never called.

A detective Mark didn't know well, a newer woman named Cecile Johnson, raised her eyebrows as if to say, *When I joined the force, I can truthfully say I never saw this one coming.*

Mark looked over at Jerome, sitting at his desk. Jerome nodded, ran his finger across his throat, then went back to getting his files together as if he might be moving desks. Mark watched him a moment—

wondering if Jerome had been fired or reassigned but hadn't told anyone yet—then he asked Cecile Johnson, "What happened?"

She told him—in detail.

Mark raised his eyebrows. He wanted to laugh out loud and say *Si Si Si was a pedo'. Just couldn't say no to his little girl*—an uninspired version of the Greek boy who *couldn't leave his little brother's behind*—but he thought better of it and said, "So where is he?"

Cop jokes could wait.

"No one knows," the female detective said.

"Wow," Mark said.

"Wow," Cecile agreed and headed home, her shift over.

As the other detectives often said, "She gives good paperwork," so they valued the time she spent in the office helping them with their reports. She would probably rather have been in the field more but knew what could happen *out there*, so she went with the flow and spent most of her work hours in the office, making reports sound interesting and credible.

Mark said, "Guess I'm back on days."

Martin looked up from his desk and said, "Guess you are." The *Fuck you, you bastard,* went unspoken.

Mark had years-in seniority. Martin would have midnight to dawn patrol.

Mark was almost through enjoying his moment when he realized Jerome had gotten up and walked over with his pile of files. He was now saying, "Step into my new temporary office." He nodded at Corlius's old permanent office and went in.

Jerome looked uncomfortable behind the desk as Mark came in, closed the door behind them, and took a seat.

Jerome pointed out, "Technically, you have seniority."

"Technically?"

"This murder thing, your shrink."

"Yeah?"

"Mark, Christ, you were fucking her."

"So I keep hearing."

Mark noticed a pack of Kools among Jerome's things. Since he didn't really want to talk about what they inevitably had to talk about, he said, "I've been meaning to ask you..."

He'd been meaning for years.

"Why you smoke so many different kinds." He looked at the Kools, then at Jerome, and said, "Most smokers stick with one. They're almost fanatical about it. But every time I see you, you've got a different brand."

Jerome shrugged and said, "I don't want to get addicted."

Mark could only come up with an, "Ah."

Jerome said, "Just so you know, it wasn't my idea. Chief made me interim Cap. It's just temporary, until they hire someone. You ask me, it won't be soon enough."

Mark pretended not to care. "Any candidates? Am I at least in the running?" he kidded.

Jerome almost laughed. Then he delivered the bad news. "Listen," he said, his discomfiture growing visibly by the second, "I gotta take your badge and gun."

Mark's smirk vanished. He'd just gotten them back—thanks to his shrink who was now apparently the reason for him losing them again. "Seriously?"

"I know, I know," Jerome said. "It sucks, but, uh, Chief's orders."

"Like you getting behind that desk," Mark snarked.

"C'mon man," Jerome said. "We go back."

"Yeah," Mark said. "We do."

"I can't do anything about this shit, Mark," Jerome protested. "I would if I could. You know that."

Mark knew he couldn't.

"Besides—"

"We had sex *once*. The doc and I."

"One too many as the chief sees it," Jerome said, without personal judgment. If all cops were as clean as Mark had been there'd be no need for IA; but most everyone fucked up sooner or later to some degree—at least got investigated after a serious enough complaint. Now was Mark's time.

Jerome said, "The thing is, buddy—"

"Buddy?"

It sounded as natural coming out of Jerome Bower's mouth as Samuel L. Jackson saying, "Golly shucks, gee whiz!"

"Yeah, yeah." Jerome sighed again.

Mark was feeling testy. "So, what? I'm a suspect? 'Person of interest'? 'Prime suspect'? What? Come on."

"Mark, see, the thing is..." Jerome was beating the bush to death.

"What? Christ, Jerry!" Mark said. "Just say it!"

Jerome finally got to the subject. "You're the *only* suspect."

Mark did not believe what he'd just heard and glared at Jerome with a look that conveyed disbelief, insult, and a fair dose of rage.

Jerome said, "You were the last one there, you left her alive—according to your statement..." He picked up a typed sheet of paper as if he was going to read from it.

Mark said, "Oh, it's a statement now. My little conversation with Marty. A statement. Very nice."

Jerome confirmed, "It is now a statement."

"Should I get a lawyer?"

"That's up to you."

"Fuck. Jerome, I can't believe I'm hearing this. And from *you*."

Jerome pressed on. "You were the last to see her alive, then you left, drank heavily, have no alibi— "

"No *alibi*?"

Jerome stared.

"I don't need a fucking alibi, Jerry. I didn't do it."

"Are you sure?" Jerome said.

"What's that supposed to mean?"

"You admitted you were drunk and didn't remember driving home. Is that accurate? Or did you not say that to Marty?"

"So?" Mark said. "I was off duty, and to tell you the truth, pretty damn confused about this whole thing."

"Killing her?"

"Jerry, stay with the program here. I didn't know she was dead yet."

"Right. You remember me calling?"

Mark paused. "Calling? What do you mean?"

"I called you, at like, four AM."

"Why would you call me at four AM?"

"I got an anonymous text. Said to call you."

"From who?"

"I don't know. It was anonymous."

"What'd your caller ID say?"

"Unknown caller."

"Okay," Mark said. "It was anonymous. What'd they say? *Text*."

"To call you."

"That's it?"

"That's it," Jerome said. "It said, 'Call your friend Mark. See what he's been up to.'"

"This is bullshit," Mark said, leaning back in his chair and throwing his hands out. "You didn't call me. And who the fuck would call you my 'friend?' After all that had gone down."

"See?" Jerome said flatly. "I didn't think you'd remember. And as for 'all that went down,' that's ancient history. Doesn't factor in. This here? This shit is uncharted territory."

Mark shifted in the uncomfortable chair. Corlius always made sure his visitor chairs were uncomfortable, assuming this would either bring out the truth quickly or ensure quick departure. Corlius wasn't a mingler.

Mark said, "So, you called me in the middle of the night and I don't remember. So what? You're saying that makes me the only suspect and I don't have an alibi?"

"That. And what you said."

Mark raised his voice to match his ire. "What the fuck did I say? Can we stop with the tautologies? I trained you better than that."

Mark had trained Jerome Bowers, it was true. At the time, there'd been no one else to do it, even though Mark only had one more year on the force. Less than a year—nine months.

They were a good team. Broke a lot of leads, had a high clearance rate, won plaudits. Got along and got by. Then came the falling out, the blaming the other for a bad arrest, the solution.

Jerome fucked up badly.

Then came absolution: he apologized, the real perp got popped, their little A-Team was split up, and they eventually decided to get along again.

If not together.

Jerome said, "Mark, you know I don't like this shit. Having to say this shit to you, do this shit to you."

"But I'm not making it easy for you, am I?" Mark said meanly. "Well, you sit in this chair and see what it feels like to have to listen to this sorry crap."

Jerome said, "I asked you how you were doing, and you said, 'I took some pills, man. I don't know. I think I did something really bad. I think I really fucked up.'"

Mark said sourly, "Doesn't sound like me."

"I'm paraphrasing. But it's pretty damn close. *You* didn't sound like you." He was now giving Mark the hard eye, the one Mark had taught him on the second day of training.

Jerome said, "I called you at two, and I called you at three, and you didn't answer."

"I was probably out of it. I stopped at a bar, I think."

"Which one?"

"I don't remember," Mark said, sounding pathetic to himself. He remembered taking one of Anne's Ambien he'd squirreled away—half of one—and passing out. The amnesia it caused in arrears.

He told Jerome.

"People sleepwalk on that shit," Jerome said. "Do weird shit. Kill people and don't remember."

"I'd remember killing someone," Mark said.

"Maybe. Maybe not. Point is, I called two, three, three-thirty, and you didn't answer until four-thirty."

"You said it was four."

"Doesn't matter. She was killed between one and three."

Mark sat still, but he wanted to run. His insides were running away already. He sat, steely and cold, and said, "I didn't kill her."

"I believe you," Jerome said. "I mean, I believe you don't think you did. But look, you know as well as I do, everybody's got a breaking point. Everyone does bad things. Everyone is guilty of something, sometime. Maybe it's just your time. Hopefully, it'll all work out. But in the meantime, you're on suspension. No desk work this time. I got them to pay you to stay home. But I have to take the car back."

"Great," Mark said with no gratitude.

Jerome lowered his voice. He warned, "And be careful. They're watching you."

"IA?"

"FBI."

Mark looked up, for the first time seeing the concern in his old partner's eyes. He said, "The Bureau? Seriously?"

"From a distance," Jerome said. So, they weren't tailing him yet.

Mark had to think that one over. "Why?"

"Because," Jerome said and paused. "There are similarities to two other cases. One in Tucson, one in Portland."

"I've never been to Portland."

"That's what I told them."

"The FBI."

"IA. They passed it on to the Feds."

"Great," Mark said, dispirited, his good morning vibe gone completely.

"Mark, I've known you almost fifteen years. I know what's in your heart. And I know your heart is heavy right now. But take the time off and enjoy it. Stock up on good beer, order out, watch ESPN all fuckin' day and night, cash your paychecks, and relax. Come out to an incident if you want, if you can't stand being cooped up. Come to mine. You know, you're always welcome."

He hadn't been the last time they'd had words.

Mark didn't say thanks, but he figured Jerome knew he was grateful for the offer. Cold jonesing after two decades of police work was not going to be easy. Not for a gifted cop, not for Mark Young, ESPN or not.

Jerome said, "But..."

Mark knew the worst was coming.

"This shit is not going away. She was one of us." Jerome paused as if considering that. "Well, she was just a fucking department shrink, but you know, it's our department, so..." He shrugged. *Anyway,* "They are dead serious about clearing this one, and you're the only thing they got."

He was clearly worried about that status.

"So, I'm gonna tell you this, old friend," Jerome Bowers said. "Get right in your heart. Make it the best it can be. 'Cause this shit is gonna get rough, and it ain't goin' away."

To make sure he was making his point, he said again, "Get it all right in your heart, man. Okay? You know what I'm sayin'? You make sure. You make *damn* sure. And if you fucked up—and I mean anywhere along the line—I don't care what you did, what you may have done, what you may have thought you may have done, what you may have done and not had a clue what it was—get it right. You see what I'm saying?"

"You're saying I need to cover my ass."

"No," Jerome said sharply. "I'm saying you need to search. Deep down in your darkest soul—and you need to face that darkness and come up with an answer your heart will accept. Not mine. Not anybody else's. Yours. You gotta dig, you gotta hurt. And it's *gonna* hurt, it's almost gonna kill you. But you gotta get down in there and dig, and dig, and dig, and face whatever it is that made you do whatever it was you told me you shouldn't have done." He paused for effect, then finished. "And then you gotta make it right—with yourself, and with your heart. That's what I'm sayin', brother."

Mark thought what Jerome was saying wasn't nearly as cryptic as it was weird, but he tried to hear the sense in it—the warning.

Jerome sat back, apparently done. "Now, gimme your gun, your backup weapon, your badge, your ID—and stay the fuck off that computer and outa mall parkin' lots."

Oh, he had to get that last dig in.

Mark knew there was no discussion he could have with Jerome or anyone else at that point that would change anything, so he put his duty weapon, ankle-strap backup, badge, and ID on the desk.

Jerome said, "Good. Now let's go check your car."

"I don't have anything in my car," Mark said, but Jerome was already opening the door and waiting for him.

Every eye in the office was on the two of them. Apparently, everyone had known but Mark.

When Jerome had Officer Dimpson search Mark's Vic, he found a cold .32 under the seat—numbers scrubbed. Every cop with more than a year had one.

Mark said, "I forgot," but he didn't even believe himself.

Jerome called him a cab and paid for the ride in advance. Mark had the driver—who looked as if he could be Jerome's brother—stop at a market and he went in. But he never came back out.

When the cabbie went in to find his detective fare, they said he'd bought a case of beer and a frozen pizza, and gone out the back, setting off an alarm.

***

Jerome Bowers left work early and made a stop at the bank on his way home. An unusually large number of late afternoon customers stood in lines. Four tellers all had customers waiting.

Jerome nodded hellos to the ones he knew and went toward the back, to his bank officer.

The painfully thin woman led Jerome into the vault, gave him his key, and left him alone.

When he was sure she was gone, Jerome muttered, "Bitch, you need to *eat*, not just *look* at the food."

He opened his big safety deposit drawer and added the thick packet of money from the night before. His box was getting full, which made him smile. He opened the top manila envelope and put the money inside, resealing it with the clip when he was done. He had written on the larger envelope, "College fund for Junior and Saleena."

Another read, "Jonelle, In the event of my death or demise. Love, Jerome."

He locked the box and left.

Chapter 27

Mark Young spent the next day lounging around the house, reading his neighbor Belton's paper. This time, Mrs. Hoddeker hadn't caught him stealing the *News*.

He tried to act as if everything was okay.

At different times, Mark thought about the active cases he knew about—occasionally even one of his own. He made a few phone calls with ideas. The case detectives thanked him politely and made notes. They knew Mark was good, that he knew what he was doing—even if he was the main suspect in the murder of their own police psychiatrist.

Even if she was hot.

Mark spent a good while thinking about Dr. Eileen Quarry. He thought about the sex, he thought about their sessions, and he thought about finding her dead body.

The cryptic message on the wall in her blood.

Again, what surprised him the most was his easy acceptance of the whole affair. "Affair," he said to himself, and laughed. His first and, he had decided, his last.

Nothing about it felt right. Seeing her corpse hadn't offered him any relief. He might have expected that, some thankfulness that he wouldn't be found out at some later, more embarrassing time. He was glad it was over, but he hadn't wanted it to end that way.

If nothing else, he was pretty sure about that part.

He pondered the message in blood. "Not if I get there first." He wrote it down and stared at it. He wondered if she had written it before she died, but that seemed highly unlikely.

No, her murderer had written it. Someone else could have come in and written it, but that was equally unlikely.

He did it. Whoever he was. But what did it mean? Get *where* first?

Mark made lists—the body dump sites, the mall abductions, his mall *adventures,* Dan's comings and goings, Jerome's, former captain Corlius's.

He'd heard that Mrs. Corlius put out a bounty on her missing husband—anyone finding him and bringing him in would receive thirty grand in cash—but Mark didn't believe it. Margaret Corlius was more the calculating type. She was probably so lawyered up that her soon-to-be ex-husband would have to have a lawyer to talk to a lawyer to talk to her lawyer's lawyer.

Mark got a good chuckle out of that one and went for his first beer of the day. Hell, it was after two. Maybe being on suspension wouldn't be so bad after all. As long as he *hadn't* killed her.

Then something struck him—and his veins ran cold.

Mark Young grabbed up his phone and scrolled through the pictures he'd clicked at the scene while waiting for the first responders—the door, the foyer, the den—until he got to the bloody message on the wall.

It looked like his handwriting. *Exactly* like his handwriting.

Now, his veins felt like ice cracking; then, just as quickly, molten lava. Pyre-like, his body burned on a pile of fear and lost memories. The nausea returned.

Mark wasn't sure whether he'd heard a knock at the door and listened closer. There it was again. He threw some handy gym shorts on and opened the door to Dan Black.

Dan said, "Hey man, got a minute for a pal?"

Mark deadpanned him. "And who would that be?" After a moment, he threw a laugh that almost sounded real. Secretly, he was glad Dan had interrupted his self-assessment and (barely) submerged terror at his own (possible) actions.

Dan said, "You got me with that one," and chuckled along.

Mark said, "I try," and let him in. Got him a beer.

Dan said, "I haven't seen these," referring to the new import label. "Where'd you come on this?"

Mark's good mood paled. "Um, a friend."

"Friends are good," Dan said and took a long draw. He made a face of approval. "Wow, that's nice. I like it."

Mark said, "Mmm," with little enthusiasm and tried not to think of Eileen handing him his first one.

Dan took another draw. It looked as if he was going to say something else about the beer—which Mark didn't want to hear—but instead he said, "Did you ever find out where your wife and kids went?"

Mark's good mood slid farther away with each word out of his neighbor's mouth. He said, "Don't want to know."

"Not even a phone number?" Dan asked, as if unable to comprehend.

Mark shook his head no. "Sick fuck gets ahold of me over some bullshit case—he's guilty, he knows he's going down, tortures me or gives me Pentothal? I don't know anything."

Simple good planning ahead for the worst possible scenario.

Dan nodded, clucked understanding. "Pentothal, wow. But if there's nothing in there to come out..." He pointed at his temple. "... your family's safe." Dan nodded as if to say, *That's smart.* He took another draw off the imported beer. "This is *really* good. Where'd you get it?"

"Store," was all Mark would say.

Dan said, "Hmmp," as if he was surprised a regular store would have such exotic beer, but that he'd have to look next time he was there.

Dan reiterated, "Real smart," about Mark's preventive planning.

Mark said, "There are some real freaks out there. Your friend Chuck was just the tip."

"Hey," Dan said. "He wasn't my friend. I just knew the guy."

"I know," Mark said. "I'm just saying, you never know. My own captain—"

Dan interrupted, almost excited. "I read that! Kiddie porn. Right there in your department." He said it as if he was sharing gossip from *The National Globe Informer.*

Mark hadn't seen it in the paper and said so.

Dan said, "No, no, not the paper. I'm sorry. I meant online, man. It's all over the place." He laughed. "What a sick perv'. He must've been some weirdo to work for, huh?"

Mark said, "He was. A bit." He couldn't decide whether he wanted to read about Corlius on the internet or not.

"Kiddie porn," Dan said, shaking his head, his laughter subsiding. "That's some sick shit."

"Not just kiddie porn. Pictures and videos he made with his own daughter starting when she was six. Ten years' worth."

Dan seemed confused. "I read they found kiddie porn."

Mark said, "I don't know." He wasn't really interested.

Dan was still confused. "On his computer at home—his wife's computer. He had some firewalled partition set up or something."

Mark said, "Oh, yeah." He remembered Cecile mentioning that.

Dan said, "Even on his computer at work. Somehow your Big Brother mainframe didn't catch it."

"No," Mark said. Cecile had mentioned that, too. Now he was certain he didn't want to know more.

He had his own problems.

Dan grunted and shook his head. "You just never know about people."

"Nope," Mark said. He realized at that instant why he had felt so little about Dr. Quarry's death. Eileen was weird—something was wrong there. All those comments about being a bad person, her allusions to a checkered history, and the rest.

What kind of a police department hired that kind of shrink, anyway?

Mine, Mark thought. There was some irony to it, maybe some humor, but he couldn't find it. So, he thought about their process.

He remembered now that in one of their sessions, she'd gone into more detail about how she had been addicted to prescription meds and booze; how that led to her abusing her son; how she regretted so much of her past and "acted out" by "going wild" at times.

Then she got him drunk and fucked him silly. *Wild, right.*

Briefly, Mark had felt manipulated and used. Now, he felt relief that his encounter with her—that relationship they didn't have—was over in a way that could never be undone. He would never be tempted again. Her "always open door" was forever closed. Finding that relief was relieving in itself.

Dan reiterated, "Nope. You just never know." Shaking his head woefully.

Or was it happily—content that he had discovered a grim truth about life?

Thinking of Eileen Quarry, Mark said, "We don't even know what we're capable of ourselves. Not really."

Eileen had said that. It now took on larger proportions. What had she really been saying? For a moment, he wondered if she'd had some perverse murder-suicide pact with another lover—some other insane patient—who got half of it right.

Or would he turn up dead somewhere too?

Dan peered at Mark oddly. "You okay, bud? That's some pretty heavy stuff—not knowing what we're capable of. Is there anything... you want to talk about?"

Mark said, "No, I'm good. Thanks." He decidedly did *not* want to talk about it.

Dan dug in. "You're just saying we never know, not even about ourselves. What we might do."

It sounded like an interrogatory, so Mark said, "Yeah. Something like that," trying to make it indirectly clear that he wanted to drop the subject.

Dan agreed by changing it. "Listen, I don't know how to say this, but..."

Mark said, "Yeah?" Thinking, *what now?* "Go on."

Dan said, "Well, it's just... I appreciate all you've done for me—as a neighbor and a friend." He looked as if he might tear up. That quick.

Then he went bleak. "I mean, I know you even thought maybe... I... might have killed my own kids."

Mark sloughed it off. "Don't take it personally. Goes with the turf. It's my job. I'm not sure I ever really thought it. Just you know, detective hunches. Usually wrong. Ice cream."

"Yeah, I know," Dan said with a wan half-laugh. "But still. You came around, saw the light and have been a good bud. I just wanted you to know how much I appreciate you giving me a second chance. Especially after I could have messed up that whole thing with Chuck—his arrest and all. Man, if he hadn't been murdered on those steps, well... I don't know what might have happened. You were right to be mad, and I just want you to know how much I appreciate that you gave me another shot, let it go, and moved on. Kept your door open so many times and hey, turned me on to this great new beer!" He toasted Mark and took a swig, finishing with a deeply satisfied, "Mmmm," at the yumminess of it.

Mark said, "Not a problem," but he was the one feeling uncomfortable now. He didn't think he'd been that charitable. If anything, he remembered being a dick. Repeatedly. The only reason he ever let Dan back in was guilt. Some friend.

Dan turned his face to the floor, as he often did, and said, "Anyway, I'm probably gonna check myself into rehab—soon as I get the nerve."

"You have a problem?" Alcohol? Drugs? Flashing the neighbors?

Dan looked up sharply. "Oh no, nothing like that. It's more, um, emotional. Psychological. You know, the file, my brain. All those concussions can add up. I've been reading about it, listening to NPR. Did you know that the most common source of concussions in the United States is girls' soccer?"

Mark said he didn't know that.

Dan said, "And one concussion, just one, can cause problems down the road. Even *way* down the road. Two and you might never be normal again. They have a compounding effect."

"You've had three," Mark said consolingly.

"Five," Dan said. "The two in country."

"I thought it was just one," Mark said. "In the Humvee—the IED attack. I mean that'd be four. I forgot that one. With the three in high school."

"Yeah, right," Dan said. "That's four, right. It was just one, the one time. In the Army." Then he looked even more embarrassed. "See? I'm all fucked up. Can't even count anymore. Like you!" He laughed with sudden pleasure, then immediately looked distressed again. He stood and began to pace, his face contorted with some internal conflict or brain-pain.

Mark said, "You're not going wacky on me, are you, pal?"

"Pal." Jesus. Listen to me. I'm getting as bad as him.

Dan said, "No more than usual," and followed it with another wan laugh. "The occasional blackout, forgetting to turn the shower off. I left the grill going all night the other night. Stuff like that. No big deal, just, you know, the headaches. It never really goes away."

"The headaches came back, huh?"

Dan said, "I could live with all that. I mean I have for ten years." An even darker cloud swallowed him. "It's my kids, Mark. I just can't... I can't shake it." He was starting to tremble. "I see their faces in the mirror. Every time I look in the mirror, they're staring back at me. I see them staring back at me. I swear. It's horrible." Dan suddenly broke down. Tears rolled down his face like acid rain. He said, sobbing, "I just can't fucking take it anymore, man! I can't..."

He didn't finish his thought.

Though he wasn't a hugger, Mark felt compelled to stand and hug Dan. It felt good to both of them, he assumed, comforting and supportive.

He said, "It's gonna be okay, Dan. It may take a while, but there's a solution out there somewhere. And you're gonna find it. I know you will." He patted Dan on the back solidly and let him go.

Dan nodded, tried to appear brave, wiping the tears. "You've been a good Mark, friend." Then he laughed and said, "I mean a good friend, *Mark.*" He looked and sounded as awky as a thirteen-year-old at his junior high prom catching himself staring at his date's breasts and saying, "Boobs?" instead of "Dance?"

Mark laughed and gave Dan another supportive, solid swat on the shoulder. "Anything I can do. Anything at all. Don't hesitate. Okay? You gonna try the VA?"

"I don't know yet," Dan said. "Thanks for the offer, though. If I can't call—I mean if I can't actually talk—I'll text. If that's okay. I don't know what the next little while is going to be like. You understand. The big unknown." He waved his hands around like the robot on *Lost in Space*, obviously trying to make light of it.

"Sure, that's fine," Mark said—though with his recent history of texts, he wasn't being wholly truthful. If he never received another text in his lifetime, it would be too soon.

Dan said, "Yeah, well," and turned to go.

Mark felt relief, but it was short-lived.

Dan turned back and said, "There is one thing you can do for me."

Everything between Mark's clavicles and his thighbones cinched up. "Sure, man," he said, but he really didn't want to hear any requests. What he wanted was to go back to sleep on the couch and wake up in a different life.

Dan stammered, "Just... I mean..." He looked lost, his eyes wandering around the room, then coming back to settle on Mark's. "Chuck did it, didn't he? I mean... he killed my kids, right?"

So, he wanted confirmation of what could not be confirmed. Maybe ever.

Mark thought it through quickly and said, "Yeah. Probably."

Lying was getting to be much easier than telling, or even seeking, the truth.

Dan said, "I mean you really think so? It would give me great comfort to know what you think, Mark—that you're pretty sure Chuck did it. Killed my kids in my house, in my backyard. I mean, it'd be better if you were certain, if you had no doubt. You saw what it looked like, man!" He looked as if he might just fall apart completely, cry and throw up, maybe have a seizure or a heart attack.

Mark said, "Pretty sure, yeah," with what he thought sounded like no conviction whatsoever. So, he added, "I mean, we don't really have any other suspects, never did, so..." He was taking a huge leap away from his usual detective's pragmatism, bred over two decades; but if there was ever a time, now was it. "Yeah," he said, expanding his endorsement for the idea. "I'm pretty sure Chuck did it. Almost certain."

The lie felt better than he had expected. He felt relief. After all, if Chuck had done it, that meant Dan hadn't. But more important, it also meant:

Mark hadn't.

A great burden lifted from his darkened spirit. It felt so good, he repeated, "I think so. I think he did."

"Oh, God!" Dan said, crying freely and hugging Mark as tightly as Mark had ever been hugged in his life. "Thank you! Thank you!"

Mark could feel Dan's hot tears on his own bare neck.

Dan pulled away, smiling from ear to ear, his eyes red and wet. He said, "Okay, then," thanked Mark again, and let himself out the back door.

Mark watched him pass the side window, round the fence, and go in his own side door—glad that he was gone, and this was over. Anne was gone, the kids were gone, Eileen Quarry was gone, and now Dan Black was gone.

Good.

Before he knew it, Quarry's case would be solved, and Mark would be an active on-duty cop again. He pined for it, but resolved to wait, convincing himself as best he could that it was all good.

All good.

Anne would come back one day with Andy and MJ. But even if they didn't, Mark would have his job back. He would be the good cop he'd always been, and that would be good. Fantastic! He might have to settle for visitation with the kids, maybe only every other weekend, but at least they'd know who he was and that he still loved them.

All good.

***

Over the next few days, whenever Mark came out to pay delivery people for groceries or take-out, he looked to see what was going on in Dan's world.

Most nights, the lights were on, but the shades were drawn. Mark would see Dan's silhouette moving past from time to time. He appeared to be naked. Of course, Mark didn't think anything about that.

He was, too.

One morning on his way out, Mark saw Dan step out onto his front porch in a nappy old bathrobe. He appeared unshaven and his hair was askew, as if he'd just awakened from a real Rumpelstiltskin.

Mark called out, "Hey, man. How's it goin'?"

Dan stared blankly as if not seeing or recognizing Mark, then went back inside without acknowledging him.

Later that afternoon, when Mark returned home from his afternoon walk, he saw Dan closing his garage door, having apparently just parked his car inside. Then he went into the house. He was wearing a short t-shirt and flip-flops.

No pants.

That night, no lights shone in Dan's house. But the next night, the lights were back on. No shadows of Dan—naked or clothed—but a light went off downstairs, then one came on upstairs shortly after. So, he was home

Mark considered going over and knocking—offer to hang out, sit and shoot the shit. Or not. Watch a game. Whatever you feel like.

Then, he decided that having Dan Black out of his life was better, no matter how bad he looked. Maybe he'd crossed over to full-on crazy. Even better that he was gone!

Mark eventually talked himself into thinking Dan was probably seeing someone, maybe a VA shrink, who had recommended heavy sedation. So, he was *probably doing much better now.*

Again: *All good.*

The next few nights played out the same. At some point, one light went off and, a few seconds later, another light came on somewhere else in the house. After a while, that light went off and two more came on.

So it went.

After a week, Mark paid no more attention, figuring Dan had checked himself into rehab and left the lights on timers. He didn't really care anymore.

He was back on Facebook.

All these silly, irresponsible young women—*girls*—telling every psychopath on the planet where they would be and when they would be there. Sometimes they even live-cam'd themselves and posted what they'd be wearing.

Sometimes they weren't wearing anything.

Mark could relate, but he wasn't stupid enough to post himself in that state of undress.

Dumb bitches just asking for it.

He could only think of his daughter MJ and hope she would never be that *stupid.* If he ever saw her again, he would have to tell her that.

Demand it.

He turned off the computer and, out of the corner of his eye, saw Dan's bedroom light go off. He didn't look to confirm it. He just didn't care anymore.

All good.

Chapter 28

When Mark pulled up to the crime site at 9:30 the next morning, he spilled his coffee and didn't even swear. He smiled at the loss and threw the cup away.

He walked to the hole in the ground, saw Jerome, and slipped up behind him silently, grabbing him by his love handles and hollering, "Gotcha!"

Jerome came out of his skin. "Jesus *fuck*! What the fuck are you doing! You scared the living piss outa me!" He dropped his Doral.

Mark laughed. Other cops laughed. Jerome did not.

Mark said, "You jumped like a guilty man." More cop humor, which usually worked the same way on all cops.

But Jerome shouted, "I was thinking of shit, man! Home shit, family shit!" He waved his hand at what was left of a badly decomposed body in the trench in front of them, the usual forensics bunch digging and dusting bones, hair, and scraps of rotting cloth.

Jerome went off. "I mean look at this fuckin' shit! It's shit, man! It's all fuckin' *shit*! Shit can happen at any goddam fuckin' minute! It's fucking *shit*!"

He stormed off, fuming, digging for a cigarette. He found a partial pack of Basic Lights, so he lit two.

Mark chortled happily, shook his head at a grinning uniformed officer, and stepped up to the death hole. Lieutenant Nancy Nann was on the scene. She looked at Mark, then at Detective Bowers' retreat, then back in the hole.

Mark said, "Being Temporary Captain doesn't sit well with him. All that added stress."

Nann stared into the hole.

Mark said, "He thinks *he* has to get into that kiddie shit, now. You know, goes with the job? I think he's really feeling it."

Lieutenant Nann continued to stare blankly into the hole. Mark thought, *Shit, maybe she liked Corlius. That would make her the only one, but it's possible*. He looked down at the remains.

"Our boy text it in?"

Nann shook her head no and said, "Homeless woman found her." As usual, Nann made no eye contact, apparently more comfortable staring at dead bodies than live ones.

Mark peered down at the bones in rotted clothing, what looked to be an older style Adidas running suit, a faded floppy Salomon sun cap, and dated Nike sneakers, all of which had probably been new at the time of death.

He said, "Found her five years ago?"

Nann kept staring into the ditch. "Something dug it up. Coyotes maybe. She saw the jacket and came over to see if it was something she could wear."

Mark guessed, "So we don't know who it is."

"Not at this time." Nann walked off without looking at Mark and started entering text into her car computer.

Mark said to himself, "Maybe it's better this way," because maybe it was.

One of the forensics guys heard him and looked up. Mark smiled broadly, took in a deep inhalation of crime site air, and walked away humming.

One cop turned to the other and said, "What got up *his* ass?" and the other cop said, "Yeah. He's kinda scary all happy like that."

Which made Mark even happier.

***

Mark slept hard that night. It felt good.

He had the blackout curtains drawn—a leftover from working nights, sleeping days. Anne had bought them for Mark for his thirty-fifth birthday. They made the room dark as night. So, when his phone started buzzing on the nightstand, Mark was disoriented. He didn't know where he was or what time it was.

He picked up his phone and looked at the red numbers on the clock radio—10:15.

Was it 10:15 at night—last night—or 10:15 this morning?

No, he had gone to bed after midnight, so it must be—

The phone vibrated in his hand.

He unlocked it and said, "Yeah?" without looking at his caller ID. No one answered. Mark realized it was a text and yawned. He opened the message screen and read:

"u found her b4 I could tell u. no fair! gues where I am?? close!!!"

Mark woke up faster than if he'd been hit with a barrelful of ice water.

He was in his pajama pants knocking at Dan's door in less than a minute. No one answered, but that didn't stop Mark from pounding more.

No one answered.

He went around the side of the house, looking in the windows, but all the shades were drawn. He still had his phone in hand and read the text again.

"u found her b4 I could tell u. no fair! gues where I am?? close!!!"

Mark pounded on a window.

No one answered.

Seeing the detached garage, Mark moved to the solid door. Locked.

"Goddammit!"

He hurried around the side to where he knew there was a window and peered in, wiping the grime so he could *see* into the dark...

...empty garage.

"Cocksucker," he muttered. "We are *not* playing this."

Mark stormed across Dan Black's small back patio to the kitchen door and started pounding again. This time he didn't wait for no one to answer.

"Dan! Open up! If you're in there, open the goddam door! This shit isn't funny!"

He pounded until his fist hurt.

No one answered.

He turned around, searching for a rock to break out a window. He found one by the fence, came back to the kitchen window over the sink and started to swing the rock when it hit him.

"What the hell am I doing?"

He was over this—*so* over this. Why was he wasting his time on an empty house? *Dan's in rehab, like he said.* His car was gone, his house was empty, no one was home, and the lights were on timers.

Mark started to laugh at himself, at his overreaction. He laughed harder—until he remembered the text message.

"u found her b4 I could tell u. no fair! gues where I am?? close!!!"

He stopped laughing and looked closer—as if trying to see what he might be missing in the text—only to realize it wasn't in the text. What he was missing was *around* the text. The phone...

... was not his.

Where had it come from? Why was it on his nightstand? How did it get there? And if this wasn't his phone, whose was it? Who was calling him? How did they get this number? Whose number was it? Where was *his* phone? And—

The phone vibrated in his hand. This time, he checked the caller ID first. It read:

"Incoming call from Det. Mark Young."

Someone was calling Mark from his own phone to this anonymous phone he'd never seen before, which had been on his nightstand for he had no idea how long. Had he been carrying it around without noticing the switch? *Using* it? Who had he called on it?

No wonder he hadn't been getting any calls back.

Mark scrolled to "Contacts" to see whose phone it might be. "No contacts," it read. He checked the minutes—"3,024 minutes remaining." Okay, that was weird. A mobile phone with no numbers and enough minutes to call Bangkok every day for a—

Mark stopped and looked up. He heard another phone ringing somewhere and followed the sound to his house. His landline was ringing. How could he be hearing it?

Standing in Dan's side yard, Mark scanned the side of his house to find that the new, gypsy-replaced kitchen window was open. Had he left it open? He didn't remember leaving his window open. His landline continued to ring.

Mark ran for his house.

Inside the front door, he tossed the new cellphone on a chair and raced into the kitchen where he picked up the wall-mount telephone. "Hello? Hello?"

No one replied. Then there was dial tone.

Something buzzed somewhere. The cellphone on a chair in the living room.

Mark ran to it and picked it up. It let him know he had: "One text message missed."

"Goddammit, what the fuck..."

Apparently, the phone was set on two rings. He didn't remember setting it on two rings, but then he didn't remember ever seeing the phone before. Maybe someone else had set it on two rings. Who would set a phone on two rings?

It vibrated again. Mark checked the incoming source: "From an unknown number" this time. He read the text message.

"I'm not at home."

Mark ran outside in his pajama pants to look up and down the street. Seeing nothing out of place, he ran back inside and upstairs to dress. He grabbed his only remaining weapon—a Ruger .40 caliber P944 he'd picked up at a gun show with no ID and kept hidden in a panel in the closet ceiling—then ran back downstairs three at a time and out into the driveway to get in his Crown Vic, only then remembering:

He didn't have his Crown Vic anymore.

"Fucking Jerome," was all he could mutter, knowing it wasn't Jerome's fault and that cursing him wouldn't do any good. But it also couldn't hurt. Someone needed to be blamed and Mark wasn't about to admit to himself that he'd left the cold, scrubbed .32 under the seat and damn well knew it had been there but didn't believe at the time that Jerome would actually go down and *check* it.

"Fucking Jerome."

Mark took a deep, steadying breath that surprisingly seemed to help clear his mind. What to do with no car? Call a Lyft? Apply for RideShare? *Right.*

Mark looked next door and saw Phil Belton's car in his driveway—back from their trip. Mark walked that way quickly.

Belton opened the door. He was a jolly round man with pink cheeks and a full head of white hair. Retired and in his late sixties, he loved to talk—about anything.

"Mark! Hey, how goes it? How are ya!" Phil Belton said. "Look, thanks for taking care of our paper. Evelyn told me—Mrs. Hoddeker—that you were on top of it every day! Thanks for that. Although, we had Ginny's cousin Randolph on the hook for checking on things. He borrowed my lawnmower last month and didn't bring it back when he said he would, so we *prevailed* upon him to keep an eye on the house, if you know what I mean. Did you see him much? Tall, thin fella, balding, cheerless. Drives a *Shiv*-ro-lay, blue or green, dark like that, needs some wax. Well come on in, come on in, what's wrong with me, where are my manners! Let me tell you about our trip to the UP. It was cold as hell, but I have to tell you—"

Before that could happen, Mark said, "Phil, I need to borrow your car."

Phil Belton screwed up his face to look at Mark as if he had green skin with orange polka dots all over. "My what?"

"Your car," Mark said, nodding over. "Keys handy?"

Belton looked as if Mark had said the savages were circling. "I... I... um. Is this police business?"

Mark said, "Absolutely. You might say that."

"Well," Belton said, clearly displaying his confusion, "Is it 'absolute' or 'might I say that'?"

Mark was momentarily stifled. Thoughts raced through his head: *What's wrong with me? Why would I say something stupid like that? Just tell him you need his car now, get the keys, and let's go. Who called me? How did whoever it was get my phone? Where did I get that other phone? It has to be Dan Black. He said he wasn't home. But it could be anyone saying that. I should know who it is. I should have a good idea, a gut feeling. Why don't I have one? Why am I standing here staring at this sad little pink portly neighbor of mine who's such a pain in the ass, with nothing coming out my mouth to solve this ridiculous situation now?*

This in the space of a second—a metaburst.

Belton said, "Sure ya don't wanna come in and talk about it? Hear about our trip? It was the bee's knees, lemme tell ya!" He held the door open wider. "Ginny just made some cranberry-maple-nut muffins that'll make your socks sing!"

Mark had never heard that term before, but he thought it fit the Beltons perfectly. "No thanks," he said, feeling a need to be courteous for some reason—some reason that felt as though he was deep into some weird shit and did *not* want to talk about it with *anyone*.

Much less Phil and Ginny Belton.

So, he said, "Look, Phil. I just need a favor."

"To borrow my car," Phil confirmed. He looked over. He and Ginny had just bought the car not six weeks earlier. It was the nicest new car they'd ever owned—a new blue Taurus with all the convenience packages and the second to the highest end trim package. Mark knew because Phil had given the full rundown the next day.

"Yeah," Mark said—and knew he needed to lie.

He leaned closer—which, oddly, made Belton appear more nervous. He leaned away. Mark persisted in a low and confidential tone. "It's my wife. You know that she and the kids left and are in hiding."

Belton said, "No I didn't know that. In *hiding*?"

Mark said, "You knew they left," knowing that Belton did.

"Well, yes," Phil Belton said. "But... hiding?"

"Yes," Mark said. "Because of the incident."

"The *in*-cident," Belton said and nodded. He knew all about it because everyone in the neighborhood knew all about it. The whole city did.

Mark nodded. *The incident.* He said, "I have a tip as to where they might be."

"The..." Belton didn't say "murderer", but Mark knew what he was getting at.

"No," Mark said. "Anne and the kids."

Belton nodded, worry wrinkles spreading across his face like a winter windshield that just had a bucket of hot water thrown on it. He said, "Is that wise? I mean, shouldn't you maybe just... leave them alone... where they're safe?"

How the hell did this pasty little fat fucker figure that out on his own?

Mark said, "Yes, normally, yes, Phil. That's how we've been playing it. But see, the... stakes have kind of gone up—just in the last ten minutes."

"The last ten minutes? My! What happened?"

Mark said he couldn't tell him—police business and all—then said, "So, may I please borrow your car? Can you get me the keys?"

Belton looked around for help. Mark could hear Ginny in the kitchen, humming what was likely a hymn from last week's church service while clanking the tin pans on the counter to release what had to be the delicious muffins.

Phil Belton was now sweating profusely.

Mark said, "Phil. Get me the keys. Now."

"But..."

"Now."

"But..."

Mark knew he had to lie again. "If anything happens to your new car, the department will buy you a new one just like it, exactly like it. I swear. On my word."

Phil said, "But it was the only blue one they had. The salesman said it was the only one in the state, and that they weren't making them anymore, that they had discontinued Sky Laser Blue Metallic. We got the *last one.*"

"He lied!" Mark shouted, scaring Belton back, and causing Ginny to call out from the kitchen.

"Phil? What is it? Who's there?"

Mark said, "Aw Christ." Not Ginny. Ginny Belton with her church dresses and fake welcoming attitude. "Forget it. I'll check with the Hoddekers."

Mark turned and headed across the street at a jog.

Belton called out, "I can talk with Ginny here! Hold on, Mark! We don't wanna be bad neighbors. It's just, the car is new and..."

Mark was already knocking on the Hoddekers' front door. When Mrs. Hoddeker opened her door, Mark walked in without comment.

Less than a minute later, he was driving away in her plain Dodge sedan, and she was calling Mr. Hoddeker at the office.

As Mark made the far corner, the unknown phone buzzed again with a new text *from himself*:

"some-1's wif @228 Cody. Urs?"

Mark recognized the address as a rental house his brother-in-law, Smithton, used to own in Parke Village, fifteen miles away.

Mark's first and only thought was that someone had found Anne and the kids. If it was Dan, he was going to kill him. Hell, if it was anyone, he was going to kill them.

Mark felt his breakfast kicking up, wanting to leave.

And *what the fuck* was he doing! Again! Dan Black was crazy, there was no doubt about it. Who *wouldn't* have gone crazy after what happened to him? But he, Mark, had to *stop thinking* Dan Black had anything to do with any of this. It was just *stupid*! He needed to focus, to figure out who was doing this, and why. Where was he? *Who* was he? *What the fuck* was going on! *Fuck Dan Black!* Forget him. *What the fuck is wrong with you!?*

Think! 228 Cody Lane!

It made perfect sense. With nowhere else to go, Anne calls her brother and asks if anyone is in the house, explaining the circumstances. If anyone is still living there, he evicts them so his sister and her kids can hide. The only problem being:

That's an easy tie-in to run down. Anyone with a small amount of knowledge about her or her family could have found it. *That was stupid, Anne,* Mark thought, cursing. *The first fucking place anyone would look.*

So, who knew about the house? Smithton of course, but he was *too gay to kill anyone,* and it was his sister. *He loves Anne.* He would never hurt her. He'd kill himself first.

But he might hole her up. Sure.

So, who else knew about 228 Cody Lane? The list was short.

Former captain Carter Corlius (whereabouts unknown), present temporary captain Jerome Bowers (acting weird as shit lately), maybe Evelyn Hoddeker (she and Anne used to be close when they took some gardening classes), Smithton's ex-lover Greg the bodybuilder (wore black leather suspenders and a Muir cap to Easter dinner). *Who* does *that? And what the fuck was his last name? Milton? Miller? Fulton? Fuck!*

Who else had Anne told? *Damn her!*

The leap to judgment came quickly and easily. When he burst in through that front door less than twenty minutes from now, he was going to give her hell!

If she was still alive.

The kids.

Mark called the address in on his way using the phone that wasn't his. He had a tough few seconds explaining to Cecile Johnson why he had forcefully taken his neighbor's Dodge—Mr. Hoddeker had called it in—but once she understood the context, Cecile called Jerome Bowers, who called his friend the Chief of Parke Village, who in turn called the Sheriff, since the address was technically in the county.

By the time Mark got to the scene, the house at 228 Cody Lane was surrounded by Surry County Sheriffs and Parke Village cops—several in tactical assault gear.

The house was old, small, and square, sitting in the middle of a large, cleared corner lot. No cover. Mark hadn't seen the house in a dozen years, but it looked just as bleak and low-rent as he remembered it. He thought Anne's brother had sold it a long time ago, but he didn't talk to Smithton much, so he didn't really know. He didn't remember Smithton's phone number—it was stored on his missing personal phone—so he couldn't call to ask.

Not that it mattered now.

Then Mark remembered that Smithton had said he'd broken up with the bodybuilder—*Greg Hilton,* that was it—because the "big lug" had hit him. Mark had thought little of it at the time, but now that he had nothing else to go on, Greg Hilton was a name he was going to remember. Smithton was going to catch hell, too.

Anne better not be in that house.

Mark went straight to the Situation Commander, who asked, "You're Detective Young?"

Mark said he was.

The wiry, black-haired captain said, "It's quiet. There doesn't seem to be anyone inside. No movement or sounds. So, we waited for you. We knocked but no one answered."

"Okay," Mark said, and turned to face the small structure. "Do your thing. Just be careful, please."

The captain said, "Understood." Then he turned and shouted, "Team!"

The bash and breach team moved for the back door, presumably the kitchen, and prepared for dynamic entry behind their black ballistic shields. Each man was bigger than the other. No women. The largest of them held the ram. He swung it once into the handle/deadbolt area and the door swung open with a bang.

SWAT poured in.

"Police! Come out! Police! Clear! Open that door! Come out, now! Police! Put down your weapons! We will shoot! Clear! Police!"

Mark could hear the cops going room to room in the small house, shouting orders. He recognized the sound of two doors being kicked in. The intentional chaos was familiar as well.

Less than a ten seconds later, it was all over.

SWAT cops started exiting the structure. Their leader—a beefy no-neck guy who looked fifty, but with the thick, solid arms of a twenty-year-old Marine—and his second in command, a man half his size and age but no less solid, went straight to the Situation Commander.

The big one said, "We have a body."

The younger one corrected, "We have *goo*."

The Situation Commander turned to Mark. "You want us to go in first?"

A fleeting image of Anne, dead, ran through Mark's mind, then it left. Everything around him felt like police work and provided a comfort. If the body was Anne's, or one of the kids—

He paled.

The captain waited for an answer, then asked, "Okay?"

Not *Are you okay*? That would be insulting. Just confirm the original question. Everything silent and unspoken is understood in inner circles.

All the cops standing close knew this and looked away as if busy with their own thoughts of what the rest of the day would be like on their shift—giving Mark time to deal with the situation, already knowing that if he said *No, go ahead without me,* they would think no less of him. They'd be seeing their own wives in their minds. Their kids. They knew what had happened next to Mark's house, to his neighbors' kids, and about his own wife and children leaving.

They knew well.

Mark swallowed his anxiety, chasing it with his determination to *end this,* like bad tap water after cheap whiskey. He said, "Let's go." MJ and Andy were back to being alive in his mind. Mark would deal with whatever was inside this house of charnel when he saw it.

At least he hoped he would.

Chapter 29

Mark and the SWAT team went in through the open kitchen door. The smell of death hit them immediately.

In the back bedroom, the smaller of the two, a woman's clothed body was partly on, partly off the bed, draped onto the floor against the wall. She had one shoe on; the other lay on the pillow. The covers were strewn as if there'd been a struggle.

She had been dead for many days and was rotting.

Mark covered his nose and mouth and stepped closer. The body was Anne's size and build and the shoes might have looked familiar, but the dress didn't match any in his memory. She could have bought it after she left, but the style wasn't Anne's, at least not one he'd ever seen her wearing. Too churchy—more like something Ginny Belton might have worn at Anne's age.

Maybe she'd repented, gone back to the church. Anne had always said she was "spiritual, not religious," but she often spoke of missing the comfort of the church of her youth, their gentle pastor, his warm, positive sermons about kindness and goodness. Everything Mark never saw at work and could never talk about with her.

He moved closer.

The haircut was Anne's, as was the color. For a moment, Mark couldn't catch a breath. It was as if the stench of his entire life had caught up with him in this small room—every bad thing he'd ever done had converged and congealed in this awful moment, this time and place where he would have to face it all.

The police waited patiently, likely imagining themselves in Mark's shoes.

Someone opened all four windows and closed the door to the rest of the house. Thankfully, there was a breeze.

When a hint of untainted air got down into his lungs, Mark stepped closer to the body. He moved around the end of the bed, careful not to step in the blood or disturb any evidence.

Then he saw her face. The contortions of a violent, unexpected death.

The captain watched him and must have seen the glint of something in Mark's eyes, flitting across his features. Rather than ask *Is that her?* the captain said, "Do you recognize her?" careful not to say *Your wife?*

Mark said, "No."

Everyone in the house sighed relief—sorry for someone else's loss, but at least it wasn't a cop's wife, one of their own.

The captain asked, "Any ideas?"

Mark had a few, but said, "No. I don't know her." She was no one he'd seen before. That much he knew.

The captain nodded and told someone to get forensics inside and send for the coroner right away. She was decomposing quickly in the hot, closed-up tiny house.

Even as they watched.

The beefy SWAT leader said he figured she'd been here for three or four days at least. Mark asked if she'd been living here.

The guy said, "Hard to say, but probably. Toiletries in the bathroom, food in the fridge, dishes in the sink, lots of family photos out in the living room. Probably a runaway from a bad situation."

Mark could imagine the type. A husband who beat her, threatened to kill her—an alkie or a meth head. Some worthless piece of shit they'd probably already arrested once, or at least been to his house—more than once. Now this.

It wouldn't be the first time.

Mark and the captain went to look in the main room. Mark suspected, but didn't say, that they'd find pictures of Dan Black, his dead wife, and three dead children. They did not. The photos were of *Mark's* family—Anne, MJ, and little Andy.

Hundreds of them tacked on the wall in neat rows that extended out from a photo in the middle. It showed a large white farmhouse, seen from the side, where a young boy and his younger sister posed grimly joyless by a folding chair and an old swing in a tall tree.

Mark's knees buckled.

Mark walks into the side yard of the house he grew up in. He sees his father Al—a tall, mean man in work khakis—shoving a young boy into a folding chair on the shaggy grass. A rusting lawnmower rests near a tire iron and other junk. A tall tree with the rope swing. Weeds.

The boy is Mark at eleven. His nine-year-old sister, Maytha, swings on a board hung from the big oak on heavy ropes. She happily sings an alphabet song from their youth, with different words.

"A is for abuse."

Young Mark Young is now bent over the folding chair, pants to his knees – his father beating him with a belt.

"B is for brave."

Young Mark stands, defiantly buckles his pants and glares at his father. His father laughs.

"C is for chicken."

His father catches a live chicken by its neck.

"D is for dead."

Mark's mother appears from a fog, behind his father. An aura forms around her head.

"E is for everyone."

A woman walks into the yard with three children. She is the dead woman from 228 Cody Lane, and her kids are Dan Black's.

"F is for fear."

The dead woman looks around nervously. The kids look up at her, pleading for mercy.

"G is for grave error."

Mark's mother looks over to where her tombstone now stands. It reads "Mrs. Albert Collin Young" with the dates, and below that, "natural causes." The letters "un" carve themselves into the stone at the beginning of the second line.

"H is for horror."

The dead Cody Lane woman finds the source of her fear – a man turned away with a gun to the back of his own head – the suicide uncle.

"I is for ideas."

A man's mouth smiles. He has an idea and raises the bloody axe, blocking his face.

Maytha sings, "J is for justice."

Young Mark realizes he's wearing a policeman's badge. It looks large on his small chest.

"K is for killer."

The man's eyes are tight above the axe blood. He flashes a look at Mark's father, whose eyes are also tight. Then, he throws a quick sideways glance at his son, and young Mark's eyes go tight too.

"L is for loving."

The Cody Lane woman is now off to one side, alone. Mark's mother stands behind Dan's children, her hands on the shoulders of the outside two. The youngest one, the boy in the middle, looks down at his small bloody penis on the ground, then cranes to look up at Mark's mother.

She smiles down at him as if to assure him that he and his sisters are safe in her arms. Large angel wings unfold behind her back.

Mark's little sister sings, "M is for – "

Dan's three children calmly say, "Murder."

There is ruffling under their shirts as wings strain against the fabric.

"N is for nothing."

Mark's father displays an open hand.

"O is for obvious."

An axe appears in his father's open hand. He swings it at the chicken's neck. Blood sprays across young Mark's face.

"P is for punishment."

The female victim from 228 Cody Lane stands still, upright in her church dress as her head falls off and rolls onto the ground. Her eyes flicker. Her body remains standing.

"Q is for quiet."

Everyone stares in a different direction, silently avoiding eye contact. Admitting nothing.

"R is for realization."

Young Mark cocks his head as if noticing something he hadn't before.

"S is for sickness," Maytha sings with sadness.

The suicide-uncle/man with the axe is now Dan Black. He's wearing a straitjacket. He easily removes it and offers it to young Mark, who puts it on. It hangs loosely. His clothes fall away underneath.

Maytha swings and sings, "T is for truth!" Happy now.

Young Mark, now in a straitjacket that fits, stands before the side of the old house, which is now plastered with the same family photos from the 228 Cody Lane living room, spread out like rays of a heavenly sun, glowing golden. His young face is bathed in glorious light. He grins wide, comforted.

"U is for understanding."

Young Mark, back in a too-large straitjacket, stands in the Cody Lane bedroom by the dead, rotting woman. She opens her eyes and looks up at him. She mouths, "I forgive you."

Maytha sings, "V is for vic-*tory!"*

Black walks away with an anonymous woman and two children to Mark's plain-wrap Crown Vic with the scratched hood. Maytha swings higher, singing her song at the top of her lungs.

"W is for weathering the storm!"

The sky goes black above the old house. A massive black funnel cloud snakes down as if alive, lapping at the woman and her kids – the family young Mark now recognizes as his own in the future.

Maytha shakes her head and sings sadly, "X is for Xs."

Anne, MJ and Andy look back woefully with cartoon Xs in their eyes, marked for death.

Finally, Maytha sings with renewed enthusiasm, "Y is for Young Mark Young, young no more! Yes!"

Mark is an adult again – nude, covered in blood, staring ahead with blank acceptance. Everyone is dead – Mark's father and mother; the Cody Lane woman and Dan Black's children; Anne, MJ, and Andy all with Xs in their eyes.

Dan Black smiles, swings a new hunting rifle around at an impossible angle and shoots himself in the back of the head. He slumps forward, dead.

Maytha laughs, swings harder, lets go, flies up into the black tornado and is sucked away. Mark stands alone. Sad. His mouth moves as a woman's voice says:

"Z is for – "

"Zebra four-seven-five," the female cop said, walking past. "Copy. Go ahead."

A radio crackled loudly.

Mark woke up on the floor with the Situation Commander, SWAT leader, and two other Kevlar-swathed cops kneeling around him.

The captain said, "EMS is on the way. How do you feel?"

For a long moment, Mark didn't know how he felt or where he was. Then he saw the photos on the wall.

He tried to sit up, but his head swam – and hurt like hell. He groaned.

"You hit your head on the coffee table," the huge SWAT cop was saying. "Took a pretty good shot. You might have a concussion there." A serious type, he added. "You probably want to get that looked at. Pop like that can fuck your well-being all to hell."

He nodded and walked off. Mark noted a scar on the back of the bald man's head—as if someone had shot him there.

Mark lifted himself up on one elbow and felt the golf-ball-sized lump on his own head. At least there was no blood.

The captain said, "Why don't you just lie there until the EMTs get here and check you out."

Mark said, "I don't know... what happened. I was... we walked in and..."

They waited. Finally, one of the other cops said, "You just dropped, man. One second you were standing, the next you were down—*bamm* on the coffee table. I've never actually seen anyone go out like that."

Another cop nodded, a new one. Apparently, she'd never seen it either.

Mark looked at the young guy who'd made the comment as if to say *You're not helping.* The young cop turned away, as did the young woman.

A second later, Mark heard a familiar voice.

"Hoh-lee-*fuck*." Jerome had come in and was looking at the photos on the wall, hands on his hips, smoking a Chesterfield.

A cop announced, "EMS is here."

A few seconds later, the two EMTs were inside, kneeling down as the Situation Commander and his people moved aside to make room.

He informed the paramedics, "He lost consciousness. Fell and hit his head on the coffee table."

One of the EMS guys said, "That's quite a knot." He was used to dealing with civilians in distress and had developed a calmative approach. "Have you been drinking, sir, or taken any kinds of drugs we should know about?"

Mark said, "No. I'm a cop. Detective. On... leave."

He glanced at Jerome. Jerome turned away.

The EMT said, "Sorry. They didn't say."

Mark said, "Can you help me up?"

"I'd rather check your vitals first, if that's all right."

"I'm fine. Just help me up."

Though they likely didn't want to, they did his bidding.

Jerome said, "You sure you're okay, man? You look awful pale."

"I'm fine," Mark told him. "I didn't have any breakfast, came straight here—"

"And saw those," Jerome said, nodding at the Young family pics covering the wall. He turned to the Situation Commander and his

SWAT team. "I think we'll be all right here. I'll catch him if he falls again."

Mark glowered at his former partner and old friend, but everyone left.

The EMS guy said, "We'll be outside a few minutes if you need us."

Mark said, "Thanks," and watched them go.

Jerome said, "It's ripe in here. Body in there?" He nodded at the bedroom.

Mark said, "They closed the door."

"Good thing."

Mark looked over, happy it was closed, too; but he could still see what was inside that room in his mind. Clearly.

"So," Jerome said, returning his attention to the wall. "You got any explanation for this crazy shit?" He added, "Sorta looks like sun rays—goin' out from that old house or something. Like the sun. Like rays of the sun. Sunbeams."

Mark had to look to see that he was talking about the arrangement of the photographs—just like in the dream, only without the glorious glowing light. He hadn't noticed before.

"Explanation?" Mark said.

"Ideas, whatever," Jerome said.

"How'd you get here so fast?" Mark asked him.

Jerome said, "I was close by. Cecile called me."

Mark said, "Cecile, yeah." He remembered calling her. Most of it was coming back, slowly.

Jerome looked at the wall of Young family photos as a splash of sunlight broke through the clouds outside and fell across the wall. He said again, "So... no thoughts? Words of wisdom?"

Mark shook his head. No words of any kind came to mind, wise or otherwise—though countless thoughts swirled like broken sticks in an eddy.

Chapter 30

After he was sure no one had any more questions, thoughts, explanations, or ideas, and that no one was following him, Mark turned off the highway for his father's house, the old one from the dream—the disturbing dream that always and never changed: always the same faces and events, never any significant differences.

Until today.

Long abandoned, the old home place had come into ruin. The windows were broken and weeds had taken over. The wooden swing hung by only one rope, its wooden seat long rotted. Three old tires, a broken shovel, and a rusted lawnmower engine lay scattered about. Fortunately, out here in the country, no one paid much attention or asked Mark to clean it up.

He'd wanted to sell the place many times over the years, but his sister had fought him on it. Maytha lived out of state, so it was easy for her to say no to "unloading" the farmhouse. Mark honored her wishes, even if he thought she was being foolish and told her so—a source of many family arguments.

He had managed the conflicted feelings in his mind by not going to the farm anymore. He hadn't been in years, maybe a decade. Their father had died before Mark graduated college—a massive heart attack—thirteen years after Mark's mother passed.

Mark didn't miss either one of them. His father had beaten him, and his mother never intervened. His sister had been spared, so she "just didn't feel right about selling the place." She "missed Mom." They never discussed Dad. Maytha knew what Mark had endured, but she didn't know about Mom's voluntary blindness.

So, the property sat, a hotbed of nasty memories that Mark avoided like a mad dentist. Though he sometimes felt a hint of regret. At one time, the farm had been big, productive, and picturesque—the white two-story house large and stately.

Mark's great-grandfather on his father's side had emigrated from middle Europe and purchased the original 250-acre spread just before he died. His son, Mark's grandfather, made the farm a success and built the house—grand for its time—when there was nothing around for miles. Years later, the spreading city lay just a few miles beyond the farm and their small hometown.

Mark's grandfather had been a hardworking man like *his* father, Mark's great-grandfather; but he also inherited a mean streak as wide as his conscientiousness. He *forced* the land to give him what he wanted and did the same with his children.

Mark's father had received almost daily beatings himself for most of his youth until he'd had enough. At seventeen, he hit his father with an axe handle and almost killed him. They never spoke again. Mark's grandfather moved into town with Mark's aunt, his father's only sister, where he died within a year—she said, "Of a broken heart." She said he missed the land.

Just not the family.

The truth was that he drank himself to death. He'd always been a hard drinker, as had his father before him. Mark's father carried on the family traditions, but without the drive to succeed offsetting his alcoholism or offering any type of redemption.

"He was just a lazy, mean man," Mark had told Eileen Quarry once, not feeling anything in saying it. His father had had no interest in hard work on the land or anywhere else. So, to feed the family, he sold off the farm a few acres at a time until only two and a half acres around the old house remained, which he let go to ruin before he died. Maytha married and moved away, so Mark left it as it was.

In the heat and wet of the decades, trees grew like weeds until the place became nearly invisible from the road. Hemlock and cedar row-hedges had become enormous green walls that hid the house and lined the driveway. Nothing to the side or back of the house could be seen from any direction. Driving past, someone might catch a glimpse of a gable or broken vane on the barn roof; but otherwise, save the fetid memories, the old home place might as well not have been there at all.

The perfect place for kept secrets.

When Mark pulled the Hoddeker's tan Dodge sedan into the overgrown driveway, it all came back like food poisoning, but he knew this was where he had to start. Ruger in hand, he moved as if walking point in war—slow, guarded, alert—around the right side of the old two-story until he had a full view of the broken swing, the debris, the dilapidated barn, and back of the house.

Fortunately, there were no photos on the wall, but there were footprints in the grass—several sets—so more than one person had been here.

Recently.

A trail led to the back door, which lay ajar. Mark pushed it open with his foot, stuck his gun in and looked around. The old table was still there, and the rusted stove, but most everything else was gone, probably looted.

As Mark made his way through the bottom floor and up the dusty, creaking stairs, he could remember every time his father beat him on each stair, the landing at the top, and in every room upstairs.

The last room Mark came to was his old bedroom, which he'd last slept in the night before the day he turned eighteen. The next morning, he walked away and never came back. His sister called him at State when "Dad died," and Mark went to the funeral for her, but he didn't say three words to anyone. As soon as the preacher finished, Mark left.

When Maytha came back for the burial three days later, Mark looked at his mother's headstone, felt nothing, and did not forgive her in his head or heart. He felt better for it, for not forgetting. Time does not heal all wounds—not if they're deep enough.

Not if they still feel as real as they did on this morning.

Mark looked around his old bedroom, seeing everything that was no longer there, remembering it all. He felt nothing other than a wish that either none of it had ever happened or he could be blessed with amnesia.

He then went back down the stairs and into the basement. Two small, dirty windows provided all the light—just enough to see there was nothing down here but spiders and their webs, unmolested.

When he found no one and no clues in the house, Mark went back outside and had started for the barn when he saw mashed grass around the storm cellar door, which was latched shut.

With a new brand-new padlock.

Swinging around to make sure no one was watching him—or about to attack—Mark kicked at the lock. It didn't give, but he heard a whimper from inside and knew instantly who it was.

"MJ?"

His daughter grunted frantically below, making strange sounds as if screaming through a thick mask of cotton balls.

"Hang on! Hang on, baby! I'm gonna get you out!" Mark looked around just as frantically for how he was going to do that. "Daddy's here. I'll get you out! Don't worry!"

Mark spotted the old tire iron leaning against the tree with the broken swing. Had it always been there, or had he presaged it in his blackout version of the dream back on Cody Lane?

He was ready to shoot the lock, but knew that was dangerous, so the tire iron was perfect. *However the hell it got there.* He holstered his P944, ran to the tree, and came back with the tool. After three tries, he busted the entire latch out of the old wood, padlock and all.

Mark swung the creaky, angled door open and ran down the steps into the darkness. "Are you okay, baby? MJ? Talk to me."

MJ couldn't talk because her mouth had been duct-taped—as had her wrists and ankles. The tape was wrapped several times around her head and was fouled badly in her hair.

Her eyes flared wide with fear.

This was one of the few times Mark wished he carried one of those super-macho hunting knives with the serrations for skinning hides and scoops to avoid suction when stabbing an animal. Lots of cops did, but Mark never saw the need.

They lived in the city, for Chrissake.

He bit at the duct tape next to MJ's face and made a notch, which he then carefully but quickly extended down until the tape was severed. He eased it off her skin as delicately as he could.

"Daddy!" she cried.

"Are you okay?" He held her.

"There were *spiders*." She burst into tears.

"I know," her father said. He could see them everywhere in the dank pit. "I'm sorry. Let me get your hands."

MJ turned so that her father could bite and remove the tape. Then her feet.

"Where's your mother and Andy?" her father asked her.

"I don't know," she said. "I woke up in here. The spiders were on me." Her teeth were rattling from terror and relief. Pent-up tears streamed down her cheeks.

Mark told her, "It's gonna be okay, Mary Jennifer." He hadn't called MJ by her full name in years. Somehow, there was comfort in it now. He hoped she felt the same. "I'm gonna carry you out now, okay?"

MJ gave a small smile and Mark lifted her. He started up the stairs.

"Are Mommy and Andy gonna be okay?" MJ asked as she squinted at the hard light above.

As they crested the steps, Mark said, "Yeah, baby. Don't worry. Daddy's here and he's gonna take care of every—"

Wham!

The shovel came down hard on the back of Mark's head. He tried to save his daughter from falling, but his arms went as limp as his legs. MJ spilled onto the grass and Dan Black had Mark's Ruger in his hand, his foot on MJ's throat.

Mark's head was swimming worse than in the Cody Lane house. At least he didn't pass out this time. He knew he hadn't because he could clearly hear Dan Black saying, "I know what you did."

Mark could also hear himself saying, "What?" as if calling into an empty fifty-five-gallon drum, and MJ crying, muted into the grass.

Dan seethed. "You don't even know what you did! Do you?!"

That much was true. Mark had no clue about anything at that moment. He didn't even know why his head was hurting, what Dan had done to him. Dan's voice sounded as if it was coming from a distant echo chamber—another room, another place.

MJ shouted angrily, "He didn't do anything, you asshole!"

Mark had never heard her say "asshole" before.

Dan said to her, "What do *you* know? You're just a little girl. A stupid little girl. You don't know how bad adults can be yet." He sounded angry—angry as hell. "But you're about to learn. Daddy's gonna teach you. Now get up. *Up*!"

He hadn't given her time to move; now he was yanking her up by the tape in her hair. She yelped and struggled.

Mark warned him, "Leave her the hell alone!" but he couldn't have shoved his hands through warm pudding, if he could even find the bowl.

Dan kicked him and ordered MJ to, "Help him up! Pitiful loser that he is. Up!"

He kicked Mark again. MJ shouted for him to stop and helped Mark to his feet. They headed for Evelyn and Fred Hoddeker's Dodge.

Chapter 31

Dan made Mark drive. Mark's head was killing him, but he figured if he didn't drive, Dan would kill him and drive himself. MJ rode in the back. Mark asked where they were going, but Dan said only, "To where the answers are."

After a few minutes, Mark's headache was reduced to a dull throbbing, so he said, "What are you doing, Dan? I mean, have you thought this through? A police officer? His family? I know you've had mental problems, but seriously. A cop?"

Dan acted as though he hadn't heard a word. He looked out the window as if they were all on a pleasant Sunday drive in the country and he was lost in happy thoughts on his way to church.

Mark tried to sneak a look at MJ in the backseat, but Dan had seated her behind Mark and turned the rear-view mirror slightly to the right.

Dan looked over at Mark and nodded. He said, "It took me a while to figure it out."

"Figure what out?" Mark said.

"The whole thing. You. Them. It. The doctor. All of it. The whole thing. Kit and caboodle."

"What are you talking about, man?" Mark wasn't following.

"*You*, man! The whole thing!" Dan said, excitedly happy. "You're the key. Well, you're the thing. The whole thing. The man. The guy. I don't know how I missed it." He shook his head.

"The key to *what*?" Mark said impatiently. "What the *hell* are you talking about?"

Dan looked at him squarely. "The mystery. The murders. The death and destruction. Everything. Me, you, her." He nodded back at MJ. "My kids."

"I'm the key," Mark said, doubtful, skeptical—certain that Dan had officially lost his mind.

"Oh yeah." Dan laughed. "I can't believe it took me so long to figure out." He stopped laughing. "But then, you didn't figure it out either and that's your job."

"Yeah?" Mark said sarcastically, indicating that he believed Dan even less now than two seconds ago.

"I mean, I can't really blame you," Dan said. "You were too close to it. Like me. Right there! Couldn't see it!" The amazement rang clear in his voice. Then he said calmly, "Turn here," and pointed to the right side of a Y in the road.

Mark followed the driving directions and said cynically, "But now you know."

"Oh yeah," Dan said, nodding. "Now I know *exactly*."

"Good," Mark said. "So why don't you turn yourself in and we can all go home?"

Dan laughed out loud. "Me? Turn *my*self in?" He laughed even harder. "You're hilarious, Mark. You just think you can say anything." He lowered it to a chuckle. "Turn myself in." He pointed to the right again. "And here."

Mark made the turn.

Dan leaned over the backseat in a friendly manner and said to MJ, "Do you know what a rubric is, honey?"

MJ hazarded, "A puzzle?"

"Yes!" Dan said. "A puzzle. Smart kid! Your mom was right."

Mark said, "Where is her mother?"

Dan looked at him.

"Where is Anne?"

Dan continued to stare at him a moment, then turned back to face MJ again. He scrunched up his face at her. "Unless you're thinking of a Rubik's cube. You're not thinking of a Rubik's cube, are you?"

"No."

Dan said, "Good. Do you know what else it is, a rubric?"

"No."

Dan turned to his driver. "Mark?" he said patronizingly, like a demented gameshow host.

Mark gritted his teeth harder than he thought possible and tried to sound calm. "No."

Dan said, "A title. A name. A label for something important. A *legend*."

Mark said, "So now you think you're a legend?"

"No, no," Dan said. "Not me. *You*." He smiled wide. "You still don't know, do you?"

"Know what?" Mark said, out of patience entirely. He hazarded a guess. "You killed them all."

"No," Dan said. "*You* killed them all."

Mark chanced a dead-on hard look, the face he put on to challenge a lying arrestee—but something suddenly felt dead wrong.

Dan seemed to sense it. He nodded, grinning, and said, "Uh-huh." Leading.

MJ said, "What does he mean, Daddy? Who did you kill?"

Before Mark could respond, Dan said, "Yeah, Daddy. Who did you kill?"

Mark was beginning to sweat. He had almost forgotten the pounding in his head.

Dan said, "You don't know, do you? You don't remember. You don't remember anything, do you? All that booze and those pills. The scotch, the fancy imported beer. The Ambien."

"What's to remember?" Mark said.

Dan said, "How many concussions have *you* had?"

Mark turned away, looked out his driver's window, and ground his teeth so hard he lost some porcelain.

Dan nodded jovially and turned back to MJ. "It's also a color: rubric. Red. Like blood." He raised his eyebrows and nodded at her.

Mark could sense MJ's fear and pictured her trying to shrink herself up even smaller, to fold into the seat and become invisible.

Dan turned his gaze back to her father. "See how it all fits together?"

"No," Mark said. "Is there a point to any of this?" He made certain to sound angry and out of patience, but all he could feel was the puddling sweat under his shirt.

Dan said, "Of course there is. Turn in here." They were almost at a lone country church, small and white, pristine in the flat open green of the land.

The sky shone a vivid blue, cloudless. Clear as Jesus.

Dan said, muddying up everything, "It's a puzzle. A very difficult puzzle involving blood and legends, names and places, people and their misdeeds. The inhumanity of humanity."

Mark said, "I don't think I'm up for playing games." What he was up for was killing Dan Black and ending all of this—whatever it was, what it had become—even if it meant erasing himself.

His *memories* or lack of them.

Dan said, "Not a game, Mark. A puzzle. They're different. Pull in here."

He indicated the last space, from which they could see that another car was parked around back in the pastor's spot. Mark was momentarily hopeful, but no one was visible.

Then he realized the silver car was Dan's Mazda. He'd already been here. How had he gotten back to the farmhouse?

"In we go!" Dan said jubilantly and got out. He held the Ruger on them.

As they walked toward the front doors of the vestibule, Dan said, "All good puzzles involve clues. The good ones, the good puzzles, like great stories, have satisfying conclusions—after some great sacrifice, of course." He then said politely, "MJ. If you would be so kind as to open the door for your father so I can keep my eye on him."

"Yes, sir," she said.

Dan beamed. "You hear that, Mark? Despite you, she is a pleasant, well-mannered young lady. She learned patience and respect in spite of your awful ways. Despite you being a horrible father."

MJ said, "You say spite too much and he's not a horrible father, he's a good father."

"Sure he is, honey. You keep telling yourself that. But we all know better. And if we don't, we will!" He was ebullient, delighted with his gambit.

He waved the gun at Mark to lead the way inside. Mark went through the first set of doors. Dan nodded at MJ to follow, but said in a low voice, "You keep being nice or I won't save the bad part of the story until later."

MJ kept her fear to herself and went inside. Dan followed.

When Mark opened the inner doors, he heard Andy say, "Daddy? Daddy!"

Mark looked up to see that his son had been attached to the large cross behind the altar as if crucified.

Mark said, "Jesus Christ. Andy!" and ran to get him.

Dan laughed, said, "That was a good one," and fired the .40-cal Ruger.

The sound was overwhelming in the small, reverberant sanctuary and did its job. Mark stopped short. Plaster rained down from the ceiling on him and MJ.

Dan said calmly, "Right. Not so fast."

Mark glowered. MJ clung to her father. He put his arm around her.

Dan said, "Sweet. Touching. But we're in a church here. I think a confession is in order. Anyone?" He looked around. "Mark?"

Mark said, low, "That's a Catholic thing. This is a Methodist church."

Dan said, "So there is *Method* to this madness," with eyes and lips wide.

Mark had had enough. "What the fuck do you want!"

Dan yelled, "In a *holy* place?! In front of the *kids*?!" As if he was actually shocked.

Mark said, even lower than before, "What... do you want?"

"That's better," Dan said. "You need to show respect for the church and its antiquities." Then he asked, "Is that the right word?" He pondered it. "You know what I mean. Its hallowed practices." He thought again. "Do I mean hallowed?" He pretended to be puzzled and said, "It's puzzling, isn't it? Like a rubric!"

Mark repeated. "What... do you want?"

Dan said casually, "It's simple, really. I want the murderer of my children to pay for his sins. What better place to start the road to redemption than a church?" He pointed around with the Ruger. "And not just any church, either. Right, Mark?" His voice went sing-songy. "You know what I mean? Do you, do you?" Then he said in his normal voice, "Yes. You *do*."

Mark broke out in fresh sweat.

> *Mark is twelve, his sister ten. They are in church, the same church, sitting next to their father who somehow looks even colder and meaner. Every man around them is wearing a dark suit, every woman a somber dress.*
>
> *Their father wears a khaki workshirt. Stained.*
>
> *They are all looking straight ahead where, under the same large wooden crucifix, Mark's mother lies in a coffin. Her death makeup is heavy.*

Dan said, "Killed herself, huh?" He was asking Mark. Then he looked at MJ on the floor and Andy on the cross. "That was the official report, kids." He nodded as if letting them in on the facts. "'Cause you know: her brother, your father's uncle, your great-uncle, killed himself too. So, it was a natural fit—the natural thing to say, the natural conclusion. Suicide being natural. In your family."

MJ shifted with the youthful discomfiture at hearing the word—the concept of self-death, of choosing to die, then doing it. She looked at her father for explanation.

He looked at Dan, imagining Dan's immediate death.

Andy said pitifully, "Can I get down now, Daddy?"

Dan screamed, "Not yet! Shut up!"

Then he turned back toward Mark, quiet and pensive. "Strange thing, though," he said, again as if pondering the situation. He scratched his forehead. "The angle of the bullet—you know, its, uh, trajectory—came from down low, from... behind." Using Mark's gun, he contorted more than was necessary to get the gun behind his back and down at a level even with the back of his knees. "Like this. Like... *bang!*"

The kids jumped. Even Mark jumped. "Goddammit, Dan. That isn't fucking funny," he said.

"*Church*!" Dan screamed at him.

MJ started crying. Andy started crying. Mark continued sweating and glaring. He told Dan to, "Lighten up, man. They're kids."

"So..." Dan said, careless, and re-contorted to show where the shot might have come from. "It's kind of low. Like a small person might have done it. Might have shot his mother." Dan then acted as if he had made an unconscious error. "Or his wife, I meant to say. I'm just saying, it's kind of weird, huh? Mother, wife, dead, suicide, low shot she couldn't have made..." He stared, holding the look of question.

No one moved.

Dan said to Mark, "You're sweating."

Mark was sweating *a lot*.

MJ said, "What's he talking about, Daddy? Did Mommy... shoot herself? What happened? Did you shoot her?"

"Honey, no," Mark said. "He's talking about your grandmother. You never knew her. You never met her. She... died—"

"She was shot to death," Dan cut in.

Mark went on to MJ, undeterred. "The service was held here in this church."

"Did she kill herself?" MJ asked.

Mark answered her, but his eyes never left Dan's. "That's what the forensics report said, sweetheart."

MJ said, "Like Dr. Maltese?"

"Right," her father said. Dr. Maltese was a doctor who did autopsies for the department. "Like her."

Dan said to MJ, "But!" and made her jump again. Then he said, "Do you know who did your *granny's* autopsy? Sheriff Booker T Gladstone. Really! See, in some places, the police departments can't afford a real doctor, or they have a law that says the coroner doesn't have to *be* a real doctor, that it can be just about anyone. So, in those places—places like, well, right here in this little hick town, just outside the Big City!—sometimes the Sheriff appoints *himself*! That's what Booker T Gladstone did. You know who voted for *him*? Who went out door-to-door for him, getting votes from all his alcoholic wife-beating friends? Your Grampa! Your daddy's daddy! Isn't that fascinating?"

MJ's brow furrowed, but it was nothing compared to Mark's.

Dan said, "So when your grandmother, Mama Bee, they called her, when she died, Sheriff Booker T—that was really his name by the way—do you know anything about Booker T and the MGs?"

Mark could stand no more. "Dan! What are you doing?"

"Telling the truth!"

"They're *kids*!"

"Right!" Dan shouted back "And they need to understand what they might become when they get to be adults! They need to know about gene pools. About inherited traits. Like suicide. Like *murder*! Hell, they need to know about Booker T and the MGs! Their sound was classic! 'Green Onions?' I mean c'mon. Classic! And they were one of the first integrated soul bands. They had white guys!" Dan turned to MJ and said, "He's *colored*, ya know. Booker T. Not *Sheriff* Booker T, now. He was *white*-white. A real redneck cop. Not like your daddy. He'd never be racist. He'd even be okay with you being in a colored soul band! Say, Booker T and the MJs. Get it? Cool, huh?"

Mark shouted, "All right, I've had enough of this shit!"

"*Church*!" Dan screamed. He raised the Ruger, aimed at Mark, and cocked the small hammer.

Mark stood still. "May I at least get my son off that cross?"

Dan said, as if marveling at the notion, "Your *son* on the cross? Your son on the *cross*? Oh my. I hadn't thought of that." Of course he had. And further, "That makes you... well... God!"

Mark hung his head and muttered, "Aw, Jesus, Dan."

"No, no, no, Mark!" Dan spurted. "Not Jesus. Well—I mean, holy trinity notwithstanding..." He waved the gun and shrugged like a comedian. "Your *son* on the *cross* is what I'm really saying. That it makes you God. I mean, at the very least, it gives you the power over life and death. Doesn't it?"

Mark didn't respond.

"Like with your *mother*?" Dan asked *innocently*.

Then he looked at Mark's daughter and said, "So anyway, MJ, to finish the story. Granny was shot in the head by nobody really knows who and the Sheriff was the coroner, but wasn't a real coroner and didn't know shit about—"

"*Church!*" MJ yelled at him.

For a moment, Dan was dumbstruck. Then he laughed as if he'd just heard the funniest thing in his life. "Oh my God! She's a stitch, Mark! Where did she get that sense of humor when you are so completely and utterly humor*less*!" He looked at the girl. "That was priceless, MJ." He shook his head as if thoroughly enjoying her gibe and went on. "Anyway, blah-blah-blah, Granny, the gunshot, Grampa on the floor with a gun, or maybe a kid has the gun and hates his mother for something, maybe letting his father beat him... I don't know, it's all pretty murky stuff. No one knows for sure." He shook his head as if he was trying to comfort them.

MJ was not comforted. "I don't understand what you're saying."

"It's okay, you will." Dan was apparently done for the moment and told Mark, "You can get him down." He waved the .40 at Andy, over the altar.

Mark turned away.

Instantly Dan said, "Wait a minute, wait a minute!"

Mark's shoulders drooped and he stopped. He turned back slowly to find Dan walking toward him, saying, "I didn't finish the other part of the story, the puzzle piece. I got the one, the puzzling puzzle piece, but I forgot the other—the God part." He came very close, holding the gun up to within an inch of Mark's nose. "The part where you're God, where you hold the fate of another man's life in your hands."

Mark's eyes never left Dan's, which never left Mark's.

Dan said, "The fate of lots of men. And women. And children."

Mark said, "I'd say you're the one holding the tool of fate right now. Dan."

Dan's expression didn't change for several seconds, then he said, "Good choice. Cut him down." He was so confident he turned his back on Mark.

It took everything Mark had not to attack.

Dan said, without looking back, "Another good choice. Mark." Then he yelled, "Cut him down! Get your boy off the goddam cross!" He spun around quickly and warned MJ, "And if you say 'church' again, I'll blow your little fucking head off." He pointed the gun at her.

He looked serious. MJ didn't move.

Dan laughed out. "I'm kidding! I wouldn't hurt a kid!" He lowered the gun. "That's your daddy's job."

Mark tried to ignore Dan but couldn't. He dared not.

He climbed up on the altar and bit at the duct tape to start a tear and get Andy off the cross. He asked his son, "Did he put you up here?" while gently removing the tape.

Andy said, "I don't know. I was asleep."

Dan said, "How'd that happen? Did you dope them, Mark? Give them some of your meds? Some of the strong medications your psychiatrist prescribed for you when you were sick?"

MJ said, "You went to a psychiatrist, Daddy? When were you sick? What was wrong?"

Mark turned to her and said, "Nothing, honey."

Dan said mockingly, "Oh yeah, *something* honey!"

"What, Daddy?" MJ was more worried than ever.

"Nothing, sweetie. I promise. After I shot at the man that night—" Mark snapped a look at Dan.

Dan said, "Don't look at me. I didn't shoot at anyone."

Mark looked back at MJ. "After that night—you remember, right?"

MJ nodded slightly, probably not *wanting* to remember.

"The department made me go see a psychiatrist."

Dan said, "And well they should! You were *nuts* to be shooting up your neighborhood like that. *Our* neighborhood. What if I'd been out there walking around? You might've shot me, or some innocent person in the neighborhood. Old Mrs. Hoddeker. What if you'd shot her? You like Mrs. Hoddeker, don't you, MJ? Your daddy stole her car."

MJ looked at her father, askew.

Mark said, "I didn't steal it, MJ. I borrowed it."

"Walked right in and took it from her," Dan said confidently.

So, he *had* been watching.

"Well," Dan said, "don't worry. Your daddy's shrink straightened him right out. And I mean straight out! Right, Dan? I mean Mark. Straight as an arrow. Right out. *Bamm!*"

He rocked his hips as if *doing it.*

"That's enough," Mark said—but he was thinking, *How the hell does this guy know so damn much about everything?*

He finally got Andy loose and soothed him with, "It's going to be okay."

Andy nodded, but Dan yelled, "It is *not* going to be okay! Mark! It's not! It never can be okay again! Not after what... you... *did*!"

He paced in a small circle in the main aisle between the pews and said, "You have no idea what it's like to lose your children, Mark. Three of them. All three. *Three children*! To have them murdered in your home. Outside your home. 'In your own backyard,' like they say, only *literally.* While you're *there.* And you can do nothing to stop it. Nothing! There is *nothing you can do to stop it!"*

Silence fell into the church like a sour prayer.

Dan reiterated, "It's not going to be okay in any way. Now, let's go."

Once he had everyone back in Mrs. Hoddeker's tan sedan, the kids reflexively reached for their seatbelts. Dan told them, "No seatbelts, kids. We don't want Daddy crashing into light poles on purpose." He put his own seatbelt on and told Mark, "You either. No belt."

Mark looked at him blankly, started the car and pulled out of the church lot.

No one would find the dead minister in the baptistry for ten hours.

Chapter 32

The throbbing in Mark's head returned once he had to concentrate on driving. The dull, flat ache had become deep, pulsing pain, as if his brain were on fire and somebody was inside his head stomping out the flames.

As if sensing that, understanding it, *feeling* it, Dan said, "Hurts, huh? Down deep. The kind of pain a man can't forget."

His parody of Mark fell on angry, deaf ears. Mark refused to look at him, but Dan was right. The pain was awful—from all of it.

Dan told Mark where to turn, then sat quietly as they drove along the old road next to the swift, wide river, gray under a darkening sky.

Mark finally asked the obvious. "Where is she?" The only one still missing. Mark's hope that she was alive had increased when he took Andy down from the cross.

Dan said, taking in the scenery as if on summer vacation, "You mean Anne? Your wife? Mother of your two beautiful children? Your two children who are still alive?"

He looked at Mark with the same feigned innocence he'd been irritating Mark with for over an hour. Mark looked away and drove in silence.

Dan said, "Am I becoming tiresome?"

Mark said nothing.

Dan said, as if he was deeply put out, "It just gets so hard to remember sometimes—you know, the details. What's really important. You know what I mean. It happens to you all the time."

Mark exploded. "I don't know what the *fuck* you're talking about!"

Dan looked back at MJ and shouted, "*Car!*" and laughed.

MJ made a mad pouty face at him and Dan returned it. Then he looked over at Mark. "Of course you don't. And again, with the kids! The language! It's no wonder they're so screwed up. What kind of a father *are* you?"

Mark said, "The kind whose kids are still alive." As nasty a thing as he'd ever uttered in his life.

Little Andy went along with it. "Yeah," he said, "and we're not messed up in the head," clearly recalling what his sister had said at the breakfast table a few weeks before.

Dan watched MJ high-five Andy in the back seat but said nothing. He stewed for a few seconds—then he laughed. "You almost had me, there, Mark. I almost wanted to kill you just now." He chuckled some more. "Good job, good job! Little poke, there. Jab to the jaw! Pow! Well done." He sighed. "But alas, that would ruin everything."

Mark said, "Yeah? Why's that."

"Because then neither of us would be getting what we want."

"And what's that?" Mark bit.

"Closure," Dan said. "Solution of the rubric." Then he said sharply, "Pull over! Now!"

Responding more out of reflex than reason, Mark whipped the Dodge off the road onto the shoulder. There was just enough room for all four tires on the grass. A heavily weeded bank led down to the water with a few trees here and there—enough to block the road from view of someone down below.

Dan pointed Mark's gun at Mark's head and said, "Everyone out, down the bank. Chop-chop! Let's go or I blow your daddy's brains out all over old Mrs. Hoddeker's nice car. Out!"

The kids jumped out, looking scared.

Dan yelled, "Down the bank! To the water! Go! We're right behind!" He waved the Ruger at the ignition. "Turn it off. Wastes gas."

Mark had wanted to leave it running in case there was a chance to make a run for it, but he turned off the car in deference to dying. Dan held out his hand for the keys. Mark handed them over.

Dan said, "Thank you," in a nasty tone, and Mark got out.

Dan got out on the other side and hollered down to the kids, "Don't try running away or it'll be your fault when I shoot your daddy in the head!"

Mark looked across the roof of the car. "What the fuck are you doing, Dan?"

"Making sure that vengeance is done and done properly in the eyes of the Lord," Dan said.

"Christ." Mark shook his head and walked around the back of the car.

Dan said, "You keep saying that. I didn't know you were so religious."

"Yeah, that's fuckin' hilarious." Mark got as close to Dan as he thought he could with his own gun pointed at his face and said, "You hurt one hair on the head of either of my kids and I *will* kill you."

Dan shrugged. "I already did that and I'm still alive. Now, quit bragging about what a great father you are when we both know you're not, and go down the bank before I kill one of your precious children in front of you."

Mark was again reduced to glaring.

Dan said, "Or maybe *you'd* like to do it. Kill one of them in front of *me*." He stood, relaxed. "It's always an option." He paused seductively. "You're a take-charge kinda guy, Mark. Everyone knows that. Might save them some pain later. You never know... about anything. Right?"

When Mark said no more, Dan said, "That's what I thought," and nodded toward the river.

Mark went.

Dan yelled over his hostage's head, "We can see you kids, so no monkey business!"

MJ and Andy probably wanted to conspire but wouldn't know where to start, so they stood still as their father joined them. Dan ordered them into a neat row with the barrel of the gun. They were just two feet from the rushing water. The river was a good forty yards across at this point, deep and fast-moving.

Mark sighed. "What are we doing?"

Dan said, "I gotta take a leak," and unzipped his pants. He pulled his penis out and immediately started urinating.

Mark turned his shocked kids away.

"What?" Dan said. "Are you one of those uptight families that pretend natural bodily functions don't exist?" He shook his head in mock puzzlement. "Jeez, how are you ever going to explain death to them? Mark."

He peed and peed and peed and peed. It seemed as if it would never stop. He said, "Man, I really had to go, huh kids?" He pretended to be making arcs in the air or writing his name. "Nothing like a good wee-wee, huh?" He repeated, "Wee-wee," and laughed.

Mark acted disgusted and turned away—but he could see MJ's eyes and she could see his. He moved his eyes to the side, towards the river.

MJ looked closer, as if she knew he was trying to tell her something but didn't know what.

Mark flipped his eyes toward the rapidly moving water again. Twice.

MJ looked at the water without moving her head.

Dan was still peeing. He said, "Phew, iced tea. It just does a number on me. Number One! Get it kids? Number One?"

Andy nodded reflexively and looked back. Dan made his eyes wide and wiggled his dick proudly.

Andy looked away.

Dan announced, "Last drops!" and flipped them off. He'd started to tuck when Mark turned and took a step toward him.

Leaving his cock out so he could raise the gun, Dan said, "Don't do anything stupid, Mark. It's too early. Someone could get hurt." There was no humor or irony in his voice.

Nor was there in Mark's. "No. We wouldn't want that."

"Not yet," Dan said and smiled. He brazenly lowered the gun to tuck himself in.

Mark made his move. It wasn't one Dan could have expected.

As Dan raised the gun again, Mark put the butt of his hand over the muzzle of the .40 and shouted, "MJ, go!"

On his command, MJ leapt into the surging water. The current instantly sucked her under and she disappeared.

Mark shoved on the muzzle. The gun went off and a bullet went through Mark's hand. Andy screamed and hit the dirt. Mark growled from the pain but pushed harder, shoving the slide off the back of the gun, rendering it useless.

Now Dan realized what Mark was doing—what he had done.

He dropped the bottom half of the Ruger, took a step back, reached around behind him and pulled a Smith & Wesson .357 revolver from the back of his pants.

He fired the gun right next to Mark's ear, deafening him, then dodged around him like a dancer and put the big-bore magnum to little Andy's face. Mark dropped the useless slide on the ground, his hand bloody and hurting.

Dan shoved the fat magnum muzzle against Andy's temple and yelled, "Don't make me do it, Dad! Not now! Not when we're so close!"

Mark's head hurt, his hand hurt, blood ran off his fingers, and he could hear nothing but deafening ringing on the right side of his head.

But the good news was that he could see past Dan, to the other side of the river, down a few hundred yards where MJ was climbing out of the water onto the opposite bank. Dan must have sensed what Mark was seeing because he snuck a quick look, just in time to see MJ top the bank and run off into a narrow field for the woods beyond.

There would be houses somewhere.

For the briefest moment, it looked to Mark as if Dan might snap—Mark imagined thoughts of killing Andy, then Mark, running through Dan's addled brain like bad meth.

But Dan caught himself and managed a small laugh. "Nice. Good. Good job. You win that round. I forgot about the swim team. My bad. She medaled in the hundred meter just last spring. Yeah, my bad, my bad, you win. Uh-huh. You win that round. Well done! *Dear god in heaven*!" He shouted the last words to the clear sky.

Mark said flatly, "May I have my son now?"

Dan looked at Mark's bleeding hand—the hole in it—and said, "Was it worth it?" He had a hazy look of appreciation in his eyes, like a happy torturer thinking he'd done the right thing.

Mark said, "You bet your fucking life."

Dan hollered with glee, "You're on! It's a bet!"

***

Dan marched the two Youngs back up the bank to the car. Andy got in the back and put on his seatbelt automatically—as kids do—but he was probably just emotionally and psychologically numb. He stared straight ahead at the back of the front seat.

Dan gestured at Mark's bleeding hand. "You don't have AIDS, do you?"

Mark said, "I need a rag or I won't be able to hold onto the steering wheel."

Dan thought a moment. "Well, I suppose you have a point. We don't want to get in a wreck and all die. Not *now*." He reached for the glove compartment. "Let's see if Mrs. Hoddeker left a hanky or anything in here." Sure enough. "Look at that!" Dan said as he pulled out the dainty handkerchief. "Old ladies, huh? Gotta love 'em."

He held the hanky out to Mark, but when Mark reached for it, Dan snatched it back, grinning. Then he handed it to Mark for real. "Just messin' with you, man. You know, like buddies do."

Mark wrapped the cloth around his hand.

Dan dropped his grinning baboon act and said plainly, "Drive."

Mark said, "Where to?"

Dan said, "That's for you to figure out."

Where Anne was.

Mark turned the key and decided to start at the beginning. He put the bland Dodge in Drive and drove three miles to their old high school in town—what was left of it—passing the deteriorating stone structure slowly. Dan looked over at the building, then turned to face forward again.

Mark kept driving.

Next, Mark drove to a run-down neighborhood and parked in front of a small, old house with cement shingles on the sides and asphalt on the roof.

Dan said, "Your first little love nest." He didn't look. Mark realized he didn't have to; he'd already been by.

Mark continued driving, his mind running every combination he could conjure. Since Dan wasn't yelling or telling Mark he was wasting time going in the wrong direction, going to a different town or a different *part* of town, he kept driving.

Dan started singing, one note, with the words, "Labba-dabba-dabba," then an octave lower, "Hooba-dooba-dooba-dooba," then a thirties-style climbing melody, "Labba-dabba-hooba-looba-dooba-doo," that ended low.

Mark looked at him.

Dan shrugged playfully and said, "I don't know. I just like to make things up sometimes."

Mark said, "Yeah, I noticed," and Dan giggled cutely like a ditzy flapper.

He kept singing his made-up song, but lower, to himself, which gave Mark some relief—and time to think while driving.

He knew to avoid the main drags. If Dan had any suspicions that Mark was trying to attract attention, the gun would come into play immediately and Andy might be shot—so Mark drove on.

He correctly guessed the way at a crossroads around the back side of town. He knew he'd guessed right because when he hesitated, then turned left, he saw Dan smile slightly and sing his idiotic tune a bit louder.

Then Mark guessed wrong, pulling up to the cemetery where both his parents were buried.

"No, no, no!" Dan said, clearly frustrated. "We're done with that part of the story, Mark! Come on, man. Think! Think ahead. Think fast. Think it through! You can do it! I know you can!"

And he sang some more.

Then he flopped around in his seat to face Mark. "Do you really think I would do something so melodramatic as stage the final scene, the last piece of the puzzle, in a *cemetery*? What, do you think I'm

Stephen King? Come on! This is bigger than that, different than that, more real than that. This is real life, not some fake scary story. This is real terror. We are dealing with everyone's deepest emotions here, Mark. Everyone's deepest fears."

He paused, then said, *asked*, "What do you fear to lose the most, Mark? Your job, your family? No! Your mind. That's what scares you the most, Mark. That you've lost your grip on reality, Mark. That you've lost control, Mark.

"You're a control freak, Mark. I can tell. All this shit, these cheesy little theatrics I'm pulling, they bother you, Mark. Not because they're a pathetic waste of everyone's time, but because you can't do anything about them. About any of it. I hold all the cards.

"I know everything there is to know about you and your precious little family, Mark. Everything!"

Mark finally cut in. "And how *do* you know all this?"

"A little bird told me," Dan said with a sardonic smile. "A little bird who knows everything."

Mark understood. "Anne." It pained him to say it—to think it.

Dan said nothing but smiled like an ass—all part of the act—and sang, "Labba-*dab*ba-hoobo-*loo*ba-dooba-*doo*!"

Mark said, "She didn't tell you where she was." That was not possible.

"No, no, of course not," Dan said. "*My* wife told me where she was just before you killed her."

"I didn't kill your wife!"

"Oh yes, you did," Dan said. He leaned closer and spoke softly. "You really don't remember, do you? You honest-to-god have no idea what this is about, do you?"

Mark said, honestly, "No."

"It's about *you, you dumb fuck*!" Dan was suddenly red in the face and spitting.

Andy started crying again.

Dan leaned over the backseat and screamed at him. "Shut up! Shut up! You cry one more goddam little goddam tear, and I'll fuckin' kill your father! Your worthless, murdering father!"

Andy pinched up his face as tightly as he could, but the tears continued pouring from his quivering little body.

Dan turned back to Mark. "This is about you, Mark. You and me and all you did and all you didn't do and how you're a lousy father and a terrible cop. That makes you a worthless human being. Not *even* human. Like some beast. Some heartless, soulless, useless *animal* that should be shot. Put to death for being so completely fucking worthless." He got close again. "Everything is going to get sorted out, though. You will understand, and you *will* be held accountable. This much I promise." He looked at his watch.

Mark knew why. MJ would likely have found a sympathetic ear by now. Calls would have been made. People—probably lots of people—were out looking for the Hoddeker's beige sedan. No doubt, law enforcement had the license plate number and had posted a BOLO.

Time had to be running out.

Dan sat back in his seat and looked forward, showing his obvious intent to speed things along. "Okay," he said. "Let's say you're a little bird and you're cooped up in a cage. Now, that sounds bad, because you don't like being cooped up."

"Anne is terrified of small spaces. She has claustrophobia, you fucking maniac."

"Right," Dan said calmly. "But what if this little, special, loving bird was cooped up in a very special place? A place that was so special to her that she could hold those memories in her heart and they would carry her through the worst ordeal of her life? A place only someone equally special to her would know about.

"What about *that*?" Dan looked at Mark. Mark looked at him.

Then Mark floored it. Dan smiled.

They had been so close.

Chapter 33

In less than three minutes, Mark pulled into the old train yard with the abandoned grain silos and rusting water tower. Everything was decomposing. The side rail hadn't been used in twenty years. Tornadoes from a decade before had torn roofs away, leaving twisted metal trusses that looked like ancient mythical beasts, writhing and dying. Dead.

The county had long ago condemned the entire site and posted numerous signs declaring the area "Unsafe!" and warning the curious to "Keep Out!" due to the "Possibility of Injury or Death!" Everyone stayed far away.

So, there was no one for miles.

"Much better," Dan said sarcastically. "I only had to give the whole piece to you." He sighed. "But some of us need help from time to time." He turned to Mark. "You're just lucky *you* got it. Just in time." Then he said exuberantly, "Everybody out for the grand finale!"

Dan hopped out of the car and strolled around, taking in the sights as if he was in the gardens at Versailles—the version with collapsing warehouses, junked trucks on blocks, an old rail office, crumbling repair shop, and twin dilapidated silos.

The tall water tower.

The ladder was so rusted that kids had even stopped going up to add graffiti. Not that there wasn't plenty—just none newer than five years ago.

Dan shaded his eyes, looked up, and said, "So romantic. What a great place to lose your cherry. So great was it that the young couple came back years later. Right here! Where a strong young swimmer was conceived. A swimmer who won't get to see the end of the story, the solution to the puzzle. Too bad, really. I mean, it's sad." He pretended to be sad, then he perked up again. "But her time will come!"

Mark watched Dan's performance carefully. Anne could be anywhere, in any one of the buildings or silos. All would be terrifying to her if she was confined inside, but when Dan made his little love speech and grinned wide, Mark knew for sure.

He ran for the tower, Andy right behind, trying to keep pace.

Dan shouted after them, "There's no rush! Really! Not *now*." He ambled that way. "Not anymore."

Is Anne dead? was all Mark could think.

Dan shouted ahead, "If she's dead, it's your fault, Mark. All your fault!"

Mark was at the ladder and starting to climb when a gunshot pinged into the metal not a foot from his head. "Jesus!"

"There we go with the religious references again," Dan said as he sauntered closer. "I had no idea, Mark! None whatsoever. You're a true believer."

Mark stood still, trembling with hatred. He put his hand on the ladder again, but Dan said, "Hold up. You and Jesus, your son there."

Looking worried, Andy said, "Daddy, don't leave me here."

Dan said, pouting, "Yeah, Daddy. Don't leave him here."

Mark understood. "He can't climb up that," he said. "He's afraid of heights." The tree in their backyard was a molehill to this mountainous tower.

"Exactly why he's going first!" Dan said, obviously proud of his plan.

Mark stepped back onto the ground, wanting desperately to attack Dan. To kill him where he stood. But Dan was just far enough away to guarantee that Mark would take the next shot to his head or body, then Andy would really be left alone. So, instead, he said, "You have all our little fears catalogued and worked into your stupid game."

"It's not stupid, and it's not a game," Dan corrected. "No, I already told you that." He turned to Andy. "What is it, And'?"

"A rubric?"

"Right! A rubric! Right at the end of the mystery!"

Mark had never seen Dan so happy.

"Up, up, up, up, up you go, Ando-Man! Up the tower of fate!"

"Nobody calls me that," Andy said.

"Well, I do!" Dan said. "Because I have *this*." He held up the .357. "I get to call you anything I want! See? It's all so easy! I just don't understand why your father keeps denying that he understands everything we're doing here and *why*. It's like he's pretending not to care, Rando. Not to care about you or me or *anything*."

Andy said, "I don't care about you. You're mean. You locked your kids in the basement and beat them with chains."

"No," Dan said patronizingly. "No, no. That's just a dirty, vicious little rumor." He paused. "I never used *chains*."

Andy stared blankly.

Dan said, "That's a joke, Andrew."

Andy looked at the ground.

"No sense of humor," Dan said. "Just like your old man." Dan sighed heavily, dramatically. "Anyway, we gotta get going. Let's go. One rung at a time. Come on. Go!"

Andy didn't move.

Dan aimed the revolver at Mark and said, "Move aside. Go on, go on." He waved Mark away.

Mark moved away.

"Farther," Dan said.

Marked dragged himself away to a spot he guessed satisfied Dan's needs.

Dan said, "Perfect," then he stuck his gun in his pants and lifted Andy onto the third rung of the rusty ladder. "It's safe, Andy-Man. I've been up and down it at least once." He looked back at Mark and grinned.

Mark said, "Jesus, Dan. He's a kid."

Andy clutched the rails as if he were already halfway up the tall ladder.

Dan said, "Oh, that's good, that's great. Touché! Jesus, the kid of God. God speaks! It's all so... spiritual and perfect. Warms your heart, it really does." Then he turned to Andy and said, "Now go on up or Daddy dies." He stepped away, pulled out his gun and aimed at Mark.

Andy said, "But I'm afraid of high places."

"Yeah," Dan said, "it's called acrophobia. Daddy's crazy-head doctor knew all about it. She knew lots of big words that you don't because you're just a dumb little kid. But let me ask you this, And-o: Are you more afraid to climb the ladder—or see me shoot your daddy in the face and kill him? Think fast! There'll be lots of blood!"

"I don't know," Andy whined.

"Then Daddy dies." Dan cocked the hammer back.

Andy insisted, "But I'm afraid!"

Dan fired.

The bullet zinged past Mark's ear and crashed into a building behind him. The tinkling of glass followed. Andy whimpering.

Dan cocked the heavy Smith & Wesson again.

Andy was crying openly again. He said, "It's too hard for me!"

Dan said, like a smart bully, "You're just a big chicken. I'm telling you, if you don't do this, and your daddy dies because of it, you'll blame this on yourself the rest of your life. And let me tell you, from experience, those things don't go away. You never get over them, do you, Mark? You know, when someone dies. Someone in your family..."

> *Mark's sister is playing with dolls on the floor. Their mother is at the kitchen sink, doing dishes. Father is at the table, silent in his work khakis, cleaning his new hunting rifle – the one Dan used in the dream to kill himself.*
>
> *Mark runs into the kitchen, laughing, playing. Trips over a doll and falls into his father's chair.*
>
> *The gun goes off.*
>
> *It hits Mother in the back of the skull and blows the top of her head off – blood, bone and brain tissue splatter the ceiling. She falls forward into the sink, face-first on the edge, then rolls back and drops to the floor, dead. Red pours from her fatal head wound.*
>
> *The family stares in horrified silence.*

Dan said mockingly to Mark, "'Thing like that stays with a man a long time.'" Then he turned to Andy. "Up. Now. No more whining."

Dan stepped away and told Mark, "Help him. Let's go. Time's a'wasting."

Mark was so full of hate and confused turbid memories, he wasn't sure he could walk. But he found enough focus to come over and put his hands on the sides of the ladder around his son's body.

"Go on, son. I'll be right behind you. I won't let you fall. I promise."

Suddenly Dan was close. Mark could feel the barrel of the revolver pressed against his back. If Dan were to shoot that big .357, the bullet would go clean through Mark and Andy both.

Dan whispered, "This is really the best thing—for you and your family. You have to come clean, Mark. You have to tell them how you let them down, how you let down so many people—including me. *Especially* me. And how so many people are dead, all because of you. In your heart, you know you're an awful killer. A murderer of the worst sort. An apathetic, blind-to-himself, selfish bastard who let everyone down and now everyone's dead or dying. It's only a matter of time and truth." He stepped back, raised his voice, and said, "Up we go! Don't look down."

Andy climbed shakily, Mark close behind, keeping his chest against his son's butt to give him confidence. It seemed to be working.

Once they were a safe distance ahead, Dan tucked his gun in his pants and followed.

When the climbers reached the catwalk that circled the water tank a hundred feet up, Dan told them to move around to the right where another rusted ladder would take them onto the top of the tank, another twenty feet.

No railing.

The wind had kicked up in anticipation of an approaching cold front. They could see the leading edge working its way toward them. If they were still up here when the storm hit, the old enamel would be slick as owl snot and down they would go.

Andy grabbed each rung as if it would be his last and his father stayed close. On the last rung before the ladder curved around onto the top of the tank...

Andy slipped.

Mark caught him, but they both almost went tumbling.

Dan was right behind to cheerlead. "Good save, Dad!" he shouted happily, as if at a high school basketball game. "Now keep going. Up on top and across to the other side." He warned, "I will have my big gun on you."

Poor little Andy was so scared he peed himself, and it ran down onto Mark's pants. "I'm sorry, Daddy," he said. "I couldn't stop it."

"It's okay, son," Mark said. "Doesn't matter a bit. Just keep going. I'm right here."

When they reached the top and moved across, Dan came up, his .357 leading the way. He pretended he'd only just noticed. "Did you pee all over yourself, Ando? Jeez, it's just a little ladder." He moved closer. "Look down over the side. It's not so bad—a hundred and twenty feet. The architects wanted it to be exactly a hundred and twenty feet. And it is!" He grinned. "Don't you love it when things work out perfectly!"

Andy didn't look down.

Mark said, "Where is she?"

The increasing wind pushed at their bodies and made them unstable. The tower creaked, rattled, and shook. They could feel the damn thing swaying.

Andy clung to his father's leg.

Dan acted put out again. "Where else, Mark? Jeez. You think I'd bring you all the way up here for nothing?" Dan pretended to think that over and said, "Well, of course you do, but I wouldn't. I promise. We're almost there."

Mark looked over at the low, square entry hatch off to one side that opened upwards so someone could go down into the tank. He said to Dan, "You are a sick fuck."

"Me?" Dan said. "*You're* the killer."

Mark glared, then sat Andy down carefully, knelt with him and said, "Just sit here, son. Don't move. I'll be right back. I'm going to get Mommy. Okay?"

Andy gave a tiny nod. Wind shoved at him even as he sat.

Dan said, as if admiring Mark, "You're so good with kids. They trust you, inherently. Like that little ginger girl! Remember her? At the mall? You could've told her anything and she would have believed you." He seemed to marvel at that. "It's kind of creepy, isn't it?"

Mark stood and said, "She better be alive."

Dan pretended not to understand. "The little ginger girl? No, she's dead, Mark. You killed her. You don't remember?"

When Mark didn't bite, Dan said, "Oh, you mean *Anne*, your lovely wife. Now, that's a different story."

Mark couldn't help himself. He had to say it again—"She better be alive"—because at this point, he really didn't know what else to do.

Dan said, "Listen to you. Repeating yourself. Making demands. This is *my* rubric, dude. Get a move on. Go get your wife. Try not to kill her like you did mine."

"I did not kill your fucking wife!"

"Mark! Language! Your son! I know we're not in a church, in your church, you crazy little God, you. But still. Have some respect."

Mark clenched his teeth and went over to the horizontal door lid which stuck up six inches above the aerial tank. He pulled up on it, only to realize it was secured with the same kind of padlock Dan had used on the storm cellar door where he'd left MJ.

Mark said, "It's locked." He had moved beyond hatred at this point into something entirely different. Something new. More powerful than hate. Some opaque acceptance for whatever horrible thing was going to happen next, which tempered his temper and made him start thinking logically.

Dan had the key—didn't he?

Dan looked confused a moment, then said, "Oh! I have it. It's right here, hold on." He dug in his pockets dramatically, as if confused even further. "Well, I *thought* I had it. It was right here." He dug some more but produced no key. He shook his head and sighed as if baffled and apologetic. "Now, Mark, I am *sure* I brought that key. I could have sworn I put it right here in my left pocket." He looked up, grinning joyously. "Right in my left. Get it!"

Mark stared, certain this was just part of the game, and waited.

Dan dug in his pocket again and pulled out the key. "Ah! There it is. See? I knew I wouldn't forget something so important. Here."

He threw the set of keys to the side. They slid across the peeling enamel as if they were on ice.

"Daddy!" Andy yelled.

Mark stood up and dove for the key ring—caught it just before it went over the edge. He closed his eyes and sighed.

Dan said, "Did I say 'Good save, Dad' already? Yeah, I think I did. But nonetheless: Good save. Dad. Mark."

Mark refused to look at Dan anymore. He went back to the tank lid, opened the padlock with the third key, and threw the lock over the side.

Dan pretended to be surprised by that move by pretending to watch it go. "Oh. Good idea. That way I can't lock you up down in there with her. Great idea, yeah. Good plan. Dad. Mark." Then he said, "Unless I had another lock—say one that went with that second key there..." He pretended to look over the side.

Still refusing to look or to play along, Mark threw open the lid and said loudly, but not so loudly as to scare her, "Anne? Are you down there? Are you okay?"

No sound came back.

Mark swung around. "If she's not all right, we're going over the side together," he said to Dan.

Dan said, "Fine with me!" with the joy Mark had come to expect and detest.

Mark turned back to the black hole and said, "Anne, I'm here with Andy and Dan."

"Ah," Dan said. "Clever. She's been warned." Then he scoffed, "As if that will make any difference." He laughed cruelly and added, "Maybe she can't hear you."

Mark looked at him.

Dan said, "Maybe she's deaf—or 'deaf' has taken her. 'Deaf' like death, like ghetto idiots say. Inbreds from the *Souf.* You know, *Norf* Cair-*line*-uh. Redneck illiterates. You know the type, Mark. Grew up in the country in a quaint old farmhouse. *Hyuck-hyuck-hyuck.* 'Ooops, shot Mom!'"

Mark ignored him and started down into the dark, musty tank on the rustiest ladder yet.

As if to entertain himself, Dan leaned down close to Andy. "Your Mommy's just like you. She's afraid of things, too. She puts on a brave face, but she's just as big a scaredy-cat as you are. Like your sister's afraid of spiders and you're afraid of being up here. Well, Mommy's claustrophobic. She's afraid of being *in there*."

Andy said defiantly, "I know. Daddy said that."

Dan feigned surprise. "You were paying attention! You weren't just peeing all over yourself." Then he played supportive uncle. "Very mature. You're growing up already! So soon! Before you know it, you'll be as big a scaredy cat as your daddy. He's afraid of *everything*. Especially himself. He's just too scared to show it."

Andy sulked and looked away. Dan laughed as the wind pushed at him. Mark descended.

Down in the tank, he lowered himself carefully on the old, slippery metal rungs twenty feet down until his feet touched the floor. Then he saw her.

Anne lay in a fetal ball in the corner, not moving.

Mark moved to her and tried to turn her toward him, but she didn't budge. Dan had taped her in such a way that she couldn't move a millimeter and tied her to the water tank's depth gauge so she couldn't turn away or roll over. Her eyes were fixed, wide.

At least she was alive.

"I'm here, okay? I'm here to set you free and get you out of this damn thing. Okay?"

She didn't move. She couldn't.

A loud *ping!* startled them both, then Dan hollered down, "That'll save you some time."

Mark looked, saw the knife, and took it.

Dan said into the opening above, "Just don't think about using it on me. I'll be on the other side of the tank up here when you bring her up. Jus' me'n'Andy!"

Mark began cutting Anne's bonds.

Dan said, "You come up first, show the knife, then throw it over the side. Then you can come out and help your lovely wife. Pretty damn dark in there, huh? Dank and stinky. All that mildew. Like a cave. No bats, though! That's the good news..." His voice trailed off. He must have moved away from the opening.

As Mark worked feverishly in the faint light to cut the many bonds on his wife, he told her, "MJ got away. She swam the river like a champ. Made it to the other side and ran away. She's fine. Andy's up there. He's scared of being so high, but he's hanging in."

He didn't mention his own throbbing skull or gunshot hand.

Bang! A gunshot so loud and harsh Mark almost shit his pants. Anne might have if she wasn't blatantly numb to any feelings other than sheer terror.

Dan was back. He hollered down, "Fuck me that was loud. Everyone okay?" He pretended to peer in with interest. "It was a bitch getting her up here, let me tell you. It's a long damn way, and she bit me. Mark, she *bit* me. I had to give her three Xanax just to be able to carry her up here and get her down in there. Good thing I didn't feed her for four days."

Mark almost had Anne free.

Dan said, "But you see, they're all alive. I didn't hurt them, Mark. They're innocent. You're the one I'm after. You're the guilty one. Mark."

He moved away again. Mark could hear his footsteps on the hollow steel above.

The wind howling into the hole.

Mark removed the gags from his wife's mouth and Anne spilt her fears. "But he... he's afraid of heights... he's got to be terrified!" As bad as she had it, she was only concerned with her son's condition.

Mark appreciated that and assured her, "He did great. He's gonna be okay."

He helped Anne to her feet, only now realizing she was handcuffed. "Shit." As her legs were shaky, Mark had to hold her up.

He yelled up at the open hole, "She's cuffed, goddammit! Dan! Where's the key! Dan! Damn it, you freak!"

No sounds came from above. Were they even still up there? Mark hollered up, "Andy! Andy, are you up there? Are you okay, son?"

Nothing.

Anne screamed, "Andy! Andy, answer me! Andy it's me, Mommy! Are you okay?!"

Nothing.

Mark said, "Fuck." His brain refused to work, again. He said to his wife, "Okay. We're going up now."

Anne looked terrified.

He said, "We're getting out of here. Okay?"

Anne didn't respond.

He said, "I'll think of something. I promise."

His own promises felt empty.

He guided Anne to the ladder, her legs seeming stable now. As to her hands being restrained, he told her, "I'll hold you against the ladder—you just go up one rung at a time, one foot then the other. I'll make sure you don't fall. Okay, Anne? You understand?"

They stood at the base of the ladder. She turned to him and said, only now crying, "He made me tell him everything about us—about you—or he'd kill them, the kids."

"I know," Mark said. "It's okay. You had to. He didn't give you a choice."

Anne asked with desperation, "Why is he *doing* this?"

Mark said honestly, "I don't think I know. He's out of his fucking mind is all I see." He sighed. "Okay. Here we go."

He nodded at the ladder for her to start up. She looked at him, befuddled and shaken, as if searching for an answer, any glimmer that might give her some hope, that might make her feel the slightest bit better about anything that had happened.

Anything that was going to happen.

Mark knew her well enough to read her thoughts. And he knew himself well enough to know there was nothing he could say that would make either of them feel any better at that point. All he could come up with was, "We'll get through this. We always do."

Though she didn't appear to believe him, Anne nodded, then turned to start up the twenty-foot ladder, crying.

Climbing the slippery ladder without the use of her hands, which were still cuffed behind her, was not easy. But Mark did as he promised and swathed her in a warm embrace, keeping her against the cold metal, giving her just enough room to raise one foot at a time.

When they neared the top, Mark shouted up, "She's coming up first. It's the only way we could do it. But here's the knife."

He tossed it past her, up onto the top. They heard it land and clatter away. Still, no human sounds came from above them. Mark had only one thought.

Has Dan grabbed Andy and fled? Or worse.

Jumped with him.

Chapter 34

At the top of the ladder, with her wrists locked behind her back, Anne had to surrender to Mark's helping hands as he shoved her out of the hole onto the top of the tank. It didn't take her long to get righted and find Dan on the far side with Andy. They were by the edge, the increasing wind shoving at them, little Andy stiff and afraid to look down, Dan grinning as though he'd won the lottery.

Anne yelled, "Goddammit, you let him go! You fucking evil bastard!"

As she started for them, Mark yelled, "No!" and caught her by the cuffs.

Dan said, "The mouths on this family. Um-mm-mm."

Anne said, "You sick, evil fuck. I'll kill you myself if I get the chance."

She lunged again, Mark barely holding her back.

"Anne! That's not the way," he said, even if he wasn't yet sure what the way was.

Dan said, "Listen to your husband, Annie. We don't all want to fall to our deaths, do we? Maybe certain ones of us, but not all. That isn't necessary."

Anne screamed, "What do you *want*!"

Mark said, "He doesn't know. He's just making this shit up as he goes along."

"Now, Mark," Dan said, pretending to force patience. "How could I possibly have made all this up as I went along? You're a cop. You know how hard it is to find out as much as I had to about you and your family, then plan out every step so that it would all work flawlessly—so that we would all end up here, facing each other and the truth." He conceded, "I did lose MJ, you're right. That was a mistake. And I let you get close enough to get shot in the hand. That was bad. My bad." He nodded culpability.

Anne looked at Mark's hand. "Oh no. Are you okay?"

"Okay enough," he said. *To finish this.*

"But overall," Dan started—then interrupted himself. "This family. This... complete dedication to our Lord and Savior is... is really touching. I mean that from my heart."

He put his hand over his heart—his hand that held the .357 magnum.

Anne looked to Mark, lost. Mark shrugged and shook his head. *Don't ask me.*

Dan laughed. "Anyway, you have to admit: All this took some brilliant planning along with extensive research. We're talking legwork, Mark. Shoe leather, Mr. Detective. You know what I'm talking about. I was your life until you fucked it all up. You know what I mean."

Mark said, "No. But I know about good detective work and that I have apparently done a sorry-assed job in that department to have let any of this happen."

"Ah, that's it, that's it! That's what I'm looking for!" Dan said. Then he lowered his voice, teasing, "You're getting *clo*-ser." He allowed, "Of course, it wasn't technically your case, so, you know, you were somewhat hamstrung as to what you could do. I understand that. I'll give you that. Plus, investigating your*self*? Who can really do that? How can you remain objective? That would be the very definition of *sub*jective, right? I know I certainly couldn't investigate *my*self. I've tried. Can't do it. It's not possible. Not when it comes to my own shortcomings. *Ours*. We all have so many.

"But *yours*? Whoa. Limitless. I mean, you don't even have a clue. Mark." He waited in feigned impatient silence for Mark to move the solution ahead.

Mark obliged. "Dan. I've had enough of your story, puzzle, rubric, whatever the hell you think it is. Just spit it out. What do you want? You want me to jump off here to save my family. Fine, I'll jump. You want me to eat the end of your gun and die on top of this goddamn tank, great. Let's go. You want me to shoot myself? *What*?"

Anne looked at her husband as if unable to believe he'd just said tall that. Seeing no answers, she turned back to Dan and said, "What is going on here? I mean, really? What the hell is this all about? Did Mark do something to you? To someone else? What? What could it possibly be? You kidnapped me and my two children, left me in this damn tank for two days unable to move an inch, thinking I'd die in there for sure. For what? For *what*?!"

"For the truth!" Dan said, meeting her tone—then he toned it down. "That's all. Just the truth." He looked at Mark. "As to your generous offers: none of the above."

"Then what?" Mark said.

"Do I want? For you to *think*. Mark."

Mark wished Dan would stop separating his name that way. "About what?" he said with little patience.

"About everything. Everything you did, everything you didn't do, and everything that happened."

Mark said, "You said that before. Several times."

"Then do it! Think! Solve the rubric! Mark!" Dan paced.

So close to the edge.

Anne kept her eye on Andy, and Mark kept his eye on Anne. If she moved quickly, lost control, Dan might shove Andy over the side, or Anne, or both. Then, Mark would tackle Dan, go over the side, and *everyone* would be dead.

Not the solution he sought.

On the move, Dan asked, "Why are you here? What did you do? Mark."

"I don't know!"

"Then figure it out!"

"Quit saying that! How can I figure it out if I don't have a fucking idea what you're talking about!"

"But you *do*. You do! You know everything!"

"I don't know *anything*!"

"Sure you do. You know everything. You *did* everything! Figure it out! Solve the rubric!"

Mark turned away in frustration. His hand ached like frostbite all the way to his shoulder. His head ached to its core. His soul felt soiled, set on fire, and burned until nothing was left but a charred shell, like the week after a five-alarm fire.

What did it matter in the end? All was lost, either way.

Now he realized that his wife was staring at him—blank, confused, alarmed. She said, "What is he talking about, Mark? What did you do?"

"I don't know!" Mark said in loud frustration. "He won't tell me!"

Dan shouted, "Because you have to figure it out on your own or it doesn't count! It's no good! I. Can't. Help. You!" He shook his head. "You have to do this yourself. Mark. I've already done the heavy lifting—literally, getting that hand-biting *bitch* up here. Now you have to do the rest. You. Mark Young. Not me."

Mark threw up his hands. "I give up. I don't have a clue. I didn't kill your wife—"

"Ah, but you did! You just don't remember how!"

Anne said, "You killed Dan's wife?"

"No," Mark said, trying to maintain his calm, but feeling it edging away.

"Yes you did, yes he did," Dan said calmly. "In the house on Cody Lane—two twenty-eight Cody Lane. My wife. Strangled, her throat slashed. Dead." He kept looking at Anne.

Mark said, "That was your wife?"

"Yeah, and you killed her, Mark. Didn't think twice about doing it, either."

Anne turned to Mark. "My brother's house?"

Mark nodded.

She said, "You killed his wife in my brother's house?"

"*No!*" Mark shouted, sweating badly. "I did *not* kill her!"

He was emphatic. But again, if he was totally honest with himself...

Mark Young was honest to a fault; he was known for that. Wasn't he? Yes, he was!

And yes, if he was totally honest right now, the truth was that he *couldn't* remember. Not now. Not anymore. Not in these conditions. And hadn't Anne's brother Smithton *sold* that house years ago? It wasn't even *his* anymore. *Was it?*

Anne said, sounding shocked, "In Smithie's house? What happened?"

Dan said casually, "He killed my wife."

"I did not kill your fucking wife! Quit saying that!"

Dan sang, "You killed my wi-ife. You killed my wi-ife."

Mark howled in anguish, nothing else left.

Dan encouraged, "Come on, Markie. Think back. Remember all the horrible things. All the awful, evil, horrible things. How they happened. What you did."

Mark gritted his teeth and stammered, "I... don't know... what... you're talking about." He suddenly felt deep fatigue, total exhaustion, as if he was ready to jump if that would end it.

Dan said, "Come on, Markles. You can do it. Fight through all the booze and the beer, the antidepressants and the Ambien. Dig down *deep*, baby!"

Anne said to her husband, "You're on antidepressants and Ambien?"

Mark stammered, "Just... one. A few. I... Just a half at a—"

"Stop it!" Dan shouted. "Mark!" He paced again. "Level with her. She's your wife. Your dearly betrothed. Tell her the truth! Mark! Tell her what you did! Tell her all of it, man! Mark!"

Confusion and fear that maybe he'd done something he couldn't remember, something horrible, clouded Mark Young's memory, fogged his cognition, muddled his processes. He stood speechless. Stumped.

Dan said, "What. Did. You. Do?" Then he added, "And how? How did you do it?"

When Mark stood in bewildered silence, Dan grabbed little Andy and shouted, "Think and tell me the answer or I will throw your son off this tower, a hundred and twenty feet to his death! Right in front of you! Right now! No second thoughts!"

Anne started crying. "No! Please. Don't. He's an innocent child."

"No one is innocent here!" Dan screamed. "Not even the little children! They make us do the things we do for them! All for them!"

Anne recoiled, then turned to her husband. "Mark, what is he..." She seemed as lost as Mark did. She closed her eyes and said, "Just... tell him what he wants to know. You have to. You have to tell him what you did." She looked earnestly into her husband's eyes. "I know you. I know you can do this. Tell him want you did."

A loving command—from a loving wife and mother.

Mark continued to sweat profusely. Perspiration dripped off him even in the cool, stiff wind—flying away like rain in a storm. Rain from the approaching storm.

The storm already here atop this tower.

Mark's brain had locked up. He needed to unlock it, somehow. He needed to *think*. To work through this, whatever the personal cost. His family's lives were at stake.

His.

And he knew Dan wouldn't stop here. He would get away, find MJ, and kill her, too. Then he would kill himself. It was the only logical conclusion.

If any of this was logical.

Dan said, "What did your shrink tell you?" He looked at Anne but spoke to Mark. "After you fucked her and before you killed her."

Anne snapped a look at her husband. Mark didn't know what to say, even how to approach it—certainly not here. He wasn't about to bring up Floyd Matson now, the recent picture of him on Anne's computer, or even why he was looking at her private pictures and wondering what she saw in Floyd Matson from Georgia.

Not here and now.

Dan grabbed Andy and shoved him toward the side, shaking him—*ready to toss him off.*

Anne screamed, "Mark! Please!" *Whatever it is, you have to tell him. To tell* me. *Do it! Say it! Now!*

"I'm trying!" Mark said, clearly hearing what she hadn't said aloud.

He was trying harder than he ever had at anything. He played through every event that had transpired in the last weeks and months, starting with the murders of Dan's children, the unknown man in the hoodie throwing a redwood table through the kitchen window, Mark chasing him, shooting at him in the night, crazy and unprofessional.

He thought through the discoveries of all the bodies, Dr. Eileen Quarry and the other women, the children. The little ginger girl. Chuck's arrest and murder. *Dan's wife's body* in the Cody Lane house and how he had no idea who she was because he had never seen her out of the house—probably because Dan never let her out. Finally, not knowing where his own family was so that he could protect them, and the months of agony that had caused him, all alone.

Then all of this today.

Mark figured he had alibis for most of the murders—at least he thought he knew where he'd been when each one occurred. And unless he was crazier than Dan appeared to be, he hadn't been at any of the murder sites prior to their discovery. As far as he knew, he'd had nothing at all to do with any of them until he found out about them later, doing his job—poorly, maybe, but still doing his job.

As far as he knew.

He had been drinking a lot, taking Anne's Ambien—and other pills he found or was prescribed. Mixing them together in a potent cocktail guaranteed to cause memory loss. Or worse. He didn't remember Jerome calling him the night of Eileen Quarry's murder. That was true—if Jerome wasn't *making it up!*

No, Jerome wasn't a liar, except about his cigarette addiction.

But Jerome was also lying about something else, Mark was certain—something bad, something dark—keeping a secret from his old partner and everyone else. Maybe *he* did it; maybe *Jerome* committed these murders. He could have. Anyone could have.

What about his captain? Corlius the child molester? His own daughter. If he could do that, he could do *this*. Where was *he* on all those other nights? Home masturbating to kiddie porn or out killing? There was no way to know—not here, not now. Maybe ever. Maybe he did do it. Maybe he didn't! Maybe Mark...

Sweat poured in the rising wind and dripped onto the rusting top of the old water tank and blew away and did nothing to cool Mark's burning skin.

Where *had* he been the night Eileen Quarry was murdered? Wasn't he out driving around? Wasn't he unaccounted for? Had he taken pills and gone to a bar or gone to a bar and taken pills? When had he taken the pills and why had he taken them? Could he have gone back and murdered her? Would he have murdered her to cover up that he was *fucking* her? Not only that:

What the fuck is *Jerome doing?* Why was he calling Mark in the middle of the night—repeatedly—in the exact timeframe during which Dr. Eileen Quarry was being murdered? Wasn't Jerome supposed to be working a case somewhere on *dayshift*? Why was he even up at 3:00 in the morning? Shouldn't he have been home, asleep?

So, *his* whereabouts were unknown as well. And *so what!* if Mark couldn't remember where he was or what he had done that night? It was one night. It was a total coincidence! Jerome could have murdered Eileen Quarry. Sure! It could have been Jerome all along!

Yeah! Jerome! Fucking Jerome!

Dan interrupted, "All of those nights," as if reading Mark's mind. "Any of those nights. Where were you? What were you doing, Mark? Think back. Think hard. Think and tell us. What. Were. You. Doing? Mark."

Mark looked up with growing panic and depthless doubt. Dan's intentional rhythms were working on him, wearing him down, wearing him out.

He had to come up with something to save his son, his wife, MJ. His *family*. He was ready to say anything, anything at all that came to mind.

Mind! Work! Come on, brain!

Where had he been, really? Again, if he was honest to his marrow, he could not swear one hundred percent that he could place himself anywhere for certain at any one of those events. Anywhere *else*.

Not now. Not here. Not after today. *All* those days, this month from hell. How many days were there? How many had there been? How many murders? How many nights? Was it one month or many?

Now, they all ran together. Where was one? Who was the other? Why was he doing whatever it was he'd been doing at that time? What the *fuck* was he doing fucking Eileen Quarry when he loved and missed Anne so much? Why had he killed her? Eileen, not Anne. Anne was still alive, right?

He had to look, to make sure. *Losing my mind.*

Yeah, Anne was alive. *Good.* But Eileen Quarry was definitely dead. He'd seen her dead body. Hell, he *discovered* it! That alone was suspicious. Why him? *Why did I kill her?*

Where did that come from? Why would he even say that to himself? Why would he ask himself something *so completely fucking insane*?!

An answer came: Because no one looked back from the mirror.

No one was there. Just like those sociopaths who murder without feeling. Why had he felt nothing—for *years*? How could he go on, day after day, night after night, investigating death while filled with life, so blithe and carefree? How could he even face life with all that death around him? Why did he feel nothing anymore? Why didn't he see anybody other than himself in those mirrors?

Why was he stalking girls in parking lots—and getting *caught*? Was it a plea for help? Begging to get caught? *Stopped*? The classic cry for help from a serial killer? *Stop me! Please stop me before I kill again!* Like some crappy late-night B-movie.

Why *didn't* Mark ask for help all those years? Why did it take shooting up his neighborhood for him to be led to help? Then, why did he not *accept* it—fully, wholly, *happily*? Why did he *kill* her? *Why did I—*

Mark threw up.

Andy winced and wrinkled his nose. He'd never seen an adult throw up.

Dan laughed and said, "Now we're getting somewhere."

Chapter 35

Anne looked at Mark—bent over, hands on his knees—her wide eyes wild with accusation and unsavory imagery of fucking and killing, bodies naked and dead.

Mark looked up and saw it, helpless to stop her thoughts. He sagged, dying inside.

"That's it, Markles," Dan said, leading. "Stay with it. Put me in the picture. Figure me into your fears. Me, your friendly neighbor who would *out* you for what you really are."

Mark wiped his mouth, licked his dry lips, and sweated more.

Dan yelled, "Think of me, goddam you! Me! Me! Me!"

Mark looked at Dan Black and followed his directions.

He thought of Andy's bicycle landing on the hood of his Crown Vic that morning, telling Anne about it, his kids, and what they'd said about Dan Black, the mean man next door. His kids.

Poopypants the child beater.

He thought about Dan's moods and Dan's friendship. Dan's loss and how he grieved and seemed to have fought his way back to normalcy—or some shallow version of it. How he faded and slipped away but sought help. How they'd laughed and drank beer together, watched ballgames that had long been played so they knew how they would turn out, how that gave them both comfort—no mystery about what might happen.

Comfort in not knowing.

How they comforted *each other* in their mutual loss of family. How Dan's was worse. So much worse. Unimaginably worse.

Still, even now, Mark could not begin to guess what that felt like—even if Dan had brought him so close to that precipice today. Mark's family was still alive and Dan's was dead forever. That part had not changed. That part was consistent throughout. That part lived in Hell.

In Dan Black.

Again, if Mark was wholly honest, his own moods had become no less unpredictable, shifting this way and that on a whim, triggered by a lead, a new body, *a loud noise.*

His suspicions of his neighbor had turned out to be wild hunches that never led anywhere except to the poor man who'd just lost his three children to a serial child murderer *eating ice cream in The Mall, for Chrissake. Vanilla ice cream!*

Served by a demented pedophilic *clown*.

How Dan was the first to offer an olive branch, to say, "I heard you lost your wife, I'm sorry. Mine left two days ago." He was the one who'd reached out. The aggrieved, lost neighbor reaching out to Mark. But Mark had been snide, rude, uncouth. Mark, whose family was still alive. Just hiding safely somewhere.

Until Dan found them.

Mark looked up, across the tank at Dan, most of the nausea swept away with the winds of the storm that was so near now. The first droplets of rain fell randomly on the back of his neck and arms.

His wounds.

Dan's face.

Dan smiled again. "You're getting closer," he said. "Almost there." He chanted, "Go, Mark. Go, Mark. Go, Mark!"

Dan was suddenly reenergized, as if all the electrical energy from the approaching storm was driving straight into his brain, his being, his purpose.

He sang that damn song again. "Labba-dabba-*dab*ba. Hooba-dooba-*doo*ba-dooba. Labba-*dab*ba-hooba-*loo*ba-dooba-*doo*, that's *you*! Mark!"

He made a Durante face, threw a tap-dancing pose, and said, "Gotcha."

Mark's eyes searched the horizon for a clue, but all he saw was flat earth, a curved horizon—black clouds and personal doom, all coming for him.

Dan nodded wildly, euphorically, endorphins apparently racing through his bloodstream like canned lightning. "*Boo-ya*!" he shouted, as if feeling every bit the liberating Marine again.

"I thought you were Army," Mark said.

Dan shrugged as if to say, *All the same. We train, we go, we kill, we come home fucked up. All the same. But this!*

He said, "It's good, huh? Right there! I can see it. I can see it now! You got it. You got it!"

Anne said, "Mark?" obviously trying to see what Dan was seeing.

Mark flashed her a quick look that likely conveyed nothing more than annoyance, then shifted his concentration back to his neighbor.

Dan said, "Good, good!" his excitement growing. "That's it! Stay with that!"

Mark hit a snag.

Dan saw it and said, "Even better! Excellent!"

Mark stared at his former neighbor. What the *hell*? What was he up to?

Mental gears started turning in a new direction.

"Yeah, yeah, that's it. There you go," Dan said, as if once again reading Mark's mind. "Great neighbors share great secrets. That's what makes them so great! Labba-dabba-*dooooo*!"

Yes, Mark *had* been a great neighbor to this loon. He had been kind and forgiving, generous to a fault. Had he not? Had he not gone out of his way to help this man with the brain injury—the TBIs and the Post Traumatic Stress—even after learning about it all? *Because* of learning about it all. He'd all but pampered Dan, let him back in every time, didn't even report him leaving his kids' clothing at Chuck's house.

Dear god, that had been bad. Everything almost came crashing down that day. But he kept on and kept trying to help his grief-stricken neighbor Dan Black.

What else? There had to be something, some reason for all this madness. *What?* What had he done?

When the department sent him to therapy, Mark went. He cooperated. He did as he was told and told his doctor all his secrets—at least the ones she asked about. He held back nothing.

He even sought her help in trying to solve the murders of Dan's children. So, what the hell was Dan talking about Mark being culpable? What the hell was he so angry about? So crazed? Why was he saying Mark had killed all these people when Mark himself was *pretty damn sure* he had not?

Sure, he'd stalked those young women online and at The Mall, but it was for their own good. He never hurt one of them, never even considered it.

Had he?

He couldn't remember for sure now, but he just didn't feel in his gut that he had. If he'd murdered them, even one of them, he was *pretty damn sure* he would remember at least part of it. *Something!* Some detail, some faint recollection. But:

Nothing. He had nothing.

He didn't see anything in the mirrors except himself—that was true—yes.

Wait.

Himself. All he saw was himself. *Myself, that's right! I saw myself!* He was expecting to see *more*. Eileen Quarry had led him to believe there was more—more to see, more to feel—but there hadn't been. *There wasn't!*

Mark felt nothing, true. But he saw himself. *Just* himself.

A flood of relief flooded Mark Young on the tower as the raindrops increased in size and frequency.

"We're almost there," Dan said, his eyes flaring like exploding dark stars.

Mark thought, *Okay, seeing myself was good.* Seeing himself did not make him a killer. Neither did feeling nothing on his job. It just made him a good cop—if a hollow man. Dr. Quarry had planted the idea and he'd accepted it. *Damn shrinks.*

Had he accepted more? More ideas? *Murderous* ideas?

What the hell was she talking about that night? "I'm not a good person." *I'm a bad person. You shouldn't like me. You* should *judge me.* Who did *she* kill? Maybe she deserved to die. Maybe she was the killer.

Holy shit!

"No!" Dan shouted, shaking his head, apparently seeing the shift. "No, no, *no*!" He paced. "Think, Mark. Think! Make it work. Make it *happen*, brother!"

For a fleeting moment, Mark considered that he'd sensed Eileen Quarry's need to be killed, her *desire*, and had killed her because he felt justified, because she wanted it—because somehow, in a thinly disguised way, she had *asked* him to. *Begged* him to kill her. If he did, if he had, that could mean he had killed before. That maybe he had killed those other women and children and who knew who. Only:

They had all happened *before* he started seeing Dr. Quarry.

Shit!

"No! Stop it!" Dan declared again with confidence, as if he knew that Mark was veering off course. He was looking into Mark's mind and seeing it!

Fuck! How is he doing that? What did I do?

Mark felt the nausea rising again but fought it away. *Focus!* Had Eileen Quarry, his doctor, planted—

"No, no, no, no, no!" Dan screamed and paced wildly—slipping, regaining, pacing more.

Andy stood stock still, obviously terrified to chance moving.

Mark bit down hard on his teeth, realizing at this moment that he had hated Dan Black from the first moment Dan offered to be friends.

And he had never trusted him.

More important, his hunches had been right. Sure, he followed Dan to The Mall where he only ate ice cream—bought from a *child murderer*! So, the hunch paid off. We don't always see how at first blush. But he'd had the hunch, followed Dan Black for some reason, and stumbled on a killer clown. It doesn't get better than that.

Well, much better.

Dan was guilty of something. Mark knew it. Now, he *only* had to figure out what it was.

He had circled around, the long way. He now felt confident that he hadn't killed anyone. It was what he wanted to believe, so he chose to believe it. He had run every scenario he could think of, and nothing had come of it.

That was what he said now. "I didn't do anything."

And Dan Black said, "Correct."

Chapter 36

Mark's response to all that had happened over the last several hours was, "What?"

Dan said, with no emotion whatsoever, "Ding, ding, ding. We have a winner." He let Andy go and tossed the handcuff keys to Mark.

Mark freed Anne, and Andy ran into her comforting arms. They both cried.

Dan said sadly, "Mark, my friend. My good friend. You could have done something. You *should* have done something. But you did nothing.

"You could have stopped me. You could have used your good cop's intuition to know that I was bad. That I was sick. That I was a killer, and that I was going to kill again. But you didn't do anything. You ignored the voice in your head, the voice of righteousness." Sadness came into his eyes, mixed with outrage. "I had to kill my own wife just to find out where *your* wife went. You see? If you had just asked your own family where they were and told me when I asked, my wife would be alive like your wife is now. *You* killed her! You see? You killed her. *You* killed my wife!"

Mark looked at Anne. "You told her where you were? The wife of this fucking *maniac*?"

Anne sighed heavily and wiped a tear. "Where we were going, yes."

Mark couldn't believe it. He had made everything so clear, so perfectly clear, why even *he* wasn't supposed to know. But Anne had told the sad neighbor lady she hardly even knew—the wife of the murderer—"Where you were going to *hide*?!"

Anne met his gaze a moment, then hung her head. "I was mad at you, I was confused. I thought someone should know—someone I didn't know well, someone who wouldn't tell you because you didn't know her."

Mark shouted, "*You* didn't know her!"

Anne shouted back, "She was afraid! She suspected her husband had killed their kids but was afraid to say anything because she didn't have a shred of evidence, just her own paranoia!

"So, I advised her to run away. She asked me how she could ever do that—and I told her." Anne looked up at Mark, clearly guilt-ridden. "I told her how we were going to do it and how we weren't telling anyone."

Dan said, "Yeah, I beat that nonsense out of her."

Mark looked at Dan. "So, you knew where your wife was all along?"

"Yeah, I followed her," Dan said with a shrug. "But I didn't know that she knew where Anne was with the kids. That took a while, some pondering, you know. It's part of the puzzle. Then I remembered seeing them talking one day out front, and I thought how strange that was. Emily never talked to anyone. I wouldn't let her. And she was crying—in front of someone we didn't know. Strictly forbidden. Never let the enemy see your weaknesses.

"Once I realized she had disobeyed me, the rest came easy."

Disobeyed.

"Killing her was easy?" Anne said, sounding sickened by the notion.

Dan shrugged that off as well. "Killing anyone is easy," he said. "You just make up your mind and do it. Once you learn that, once you do it once, it's easy. Sad, isn't it?"

For the first time, Dan seemed a broken man—broken of spirit, hope, and humanity.

Anne looked at her husband and said, "I'm sorry. I know you said—"

Mark said, "It's okay."

"No, it's my fault," Anne said, realizing her part in the play. "Oh my god. It's all my fault." Her tears renewed. "Christ."

Dan rolled his eyes dramatically. "You can't blame yourself, hon'," he told Anne. "You're a woman. Women can't help themselves. They blab about anything that pops into their simple little minds. Just like children.

"Your husband gave you specific orders, a well thought out plan that would protect you and your family from, well, me. But you disobeyed him, just as my wife disobeyed me.

"And for that," he said, "We all must pay."

Was he going to kill them all now? Was that his whole sick plan?

Dan looked at Mark and said, "But you can't really blame Anne, can you? She was just being a silly female. But you're a man, Mark. A trained police officer. And you did nothing. *Nothing*!

"All the signs were there, Mark. I was giving them to you on a *platter*! I came to your house and offered myself to you. All you had to do was ask me a few questions, just a few. A few clever cop questions that I couldn't have answered. And you would've had me. Easy-peasy."

"It wasn't my case," Mark said.

"Oh," Dan said pitiably. "It wasn't your case. Right. It was that worthless public servant Martin Coor's case. Detective Martin Coor, the most incompetent idiot of a civil servant I've ever seen. He couldn't get a job in the DMV giving eye tests to blind people and get it right. You know the depth of the questions he asked me. He'd say..." Dan mimicked Coor. "'Mr. Black, I'm sorry to trouble you again with all the grief you must be feeling over' *killing your own goddam kids in your own goddam backyard*!

"*Detective* Coor would say, 'I know this is a difficult time, but can you tell me, please kind sir, how it was that you didn't wake up?' And I would say, 'I'm a deep sleeper.' And he would say, 'Well, okay then.' And he'd ask me what I had for breakfast."

Mark nodded inside his own head. He'd never thought much of Martin Coor as a homicide investigator, though he might have asked a suspect what he'd had for breakfast to throw them off, skirt around the real question, then come back at it from an oblique angle. On the other hand, Marty Coor had probably actually wondered what Dan had for breakfast.

He was probably hungry.

Dan continued his insulted act. "You know, he never asked me—never even came over to feel me out—when your girlfriend Dr. Quarry got murdered in her own den. Not one question about your behavior. Can you imagine that? Here we're friends, we've been through this... this... thing together." He made a sour face that Mark took to mean his children being murdered. "And he doesn't even think to ask me anything about you. At all! And did he consider me as a suspect? No! He didn't even ask me if I knew your shrink or where I was that night. He didn't ask me where *you* were that night! And you had just fucked her and left her there for me to kill with a goddam Crate and Barrel bar-b-cue skewer! Right there in the drawer with her Williams-Sonoma corkscrew. 'Eileen, where can I find a can opener?'

"'Right there in the drawer by the stove, Daniel.' *Daniel*. She fuckin' called me Daniel." He laughed, though in the wind it sounded a little like crying. "Here you had just fucked her—I could *taste* you in her. Tasted like shit, by the way. What, do you eat garlic by the wheelbarrow?" Dan looked disgusted. "I didn't want to mingle with that shit. I had to fuck her in the ass." Then he laughed again. "Not that she knew at that point, or cared."

Mark and Anne shared a look. In it, he conveyed his apology and she her forgiveness. Then, they turned back to Dan.

He said, "I just knocked on her door and said, 'Hey, I'm that friend of Mark's who lives next door to him, the one whose kids were murdered.' And I looked a little sad and pitiful and I said, 'Mark suggested that I might talk to you about all the pain and suffering and loss and horrible thoughts and nightmares and... you know, bullshit. She was dead before she finished her stupid glass of 'port.' Rich bitch. What an arrogant cunt. Women. I'm tellin' ya, man. Worthless.

"She was a pretty good fuck though, I have to admit. Even dead."

Dan looked off as if trying to remember something. "Wait, wait, wait. I think I fucked her first then killed her." Then *thinking* more. "No, that was that other bitch." Then looking at Mark and Anne. "You know, truthfully, I can't remember. They all run together. Right, Mark? Mark? Mark?" He turned his attention to, "And Anne? Little Annie Fannie. Does Mark fuck you in your ass? I'll bet he wants to. I'll bet he wants to kill you first. All men do. We're all the same."

Anne said, "Fuck. You. I know what you're trying to do."

Dan said, "No you don't. You don't have a fucking clue. You are clue-*less*." He scoffed. He spat. It ran down his chin in the wind. He farted. "Fuckin' whores, all of you. Little MJ? Just a whore in the making. I get off this tower, she's bent over a barrel takin' it up the shitter just like every one of them, loving it."

Mark blew up. "Goddammit! Jesus Christ, man! What the fuck are you trying to do! Do you want me to *arrest* you, is that it?"

Dan mocked him openly. "Oh sure, *now* he wants to arrest me. It's a little late, don't you think? Mark? Where was all that good police work then? You're only a notch better than that idiot Coor.

"By the way," Dan added, "you'll find his body in the reservoir. I fucked him, too."

Mark stared.

Dan laughed. "Ah, I'm just kidding. I don't fuck men. That's disgusting."

It wasn't clear whether he really thought that or not, whether he had or had not.

Nothing was clear at that point.

Dan shook his head and said, "But I'll tell you this. He was a weaselly little fuck. Changed his routine every few days. What's up with that? What's he into?"

"I don't know, Dan," Mark said. "You're the expert in these areas."

"Yeah," Dan admitted, then shook his head. "He's into something." He seemed bothered that he hadn't figured it out yet.

Mark said, "Well, when you find out, let me know."

Dan said, "Oh yeah, yeah, sure. Only that's never gonna happen. Right, Annie?"

Anne looked as if she had fallen into a parallel universe, a flat brane where nothing made sense and every word out of everyone's mouth was vile and misleading, hurtful and grim. Mark felt the same.

Rain began to pelt them. The wind tore at their clothes.

Something occurred to Dan. "Oh, Mark. Your old partner, Jerome the *nee-grow*? He's selling dope to put back money for his kids' college fund."

"How do you know that?" Mark asked, stupefied. How could Dan *possibly* know that?

Dan shrugged. "I know everything. But *you*! Following me to the mall. Christ. You thought I didn't see you the whole way, two cars back, then almost running into me at the light? I thought you clipped that dump truck." He found that hilarious—laughed like a loon—then went on. "Going all stealth on me and I walked up to *you*. Scared the piss outa you, didn't I?" He laughed again. "Then you're all, 'Oh, I was just following you on a hunch. Being a good cop, following my good cop hunches.' All tough and interrogative. Lousy cop. Shitty cop. *Horrible* cop!"

"How did you know about Jerome?" Mark asked again. It stuck in his craw.

"I just asked around. Tailed him one night. No one easier to tail than a cocky cop. I saw him make the drop, collect his envelope, and skulk off into the night.

"Mind you, I don't blame him. Times are tough. I wouldn't want to have to pay for my kids' college education, either. You know, if they were alive. But I've alleviated myself of that burden. They'll never go to college, never ask for money, an apartment, a car, dorm room, books." He went full rage again. "You let me kill my own kids, Mark! You did nothing to stop me!"

Mark protested, "I didn't know you then!"

"I threw your kid's bike on your car! I was an antisocial miscreant! I locked my kids in the basement and beat my wife! I got in your face every chance I got, and you just ignored me! I killed your bushes with gasoline! And you didn't think anything of it!" He mocked Mark's voice. "'Yeah, I don't know, Dan. I think they have a plant disease, or bugs.' Fucking idiot!"

Anne said, "You put gas on our bushes?"

"Yes! And I killed your dog!"

Andy said, "You killed Fluffy?"

"Yes, you snotty little asswipe! I would have killed you that night, and your mommy and your big sister, if your daddy wasn't such a complete loser jerkoff that he left his cellphone at home and had to come back for it."

Mark looked at him, putting it together.

Dan said, "Yes, it was me! Of course it was me! But you're such a lousy shot, you fired twelve rounds and didn't even wing me. Didn't come close! You shot up every fucking house in the neighborhood but *mine*, and I was the one you were *after*!"

Mark said defensively, "I was running after you and... wound up. I lost you."

Dan took a step closer and yelled, "I hopped over my back fence! I was standing in my own backyard and watched you run past, you dumb fucking asshole! That's why you 'lost' me! You didn't even look! Right there, not ten feet away! You could've had me! Jesus!"

Mark pictured it all clearly—and wondered why he'd fired the additional nine shots. What the hell had he been shooting at? What had he thought he'd seen if no one was there? It just made the whole thing feel worse—Dan in his backyard, watching Mark run past shooting at shadows.

Dan shook his head. "All the signs were there," he said. "I had no solid alibis for anything, and you let me slide. You let me go on killing. Lydia Hamilberg, Emily Farrington, Anna Jacobs-Crowley, the little redhead twerp with her stupid braces. All of them. For years! You had every case at some point and never got within a mile of me. I had to move *next door* to you to get your attention, and even then you never even had a fucking clue. Just your vapid, idiotic 'cop hunches.' Pathetic." He spat the words.

Then, Dan Black lowered his voice. "You're a shitty cop, Mark. A very... shitty... cop."

He raised the gun—aimed at Mark.

Anne yelled, "No!"

At the last second, Dan swung the gun slightly to the side and fired, hitting Anne. She spun and dropped to the tank. Andy screamed, "Mommy!" and Mark dropped to his knees by his wife.

"Annie, baby. Talk to me."

Dan shook his head in disgust. "She's all right. You see what a shitty cop you are? It's just a flesh wound. You couldn't even *tell*!"

Mark checked. Sure enough, Dan had shot Anne in the fleshy part of her upper arm, just below her shoulder. She'd have a scar, but it wouldn't even bleed much in the meantime.

"I'm okay, I think," she said.

"Of course you are, you stupid bitch," Dan said. "Why do you think I go the range five times a week? I can shoot the balls off a fly at fifty feet. Your fat ass is a piece of cake."

Mark realized then that Dan could have shot him at any moment with deadly accuracy. He had missed on purpose—like when he'd hit that ladder down below just inches from Mark's head and fired past him when he stepped away.

Any one of those shots.

Mark stood up, his head swimming in irrational thoughts. "You're fucking crazy."

Dan said, "Yes! And you see the lengths I have to go to to wake you up to that?! I had to *shoot* your wife to inspire you to action! To play *God*! Mark." Dan took small steps toward Mark. "I've been working you all along! Don't you see?" He was almost whining. "All the lies?"

Then he told Mark what really happened in Afghanistan.

The Humvee is upside down, the Gunner is dead, the Afghani kids and the one Afghani man are watching.

Dan kills them all.

Then he kills his wounded driver and Shotgun.

He drops his weapon and walks away.

Dan told Mark about the first text message.

In the mall restaurant, the hostess, waitpersons, and cooks are all busy, preparing for the noon crunch. A few customers are in the front room. In the back, three teenage girls giggle and run for the ladies' room.

Dan walks past and takes the cellphone left behind.

No one notices.

He described the many murders he committed once he returned home from the wars.

1) He buries the woman with Nikes in a vacant lot near the projects.

2) He grabs Emily Farrington, twenty-three, from a street by a park. No one notices as Dan drags her into the bushes, strangles and rapes her, then buries her in the hole he has ready.

3) Dan is in a small boat on the lake. He rolls Linda Hamilberg's nude body, wrapped in chains, over the side, picks up a pole and casts his plug to fish for bass. Pops a cold beer.

4) Dan is digging in the new, soft dirt under the "Covington Downs" sign. A girl's nude body lies nearby awaiting burial.

5) Riverside. Using the coordinates Dan gave the police, he buries Anna Jacobs-Crowley in a ready grave. He is nude in the dark, covered with her blood, but working at a steady casual pace. When he's done covering the grave, he walks to the river to rinse off, his clean, unsullied clothing nearby.

6) A young woman is shopping in a large clothing store in the mall, listless, unaware. Bored, she wanders into a back hallway for the ladies' room – and Dan has her. He bags her head, lifts her up and carries her out a back exit, throwing her into the open trunk of his car, parked just outside. An alarm sounds and a clerk comes to check it out, but he's as bored as she was, so he notices nothing.

Dan said, "I called that one in earlier today. Your boy Jerome's probably there now if he isn't dealing more dope."

There were others.

7) A family, the Piersons, are coming out of church after a Sunday sermon. In the blink of an eye, their son Maron, twelve, is gone. A second later, their daughter Avery, fourteen, is gone. The parents call their names and ask around desperately.

No one saw anything.

Later that night, Dan works nude, burying Maron and Avery – in his backyard. He looks up, sweaty, spattered with blood, to see his wife in the house playing with his kids, oblivious.

8) Dan chops his own children apart in his backyard, placing their bodies on the exact spots where the other bodies were buried earlier. The grass grew back beautifully.

Dan said, "No one even looked." He grunted. "The dogs barked and scratched, but your idiot cop cohorts figured they were barking about my kids and left."

9) Dan stands in the house on Cody Lane holding a piece of paper with the address for Anne and the kids' safe house. Dan's wife is freshly dead.

Dan blew out a tired sigh and said, "That's about it for this round, I guess."

"This round?" Mark said.

Dan shrugged. "Unless you stop me. But at this point, you have no credibility. Zero success rate. You suck. You're worthless. You won't stop me because you can't. You're not up to the job. Mark."

Mark said, "You have the gun."

Dan looked at it and nodded agreement. "Yeah," he said wistfully. "And what are we gonna do about that?"

Mark tried the sincere approach. "Dan, man, come on. We had some good times."

"Oh yeah, great," Dan said, snorting sarcastically. "Only we didn't actually have them *together*, now did we?" He looked at Anne and said, "He ever fuck you like he fucked his shrink? I watched them go at it for hours. Hours! He's a stallion, this guy!" Dan feigned admiration of the highest order.

Anne was obviously long past worrying about a fling. She said, "What is *wrong* with you?"

"What isn't wrong with me?" Dan asked rhetorically.

"But *why*?" she asked as if nothing else came to mind.

Dan shrugged. "Brain injury. That's what I tell myself. I mean, I did hit my head, that much is true, and it could have triggered something, anything. Who knows? But Mark's little sob story about getting the belt a few times from his mean daddy, and seeing his mommy die in an unfortunate gun accident of which he was a critical part, the main player? Shit. Child's play to what I went through. Why do you think I enlisted the day I turned seventeen? I forged my parents' names—I'd already killed them and buried them in the cornfield the week before. We lived in Kansas. Flat as a floor. He'd been raping me since I was two. My mother was an alkie. She took her turn."

Mark said, "You're making this shit up. You were raised in the suburbs and went to parochial school. I'll bet you didn't even play basketball." He was guessing.

Dan went on, speaking matter-of-factly about his childhood as if discussing normal activities for a kid. "I killed dogs and cats. A few horses. You know, for the kick. Wasn't much after a while, so I killed some old lady in a house fire. Watched her burn up trying to get out on her walker. After that, like I said, it wasn't so hard. My parents—I thought that might be harder. But the minute they got on their knees and begged, I knew it was over. They had it coming. I used his own .22 on them." He laughed. "Then the army 'taught me how to kill.'" He laughed harder. "Hell, I coulda taught *them* a few things!"

He settled down. "Then they sent me out to get blown up by a roadside IED and I ended up killing my buddies because..." He paused, reflecting. "You know, I really don't know the 'because.' I have no excuse. I just did it and walked away, and the Army gave me some aspirin, sent me back to kill some more, and here we are." He continued, ruefully, "So you see, I have every excuse. But you: Mark Young. You have only one. And that was an accident. It really doesn't stack up to what I've been through. It was just enough to make you want to be a cop to 'avenge all the wrongs in the world'—but not enough to be a very good cop."

Mark said, "So you gave up your friend Chuck just to steer us away from you. You really enjoyed those snuff films he liked to show to his friends."

"Oh, there were no friends," Dan said. "Chuck have friends?" He laughed. "He was a sick child molester. Mark. They don't hang out in groups and eat pizza and drink beer. Jesus." He laughed as if to say Mark was a complete moron. "He was a loner. Like me. I went in for ice cream one day, saw the way he looked at a little girl—that first one that he took at the mall and killed. Not the first one he killed, just the first one from the mall." He added, as if being precise, "And not the one you stumbled on, the first one, the black kid." He seemed to be thinking back. "Did you ever find her body?"

Mark said, "No. Do you know where it is?"

"No," Dan said. "I didn't ask Chuck his business. But you might try looking up on the north side of the lake, around Claughton Harbor, Shores whatever. He always talked about that place like it held special meaning to him."

Mark said, "And the ginger girl?"

"Oh, pure Chuck. But after you followed me there, I knew you'd be asking questions about her at some point, so I asked Chuck for details. Fuckin' idiot told me everything. He was happy as a goat in a scrapyard." Dan chuckled. "And you played along beautifully, I must say. But we *nailed* his ass, didn't we? We did it together, man." He shook his head. "One thing I can't countenance is a child molester. Guy who fucks kids needs to go." Dan said it as if there was some honor in the thing. He moved closer.

Mark said, "So you just got lucky when her father killed Chuckie on the courthouse steps."

"We all get lucky sometimes," Dan said. "Even you." He thought for a moment. "Well, most of us."

His face went dark, and he said with disgust, "You could have stopped me a hundred times. Mark. But you didn't. Mark." He raised the gun. "You're pathetic. Mark. You don't deserve to live. Mark."

He was close. He cocked the gun to kill.

Mark stepped forward quickly.

He grabbed the .357 as he had the semi-automatic, but this time, full around.

Dan looked down and saw why. With Mark's hand holding the cylinder and his thumb in the hammer, the gun was rendered useless. Not a single shot this time.

Dan reacted quickly. He released the gun, grabbed Mark's belt, and dove for the side of the tank. He yelled the whole way, like a deranged Saints linebacker tackling for a bonus.

They went over the side as one.

Chapter 37

Anne screamed, shoved Andy down to sit, and ran to the side. Rain slapped them and the windward side of the tall, rusty tower.

Dan had landed long-ways on the catwalk rail, so it didn't break his back, but Mark fell on top of him, and now their momentum carried them over.

Contorting almost in two, Mark grabbed the railing with his good hand while Dan slipped past him, grabbing at anything.

The reflex not to die is strong. Even in a hopeless killer.

Dan grabbed the wrist of Mark's gunshot hand and held on with both hands.

Anne yelled from above, "Let him go!"

Mark yelled up to her, "Go down, go down! Climb down now! Take Andy!" His brain was working again. All doubt had left. "Go! Now! I got this."

Dan looked down, his feet swaying back and forth 120 feet above the concrete ground. He looked back up at Mark. For the first time all day, Dan looked scared.

Mark was calm again. Finally.

Dan said, "Look at you. We both could die. Right now. We both probably will—if I have anything to do with it." He laughed briefly, then said with admiration, "But there you are, so calm and in control."

Mark wouldn't trust anything Dan said from now on. He said, "It's going to be all right. Just—"

Dan shouted, "It's not fucking going to be all right, Mark! When are you going to figure that out! It's too late for that." His tears started and he thrashed, almost falling. Then he grabbed even more tightly. "Don't let me fall, man. Mark. Please. I don't want to die like this."

Mark said, "I got you. Just don't do that again or you might take us both down."

He checked his grip on the rail, then told Dan, "So just... hang on. I'll get us both down safely." But he knew three things that gave him doubts.

One, accomplishing that would be a small miracle; still, he was determined to do it whatever it might take or mean. Two, Dan would get a fair trial, whatever that meant for a soulless man who'd committed multiple murders, including his own wife and children, and confessed to them all. Three, Dan would get the death sentence in their state; but even with that, he might live out his appeals and die in prison an old man.

Mark thought about letting go, but his job as a police officer was to keep Dan calm and get him up onto the catwalk, then back down and into custody. As Dan had said before, if Mark was anything, he was a cop through and through.

Good or shitty.

Mark would not let go. He didn't have it in him. Now, he remembered why.

But he was sweaty and wet from the increasing rain. So, when Dan tried to pull himself up, his hands slipped. He yelped and his eyes flared.

Mark managed to grab his shirt collar and hold tight. "I got you!"

"Oh, Jesus," Dan said, clutching Mark's arm, swinging wildly. He cried more. "Look at me," he said. "I'm the pathetic one. I just shit myself." He was bawling now. "All I did. All the killing I did with no feeling whatsoever, and here I am scared to death. So selfish." He shook his head, then nodded. "This is what all those people felt just before I killed them." He snorted at the irony. "Never thought I'd be here. Never crossed my mind. Just shows to go ya." He chuckled again through the tears.

Then he hardened. "I'm not going to be one of those whining faggots in prison for the rest of my life, swearing I didn't do it and filing appeal after appeal until I die of cancer or someone frags me in the shower. Fuck them!"

Mark said, "Try to stay calm. Dan. I'm going to pull you up slowly—enough so you can reach out and grab this rail post, okay?"

Dan looked up, his eyes filled with tears and fear. "Okay," he said weakly. "Why are you doing this for me after all I did—to *you*?"

Mark said, "You were right. I was a lousy cop before. I didn't do the right thing, what I was trained to do, what I felt in my gut. But all that's behind us. My job now is to save your life."

"So they can kill me later," Dan said.

Mark said, "That's up to the jury and the judge. You never know. Now, I need you to focus."

Dan grunted darkly, looked down past his swaying feet in the wind and rain. The ground far below.

Mark said, "It's gonna be tricky. All about the timing. Okay? I'm going to have to shift a little. It'll feel like you're slipping away, but you're not. We're just going to change our grips a bit, then I'm going pull you up. Okay? Ready? Here I go."

Mark carefully shifted his body position so that his midsection was wedged against a rail pillar. "So far, so good," he said. "Now you."

Dan, crying fully, said, "Thanks, friend. You've been a great neighbor. But you've done enough." He smiled—and let go.

Mark had a good grip on Dan's shirt, and thankfully it was strong material. Still, he was angry as Dan swung, hands free. "Dammit! Reach up! Grab my wrist! Do it!"

When Dan reached up, he had the pocketknife in his hand. Mark saw it just before Dan stabbed him in his good hand, in the fleshy part by his thumb.

It hurt like hell.

"Goddammit!" Mark shouted, and held on for all he was worth. "Stop it!"

Dan said, "Thanks for everything. I mean it, buddy."

He pulled the knife out and swung it again, this time stabbing the short blade into the side of Mark's hand and slicing down. Mark howled and let go of Dan. He couldn't help it.

Dan fell away.

Mark watched as Dan smiled up, then rolled over seconds before hitting the ground. Mark saw the blood blow out from 120 feet up.

Then he looked up and across the yard to see the police cars streaming in from three directions at high speed. He hadn't heard them, he was so focused.

Lifting himself back onto the catwalk, Mark looked down to see Anne and Andy just reaching the ground. Anne turned Andy away from the grim sight that was Dan's crumpled dead body. All that it meant.

As the first police cars pulled in and screeched to a stop, Mark saw MJ leap out the back of the second one and run to her mother's arms.

THE END

ABOUT THE AUTHOR

Author Glenn A. Bruce, MFA, is an award-winning writer-director who began his career in Hollywood, where he wrote the hit movie Kickboxer as well as episodes of Walker: Texas Ranger, Baywatch, plus many more. He's had over fifty short stories and essays published internationally, and recently completed his 32nd novel. Glenn taught screenwriting at Appalachian State University for over a dozen years, and recently returned to his home state to once again be a Florida Man.

You can follow Glenn online at:
Website: www.GlennABruce.com
Goodreads: Glenn A. Bruce
IMDb: Glenn A. Bruce
Facebook: @GlennArdenBruce
Instagram: @GlennArdenBruce
Twitter: @GlennArdenBruce

WHAT'S NEXT?

Glenn A. Bruce always has at least one book in the works, so please stay tuned to developments and plans by subscribing to our newsletter at the link below.

www.EvolvedPub.com/Newsletter

MORE FROM EVOLVED PUBLISHING

We offer great books across multiple genres, featuring high-quality editing (which we believe is second-to-none) and fantastic covers.

As a hybrid small press, your support as loyal readers is so important to us, and we have strived, with tireless dedication and sheer determination, to deliver on the promise of our motto:

QUALITY IS PRIORITY #1!

Please check out all of our great books,
which you can find at this link:

www.EvolvedPub.com/Catalog/

Thank you!

CPSIA information can be obtained
at www.ICGtesting.com
Printed in the USA
LVHW100017010522
717630LV00006B/553

9 781622 538324